CLARKESWORLD

CLARKESWORLD YEAR 5

EDITED BY NEIL CLARKE & SEAN WALLACE

WYRM PUBLISHING

CLARKESWORLD: YEAR FIVE

Wyrm Publishing
www.wyrmpublishing.com

For more information, contact Wyrm Publishing:
wyrmpublishing@gmail.com

ISBN: 978-1-890464-24-0 (trade paperback)
ISBN: 978-1-890464-23-3 (ebook)

Visit Clarkesworld Magazine at:
clarkesworldmagazine.com

*For Cynthia, John D., Terra, Aimee, Jason, Jamie, Cheryl W.,
Rebecca, Halsted, Justin, Nayad, Daniel, Paul, and Sean M.
—Thank you!*

Contents

INTRODUCTION, Neil Clarke 7

GHOSTWEIGHT, Yoon Ha Lee.. 9

PERFECT LIES, Gwendolyn Clare 27

TYING KNOTS, Ken Liu.. 41

SEEING, Genevieve Valentine... 53

SALVAGING GODS, Jacques Barcia 65

LAYING THE GHOST, Eric Brown... 75

THE CHILDREN OF MAIN STREET, A.C. Wise.................................. 89

DIVING AFTER THE MOON, Rachel Swirsky............................... 99

THREE ORANGES, D. Elizabeth Wasden 109

MATCHMAKER, Erin M. Hartshorn.... 117

TRICKSTER, Mari Ness..131

THE BOOK OF PHOENIX (EXCERPTED FROM
           THE GREAT BOOK), Nnedi Okorafor............................. 149

THE ARCHITECT OF HEAVEN, Jason K. Chapman 165

FROZEN VOICE, An Owomoyela 177

TROIS MORCEAUX EN FORME DE MECHANIKA, Gord Sellar......... 185

PACK, Robert Reed... 195

SEMIRAMIS, Genevieve Valentine 205

WHOSE FACE THIS IS I DO NOT KNOW, Cat Rambo........................... 215

THE TAXIDERMIST'S OTHER WIFE, Kelly Barnhill 225

ON THE BANKS OF THE RIVER LEX, N. K. Jemisin 233

SIGNALS IN THE DEEP, Greg Mellor... 243

THE FISH OF LIJIANG, Chen Quifan (translated by Ken Liu)................ 255

CONSERVATION OF SHADOWS, Yoon Ha Lee 267

THE CARTOGRAPHER WASPS AND THE
           ANARCHIST BEES, E. Lily Yu 275

ABOUT THE AUTHORS 283

CLARKESWORLD CENSUS 289

ABOUT CLARKESWORLD 293

Introduction
NEIL CLARKE

While collected here for the first time as an anthology, all of the stories in this book were originally published in *Clarkesworld Magazine* between October 2010 and September 2011. This volume represents all of the original fiction from our fifth year of publication. If you've never read *Clarkesworld,* this anthology will serve as a good introduction to what you can expect to find in our monthly issues. More details about our magazine may be found at the end of this anthology.

While many of the stories in this volume have been honored as selections for Year's Best anthologies, the two that bookend this anthology have received nominations for some of our community's biggest awards:

"Ghostweight" by Yoon Ha Lee
- Finalist: Sturgeon Award

"The Cartographer Wasps and the Anarchist Bees" by E. Lily Yu
- Nominee: Hugo Award for Best Short Story
- Nominee: Nebula Award for Best Short Story
- Nominee: World Fantasy Award for Best Short Story
- Finalist: Locus Award for Best Short Story
- Nominee: WSFA Small Press Award

Congratulations to Yoon and Lily, and thank you to all our authors. We're honored to have been entrusted with your work.

And now for the best part, let's go read some stories . . .

Neil Clarke
October 2013

Ghostweight

YOON HA LEE

For Charibdys

It is not true that the dead cannot be folded. Square becomes kite becomes swan; history becomes rumor becomes song. Even the act of remembrance creases the truth.

What the paper-folding diagrams fail to mention is that each fold enacts itself upon the secret marrow of your ethics, the axioms of your thoughts.

Whether this is the most important thing the diagrams fail to mention is a matter of opinion.

"There's time for one more hand," Lisse's ghost said. It was composed of cinders of color, a cipher of blurred features, and it had a voice like entropy and smoke and sudden death. Quite possibly it was the last ghost on all of ruined Rhaion, conquered Rhaion, Rhaion with its devastated, shadowless cities and dead moons and dimming sun. Sometimes Lisse wondered if the ghost had a scar to match her own, a long, livid line down her arm. But she felt it was impolite to ask.

Around them, in a command spindle sized for fifty, the walls of the war-kite were hung with tatters of black and faded green, even now in the process of reknitting themselves into tapestry displays. Tangled reeds changed into ravens. One perched on a lightning-cloven tree. Another, taking shape amid twisted threads, peered out from a skull's eye socket.

Lisse didn't need any deep familiarity with mercenary symbology to understand the warning. Lisse's people had adopted a saying from the Imperium's mercenaries: *In raven arithmetic, no death is enough.*

Lisse had expected pursuit. She had deserted from Base 87 soon after hearing that scouts had found a mercenary war-kite in the ruins of a sacred maze, six years after all the mercenaries vanished: suspicious timing on her part, but she would have no better opportunity for revenge. The ghost had not tried too hard to dissuade her. It had always understood her ambitions.

For a hundred years, despite being frequently outnumbered, the mercenaries in their starfaring kites had cindered cities, destroyed flights of rebel starflyers, shattered stations in the void's hungry depths. What better weapon than one of their own kites?

What troubled her was how lightly the war-kite had been defended. It had made a strange, thorny silhouette against the lavender sky even from a long way off, like briars gone wild, and with the ghost as scout she had slipped past the few mechanized sentries. The kite's shadow had been human. She was not sure what to make of that.

The kite had opened to her like a flower. The card game had been the ghost's idea, a way to reassure the kite that she was its ally: Scorch had been invented by the mercenaries.

Lisse leaned forward and started to scoop the nearest column, the Candle Column, from the black-and-green gameplay rug. The ghost forestalled her with a hand that felt like the dregs of autumn, decay from the inside out. In spite of herself, she flinched from the ghostweight, which had troubled her all her life. Her hand jerked sideways; her fingers spasmed.

"Look," the ghost said.

Few cadets had played Scorch with Lisse even in the barracks. The ghost left its combinatorial fingerprints in the cards. People drew the unlucky Fallen General's Hand over and over again, or doubled on nothing but negative values, or inverted the Crown Flower at odds of thousands to one. So Lisse had learned to play the solitaire variant, with jerengjen as counters. *You must learn your enemy's weapons,* the ghost had told her, and so, even as a child in the reeducation facility, she had saved her chits for paper to practice folding into cranes, lilies, leaf-shaped boats.

Next to the Candle Column she had folded stormbird, greatfrog, lantern, drake. Where the ghost had interrupted her attempt to clear the pieces, they had landed amid the Sojourner and Mirror Columns, forming a skewed late-game configuration: a minor variant of the Needle Stratagem, missing only its pivot.

"Consider it an omen," the ghost said. "Even the smallest sliver can kill, as they say."

There were six ravens on the tapestries now. The latest one had outspread wings, as though it planned to blot out the shrouded sun. She wondered what it said about the mercenaries, that they couched their warnings in pictures rather than drums or gongs.

Lisse rose from her couch. "So they're coming for us. Where are they?"

She had spoken in the Imperium's administrative tongue, not one of the mercenaries' own languages. Nevertheless, a raven flew from one tapestry to join its fellows in the next. The vacant tapestry grayed, then displayed a new scene: a squad of six tanks caparisoned in Imperial blue and bronze, paced by two personnel carriers sheathed in metal mined from withered stars. They advanced upslope, pebbles skittering in their wake.

In the old days, the ghost had told her, no one would have advanced through a sacred maze by straight lines. But the ancient walls, curved and interlocking, were gone now. The ghost had drawn the old designs on her palm with its insubstantial fingers, and she had learned not to shudder at the untouch, had learned to thread the maze in her mind's eye: one more map to the things she must not forget.

"I'd rather avoid fighting them," Lisse said. She was looking at the command spindle's controls. Standard Imperial layout, all of them—it did not occur to her to wonder why the kite had configured itself thus—but she found nothing for the weapons.

"People don't bring tanks when they want to negotiate," the ghost said dryly. "And they'll have alerted their flyers for intercept. You have something they want badly."

"Then why didn't they guard it better?" she demanded.

Despite the tanks' approach, the ghost fell silent. After a while, it said, "Perhaps they didn't think anyone but a mercenary could fly a kite."

"They might be right," Lisse said darkly. She strapped herself into the commander's seat, then pressed three fingers against the controls and traced the commands she had been taught as a cadet. The kite shuddered, as though caught in a hell-wind from the sky's fissures. But it did not unfurl itself to fly.

She tried the command gestures again, forcing herself to slow down. A cold keening vibrated through the walls. The kite remained stubbornly landfast.

The squad rounded the bend in the road. All the ravens had gathered in a single tapestry, decorating a half-leafed tree like dire jewels. The rest of the tapestries displayed the squad from different angles: two aerial views and four from the ground.

Lisse studied one of the aerial views and caught sight of two scuttling figures, lean angles and glittering eyes and a balancing tail in black metal. She stiffened. They had the shadows of hounds, all graceful hunting curves. Two jerengjen, true ones, unlike the lifeless shapes that she folded out of paper. The kite must have deployed them when it sensed the tanks' approach.

Sweating now, despite the autumn temperature inside, she methodically tried every command she had ever learned. The kite remained obdurate. The tapestries' green threads faded until the ravens and their tree were bleak black splashes against a background of wintry gray.

It was a message. Perhaps a demand. But she did not understand.

The first two tanks slowed into view. Roses, blue with bronze hearts, were engraved to either side of the main guns. The lead tank's roses flared briefly.

The kite whispered to itself in a language that Lisse did not recognize. Then the largest tapestry cleared of trees and swirling leaves and rubble, and presented her with a commander's emblem, a pale blue rose pierced by three claws. A man's voice issued from the tapestry: "Cadet Fai Guen." This was her registry name. They had not reckoned that she would keep her true name alive in her heart like an ember. "You are in violation of Imperial interdict. Surrender the kite at once."

He did not offer mercy. The Imperium never did.

Lisse resisted the urge to pound her fists against the interface. She had not survived this long by being impatient. "That's it, then," she said to the ghost in defeat.

"Cadet Fai Guen," the voice said again, after another burst of light, "you have one minute to surrender the kite before we open fire."

"Lisse," the ghost said, "the kite's awake."

She bit back a retort and looked down. Where the control panel had once been featureless gray, it was now crisp white interrupted by five glyphs, perfectly spaced for her outspread fingers. She resisted the urge to snatch her hand away. "Very well," she said. "If we can't fly, at least we can fight."

She didn't know the kite's specific control codes. Triggering the wrong sequence might activate the kite's internal defenses. But taking tank fire at point-blank range would get her killed, too. She couldn't imagine that the kite's armor had improved in the years of its neglect.

On the other hand, it had jerengjen scouts, and the jerengjen looked perfectly functional.

She pressed her thumb to the first glyph. A shadow unfurled briefly but was gone before she could identify it. The second attempt revealed a two-headed dragon's twisting coils. Long-range missiles, then: thunder in the sky. Working quickly, she ran through the options. It would be ironic if she got the weapons systems to work only to incinerate herself.

"You have ten seconds, Cadet Fai Guen," said the voice with no particular emotion.

"Lisse," the ghost said, betraying impatience.

One of the glyphs had shown a wolf running. She remembered that at one point the wolf had been the mercenaries' emblem. Nevertheless, she felt a dangerous affinity to it. As she hesitated over it, the kite said, in a parched voice, "Soul strike."

She tapped the glyph, then pressed her palm flat to activate the weapon. The panel felt briefly hot, then cold.

For a second she thought that nothing had happened, that the kite had malfunctioned. The kite was eerily still.

The tanks and personnel carriers were still visible as gray outlines against darker gray, as were the nearby trees and their stifled fruits. She wasn't sure whether that was an effect of the unnamed weapons or a problem with the tapestries. Had ten seconds passed yet? She couldn't tell, and the clock of her pulse was unreliable.

Desperate to escape before the tanks spat forth the killing rounds, Lisse raked her hand sideways to dismiss the glyphs. They dispersed in unsettling fragmented shapes resembling half-chewed leaves and corroded handprints. She repeated the gesture for *fly*.

Lisse choked back a cry as the kite lofted. The tapestry views changed to sky on all sides except the ravens on their tree—birds no longer, but skeletons, price paid in coin of bone.

Only once they had gained some altitude did she instruct the kite to show her what had befallen her hunters. It responded by continuing to accelerate.

The problem was not the tapestries. Rather, the kite's wolf-strike had ripped all the shadows free of their owners, killing them. Below, across a great swathe of the continent once called Ishuel's Bridge, was a devastation of light, a hard, glittering splash against the surrounding snow-capped mountains and forests and winding rivers.

Lisse had been an excellent student, not out of academic conscientiousness but because it gave her an opportunity to study her enemy. One of her best subjects had been geography. She and the ghost had spent hours drawing maps in the air or shaping topographies in her blankets; paper would betray them, it had said. As she memorized the streets of the City of Fountains, it had sung her the ballads of its founding. It had told her about the feuding poets and philosophers that the thoroughfares of the City of Prisms had been named after. She knew which mines supplied which bases and how the roads spidered across Ishuel's Bridge. While the population figures of the bases and settlement camps weren't exactly announced to cadets, especially those recruited from the reeducation facilities, it didn't take much to make an educated guess.

The Imperium had built 114 bases on Ishuel's Bridge. Base complements averaged 20,000 people. Even allowing for the imprecision of her eye, the wolf-strike had taken out—

She shivered as she listed the affected bases, approximately sixty of them.

The settlement camps' populations were more difficult. The Imperium did not like to release those figures. Imperfectly, she based her estimate on the zone around Base 87, remembering the rows of identical shelters. The only reason they did not outnumber the bases' personnel was that the mercenaries had been coldly efficient on Jerengjen Day.

Needle Stratagem, Lisse thought blankly. The smallest sliver. She hadn't expected its manifestation to be quite so literal.

The ghost was looking at her, its dark eyes unusually distinct. "There's nothing to be done for it now," it said at last. "Tell the kite where to go before it decides for itself."

"Ashway 514," Lisse said, as they had decided before she fled base: scenario after scenario whispered to each other like bedtime stories. She was shaking. The straps did nothing to steady her.

She had one last glimpse of the dead region before they curved into the void: her handprint upon her own birthworld. She had only meant to destroy her hunters.

In her dreams, later, the blast pattern took on the outline of a running wolf.

In the mercenaries' dominant language, jerengjen originally referred to the art of folding paper. For her part, when Lisse first saw it, she thought of it as snow. She was four years old. It was a fair spring afternoon in the City of

Tapestries, slightly humid. She was watching a bird try to catch a bright butterfly when improbable paper shapes began drifting from the sky, foxes and snakes and stormbirds.

Lisse called to her parents, laughing. Her parents knew better. Over her shrieks, they dragged her into the basement and switched off the lights. She tried to bite one of her fathers when he clamped his hand over her mouth. Jerengjen tracked primarily by shadows, not by sound, but you couldn't be too careful where the mercenaries' weapons were concerned.

In the streets, jerengjen unfolded prettily, expanding into artillery with dragon-shaped shadows and sleek four-legged assault robots with wolf-shaped shadows. In the skies, jerengjen unfolded into bombers with kestrel-shaped shadows.

This was not the only Rhaioni city where this happened. People crumpled like paper cutouts once their shadows were cut away by the onslaught. Approximately one-third of the world's population perished in the weeks that followed.

Of the casualty figures, the Imperium said, *It is regrettable.* And later, *The stalled negotiations made the consolidation necessary.*

Lisse carried a map of the voidways with her at all times, half in her head and half in the Scorch deck. The ghost had once been a traveler. It had shown her mnemonics for the dark passages and the deep perils that lay between stars. Growing up, she had laid out endless tableaux between her lessons, memorizing travel times and vortices and twists.

Ashway 514 lay in the interstices between two unstable stars and their cacophonous necklace of planets, comets, and asteroids. Lisse felt the kite tilting this way and that as it balanced itself against the stormy voidcurrent. The tapestries shone from one side with ruddy light from the nearer star, 514 Tsi. On the other side, a pale violet-blue planet with a serenade of rings occluded the view.

514 was a useful hiding place. It was off the major tradeways, and since the Battle of Fallen Sun—named after the rebel general's emblem, a white sun outlined in red, rather than the nearby stars—it had been designated an ashway, where permanent habitation was forbidden.

More important to Lisse, however, was the fact that 514 was the ashway nearest the last mercenary sighting, some five years ago. As a student, she had learned the names and silhouettes of the most prominent war-kites, and set verses of praise in their honor to Imperial anthems. She had written essays on their tactics and memorized the names of their most famous commanders, although there were no statues or portraits, only the occasional unsmiling photograph. The Imperium was fond of statues and portraits.

For a hundred years (administrative calendar), the mercenaries had served their masters unflinchingly and unfailingly. Lisse had assumed that she would have as much time as she needed to plot against them. Instead, they had broken their service, for reasons the Imperium had never released—perhaps they didn't know, either—and none had been seen since.

"I'm not sure there's anything to find here," Lisse said. Surely the Imperium would have scoured the region for clues. The tapestries were empty of ravens. Instead, they diagrammed shifting voidcurrent flows. The approach of enemy starflyers would perturb the current and allow Lisse and the ghost to estimate their intent. Not trusting the kite's systems—although there was only so far that she could take her distrust, given the circumstances—she had been watching the tapestries for the past several hours. She had, after a brief argument with the ghost, switched on haptics so that the air currents would, however imperfectly, reflect the status of the void around them. Sometimes it was easier to feel a problem through your skin.

"There's no indication of derelict kites here," she added. "Or even kites in use, other than this one."

"It's a starting place, that's all," the ghost said.

"We're going to have to risk a station eventually. You might not need to eat, but I do." She had only been able to sneak a few rations out of base. It was tempting to nibble at one now.

"Perhaps there are stores on the kite."

"I can't help but think this place is a trap."

"You have to eat sooner or later," the ghost said reasonably. "It's worth a look, and I don't want to see you go hungry." At her hesitation, it added, "I'll stand watch here. I'm only a breath away."

This didn't reassure her as much as it should have, but she was no longer a child in a bunk precisely aligned with the walls, clutching the covers while the ghost told her her people's stories. She reminded herself of her favorite story, in which a single sentinel kept away the world's last morning by burning out her eyes, and set out.

Lisse felt the ghostweight's pull the farther away she walked, but that was old pain, and easily endured. Lights flicked on to accompany her, diffuse despite her unnaturally sharp shadow, then started illuminating passages ahead of her, guiding her footsteps. She wondered what the kite didn't want her to see.

Rations were in an unmarked storage room. She wouldn't have been certain about the rations, except that they were, if the packaging was to be believed, field category 72: better than what she had eaten on training exercises, but not by much. No surprise, now that she thought about it: from all accounts, the mercenaries had relied on their masters' production capacity.

Feeling ridiculous, she grabbed two rations and retraced her steps. The fact that the kite lit her exact path only made her more nervous.

"Anything new?" she asked the ghost. She tapped the ration. "It's a pity that you can't taste poison."

The ghost laughed dryly. "If the kite were going to kill you, it wouldn't be that subtle. Food is food, Lisse."

The food was as exactingly mediocre as she had come to expect from military food. At least it was not any worse. She found a receptacle for disposal afterward, then laid out a Scorch tableau, Candle Column to Bone, right to left. Cards rather than jerengjen, because she remembered the scuttling hound-jerengjen with creeping distaste.

From the moment she left Base 87, one timer had started running down. The devastation of Ishuel's Bridge had begun another, the important one. She wasn't gambling her survival; she had already sold it. The question was, how many Imperial bases could she extinguish on her way out? And could she hunt down any of the mercenaries that had been the Imperium's killing sword?

Lisse sorted rapidly through possible targets. For instance, Base 226 Mheng, the Petaled Fortress. She would certainly perish in the attempt, but the only way she could better that accomplishment would be to raze the Imperial firstworld, and she wasn't that ambitious. There was Bridgepoint 663 Tsi-Kes, with its celebrated Pallid Sentinels, or Aerie 8 Yeneq, which built the Imperium's greatest flyers, or—

She set the cards down, closed her eyes, and pressed her palms against her face. She was no tactician supreme. Would it make much difference if she picked a card at random?

But of course nothing was truly random in the ghost's presence.

She laid out the Candle Column again. "Not 8 Yeneq," she said. "Let's start with a softer target. Aerie 586 Chiu."

Lisse looked at the ghost: the habit of seeking its approval had not left her. It nodded. "The safest approach is via the Capillary Ashways. It will test your piloting skills."

Privately, Lisse thought that the kite would be happy to guide itself. They didn't dare allow it to, however.

The Capillaries were among the worst of the ashways. Even starlight moved in unnerving ways when faced with ancient networks of voidcurrent gates, unmaintained for generations, or vortices whose behavior changed day by day.

They were fortunate with the first several capillaries. Under other circumstances, Lisse would have gawked at the splendor of lensed galaxies and the jewel-fire of distant clusters. She was starting to manipulate the control interface without hesitating, or flinching as though a wolf's shadow might cross hers.

At the ninth—

"Patrol," the ghost said, leaning close.

She nodded jerkily, trying not to show that its proximity pained her. Its mouth crimped in apology.

"It would have been worse if we'd made it all the way to 586 Chiu without a run-in," Lisse said. That kind of luck always had a price. If she was unready, best to find out now, while there was a chance of fleeing to prepare for a later strike.

The patrol consisted of sixteen flyers: eight Lance 82s and eight Scout 73s. She had flown similar Scouts in simulation.

The flyers did not hesitate. A spread of missiles streaked toward her. Lisse launched antimissile fire.

It was impossible to tell whether they had gone on the attack because the Imperium and the mercenaries had parted on bad terms, or because the authorities had already learned of what had befallen Rhaion. She was certain couriers had gone out within moments of the devastation of Ishuel's Bridge.

As the missiles exploded, Lisse wrenched the kite toward the nearest vortex. The kite was a larger and sturdier craft. It would be better able to survive the voidcurrent stresses. The tapestries dimmed as they approached. She shut off haptics as wind eddied and swirled in the command spindle. It would only get worse.

One missile barely missed her. She would have to do better. And the vortex was a temporary terrain advantage; she could not lurk there forever.

The second barrage came. Lisse veered deeper into the current. The stars took on peculiar roseate shapes.

"They know the kite's capabilities," the ghost reminded her. "Use them. If they're smart, they'll already have sent a courier burst to local command."

The kite suggested jerengjen flyers, harrier class. Lisse conceded its expertise.

The harriers unfolded as they launched, sleek and savage. They maneuvered remarkably well in the turbulence. But there were only ten of them.

"If I fire into that, I'll hit them," Lisse said. Her reflexes were good, but not that good, and the harriers apparently liked to soar near their targets.

"You won't need to fire," the ghost said.

She glanced at him, disbelieving. Her hand hovered over the controls, playing through possibilities and finding them wanting. For instance, she wasn't certain that the firebird (explosives) didn't entail self-immolation, and she was baffled by the stag.

The patrol's pilots were not incapable. They scorched three of the harriers. They probably realized at the same time that Lisse did that the three had been sacrifices. The other seven flensed them silent.

Lisse edged the kite out of the vortex. She felt an uncomfortable sense of duty to the surviving harriers, but she knew they were one-use, crumpled paper, like all jerengjen. Indeed, they folded themselves flat as she passed them, reducing themselves to battledrift.

"I can't see how this is an efficient use of resources," Lisse told the ghost.

"It's an artifact of the mercenaries' methods," it said. "It works. Perhaps that's all that matters."

Lisse wanted to ask for details, but her attention was diverted by a crescendo of turbulence. By the time they reached gentler currents, she was too tired to bring it up.

They altered their approach to 586 Chiu twice, favoring stealth over confrontation. If she wanted to char every patrol in the Imperium by herself, she could live a thousand sleepless years and never be done.

For six days they lurked near 586 Chiu, developing a sense for local traffic and likely defenses. Terrain would not be much difficulty. Aeries were built near calm, steady currents.

"It would be easiest if you were willing to take out the associated city," the ghost said in a neutral voice. They had been discussing whether making a bombing pass on the aerie posed too much of a risk. Lisse had balked at the fact that 586 Chiu Second City was well within blast radius. The people who had furnished the kite's armaments seemed to have believed in surfeit. "They'd only have a moment to know what was happening."

"No."

"Lisse—"

She looked at it mutely, obdurate, although she hated to disappoint it. It hesitated, but did not press its case further.

"This, then," it said in defeat. "Next best odds: aim the voidcurrent disrupter at the manufactory's core while jerengjen occupy the defenses." Aeries held the surrounding current constant to facilitate the calibration of newly built flyers. Under ordinary circumstances, the counterbalancing vortex was leashed at the core. If they could disrupt the core, the vortex would tear at its surroundings.

"That's what we'll do, then," Lisse said. The disrupter had a short range. She did not like the idea of flying in close. But she had objected to the safer alternative.

Aerie 586 Chiu reminded Lisse not of a nest but of a pyre. Flyers and transports were always coming and going, like sparks. The kite swooped in sharp and fast. Falcon-jerengjen raced ahead of them, holding lattice formation for two seconds before scattering toward their chosen marks.

The aerie's commanders responded commendably. They knew the kite was by far the greater threat. But Lisse met the first flight they threw at her with missiles keen and terrible. The void lit up in a clamor of brilliant colors.

The kite screamed when a flyer salvo hit one of its secondary wings. It bucked briefly while the other wings changed their geometry to compensate. Lisse could not help but think that the scream had not sounded like pain. It had sounded like exultation.

The real test was the gauntlet of Banner 142 artillery emplacements. They were silver-bright and terrible. It seemed wrong that they did not roar like tigers. Lisse bit the inside of her mouth and concentrated on narrowing the parameters for the voidcurrent disrupter. Her hand was a fist on the control panel.

One tapestry depicted the currents: striations within striations of pale blue against black. Despite its shielding, the core was visible as a knot tangled out of all proportion to its size.

"Now," the ghost said, with inhuman timing.

She didn't wait to be told twice. She unfisted her hand.

Unlike the wolf-strike, the disrupter made the kite scream again. It lurched and twisted. Lisse wanted to clap her hands over her ears, but there was more incoming fire, and she was occupied with evasive maneuvers. The kite folded in on itself, minimizing its profile. It dizzied her to view it on the secondary tapestry. For a panicked moment, she thought the kite would close itself around her, press her like petals in a book. Then she remembered to breathe.

The disrupter was not visible to human sight, but the kite could read its effect on the current. Like lightning, the disrupter's blast forked and forked again, zigzagging inexorably toward the minute variations in flux that would lead it toward the core.

She was too busy whipping the kite around to an escape vector to see the moment of convergence between disrupter and core. But she felt the first lashing surge as the vortex spun free of its shielding, expanding into available space. Then she was too busy steadying the kite through the triggered subvortices to pay attention to anything but keeping them alive.

Only later did she remember how much debris there had been, flung in newly unpredictable ways: wings torn from flyers, struts, bulkheads, even an improbable crate with small reddish fruit tumbling from the hole in its side.

Later, too, it would trouble her that she had not been able to keep count of the people in the tumult. Most were dead already: sliced slantwise, bone and viscera exposed, trailing banners of blood; others twisted and torn, faces ripped off and cast aside like unwanted masks, fingers uselessly clutching the wrack of chairs, tables, door frames. A fracture in one wall revealed three people in dark green jackets. They turned their faces toward the widening crack, then clasped hands before a subvortex hurled them apart. The last Lisse saw of them was two hands, still clasped together and severed at the wrist.

Lisse found an escape. Took it.

She didn't know until later that she had destroyed 40% of the aerie's structure. Some people survived. They knew how to rebuild.

What she never found out was that the disrupter's effect was sufficiently long-lasting that some of the survivors died of thirst before supplies could safely be brought in.

In the old days, Lisse's people took on the ghostweight to comfort the dead and be comforted in return. After a year and a day, the dead unstitched themselves and accepted their rest.

After Jerengjen Day, Lisse's people struggled to share the sudden increase in ghostweight, to alleviate the flickering terror of the massacred.

Lisse's parents, unlike the others, stitched a ghost onto a child.

"They saw no choice," the ghost told her again and again. "You mustn't blame them."

The ghost had listened uncomplainingly to her troubles and taught her how to cry quietly so the teachers wouldn't hear her. It had soothed her to sleep with her people's legends and histories, described the gardens and promenades so vividly she imagined she could remember them herself. Some nights were more difficult than others, trying to sleep with that strange, stabbing, heartpulse ache. But blame was not what she felt, not usually.

The second target was Base 454 Qo, whose elite flyers were painted with elaborate knotwork, green with bronze-tipped thorns. For reasons that Lisse did not try to understand, the jerengjen dismembered the defensive flight but left the painted panels completely intact.

The third, the fourth, the fifth—she started using Scorch card values to tabulate the reported deaths, however unreliable the figures were in any unencrypted sources. For all its talents, the kite could not pierce military-grade encryption. She spent two days fidgeting over this inconvenience so she wouldn't have to think about the numbers.

When she did think about the numbers, she refused to round up. She refused to round down.

The nightmares started after the sixth, Bridgepoint 977 Ja-Esh. The station commander had kept silence, as she had come to expect. However, a merchant coalition had broken the interdict to plead for mercy in fourteen languages. She hadn't destroyed the coalition's outpost. The station had, in reprimand.

She reminded herself that the merchant would have perished anyway. She had learned to use the firebird to scathing effect. And she was under no illusions that she was only destroying Imperial soldiers and bureaucrats.

In her dreams she heard their pleas in her birth tongue, which the ghost had taught her. The ghost, for its part, started singing her to sleep, as it had when she was little.

The numbers marched higher. When they broke ten million, she plunged out of the command spindle and into the room she had claimed for her own. She pounded the wall until her fists bled. Triumph tasted like salt and venom. It wasn't supposed to be so *easy*. In the worst dreams, a wolf roved the tapestries, eating shadows—eating souls. And the void with its tinsel of worlds was nothing but one vast shadow.

Stores began running low after the seventeenth. Lisse and the ghost argued over whether it was worth attempting to resupply through black market traders. Lisse said they didn't have time to spare, and won. Besides, she had little appetite.

Intercepted communications suggested that someone was hunting them. Rumors and whispers. They kept Lisse awake when she was so tired she wanted to slam the world shut and hide. The Imperium certainly planned reprisal. Maybe others did, too.

If anyone else took advantage of the disruption to move against the Imperium for their own reasons, she didn't hear about it.

The names of the war-kites, recorded in the Imperium's administrative language, are varied: *Fire Burns the Spider Black. The Siege of the City with Seventeen Faces. Sovereign Geometry. The Glove with Three Fingers.*

The names are not, strictly speaking, Imperial. Rather, they are plundered from the greatest accomplishments of the cultures that the mercenaries have defeated on the Imperium's behalf. *Fire Burns the Spider Black* was a silk tapestry housed in the dark hall of Meu Danh, ancient of years. *The Siege of the City with Seventeen Faces* was a saga chanted by the historians of Kwaire. *Sovereign Geometry* discussed the varying nature of parallel lines. And more: plays, statues, games.

The Imperium's scholars and artists take great pleasure in reinterpreting these works. Such achievements are meant to be disseminated, they say.

They were three days' flight from the next target, Base 894 Sao, when the shadow winged across all the tapestries. The void was dark, pricked by starfire and the occasional searing burst of particles. The shadow singed everything darker as it soared to intercept them, as single-minded in its purpose as a bullet. For a second she almost thought it was a collage of wrecked flyers and rusty shrapnel.

The ghost cursed. Lisse startled, but when she looked at it, its face was composed again.

As Lisse pulled back the displays' focus to get a better sense of the scale, she thought of snowbirds and stormbirds, winter winds and cutting beaks. "I don't know what that is," she said, "but it can't be natural." None of the imperial defenses had manifested in such a fashion.

"It's not," the ghost said. "That's another war-kite."

Lisse cleared the control panel. She veered them into a chancy voidcurrent eddy.

The ghost said, "Wait. You won't outrun it. As we see its shadow, it sees ours."

"How does a kite have a shadow in the void in the first place?" she asked. "And why haven't we ever seen our own shadow?"

"Who can see their own soul?" the ghost said. But it would not meet her eyes.

Lisse would have pressed for more, but the shadow overtook them. It folded itself back like a plumage of knives. She brought the kite about. The control panel suggested possibilities: a two-headed dragon, a falcon, a coiled snake. Next a wolf reared up, but she quickly pulled her hand back.

"Visual contact," the kite said crisply.

The stranger-kite was the color of a tarnished star. It had tucked all its projections away to present a minimal surface for targeting, but Lisse had no doubt that it could unfold itself faster than she could draw breath. The kite flew a widening helix, beautifully precise.

"A mercenary salute, equal to equal," the ghost said.

"Are we expected to return it?"

"Are you a mercenary?" the ghost countered.

"Communications incoming," the kite said before Lisse could make a retort.

"I'll hear it," Lisse said over the ghost's objection. It was the least courtesy she could offer, even to a mercenary.

To Lisse's surprise, the tapestry's raven vanished to reveal a woman's visage, not an emblem. The woman had brown skin, a scar trailing from one temple down to her cheekbone, and dark hair cropped short. She wore gray on gray, in no uniform that Lisse recognized, sharply tailored. Lisse had expected a killer's eyes, a hunter's eyes. Instead, the woman merely looked tired.

"Commander Kiriet Dzan of—" She had been speaking in administrative, but the last word was unfamiliar. "You would say *Candle.*"

"Lisse of Rhaion," she said. There was no sense in hiding her name.

But the woman wasn't looking at her. She was looking at the ghost. She said something sharply in that unfamiliar language.

The ghost pressed its hand against Lisse's. She shuddered, not understanding. "Be strong," it murmured.

"I see," Kiriet said, once more speaking in administrative. Her mouth was unsmiling. "Lisse, do you know who you're traveling with?"

"I don't believe we're acquainted," the ghost said, coldly formal.

"Of course not," Kiriet said. "But I was the logistical coordinator for the scouring of Rhaion." She did not say *consolidation.* "I knew why we were there. Lisse, your ghost's name is Vron Arien."

Lisse said, after several seconds, "That's a mercenary name."

The ghost said, "So it is. Lisse—" Its hand fell away.

"Tell me what's going on."

Its mouth was taut. Then: "Lisse, I—"

"Tell me."

"He was a deserter, Lisse," the woman said, carefully, as if she thought the information might fracture her. "For years he eluded Wolf Command. Then we discovered he had gone to ground on Rhaion. Wolf Command determined that, for sheltering him, Rhaion must be brought to heel. The Imperium assented."

Throughout this Lisse looked at the ghost, silently begging it to deny any of it, all of it. But the ghost said nothing.

Lisse thought of long nights with the ghost leaning by her bedside, reminding her of the dancers, the tame birds, the tangle of frostfruit trees in the city square; things she did not remember herself because she had been too young when the jerengjen came. Even her parents only came to her in snatches: curling up in a mother's lap, helping a father peel plantains. Had any of the ghost's stories been real?

She thought, too, of the way the ghost had helped her plan her escape from Base 87, how it had led her cunningly through the maze and to the kite. At the time, it had not occurred to her to wonder at its confidence.

Lisse said, "Then the kite is yours."

"After a fashion, yes." The ghost's eyes were precisely the color of ash after the last ember's death.

"But my parents—"

Enunciating the words as if they cut it, the ghost said, "We made a bargain, your parents and I."

She could not help it; she made a stricken sound.

"I offered you my protection," the ghost said. "After years serving the Imperium, I knew its workings. And I offered your parents vengeance. Don't think that Rhaion wasn't my home, too."

Lisse was wrackingly aware of Kiriet's regard. "Did my parents truly die in the consolidation?" The euphemism was easier to use.

She could have asked whether Lisse was her real name. She had to assume that it wasn't.

"I don't know," it said. "After you were separated from them, I had no way of finding out. Lisse, I think you had better find out what Kiriet wants. She is not your friend."

I was the logistical coordinator, Kiriet had said. And her surprise at seeing the ghost—*It has a name,* Lisse reminded herself—struck Lisse as genuine. Which meant Kiriet had not come here in pursuit of Vron Arien. "Why are you here?" Lisse asked.

"You're not going to like it. I'm here to destroy your kite, whatever you've named it."

"It doesn't have a name." She had been unable to face the act of naming, of claiming ownership.

Kiriet looked at her sideways. "I see."

"Surely you could have accomplished your goal," Lisse said, "without talking to me first. I am inexperienced in the ways of kites. You are not." In truth, she should already have been running. But Kiriet's revelation meant that Lisse's purpose, once so clear, was no longer to be relied upon.

"I may not be your friend, but I am not your enemy, either," Kiriet said. "I have no common purpose with the Imperium, not anymore. But you cannot continue to use the kite."

Lisse's eyes narrowed. "It is the weapon I have," she said. "I would be a fool to relinquish it."

"I don't deny its efficacy," Kiriet said, "but you are Rhaioni. Doesn't the cost trouble you?"

Cost?

Kiriet said, "So no one told you." Her anger focused on the ghost.

"A weapon is a weapon," the ghost said. At Lisse's indrawn breath, it said, "The kites take their sustenance from the deaths they deal. It was necessary to strengthen ours by letting it feast on smaller targets first. This is the particular craft of my people, as ghostweight was the craft of yours, Lisse."

Sustenance. "So this is why you want to destroy the kite," Lisse said to Kiriet.

"Yes." The other woman's smile was bitter. "As you might imagine, the Imperium did not approve. It wanted to negotiate another hundred-year contract. I dissented."

"Were you in a position to dissent?" the ghost asked, in a way that made Lisse think that it was translating some idiom from its native language.

"I challenged my way up the chain of command and unseated the head of Wolf Command," Kiriet said. "It was not a popular move. I have been destroying kites ever since. If the Imperium is so keen on further conquest, let it dirty its own hands."

"Yet you wield a kite yourself," Lisse said.

"*Candle* is my home. But on the day that every kite is accounted for in words of ash and cinders, I will turn my own hand against it."

It appealed to Lisse's sense of irony. All the same, she did not trust Kiriet.

She heard a new voice. Kiriet's head turned. "Someone's followed you." She said a curt phrase in her own language, then: "You'll want my assistance—"

Lisse shook her head.

"It's a small flight, as these things go, but it represents a threat to you. Let me—"

"No," Lisse said, more abruptly than she had meant to. "I'll handle it myself."

"If you insist," Kiriet said, looking even more tired. "Don't say I didn't warn you." Then her face was replaced, for a flicker, with her emblem: a black candle crossed slantwise by an empty sheath.

"The *Candle* is headed for a vortex, probably for cover," the ghost said, very softly. "But it can return at any moment."

Lisse thought that she was all right, and then the reaction set in. She spent several irrecoverable breaths shaking, arms wrapped around herself, before she was able to concentrate on the tapestry data.

At one time, every war-kite displayed a calligraphy scroll in its command spindle. The words are, approximately:

I have only
one candle

Even by the mercenaries' standards, it is not much of a poem. But the woman who wrote it was a soldier, not a poet.

The mercenaries no longer have a homeland. Even so, they keep certain traditions, and one of them is the Night of Vigils. Each mercenary honors the year's dead by lighting a candle. They used to do this on the winter solstice of an ancient calendar. Now the Night of Vigils is on the anniversary of the day the first war-kites were launched; the day the mercenaries slaughtered their own people to feed the kites.

The kites fly, the mercenaries' commandant said. *But they do not know how to hunt.*

When he was done, they knew how to hunt. Few of the mercenaries forgave him, but it was too late by then.

The poem says: So many people have died, yet I have only one candle for them all.

It is worth noting that "have" is expressed by a particular construction for alienable possession: not only is the having subject to change, it is additionally under threat of being taken away.

Kiriet's warning had been correct. An Imperial flight in perfect formation had advanced toward them, inhibiting their avenues of escape. They outnumbered her forty-eight to one. The numbers did not concern her, but the Imperium's resources meant that if she dealt with this flight, there would be twenty more waiting for her, and the numbers would only grow worse. That they had not opened fire already meant they had some trickery in mind.

One of the flyers peeled away, describing an elegant curve and exposing its most vulnerable surface, painted with a rose.

"That one's not armed," Lisse said, puzzled.

The ghost's expression was unreadable. "How very wise of them," it said.

The forward tapestry flickered. "Accept the communication," Lisse said.

The emblem that appeared was a trefoil flanked by two roses, one stem-up, one stem-down. Not for the first time, Lisse wondered why people from a culture that lavished attention on miniatures and sculptures were so intent on masking themselves in emblems.

"Commander Fai Guen, this is Envoy Nhai Bara." A woman's voice, deep and resonant, with an accent Lisse didn't recognize.

So I've been promoted? Lisse thought sardonically, feeling herself tense up. The Imperium never gave you anything, even a meaningless rank, without expecting something in return.

Softly, she said to the ghost, "They were bound to catch up to us sooner or later." Then, to the kite: "Communications to Envoy Nhai: I am Lisse of Rhaion. What words between us could possibly be worth exchanging? Your people are not known for mercy."

"If you will not listen to me," Nhai said, "perhaps you will listen to the envoy after me, or the one after that. We are patient and we are many. But I am not interested in discussing mercy: that's something we have in common."

"I'm listening," Lisse said, despite the ghost's chilly stiffness. All her life she had honed herself against the Imperium. It was unbearable to consider that she might have been mistaken. But she had to know what Nhai's purpose was.

"Commander Lisse," the envoy said, and it hurt like a stab to hear her name spoken by a voice other than the ghost's, a voice that was not Rhaioni. Even if she knew, now, that the ghost was not Rhaioni, either. "I have a proposal for you. You have proven your military effectiveness—"

Military effectiveness. She had tallied all the deaths, she had marked each massacre on the walls of her heart, and this faceless envoy collapsed them into two words empty of number.

"—quite thoroughly. We are in need of a strong sword. What is your price for hire, Commander Lisse?"

"What is my—" She stared at the trefoil emblem, and then her face went ashen.

It is not true that the dead cannot be folded. Square becomes kite becomes swan; history becomes rumor becomes song. Even the act of remembrance creases the truth.

But the same can be said of the living.

Perfect Lies
GWENDOLYN CLARE

The only enjoyable part of my daily meeting with Losin was the view. One large panoramic viewport made up the far wall of his grandiose office—a perk of being the Director-General of the UN Interworld Relations Organization. Losin sat facing the door instead, so while he talked I stared over his right shoulder at the starscape beyond.

The Mask People's starship floated in the distance, gargantuan yet fragile, a city-sized architectural latticework sprawling in three dimensions. The vessel had synchronized its trajectory with our station's orbit, so it seemed to hang motionless against a backdrop of crawling stars. I loved the look of it—so still, so stoic. A massive, involuted shell to hide the Mask People and all their teeming emotions.

Not that it mattered how I felt. I would do my job.

Losin paused. "Are you listening, Nora?"

I don't generally look at people's faces unless I have a specific reason for reading them. Too late, I remembered how little Losin cared for my natural stoic demeanor.

I shifted my gaze to make eye contact and twisted my mouth into a reassuring smile. "Of course, sir."

"It's critical to reach an agreement with no alterations to the trade proposal. I don't care what you have to do to convince them, I want signatures on that document as is." He was in his third decade of politics and had both the gray hair and the attitude to match.

I played a quick microexpression of surprise across my face, followed by half-concealed disagreement. "With all due respect, sir, we're at the start of what will likely be a long and complicated interspecies relationship. Pushing too hard at this juncture could have unforeseen consequences." Not to mention the consequences of deliberately misrepresenting our intentions, outright lying to them, and attempting to steal from them. All of which I would soon facilitate.

"You'll play the game the way I tell you to," he said, flashing an unconscious sneer. He thought of me as his puppet, a glorified translator and nothing more.

A now-familiar flame of spite flared in my chest. To be fair, "puppet" was pretty much the job description I signed up for. I wore the title of ambassador purely to avoid insulting the Mask People with my negligible political status. Problem was, I couldn't seem to shut off my brain quite the way Losin wanted.

I also couldn't help needling him. "What shall I tell the Prime Judge if he asks to meet with you?"

Losin flinched slightly from fear of the Mask People's hyperobservant abilities. "That might be unavoidable."

"Maybe we could arrange a social event," I offered, raising my eyebrows with the suggestion. "Some polite conversation but no politics beyond 'we're glad you're here.' A short introduction would be enough to set their minds at ease."

Losin stood and poured a drink from a bottle on the credenza as an excuse to not look at me. At the same time that he resented me for every scrap of limelight he had to share, he understood I was necessary. Me with my unique deficiency, my talent for inexpression.

He swirled his scotch, trying to hide his reluctance. "Not a bad idea. I'll have my secretary put it on the schedule."

Out the viewport, a fleck of movement caught my eye. Sunlight reflected off an approaching short-range transport, the shuttle dwarfed in comparison to the Mask ship from which it came. They were coming, eager and well-intentioned. For a fleeting moment, I wished I'd quit politics and taken up life as a hermit.

"One more thing," Losin said. "We've had a rise in threats against Mask People and the Interworld Relations Organization since the trade talks were announced. Central security has cordoned off an area of the station for the Mask People, but I want you to be extra careful, especially when you're outside the secure zone."

"Of course, sir," I said, and smiled a professionally fake smile—lips a little too tight, eye muscles not quite scrunched enough. "Will that be all?"

The newest member of my personal security detail, Iman Amiri, waited outside Losin's door. He fell into step beside me as I strode down the hallway. He had a restless bounce in his step, and after a moment he asked, "What's our status?"

"The Prime Judge should be docking soon," I said. "Time to meet your first Mask People."

Protocol demanded that two more security officers meet us at the Bay Two entry hall to be present during interspecies contact. They weren't two I was particularly fond of. They belonged to the camp who referred to me as "the robot" behind my back, as if I wouldn't find out about something so inane. Amiri either hadn't picked up on the nickname yet, or had decided it wasn't worth pissing me off just to fit in with his coworkers. I hoped it was the latter; I could use someone smart to balance out these meatheads.

"New kid gets the screen," I declared, and the meathead named Gorsky passed the large, round holographic projection screen to Amiri. I controlled the screen's image wirelessly, which was very convenient for communicating with Mask People, but the chip behind my ear did little to alleviate the robotic reputation.

To Amiri, I said, "You can talk to them but they won't be listening to the words—they'll get the meaning from reading your face."

He nodded, quick and nervous. Nervous was okay—not anything the Mask People hadn't seen a hundred times before. Hostile would've been a problem, but I didn't read any of that in the microexpressions he kept trying to cover up. The trying was okay too—they would hardly notice the false stoicism overlaid atop the true emotions.

At the opposite end of the hall, a light on the wall flashed green to indicate their arrival, and the doors slid silently open to admit the Mask People.

The first feature anyone notices about the Mask People is their enormous faces. To say that a Mask Person has an enlarged face is like saying that a giraffe has an elongated neck or a blue whale is a bit heavy. Mask People are mostly face by volume, the round surface covered in feathery, dexterous appendages that they use as their primary means of communication. The facial feathers come in bright, carnival colors—tourmaline green and iridescent violet, sanguine red and sunlit yellow—though that's not why they're called Mask People. Still, the feathers are hard to miss.

Most of their musculoskeletal effort goes into supporting their massive faces, with mobility only earning a distant second place, so the Prime Judge and his entourage shambled forward in a zigzag of awkward steps. I've overheard the spaceport brats making Mask-People-tipping jokes the way my great-grandparents may have joked about cow-tipping as children. They did look rather like it wouldn't take much of a push.

Despite their innocuous appearance, the Mask People were far from harmless. Their starship came equipped with technologies that made humankind's ventures into space look like monkeys throwing sticks in the air. Nothing like an imbalance of power to make trade negotiations a little too interesting.

Humanity's only advantage was that they had me.

Following the Prime Judge, the Mask Ambassador, and their personal staff came the Mask Bearers, carrying the unwieldy cultural artifacts from which their species took their name. The masks, unlike the Mask People's true faces, bear no resemblance to carnival dress—they are plain and blank, expressionless, and large enough to entirely cover a Mask Person's face. Even the eye holes have one-way reflective glass, so the wearer can look out without anyone seeing their eyes. For a race of hyperexpressive beings, masks provide the only means of privacy.

The Prime Judge extended one long, skeletal arm to clasp hands in the standard human fashion, and I wrapped my fingers around his skinny digits with an appropriate level of solemnity. Their upper limbs always put me in mind of starvation victims. Good thing I never show what I'm thinking.

The Prime Judge greeted me in his native language, facial feathers dancing. *Well met, Human Ambassador.* Reading their language required a somewhat diffuse gaze; if I stared at any particular spot on their face, I would miss subtleties elsewhere. He was testing me, curious to see how well I understood him.

Welcome to Sol System, Prime Judge, I said, mentally puppeting the holographic Mask Person face projected by the screen in Amiri's arms. I tailored my answer to be formal and respectful but with undertones of warmth and gladness. After years of training to be able to puppet my own body, it hadn't been much of a stretch to adapt to the screen instead. The feathers on the Prime Judge's cheeks smoothed flat, surprised and impressed with my grasp of his language's emotive subtleties.

Mask Ambassador, I said, looking at the Mask Person on its left, *may I present New Security.*

I translated the Mask Ambassador's laconic greeting for Amiri and he replied with a simple "Hi." He tucked his chin and glanced up at them and down again several times, awkward and anxious for their approval. I read amusement in the slow twirl of their feathers.

The introductions continued until everyone in the room had met everyone else down to the last Mask Bearer. In their culture, ignoring someone with an unmasked face was a terrible insult—even if that person, say a human security officer, would prefer to fade into the background. The custom also meant I had to shake the hand of each person I would shortly be backstabbing during the trade talks.

By the end, I was thankful that no actual discussion of policy was planned for the day, simply a mutual confirmation of the schedule for days to come. Once the introductions were completed, the Prime Judge seemed eager to move on to his private quarters; sometimes I think they visit purely to meet new people. Did I mention how very much they enjoy their introductions? It's the people they've already met they grow tired of.

Not me, though, they don't get tired of me because they can only read what I give them. By the end of the meeting, the Prime Judge left feeling reassured and a little intrigued. An excellent first impression. I earned their trust and felt sick all the while, knowing what was to come. If my face were chained to my innermost thoughts like a normal person, I would have grimaced.

Of course, if I were a normal person, the UN never would have slapped the ambassador label on me and shipped me up here. They hired me for the job because I was the only human they could find with the capacity for becoming fluent in the Mask People's language. Also, because I was the only human who could successfully lie to them.

We had the rest of the day free, while the Mask People settled in to their temporary accommodations aboard the station. I dismissed the two meatheads and took Amiri with me when I left the entry hall. At the first major corridor junction, I turned toward the public sectors of the station.

Amiri raised an eyebrow at that, and I said, "We've got to make a stop."

The Dark Moon Café offered garish décor and mediocre-to-awful food. More cafeteria than café, it was noisy, crowded, exposed, and I loathed it. We were served lunch, and I hoped my other purpose would be served as well.

"What exactly are we doing here? This is hardly a secure location," Amiri said from across the table, displeasure showing in the crease of his brow.

"We're fishing for extremists. If they've managed to get on board, I want to know about it." The desire to do the exact opposite of what Losin instructed me to also may have contributed slightly, I admit.

"Draw them out using yourself as bait?" Amiri thought about it. "That's nuts, but it's my kind of nuts."

"If they're here, I'd rather we find them before they get a shot at the Mask People."

I watched the crowd, scanning for tell-tale microexpressions of hate or disgust. We both picked at our food. Stake-outs weren't a part of my usual repertoire, and this one gave me a strange combination of boredom and anxiety.

While he kept an eye on the exits, Amiri tried making conversation to relieve the tension. "Did you hear about the new Castillo Method results?" He'd been on the job for three weeks and hadn't yet figured me out—though he kept fishing for clues.

"Nope," I said, giving him none.

"They're having some luck with sociopaths."

I moved my gaze from the other patrons—none of whom displayed hostile intent—down to my half-eaten slice of quiche without making eye contact. "You're suggesting I might be interested in the procedure, with regards to my condition."

"They must be making progress if they can correct sociopathy now. And neural pathway realignment is noninvasive and very low risk. So why not?"

"I'd be out of a job, for one thing," I said. And then, when he didn't get it, "That was a joke."

"Oh," he said, and let himself grin.

I took another bite, chewed, swallowed. "I wonder how the sociopaths felt about the treatment."

He grinned again. It wasn't a joke this time.

I scanned the crowd once more. Either there weren't any extremists on board, or they weren't eating lunch at the Dark Moon like half the station was. It was frustrating not knowing, one way or the other. The last thing these trade talks needed was another element of uncertainty.

I forked one more mouthful, surgically removing the filling from the soggy crust, and slid the plate away. "Come on, new kid. There are other places to check."

My parents thought I was a sociopath for a long time.

I hardly ever cried as a baby, and I never once smiled. It almost would have been a relief, I think, if I'd turned out to be severely mentally retarded. But as it was, I developed more or less normally, except that I utterly failed to express emotional responses or recognize them in others. My parents went through an endless stream of baffled child psychologists, all the while waiting for the tortured animal carcasses to start showing up.

But the problem wasn't a lack of healthy emotions, simply an inability to communicate them. Finally they found a school—a special and very expensive school—that claimed to be up to the challenge, and they shipped me off. I never interacted with them outside of mandatory holidays after that. To this day I don't know if they were ashamed of me, or ashamed of themselves for assuming their own daughter was a budding serial killer for so many years.

In school, I learned most of the regular drivel, but the classes that mattered were all about facial anatomy and body language and verbal inflection. I learned how to recognize emotions analytically, piece by painstaking little piece, and how to make my own muscles mimic them.

To everyone's surprise, I got good at it—really good at it. Like an ESL student who knows better English grammar than a native speaker, I became more fluent in emotional expression than most of the people who use it naturally. The government recruited me when I turned eighteen.

Around one in four hundred people has a natural ability to read microexpressions and body language such that they can reliably tell when someone is lying. These people have been called "Truth Wizards." I can do what they do, but I can do the opposite just as well. I suppose that makes me the "Falsehood Wizard."

After a fruitless afternoon of scanning for extremists, I ate dinner in the security lounge with my staff so we could go over the work schedule for tomorrow. With each successive meeting between humans and Mask People, the anti-alien factions have spewed their xenophobic propaganda louder and louder. The station's central security screens for anyone who poses a threat, but that just means the extremists need to act smarter to slip through.

Toward the end of the meal, I was finished with the business part and the men were chatting and joking among themselves.

"Hey Amiri, check this out." Gorsky leaned over and poked me in the arm with his fork. It hurt. They all laughed when I didn't flinch, all except Amiri who looked distinctly uncomfortable.

I stared at Gorsky, and my lack of expression set them to laughing for another round. That sound filled me with a black hatred for humanity.

I picked up my own fork and jabbed it down into the meat of his thigh, metal tines sinking into flesh. Gorsky's eyes flew open with surprise and he howled his pain.

"You're fired," I said and stood to leave. "Amiri, come with me."

Amiri seemed frozen in his chair for a moment before he scrambled to fall in step behind me. As we left, I heard Gorsky yell, "It was a joke, you crazy bitch!"

I thought about re-hiring him just so I could fire him twice. I should have put that whole situation to rest much sooner, before it got out of hand. Not very diplomatic of me. I've gotten so used to being isolated and ostracized that I suppose I stopped recognizing it for what it was: suffering in silence.

Story of my life.

"That was sort of amazing, what you did," Amiri said later. It wasn't technically his shift anymore, but I didn't feel like facing the others.

We were in the sitting room of my suite—him fiddling with the settings on his standard-issue stunner and me reviewing the hundred-page-long trade proposal I'd be discussing the next day.

"It doesn't concern you that your new boss stabbed one of her other employees?" I kept my eyes on the document, half-listening for his answer.

"No offense, but if the guy can't defend himself against a pissed-off lady with a fork, he's not much of a security officer." He paused. "Why'd you do it, though?"

"I decided it was time to make a point," I said, scrolling through to the next page.

"More like four points." I could hear the grin in the timbre of his voice.

By page seventeen, I was treading water in an endless sea of legalese. The Mask People want to purchase asteroid mining rights, which is complicated enough on its own given that no one actually has a legal claim to the asteroid belt. And if they agree to trade their propulsion technology, then the very same mining resources suddenly become accessible and potentially desirable to humans, too.

Amiri interrupted again. "Wouldn't things be easier if you pretended to be normal all the time? I've seen you working, you can mimic expressions perfectly. Why not just do that with everyone?"

"Because the act is a lie." I set aside the document and looked up at him, curious to see how he'd react to my answer. "I never feel like smiling—I feel happy, and then I switch on a smile, like a robot executing an if-then command. It may look all warm and fuzzy and genuine to you, but it's not."

He cringed slightly at the robot reference, but he said, "If nobody can tell it's a knock-off, what does it matter that it's not the real thing?"

"I would know." Sometimes it made me angry—the constant expectation that I pretend to be someone I'm not for the comfort and convenience of everyone else—but not right now. He was new and still trying to figure me out, which was more than meathead Gorsky ever did for me.

In the morning, I went early to the reception room to see Director-General Losin before the Mask People arrived. His back was to the door when I came in, but I caught him unconsciously wiping clammy palms on his trouser legs. Terrified. I held out a hand to tell my security detail—Amiri and Wellinger—to hang back, and I walked up beside Losin.

"They're not psychic, you know."

He jumped, then glared down at me for startling him. "What?"

"They can't read your mind, just your face. All you have to do is stay focused on safe thoughts, safe emotions."

"I know what I have to do, Nora." Losin shifted his weight, restless, probably wondering how badly he could screw up his precious trade agreement with a single expression.

I admit, I was enjoying his discomfort. "Don't worry. They'll get bored with you pretty quick, so long as you don't look like you're hiding something," I said and smiled sweetly.

Losin got back at me by assigning one of his own security detail to hold my screen, effectively tethering me to his side to serve as his personal translator for the morning. A small crew of central-security-approved caterers were already set up, and the other human guests began to arrive in ones and twos—whatever dignitaries Losin could manage to round up on short notice.

The Prime Judge, the Mask Ambassador, and their sizeable entourage arrived at the reception hall precisely on time. Within minutes, a few of the Mask People tired of Losin's dignitaries and began to harass the caterers for introductions instead, offending the former and confusing the latter. I wished I could kick back and watch the hilarity ensue. But given that the average person could learn to recognize only a few of the most basic expressions in the Mask language, I was needed for any complicated interactions. My duties occupied my full attention.

Or almost all of it.

A movement in my peripheral vision distracted me. Across the room, one of the caterers walked with too much tension in his step and clutched his tray nervously. He was not here with the sole intention of serving appetizers.

I caught Amiri's eye, then transferred my gaze quickly to the suspect and back again. He quirked a questioning eyebrow, not able to see the signs I saw. I widened my eyes and tilted my head down, insistent. A twitch of his shoulder, ceding the point, and he slid through the crowd in pursuit.

Amiri attempted to escort him out quietly, but the caterer stood his ground and started making a scene. The room fell silent as all the humans craned their necks to see what was going on. A couple other security officers descended on the caterer, and the ruckus ended with him stunned and dragged out of the room. At the door, Amiri turned to give me a slight nod, confirming that the suspect had something on him. Not a weapon, from Amiri's expression. Poison, maybe. I'd have to ask him later.

I turned around again, intent on resuming my translator duties, but I froze when I saw Losin. His expression screamed, *That moron is going to ruin all my plans.*

I kept my own expression impassive and leaned in close to him. "Take a walk. Your face is a mess."

He scowled, I met his gaze with an expressionless stare, and after a moment he relented. He wandered off and found a group of humans to socialize with until his thoughts were back under control. Relief washed through me. At least Losin had the sense to listen when it counted.

I caught the Prime Judge watching me, and the feeling of relief evaporated. My screen-holder in tow, I closed the distance to speak with the Prime Judge.

You saw all of that, didn't you? I said, chagrined.

It rippled its facial feathers in the Mask Person equivalent of a wry smile. *Of course.*

Why didn't you point out the threat before I noticed it?

I was curious to observe how your species would handle the situation.

And? I resisted the urge to look for Losin and check whether he had his expression under control yet.

The experience was informative, the Prime Judge said with a hint of cautiousness, almost suspicion.

I wondered whether the cautiousness was a response to the threat itself, or to Losin's too-revealing reaction. Bluntness was often seen as a virtue in the Mask culture, so I said, *It is not entirely safe for you here.*

Yes, it said, at once resigned and forgiving—Losin had insisted on hosting the trade talks on the station. *It would have been safer to meet on the starship, where we have adequate protection.*

Doubt made me pause. This was supposed to be a social gathering, not a political tête-à-tête, but I needed to know more about how they viewed their own technology. *Just "adequate"? Your species could sterilize the surface of our planet if you so desired.*

The Prime Judge's feathers smoothed with genuine surprise. *Possessing the ability and possessing the intention are entirely different matters, Ambassador.*

Indeed. If only that answer would satisfy Losin.

I knew that it wouldn't. Losin was committed to a course of action, and I had no choice but to proceed as he'd planned.

The afternoon was reserved for the real work: trade negotiations. Amiri waited for me to finish lunch while Wellinger went ahead to secure the conference room. This arrangement was fine by me, since meathead Wellinger wasn't likely to forgive me the Gorsky incident any time soon. I emptied my coffee cup, tucked all the necessary documents into a slim shoulder-bag, and made eye contact with Amiri to tell him I was ready.

Before Amiri joined my staff, I used to prefer multiple escorts. They talked among themselves and I could disengage, mentally withdraw from their company. Now it seemed almost comfortable, having Amiri all to myself.

We walked the spaceport corridors toward the designated meeting space, Amiri unconsciously matching my stride. Out in public, half his attention focused on scanning and evaluating—not too vigilant to hold up a conversation, but I wasn't exactly feeling chatty with the trade negotiations only minutes away, so we walked in silence. The hallways seemed ominously long today.

I told myself I was just doing my job. The decisions had already been made by people more important and more knowledgeable than me. I was only a messenger, and none of it would be my fault. Not really.

Out of the corner of my eye, I saw Amiri tense in a way that shot adrenaline through my veins, and then all hell broke loose. The first two men closed with Amiri before he could unholster his stunner. The third and fourth stepped around them to come at me from both sides.

The one on my left said, "Eat this, bitch." The one on my right fingered the handle of his shiv and said nothing. My own fingers tensed around the strap of my shoulder bag, readying to use it as a shield.

The sound of punches landing emanated from Amiri's general direction, and his assailants fell to the ground, first one and then the other in rapid succession. He spun to face me, threw up his arm, and the other two dropped to the floor unconscious.

God, he was fast. I never even saw him draw the stunner.

Back in my suite, I sipped from the glass Amiri gave me, hand shaking. Adrenaline—one of the few biochemicals I can honestly express, since it bypasses the brain and acts directly on muscle function.

I set the glass down so I wouldn't drop it. "We need to reschedule the meeting."

"Already done," said Amiri.

"And have Gorsky forcibly removed from the station."

"Gorsky?"

"They were waiting for me. There's a short list of people who could've told them my schedule, and only one who recently took a fork in the leg."

"Point," he said, and dialed central security on his comm.

When he finished the call, he sat down across from me and leaned forward in the way people do when they're trying to read someone. Force of habit, I suppose. He said, "You okay?"

"Yes." The adrenaline high was fading and I felt too worn out to put on an act for him. "Honestly, I'm grateful for the delay."

"Uh-oh. That doesn't sound good."

I paused, considering how much to tell him. He'd saved my life; it seemed absurd to distrust him now. "In exchange for the asteroid mining rights they've requested, human technicians will be given full access to their onboard systems in the starship. And we promise not to copy any of their offensive technology, of course." I looked up, to see if he got it.

"You're kidding," Amiri said. The kid was smart, I'd been right about that. "They're going to trust us not to steal their weapon designs? That'll end well. And you're supposed to be selling this as a *good* plan?"

"We're trying to establish a relationship of trust." Trust we could exploit, of course. Never mind that, in the process of ensuring our martial adequacy against the Mask People, we might accidentally start the very war we sought to avoid. "Besides, our technicians are scrupulous and beyond reproach. That's the party line."

Amiri threw me a skeptical look. "The problem with telling perfect lies is that you might start believing them yourself."

I would have winced then, were I normal. Amiri had no idea how close he came to hitting the mark—there's nothing I fear more than the thought of the lies starting to control me, and not the other way around.

I didn't share that with him. It was my right not to. I'm a professional at leaving things hidden and I don't regret it—I tell myself I never regret it. I tell myself I like holding the world at arm's length.

"You should call Wellinger. He's probably still waiting in the conference room," I said, ending the conversation.

The next morning, Amiri was on duty again for the rescheduled negotiations with the Mask People. We arrived at the conference room without incident. Wellinger reported the room secure and I told him to wait outside the door, which was against protocol but he did it anyway. I needed complete control over the negotiations, and I didn't want his negative expressions cluttering up the room. Might give the Mask People the wrong impression about me—or the right one.

The Mask People entered through a door at the opposite end of the room, a small entourage preceding the more important political figures. The Prime Judge came in last, and he was wearing his mask.

I glanced at Amiri, who watched the masked Prime Judge with curiosity smeared all over his face. I said, "Think about something else."

"What?"

"It's extremely rude to inquire about mask wearing."

"I wasn't—"

"Your face was," I interrupted. "Think about anything else. You can think about screwing your girlfriend for all I care, just don't wonder about the masks."

He hunched his shoulders a little, embarrassed, and covered it up with a wry answer. "No pink elephants either, huh?"

I couldn't blame him though. Secretly, I liked seeing them with their masks on, peaceful and flawlessly impassive. I am like a Mask Person who can't take off the mask. I can never have an honest conversation with my own species; either it's not honest, or it's not a conversation, not the kind they want anyway. At least the Mask People understand the virtue of being hidden. Safety in isolation.

The Prime Judge's mask came off and was passed to a Mask Bearer. Then the usual extensive greetings were exchanged all around, and we settled down to business.

The first hour or so of the meeting was an overview of the trade proposal, each party confirming that we understood all of the major points. Though I didn't look at Amiri, his presence weighed on my awareness. Finally I couldn't stand it anymore, I couldn't stand not knowing what he was thinking. I threw him a sideways glance.

He smiled back at me with his eyes. It was only a momentary tensing of his lower lids, but I read warmth and confidence there. It was a smile that said, *I'm not worried because I trust you'll do the right thing.*

The smile hit me like a punch, and I was yet again grateful my reaction stayed internal. The Prime Judge only saw Amiri's half of the visual conversation. But beneath my silent face, Amiri's words from last night echoed around my brain.

I was born to lie, that much was inescapable. But Amiri had been right: I should make the lies, not let the lies make me. Even a liar can sometimes show the truth about themselves, embedded in the rhyme and meter of their falsehoods.

As the meeting progressed, I meticulously emoted a fraction less enthusiasm than formal Mask-Person etiquette dictated. Not enough difference for my human overseers to detect, but then the Prime Judge was ever so much more sensitive than they were. All I needed was to light a spark of suspicion.

We reached the end of the document and the conversation floated away from the particulars to less concrete matters. The Prime Judge asked, *How do your superiors feel about this agreement?* A question that would have seemed odd between human ambassadors, but Mask People are accustomed to always knowing how everyone feels.

They are very eager to establish economic relations, I said. Entirely true, and beyond reproach from the viewpoint of a human negotiator. But on *they,* I gave a subtle emphasis of detachment, expressing a desire to disassociate myself from them.

The Prime Judge paused, considering my meaning. *They come with honorable intent?*

They will thoroughly fulfill their trade obligations—which was also true, but not the same as a "yes."

We are concerned that trade remain peaceful and amicable.

Your offensive technology is far superior. How could humans pose a threat to you?

The Prime Judge rippled his feathers thoughtfully. *Thank you, Ambassador. I believe we have reached an understanding.*

The thing about perfect liars is they can fool anybody. You can never be sure whose side they're on.

Director-General Losin was, needless to say, extremely displeased. Shall I describe his anger? The deep scowl, the tight jaw, the jutted chin? Anger is a simple emotion to read—it so rarely tries to hide itself.

"What happened in there? You seemed to be doing an acceptable job at the start." He'd been watching on the security cam, of course. "Then suddenly they want to back out and redraft the agreement? Explain *that* to me!"

I shrugged, lacing the gesture with nervousness and confusion. "I don't know what happened, sir."

"You damn well must've screwed something up."

"They changed their minds. I have no idea why."

"And you're going to tell me with a straight face that you did everything in your power to convince them to approve the proposal?"

"Yes," I lied with ease. "Now that is something I can do."

Tying Knots

KEN LIU

古者無文字，其有約誓之事，事大，大其繩，事小，小其繩，結之多少，隨物眾寡，各執以相考，亦足以相治也。

(In ancient times, there was no writing. When people needed to make a contract or pact, they tied a big knot on a string for a big matter, a small knot for a small matter. The number of knots depended on the quantity under contract. That was sufficient to provide a record.)

—《九家易》 (*Jiujiayi*, a Chinese philosophy text on the study of the *I Ching*, probably composed during the Eastern Han Dynasty, 25-220 AD)

Sky Village:

The spirits like to play jokes on us. I have seen more in my lifetime than any *Nan* in recorded history, and yet I am also the most shortsighted, practically blind.

Five years ago, when two Burmese traders climbed up the mountain for their annual trading trip, their hair dripping with water from the hard hike up through the clouds, they brought a stranger with them.

The stranger was unlike anyone I had ever met, and there was no record of anyone like him in our archive of ropes. He was tall, taller than my nephew Kai by two feet, and Kai was the tallest man in the village. His face was pale, florid and ruddy, like a statue of an *arhat* with a painted face. He also had blue eyes and golden hair, and a nose so sharp and stuck so far out of his face that it was like a bird's beak.

Pha, one of the traders, told us that the stranger's name was *To-mu*. "He's from far away."

"As far away as Rangoon?" I asked.

"Much, much farther. He is from *America*. Headman Soe-bo, that is so far away that you cannot imagine. Not even a hawk flying nonstop for twenty days can reach it."

That was probably an exaggeration, as Pha liked to tell tall tales. But To-mu spoke to Pha in a harsh, staccato language that held a kind of music I had never heard, so he was certainly from no place I knew of.

"What is he doing here?"

"Who knows? I don't understand anything he does. Westerners are all strange, and I have met many. But he is even odder than most. He walked into Man-sam two days ago, carrying that pack on his back, which seems to hold everything he owns. He asked me and Aung to bring him to places no Westerner had been to. He offered us a lot of money. So we said we'd take him to Sky Village. Maybe he's running and hiding from an opium lord."

Pha would do anything for money, even incurring the wrath of a general with opium fields. Sometimes we sell the rice for money too, to save up for a lean year when we might not have enough rice to trade. But we don't pine after it the way Pha does.

If To-mu was trying to hide from an opium lord, then we wanted nothing to do with him. I had to watch him carefully, and make sure he left with the traders.

But To-mu did not act like a man on the run. He was loud and rude, and smiled at everyone and everything. He was always asking one villager or another to stand still while he held up a small metal box to his eyes and made clicking noises with it. He walked around and examined our huts, the narrow terrace fields, the wildflowers and weeds, and even the children shitting in the bushes. Pha translated for him as he asked the stupidest questions: What did we call this animal? What was the name of that flower? What foods did we eat? What crops and vegetables did we grow? To-mu was like a child, and did not know the most basic facts. He acted like he had never seen people.

He sought out Luk, the medicine man, and waved a stack of money at him.

"He wants you to tell him about sicknesses and how you treat them," Pha said.

The traders sometimes asked Luk for tips like this too, so this was not such a strange request as To-mu's other questions. Luk shrugged away the money, and patiently walked around with To-mu, pointing at herbs and insects and explaining their uses. To-mu held up his metal box and clicked at everything, and wrote in a notebook, as he collected the herbs and insects and stored them away in small clear bags he took out of his backpack.

We *Nan* have lived on this mountain for thousands of years. The oldest books passed down in the village—copied and reknotted with fresh hemp rope every few generations—tell the origin of our people. Long ago, our ancestors lived many days to the north, in a small Chinese kingdom. A war came, and invaders on horses tore through the rice fields, burning down our houses. The brave Elder San-pu led the survivors on a desperate run until we could no longer hear the horses' hoofbeats, and we kept on walking for another moon. We climbed onto this mountain, and made our home above the clouds. We do not bother the world, and the world, for the most part, leaves us alone.

I say "for the most part" because every year, a few traders make their way up the mountain and bring us medicine, iron tools, silk and cotton cloth, and spices from far away. In exchange, they want one thing: our rice. The large, smooth grains, unlike anything the Burmese villages at the foot of the mountain grow, are hawked by the traders as "sky rice" in the markets.

They tell their customers that sky rice is fed with the pure essence of clouds and grows in air. When I heard this, I explained to the traders that the rice comes from the terrace fields on the mountainside, and we water it by irrigation ditches, no different from how our ancestors used to do and no different from the villages below. But the traders laugh. *The buyers like our story better. They are willing to pay more because of our idea.* You can never trust traders to tell the truth.

The rice harvest had not been good for a few years. It did not rain as much as it used to, and the springs that flowed down from the peak of the mountain slowed down to a trickle in the summer. Young men with keen eyes said that they thought the snowy peaks far to the west were losing their white hair, like old men going bald. Families were now eating a lot more wild vegetables and the children helped by hunting birds and treeshrews. But even these sources of food seemed to be in decline.

I had consulted the records of rainfall and harvest for past centuries, and a drought such as this had never been recorded. Could something in the world below the mountain be causing all of this?

I asked the traders for their thoughts.

They shrugged. "We hear the weather has turned strange everywhere, drought up north in China and cyclones down south in the Irrawaddy. Who knows why? It is just the way it is."

I offered to have To-mu and the traders stay with me for the night, before their long climb down the mountain the next day. Pha and Aung always had good stories to share of the world below, and To-mu seemed a man full of interesting tales too.

I served them the last of my rice with sweet bamboo shoots and pickled ginger. To-mu smacked his lips and praised my cooking. I laughed, embarrassed. After the meal, we sat around the fire drinking rice wine and chatting.

I asked To-mu what he did. He sat quietly for a bit, scratched his head, laughed, and then said a long string of words to Pha. Pha seemed puzzled. He shrugged, and said to me, "He says he studies sicknesses and invents *proteins*—I guess that's a kind of medicine—to treat them. It's very confusing though. He says he doesn't see any sick people or make medicine. He just comes up with ideas."

So he was a healer, of sorts. That was certainly an honorable calling, and I had respect for anyone who wanted to heal others, no matter how strange he was.

I asked To-mu if he wanted to hear some of the old medicine books of the *Nan.* Even Luk, skilled as he was, couldn't hold all knowledge in his head. He often consulted the old medicine books when he encountered a disease he hadn't seen. There is much wisdom passed onto us from our ancestors, some of it bought with the lives of brave men who ventured past the line between medicine and poison.

To-mu nodded after Pha translated my offer. I got up, and retrieved the knotted clumps of the medical books. Stretching out the rope, I ran my finger down the line, and read out the symptoms and cure recipes.

But instead of listening to Pha's translation, To-mu was staring at the knotted books, his eyes wider than teacups. He interrupted Pha and jabbered at him. I could tell he was extremely excited.

"He's never seen knot-writing before," Pha said. "He wants to understand how you do what you do."

The traders have seen the *Nan* knotting for years, and grown used to it. I have also seen them record their purchases and inventory with markings on paper—Tibetan, Chinese, Burmese, Naga—different traders use different scripts. As different as they look though, the ink markings always seem to me dead, flat, ugly. The *Nan* do not write. We knot.

Knots have allowed us to keep alive the wisdom and voices of our ancestors. A long hemp rope, supple and elastic, is stretched and twisted to give it the right amount of tension and coil. Thirty-one different kinds of knots can be made on the rope, corresponding to the shapes of the lips and the tongue in making different syllables. Strung together like Buddhist prayer beads, the knots form words, sentences, stories. Speech is given substance and form. Run the hand down the string, and you can feel the knotters' thoughts in your fingers and hear their voices through your bones.

The knotted string does not stay straight. The knots put tension on the rope. It coils in on itself, twisting, bending, yearning towards a shape. A book of knots is not a straight line, but more like a compact statue. Different knots give you different shapes in the coiled-up rope, and at a glance you can see the flow and contour of the argument, the tangible rise and fall of rhythm and rhyme.

I was born with bad eyesight. I can only see clearly a few feet away, and my head aches if I strain my eyes for too long. But my fingers have always been nimble, and even as a child my father said I was a quick learner of the properties of different ropes and knots. I had a talent for seeing in my mind the way the knots would change the tension on the rope, the way the little forces pulled and pushed it into its final form. Every *Nan* can knot, but only I have the eye for seeing the final shape of the rope before even a single knot has been made.

I began as a copyist, taking the oldest knotted books that were fraying and falling apart, feeling and memorizing the sequence of knots, and then recreating them with fresh hemp rope so that every knot, every twist would be faithfully reproduced, until the rope coiled in on itself, an exact replica of the original, so that the village's children and their children would also be able to feel and learn from the voices of the past.

And later, after I became Headman and the record keeper after my father's death, I knotted my own ropes. I knotted practical things, like the prices charged by the traders from year to year so that we wouldn't be cheated, the new uses for old herbs discovered by the medicine men, the weather patterns and planting times. I also knotted other things, just because I liked the way the knotted ropes looked after I was done. I knotted the songs of the young men singing to the girls they liked, the feel of fresh spring sunlight on my face after the dark winter, the flickering shadows of the *Nan* dancing by the bonfire at the Spring Festival.

Route 128, Greater Boston:

It took a year of begging, expensive lawyers, bribes—excuse me, *extraordinary processing fees*—and even getting back in touch with acquaintances I hadn't spoken to since college who now work at the State Department to get Soe-bo the right travel documents.

He doesn't have a birth certificate? No last name? Does he grow opium for the warlords up there? Do you know anything about this guy? I gotta tell you, Tom, I'm pulling in a lot of favors for your native witch doctor. This better be worth it.

It is amazing how a few pieces of paper can generate so many headaches. Made me wish that it was still Victorian times, and I could just bring a "native" from the jungle back home without dealing with a thousand bureaucrats in two governments who didn't much like each other.

"That is a very long journey," Soe-bo had said, when I tried to convince him to come back with me on my second trip to Sky Village. "Too far for me."

The *Nan* had no interest in money. I knew that it would be useless to promise him rich rewards.

"If you come with me, you can help heal many people."

"I'm no healer."

"I know that. But that knot-writing thing you do . . . You can help a lot of people. I can't explain it. You have to trust me."

He was moved, but still uncertain. Then I played my trump card, something I knew was on his mind, the only thing he might want.

"Your rice crops are dying because of the drought," I said. "I can help you get new rice that will thrive with less water. But you have to come with me, and then I'll give you new seeds."

Soe-bo was not as terrified of the airplane as I had expected. He was such a small man to begin with, but huddled in his seat, his movements cautious and slow, he seemed even more like a child. He was calm though. I think the bus to Yangon shocked him a lot more. After sitting in one metal box that moved on its own to get you from one place to another, I guess a box that flew wasn't much stranger.

As soon as I settled him into the studio suite at the hotel next to the GACT Labs campus, he fell asleep. He didn't use the bed; instead, he curled up on the tile floor in the kitchen. Closer to the hearth, I suppose, an instinctual urge that I had read about in old anthropology books.

"Can you knot the rope so that it ends up in this shape?" I pointed to a small model sculpted out of clay. It looked vaguely like the head of a dragon. The Burmese college kid we were using as a translator shook his head—this whole set up must have seemed crazy to him; heck, it seemed crazy to me—but he translated my question.

Soe-bo picked up the model, turning it this way and that. "It doesn't say anything. The knots will be nonsense."

"It doesn't matter. I just want you to make it so that the rope folds up naturally into this shape."

He nodded, and began to twist and knot the rope. As the rope coiled in on itself, he compared the result to the model, pulled the rope straight and let it coil back again. He shook his head, and untied some knots and retied new ones.

In the lab, five different cameras were recording his progress, and on the other side of the one-way mirror, a dozen scientists leaned in to watch the tiny man and the zoomed-in image of his nimble fingers.

"How do you do it?" I asked.

"My father taught me, as his father had taught him. Knot-writing is passed down to us from our ancestors. I've pulled apart and retied a thousand books. I feel in my bones how the rope wants to tie itself."

Proteins are long chains of amino acids strung together, their sequence dictated by genes in living cells. The amino acids, knotty with their hydrophobic and hydrophilic side chains and differing charges, pull and push at each other, forming local secondary structures like alpha helices and beta sheets through hydrogen bonds. The long chain of the protein is an unstable, writhing, jiggling mass agitated by millions of minuscule force vectors until it "folds," coils in on itself to minimize the total energy in the entire chain, and thus settles into its tertiary structure. That final, stable, native state gives a protein its characteristic shape, a tiny three-dimensional clump, a modernist sculpture.

A protein's shape is what gives it its function. The "proper folding" of a protein depends on many things: temperature, solvent, chaperone molecules to help things along. When proteins fail to fold into their characteristic shapes, you get diseases like mad-cow prions, Alzheimer's, cystic fibrosis. But with the right-shaped proteins, you get drugs that can stop the uncontrollable division of cancer cells, block the cellular pathways needed for HIV to replicate, and cure all kinds of difficult diseases.

But predicting the native state of a sequence of amino acids (or, the converse, designing a sequence of amino acids that will fold into the desired protein shape) is harder than particle physics. A brute-force simulation of all the forces acting on the atoms in even a short chain of amino acids and a search through the free energy landscape will bring the most powerful computer to its knees. And proteins are composed of hundreds of amino acids, sometimes thousands.

If we can find an accurate, fast algorithm to predict and fold a sequence of amino acids into its native state, medicine will have taken the largest stride since the discovery of antibiotics. It will save countless lives—and be very profitable.

Once in a while, when Soe-bo seemed tired from the work, I would take him on an excursion into Boston. I looked forward to these excursions myself. My globe-trotting had made me into something of an amateur anthropologist, and I liked to observe the reactions of those outside of our world to the things we took for granted. It was fascinating to see the world through Soe-bo's eyes, and to discover what shocked him or didn't.

He accepted the skyscrapers as attributes of the landscape, but he was frightened by escalators. He took the cars and highways and crowds of people of all colors towering over him in stride, but he could not get over his amazement with ice cream. He was lactose intolerant, but he would endure the stomach aches for the pleasure of two scoops. He avoided dogs, even when they were on leashes, but he enjoyed feeding the ducks and pigeons in the Common.

Next, we moved to simulations on computers. Soe-bo could not learn to use a mouse effectively, and the screen tired his eyes. So we had to rig up a 3-D simulation system, complete with gloves, goggles, and adequate tactile feedback.

Now he was no longer working with his familiar knots. We had to see if his ability to predict the final shape of the chain was just the result of rote memorization of rigid folk traditions, or if the techniques could be generalized and mapped into a new domain.

Through a video feed from his goggles, we observed him manipulating the models of amino acids floating in air, learning their properties when placed next to each other. He jiggled the chains, pulled some strands apart, pushed some strands together, tucked in the side chains. To him, it was just playing a strange game.

But he did not have much success. The amino acids were too different from his knots, and he could not solve even the simplest puzzles.

The Board grew impatient and skeptical. "You really think this illiterate Asian peasant is going to provide a breakthrough? If this fails and it gets out in the papers, investors wouldn't touch us with a ten-foot pole."

I had to bring up, yet again, my track record of mining pre-industrial peoples for medical knowledge. Within the mess of old wives' tales and superstitions, there often lay hidden kernels of real expertise that could be discovered and exploited for real gains. Hadn't our bestselling drug been first extracted from those orchids used by the Taeoc Indians in Brazil? They ought to have a little faith in my instincts.

But I was worried.

For our next excursion, I took him to the Sackler Museum at Harvard, where they had a collection of ancient Asian art. I understood vaguely that the *Nan* had migrated to where they were from somewhere up north in China during the Bronze Age. I thought he might be interested in seeing the old earthenware and bronze ritual vessels from people connected to his ancestors.

The museum had few visitors, and we wandered through it quietly. A large, three-legged, roundish bronze pot in a glass case caught Soe-bo's attention, and he shuffled closer. I followed.

The vessel, called a *ding,* was etched with Chinese characters and decorative patterns composed of animal motifs, but there was something else, an even finer pattern of thin lines that covered the smoother parts. I read the little placard at the bottom of the case:

"The Chinese wrapped bronze vessels in silk and other fine cloth for storage. Over the centuries, the pattern of warp and weft in the wrapping would be left in the patina, long after the cloth has rotted away. Our knowledge of ancient Chinese weaving comes almost entirely from such traces."

I asked the translator to read this to Soe-bo. Soe-bo nodded and pressed his face up against the glass to get a closer look. A museum guard walked towards us, but I waved him away. "It's all right. He has bad eyes."

"Thank you," Soe-bo said afterwards. "They did not write with their threads, so the patterns were not intelligible. But I followed them closely, and I could hear their voices, though but faintly. A chance to hear such ancient wisdom, even if I could not understand it, is a great gift."

During our next session, Soe-bo managed to fold a reasonably complex chain. It was as if he had gained some extra insight, and suddenly things clicked for him. We repeated the experiment with a few more complex chains, and he solved them even faster.

I think he was even happier than I was.

"What changed?"

"I don't know how to explain it," he said. "In my knot-writing, knots very far from each other do not influence each other, but that is not true in your game. Hearing the voices left on the Chinese bronze helped me. The weaving pattern is made by one thread knotting back on itself over and over. But once woven into a net, a knot's tension can be felt in all directions, even by far away knots. That made me see how I had to think about this game, and change what I knew about knot-writing to make the patterns fit. The ancient voices did have much to teach me, but I had to know how to listen."

I was fine with mystical mumbo-jumbo, as long as it worked.

We played back his sessions on the computer, abstracting out his movements, inferring his decisions, systemizing his trials, compiling it all into an algorithm. This was not trivial, and it required a great deal of creativity and hard work to refine Soe-bo's instincts into explicit instructions. But having Soe-bo's movements as guide lights through the dark sea of infinite possibilities made the effort possible.

I resisted the urge to say to the Board "I told you so."

Soe-bo reminded me that I had yet to fulfill my promise. We had been working together for months, and I was so absorbed in the progress we were making that I had forgotten. I was embarrassed.

I called up Chris, who had been at grad school with me, working in the same lab. He was now at Enadyne Agro, which had a reputation for good varieties of genetically modified rice.

I explained what I wanted: drought- and altitude-tolerant, does well in acidic soils, high yield, and preferably resistant to common Southeast Asian pests.

"I have a few varieties that might work," Chris said. "But they are expensive. And we don't usually like to sell seeds to a place like Myanmar. Besides the political risk, there's no respect for intellectual property in much of Asia. I don't want to see the whole country growing our rice without paying. You know the police and courts are useless, and hiring thugs to enforce patents against peasants doesn't play well on the evening news."

I asked Chris for this favor, and promised to help with the lessons on intellectual property.

"We might have to implement a technical solution for the problem of unauthorized seeds," he added.

The *Nan* need the rice, I thought. The world is changing around them, and they need help.

I accompanied Soe-bo on his trip home and helped him carry the bags of rice seeds up the mountain. It must have been an amusing sight: the little Asian explorer coming home ahead on the trail, and me lumbering after under my load, a strange sort of Sherpa.

Sky Village:

It took me a long time to knot down the records of my trip to America, and the amazing sights I saw there. They now fill a whole shelf, and children come to me every night for more stories.

A trip like that makes you see how much a man does not understand. I thought I knew much before I left, because I had read more of the rope-books in this room than anyone in the village, but now I know better.

The rice seeds given to us by To-mu in exchange for my going to America grew like magic. The first year's harvest was bigger than anyone remembered. The rice didn't taste as good as the old rice, but we had so much more of it. We celebrated with a great festival, and everyone, even the children, got drunk. It felt good to have done this, to have brought in new seeds, new hope from outside that would fill everyone's bellies again.

Before the next planting season, To-mu came again with Pha and Aung, carrying his heavy backpack as always. Even though we had not known each other that long, I thought of him as an old friend, familiar since childhood, because I had learned so much since I first met him.

But he seemed uncomfortable, agitated. "I came," he said, "to sell you more seeds."

"Oh, we do not need more seeds." I'd learned to accept that To-mu could be very knowledgeable about some things, but had little common sense. "We saved plenty of seeds from last year's harvest."

To-mu looked away from me. "The seeds you saved will not work. They are *sterile.*"

Pha did not know how to translate this word, and To-mu had to try again. "The seeds will not grow. They are dead. You have to buy new ones."

I had never heard of such a thing. How could seeds grow into rice stalks that will not yield more seeds?

To-mu explained that there are small bits of twisted-up string in every living thing, including the seeds and including us, called *genes,* which determine how that thing grows and how it will look. The genes are strung together from little clumps that form a language that can be read.

"Like the *Nan* knots," I said. He nodded.

When someone invents a new gene, a string of new words, and puts it in a seed, that seed may have qualities that people like. The words make the seeds valuable. But the words are owned by the inventor, and other people have to pay him if they want to grow the seed. To make sure that people pay, To-mu explained, the inventor sometimes has to put in more words in that will prevent the seed from growing new seeds. So people have to pay every year.

"If you tried to grow seeds with that gene without the inventor's permission, you would be stealing from him," To-mu said. "It's just like if you walked into the inventor's house and took a bowl of rice away from him. The sterile genes are added to help people stay honest."

This made no sense. If I take someone's bowl of rice, that's stealing because that person doesn't have the bowl of rice any more. But if someone teaches me a new word with power, I haven't taken that word away from him. He still has it.

I tried to understand this better. "We have to pay to use these words that you say are knotted up inside the rice seeds." He nodded.

To-mu had told me that watching me tying knots in his game helped him. "So if you learn the words from our books, the wisdom from our knot-writing, do you have to pay us every year too?"

To-mu laughed and scratched his head. I thought he seemed nervous. "No, I don't think so. The things I learn from you are . . . old. Not protected, not by *copyright* or *patent*." More words that Pha could not translate, and I didn't want him to bother asking To-mu to explain. If I learned more words from To-mu, I might have to pay for them too. I understood enough to know that To-mu thought what the *Nan* could teach him was of no value.

I had been a fool. I thought I was doing something to help the village, but To-mu's part of the bargain came with strings tied to it. All I did was to put us into debt with a remote lord, a lord to whom we must pay an annual tribute. I had brought Sky Village as low as the peasants bonded to the opium lords.

There was nothing to be done. So we sold more rice to the traders to get money, which we used to buy the seeds from To-mu.

"The price will go up a bit next year, and the next," he said. "I had to beg my friend to give you a discount for the first few years. You might want to think about how to expand the village's economy so you'll be able to afford the seeds and buy better things. Like medicine and ice cream."

Pha said that some of To-mu's words made sense. The world was changing, and the *Nan* should change too. Some of the young men could go down the mountain to work, and Pha knew of opportunities for pretty young girls in the cities, especially if they were willing to go as far as Thailand.

I knotted a book about my conversation with To-mu. Maybe it will serve as a warning for the future, so that others will not be as shortsighted and stupid as I was.

We tried to grow some of our old rice alongside the new rice the next few years, but the old rice withered since it needed lots of water, and we had to save most of the little water we had for the new rice. People gave up. I think about the little genes twisted up inside those old seeds, the words passed down to us from our ancestors, now forgotten and gathering dust in storage sacks. Will those seeds even grow in the future, if the rain ever comes back?

To-mu has not been back since that second year. A different man now comes before each planting season to sell us seeds.

Route 128, Greater Boston:

The algorithm based on Soe-bo's techniques performed well, far better than anything in the published literature. The paper describing my research is out for peer review, now that the lawyers are done with the patent applications.

If things work out right, this may be every bit the breakthrough I was hoping for. My algorithm will speed up drug discovery by orders of magnitude and save many lives.

I haven't had time to focus on the revenue impact this will have on us, but the CFO's presentation to the Board was very well received. The ten-year profit projections from direct discovery and licensing looked like an exponential curve.

Maybe it's time for another discovery trip. I'm thinking Bhutan.

Author's Notes

The idea of tapping human pattern-recognition and spatial reasoning skills to aid the search for effective algorithms for protein-folding is described by Seth Cooper et al. in "Predicting protein structures with a multiplayer online game," *Nature 466,* 756-760 (5 August 2010).

Some features of the knot-writing system of the *Nan* are modeled on the Hangul script as well as Incan quipus and Chinese folk art knotting.

Seeing

GENEVIEVE VALENTINE

After it was over, they pulled her from the sea.

Even as they lifted her into the rescue boat she was saying, "No, no; we could have made it."

She was cradling the hand the Captain broke.

The first time Marika saw the night sky, she was terrified.

(Strange she wasn't terrified sooner. They'd escaped the city because of the water riots. The city wouldn't last long; the night swallowed it up one time too many, and then day just never came.

Maybe that's what happened to her—one terror swallowing another.)

The night sky was a battle of stars, a violent seam tearing through the center like a wound badly sewn up. The points of light marshaled in ways she didn't understand; the constellations she remembered were devoured by the hordes. Everything bled.

(This prepares her, a little, for what comes later.)

(What comes later:

A star dropping out of sight, a ship that holds three, a scattering of gold.)

It is impossible, from the ground, to look at a star.

The atmospheric interference muddies the light, drags it through the sky faster than your eyes can follow. If you're lucky—if you're at a high altitude, on a clear night, in a lonely place—this interference is perhaps a few dozen arcseconds out of alignment with reality. If it's windy, or you can't escape the summer, or you are trapped by people and lights, your problems multiply. You fall away from the truth by full seconds; you are hopelessly lost the moment you turn your face to the sky.

By the time you look up, nothing is true any more; the ghosts of the stars only flicker and shine.

Astronomers call this measurement Seeing. (Science has run out of more complicated words to explain the ways the universe has outwitted us.)

What it means: you can't trust your eyes. You can't trust your instruments. You can't trust a thing, from the ground.

• • •

They made it to a boat. At night, Marika slipped from her mother's arms and climbed to the deck to watch the sky.

Once, an old man was sitting on the railing. He was staring at something—a steady, bright star that was already setting.

The water that night was calm, past the ship's wake; the edges of the sky were mirrored clean. The star, reflected in the water's edge, looked like twins moving to greet one another.

The old man didn't turn to look at her. He didn't move at all. He watched the star setting for a long time.

When it slipped into the water, so did he.

It seemed rude that some places survived when others didn't, but Marika and her mother found a city where lights still came on. (Her mother didn't last six months there; too used to running.)

The city drafted for sciences; better than a war that only drafted cannon fodder. When the city came for Marika, she didn't argue.

(They had privatized water. Mission Control got it below market price. Marika even had enough to bathe in. She still hoarded, took furtive gulps like she didn't know when the next one was coming. It gave her away as a refugee, but she couldn't stop. Some thirsts you never get over.)

They teach Marika how to measure light.

In some ways it's interesting to discover that light has measures other than Safe and Not Safe, that there's still a world in which mathematics are of any use at all. But the more she learns about candelas and albedo and gravitational lensing and seeing and the impossibility of ever knowing anything for sure, the more thinks that every light should just be classified Not Safe.

(You know as little about light as you know about why a man would slip away into the water when the shore was in sight by morning.)

But still she negotiates the unlikelihood of Gaussian distribution in phase fluctuations, and calculates probable intermittency to gauge turbulence strength, all so that someone standing at the telescope can point the lens at the sky and know where it's really looking.

Konstantinova heads up the observation banks, and Marika tries not to look over her shoulder at the star map there. (It doesn't matter. Not her business. Not Safe.)

When Gliese 581-d transits its star, Marika is the only one still awake working, and Konstantinova says, "Well, it might as well be you—come look at this."

Marika leans in and watches the screen; it's a grainy, stuttering image replaying in a slow-motion loop, tucked into a corner and drowned out by a crawl of numbers underneath. She recognizes the numbers at the very bottom edge; the initial readings are run through her model to peel away the seeing and get as close to exact locations as their numbers allow.

"It's beautiful," Konstantinova says.

Marika knows she's only looking at the numbers.

Numbers are universal, Marika gets it. You have to rely on mathematics if you're going to get anywhere, because the universe conspires against you the moment you lift your face to the sky in some warm place on a windy plain, the atmosphere sluicing across the nightscape, your meager vision blurred by tears. Marika understands.

(But she knows, she *knows,* you can't tell a thing from the ground.)

This moment is their first point of contact.

(Only Konstantinova would know what that means, what will happen now; but it's a measurement she never takes.)

Konstantinova has a knack for transit.

She watches the map they've made, piled with F-through-M stars (warm enough to heat a planet, cool enough to last). They're tagged; the closest ones have telescopes dogging them, just in case.

(They won't be able to stay here very long. They have to pick somewhere to go where they stand a chance.)

Sometimes one of the stars has a drop in luminosity, the intensity of their light suddenly dimming. This happens sometimes when one is dying, or a flare ends, or when debris comes between the telescope and the far-off star.

But Konstantinova has a knack, and she can watch the numbers sinking and know she has a transit even before the alarm sounds.

Every time it comes she flips the switch to record, replays it in slow motion, marks the points of contact: click, click, click, click.

Every time, she thinks, *Let this be home.*

(By now the numbers are practically shapes; she can look at a column of numerals and see the corona of a star.)

During a planetary transit, there are four points of contact, moments where the circumference of the planet touches the edge of the star in only one place.

1. Just before the transit begins, when the outermost edges meet for the first time.

2. As the planet moves closer to the center, when the trailing edge of the planet has just come within the circle of the star.

3. As the planet passes the center of the transit, its leading curve touches the far edge of the star.

4. At the end of transit, the trailing curve of the planet moves closer and closer to freedom; then there is a single point of contact with the edge of the star; then the transit is over and they are parting.

(This has no real scope if you are close to the event; schoolchildren gather with shoeboxes to peer into the eclipse, that's all.

This has no meaning until you are watching your new home become a black pearl against a far-off disc of light.)

Gliese 581 is a red dwarf star, warm and small, twenty light years from the Earth. It hangs in Libra, if you're watching from the ground. It has four planets ringing it. One of them transits at the right speed; it's close enough to Gliese for light, far enough for water.

(The classification is Gliese 581-d; when people begin to pin hopes on it, it shrinks to "Gliese Dee"; to "Dee." Marika calls it Gliese 581, never mentions Dee at all.)

There is a chance Dee is an ocean planet.

In the ops bay, there is construction on a small-scale human transport. There are calculations being made.

It is a very slight chance, but these are desperate days, and people must put a lot of faith, sometimes, in very slight chances.

Sometimes when they were still running from place to place, it was a comfort for Marika to watch the sky and see there was no balance there, either. The stars you knew would roll beyond your sight and be replaced by strangers, and there was nothing you could do.

After a while she couldn't breathe in cities, wanted only to be in the wild, watching a war she couldn't win.

(The sky is a battle; stars are always falling.)

Seeing can be mitigated on cold, clear nights. From a refuge on top of a mountain, the seeing is so clear that, if you didn't know better, it might not occur to you that the star is even moving.

(You know better now; you can't trust your eyes.)

Sometimes there's no such luck, and even the Moon wavers like a coin submerged in shallow water. When seeing is at its worst, the Aristarchus crater on the Oceanus Procellarum can suffer so much distortion that it's only intermittently visible. If you know what you're looking for, and you know your numbers, you can calculate the seeing from that.

Marika doesn't learn this until it's too late. For her, Aristarchus is always just a pale dot in a black sea, washing in and out of sight; a star on dark water, or a drowning man.

Maybe the old man held out a hand as he toppled—a reflex, second thoughts— but Marika never remembers. Maybe he called for help, or tried to pull himself up before the water took him, but it might be a lie.

This moment always blurs when she tries to recall it; it wavers like the

Moon, sneaks sidelong into her imagination when she's running checklists on the three-seat ship that will carry them to Gliese 581.

(She doesn't think she was terrified watching the old man drop into the water, but she must have been; whenever he appears in her thoughts she freezes, fumbles for something to hold on to.)

When she's drunk enough and dreaming, sometimes he holds out his arm and the star-wake catches him, pulls him smoothly across the water until he disappears into the sky.

But it was only Jupiter, she thinks, not a star; you know that now.

She wakes up grieving, doesn't know why.

Marika calls it Gliese 581 because she doesn't ever want to pin her hopes on a planet by mistake.

Their spacesuits are molded in the Orlan model—a thick skin they can pull on and clamp shut—and Konstantinova thinks it's remarkably like wearing an elephant.

Apparently it's not as bad as it used to be. The gloves are more articulated, the legs less bulky. There's still no joint at the neck; the chest is stiff to support the oxygen and coolant strapped to the back.

Before Alkonost I, she and Zeke and Marika run drills until they can all get in, attach the water-coolant hoses, and seal up in five minutes; in four; in three.

Konstantinova always hears an exhale over the mike when Marika's fastened in. For a long time she thinks it's relief. Exertion, maybe. Panic, maybe. (Marika is a liability; why they're sending her up is anyone's guess.)

But once, Konstantinova sees Marika's face as Zeke seals her in: Marika frowns, brushes at the helmet's gold-coated visor like she's cleaning a dirty glass.

(The sound is a sigh. It hurts.)

Konstantinova's life support system whirrs awake.

"Clear," she says, turns her mind to important things.

"The life support system isn't active in the pods," says Zeke. "Shit. Mission Control, are you reading me?"

An acknowledgement comes back over the static; then a plan. Marika and Zeke fish around in the toolbox and do as they're told. Konstantinova takes comm, passing along a series of orders that become wild guesses.

No one panics until they realize the ambient heat from the launch melted a circuit in the outer hull that can't be set right again.

Mission Control goes quiet for a long time.

Marika and Zeke wait, holding the handrails to keep from floating away; at the comm, Konstantinova is bent over like someone punched her in the stomach.

Then the Director says, "At full speed, it's forty years to Dee. Operations calculates that it's possible to make it, without suspension, on the existing lift-support." A pause. "There's not enough for a return."

He doesn't say, We might not have this chance again, if this ship comes down in pieces. He doesn't say, You might as well take your chances, things aren't any better on the ground.

Konstantinova's visor trembles against the net of stars.

"You'll have some life support after landing," comes over the line. "A day, maybe, maybe a week. Depends how much oxygen you use on the trip. But even a day is long enough to find out if Dee is really habitable."

The Director clears his throat. "This isn't a call we're going to make, Alkonost. It's up to you."

After a long time, Konstantinova says, "No."

Zeke says, "And I'm a No. That's majority—we're no-go, Control. We're inputting a new trajectory. Confirm."

Konstantinova curses under her breath, until the roar of the atmosphere swallows the words.

After it's over, Konstantinova pulls Marika out of the hatch.

"My hand hurts," Marika says, absently.

Konstantinova says, "We broke your fingers."

(This is the second; it is nearly the eclipse.)

Marika doesn't remember anything until they play the recording.

Then she listens as Zeke orders her more and more sharply to let go of the handhold and strap in for re-entry, where are you going, the decision's been made, this is an order, don't touch the hatch, have you lost your mind, that's an order, answer me goddammit, move back *now* or I'll make you move.

"Why didn't you answer?" they ask her.

She says, "I did."

(Not then—when Zeke blocked the hatch and broke her fingers, it was Konstantinova who yelped.

But on the recorder, as soon as the Director said "It's possible to make it," she said "Go.")

They put Marika back at the computer bank, and she gauges wind resistance and plots angles and tells the telescope where it should be pointing.

(She's still good at it; she just doesn't look behind her any more where the map is, where the ghosts of the stars flicker and shine.)

It's a week before anyone talks to her.

The first person who does is Konstantinova.

"Can you move your fingers?"

Marika says, "Yes."

A week later, Konstantinova hands her a screwdriver, says, "Prove it."

• • •

Konstantinova makes her do mechanic drills at night, after the others are asleep.

So Marika drills: into her suit in two minutes, alone; flicking switches to a full-speed metronome; screwing and unscrewing panels until the pads of her fingers have no skin left.

She doesn't understand why, until she hears rumors that the techs are making modifications and repairs; that it will be going back up as Alkonost II, with three chairs up for grabs.

"They'll never crew me again," she says.

Konstantinova says, "You have fifteen seconds. Go."

It takes a year for Alkonost II to take off.

Zeke gets water-fever and dies. No one offers to replace him.

Walters gets drafted out of the pilot pool. He's surly to the techs; he can suit up in two minutes; he cries in his bunk.

Konstantinova wishes for one, just one, to be the sort of person you want beside you when you stand on a new planet.

But no one else comes, and that morning on the launch pad, it's Marika standing on her other side.

(This is the third; it's almost over.)

The launch succeeds. The pods register nominal. The life support system holds.

They make it through the asteroid belt with only one bump (a fragment of meteorite, so small that when it strikes the hull it makes a soprano ping they can hear inside).

Decision point comes after that, with the inner planets behind them and Jupiter filling the viewscreen. Along the top edge, a shadow is passing; a moon in transit.

"We are go," says Konstantinova; her feet go numb just saying it.

"Godspeed," says Mission Control.

On the ground, they've already started to leave notes, to write things down and lock them up safely in case the war gets worse while they're gone. They're making a covenant of things for their children to do when they're grown and staring at the dusty computer banks, greeting three far-away strangers.

"When we wake up," says Konstantinova, "we won't know a soul. Imagine that."

She glances behind her, but Marika's looking out at Jupiter with a crestfallen face; a moment later, Marika closes her pod like she's glad to go.

(Walters went into his right after launch, even before the asteroid field. He'd better be as good at landings as they swear he is. She doesn't put much faith in people who are surly to techs.)

Konstantinova stays up long enough to watch the ship accelerate to full speed, just in case.

Jupiter drops away, and Uranus and Neptune roll past in the distance like blue marbles, and there's a brief bright string of stones along the Kuiper belt

(Haumea whirling by), and then they're in deep space and it's nothing but her star map, as far as she can see.

It's so familiar, suddenly, that she has to calculate the luminosity of Vega from memory before she can breathe again.

(Some thirsts you never get over.)

They wake up three days shy of Gliese 581.

Konstantinova wakes a day before the others to check out the comm. The Captain should be first, she feels. Zeke would have agreed.

When Dee comes into sight, cloudy and blue and welcome, Konstantinova holds her breath, runs some numbers.

(It's an afterthought. By now the numbers are practically shapes, and she knows what home looks like.)

Walters wakes next. He looks out at the planet, sighs, and starts to dress.

Marika wakes last. As her pod cracks open she knocks it away with outstretched arms, leans out the edge and takes a few gasping breaths.

"I dreamed we hit the water," she says.

Konstantinova doesn't answer. People's dreams are their own business.

The navigation system is working and the life support is as expected (enough air to get home, and Konstantinova tries not to shout with relief).

There's a message from Mission Control, only twenty years old, which catches up to them on the second day. A few of the old voices from Mission Control send good wishes, and introduce some new voices.

"We've been monitoring your trip, Alkonost," says one of the strangers. "Everything looks good; watch fuel usage on your way in, so you can make it back up all right if the gravity's stronger than estimated. Let us know when you wake up. Good morning, and Godspeed."

Konstantinova sends a message back. Beside her, Marika looks grimly through the viewscreen, where Gliese 581-d is spinning in the glow of their new home star.

They suit up and take positions for landing; it's so instinctive now that Konstantinova smiles.

(She spent forty years dreaming of setting down on Dee, and after all that practice the comm switches feel like her own fingertips.

She never got to the part where they step out on a new world; not enough imagination left over.)

The checklist goes well until the very last moment, until Dee's gravity has already caught them and they've begun the slow, inevitable fall.

"The third shock absorber isn't running," says Konstantinova. The words sound distant; disbelieving.

"We can land with two," Marika says.

Walters says, "Not on water; if we're off by more than a few degrees the surface tension will knock us over before we even touch down. We'll slam into the water and be pulverized by impact." He's not disbelieving; he sounds like that's just what he's expected all along.

"Then you'd better do your job, I guess," Konstantinova snaps.

"What's wrong with it?" asks Marika. "It froze?"

Konstantinova frowns at the diagnostic. "Doesn't look like it. The mechanism still registers. Something must have broken loose while we were sleeping. Maybe we can open the nav panel in the back and -"

"In the asteroid belt," says Marika. "Something hit the hull."

"After last time, there better not be a fucking thing wrong with that hull," says Konstantinova.

"But it sang," Marika says quietly.

All at once Konstantinova has a vision like a reel of film, as a sliver of rock careens into the hull, as a few grains slice through the hull and nick the fuel line, as forty years of a microscopic accident converge on them at once when there's not enough pressure in a valve.

She tries for words, and for a moment fails.

"We can't access that now," Walters says. "We're heading into the atmosphere, we'll burn up if we go out there. Let's pull out, we'll look at it from a steady orbit."

"If we pull out now," says Konstantinova, "we'll burn the fuel we need to launch from the surface of Dee and go home. So we take our chances in the water, or we take our chances on the ground."

This shouldn't be such an agony; this isn't the first time she's been here. It should get easier. This should have an answer, by now.

"All right," she manages, "pull out and circle back on a one-way trip. This is the go/no go. Vote."

She waits without turning for them to weigh in. She has a new respect for Mission Control, forty-one years ago; this is a silence that's hard to allow.

At last, Walters says, "No go. We'll take our chances in the water."

Marika doesn't say anything. Konstantinova frowns at the comm, wonders if she missed it; if Marika answered while Konstantinova was still talking.

(Marika has that habit, and her answer is always Go.)

But she waits for an answer a long time, until there is the sound of something sealing; Konstantinova sees the warning light go red under her fingers before she registers that Marika is opening the outer hatch.

Click.

(The transit is over; they are parting.)

The hairline crack is in the hydraulics panel. As Marika approaches it, moving hand over hand along the side rails, one bead of gasoline pushes through it and away.

"You won't get home," she says into her mic. "You've lost too much already."

She doesn't know if the connection is still live; she forgets if she turned it on or not, and her heart is pounding too loudly for her to hear a thing.

She grips the screwdriver in her free hand and gets to work. It's familiar by now, and the screws come apart one by one, cling gently to the magnets in the fingertips of her glove.

The suit warms up with her work; her visor fogs. She tries not to panic. There's not enough air to panic. (She disconnected—there wasn't time for anything else.)

If she lets go of the handrail, she'll vanish.

She imagines a darkness like the darkness of the boat on calm water, imagines stretching out a hand as she falls.

The screwdriver shakes; she clamps down with numb fingers to keep it from escaping, drags off another screw.

But it's useless. Her helmet is fogging up from the inside now—she can't see, she can't *see*, and there's not enough time left to hold her breath and wait for equalization, not enough oxygen left to hyperventilate and turn it into droplets big enough to see around.

She shoves the pick in at an angle, to avoid her eyes.

Three stabs before the visor cracks; another three before she can wedge the pick inside and wrench it out.

The shield winks once and spins gently out of sight, knocks away a scattering of gold where the coating has flaked off under the chisel.

She exhales, so her lungs don't explode from the decompression, and turns to the bulkhead with shaking hands. She has to work fast—she forgets how long you can last before the darkness swallows you.

(You have fifteen seconds. Go.)

The last screw opens; the panel opens.

She slices the fuel line where it's torn, shoves the healthy end of the hose back into the joint, throws the clamp shut. Stray gasoline floats past her in black pearls.

(She's freezing; her lips are numb; when she blinks her eyelids crack, snap off, go flying.)

The panel begins to vibrate as the system kicks in.

(Seven seconds.)

She slams the bulkhead shut, fumbles three of the screws back into place. It's all she manages before her fingers freeze.

Far away, Konstantinova is saying something about re-entry, about being out of time, she's panicked, she's screaming—but the last of the air escapes the suit, and then there's silence.

(Marika breathes in; her lungs collapse.)

The ship is accelerating now, dragging her.

She pulls free.

The motion spins her slightly, away from the planet towards the sky. For a moment, the full view stuns her.

She thinks, *It's beautiful.*

It's the first time in her life she's ever thought it.

(This is why: there is no seeing.

Now there is only the sky; she's looking, for an instant, straight to the stars. This is the true geography.)

The Milky Way rips through the black at a different angle; this sky is a stranger, a ceaseless riot, sharp and steady-bright.

It's a lovely war.

(Two seconds.

One second.)

After it's over, Konstantinova will emerge from the sea.

She will stand on the deck of the Alkonost; pull off her helmet; breathe.

The night will be deep. When she turns her face to the sky, to search for a place to begin with her numbers, the ghosts of the stars will flicker and shine.

Salvaging Gods
JACQUES BARCIA

Gorette found her second godhead buried under piles of plastic bottles, holy symbols, used toilet paper and the severed face of an avatar. No matter how much the scavengers asked, the people from Theodora just wouldn't separate organic from non-biodegradable, from divine garbage. They threw out their used-up gods along with what was left of their meals, their burnt lamps, broken refrigerators, tires, stillborn babies and books of prayer in the trash can. And when the convoys carrying society's leftovers passed through the town's gates, some lazy bureaucrat would mark in a spreadsheet that another mountain was raised in that municipal sanitary landfill, the Valley of the Nephilim. And to hell with the consequences.

Her father says no dead god is dead enough that it can't be remade on our own image. The old man can spend hours rambling about over-consumption, the gnostic crisis, the impact of all those mystical residues poisoning the soil and the underground streams, how children are born malformed and prone to mediunity, and how unfair it is that only the rich have access to miracles. People will do what's more comfortable, not what's best for everyone, he'd finally say. It's far easier to buy new deities than try to reuse them. So he taught her how to recycle old gods and turn them into new ones, mostly, she believed, because he wanted to make a difference. Or maybe because he was the one true atheist left in the world.

It was a small one, that godhead, and not in a very good shape. Pale silver, dusty, scratched surface and glowing only slightly underneath the junk. At best, thought Gorette, it'd have only a few hundred lines of code she'd be able to salvage. Combined with some fine statues and pieces of altars she'd found early that morning, perhaps she'd be able to assemble one or two more deities to the community's public temple at Saint Martin. The neighborhood she was raised in had only recently been urbanized, so that meant the place was not officially a slum anymore. But still, miracles were quite a phenomenon down in the suburbs.

"Hey, daddy. Found another one," Gorette said, covering her eyes from the burning light of midday. "Can we go home now, please?"

The egg-shaped thing had the pulse of a dying heart, and fitted almost perfectly in her adolescent hand. So she arranged a place for it amongst the relics in her backpack, inside the folds of a ragged piece of loincloth, and into a beaten up thurible where it'd be safe enough to survive the hour-long ride back to the city.

Her father stood next to a marble totem, sweeping the field with a kirlian detector. The pillar was part of a discarded surround-sound system with speakers the size of his chest, and served as a landmark to the many scavengers exploring the waste dump. When he heard his daughter calling him, he took his gas mask off and said "That depends," his low-toned voice coming like a sigh, tired. "Do you think this will do? We're running out of code and there are many open projects in the lab."

A plastic bag some ten yards away from her smelled of rotting flesh. Animal sacrifice, she knew, and the vultures seemed to have noticed that too. "Yeah," she lied, "It's a bit wasted, but I think it has a lot of good code in it. Never seen one of these, so I suppose it's a quite new model." She desperately needed to take that stink out of her body and today she hoped was water day. "Is it water day today, daddy?"

The old man picked up one last relic, a fang or something, and examined it close to his thick glasses. He nodded to the object and put it in a sac he carried tied to his waist. "No, it's not. The Palace said three days ago that they'd reinforce the water gods cluster, so the suburb's rationing would drop to two days. But of course that didn't happen." He finally walked to Gorette and scratched her dreadlocks, trying to smile. "Maybe you can build a water god with the godhead you found, huh?"

Gorette made her first wish that evening, after incubating some of the new godhead's code in an altar of her own design. It was built out of the remains of a semi-defaced idol, a one-eyed marble bust wearing a tall orange hat, adorned with shattered crystals, split dragon horns, praying cords and barbed wire. That last bit just to make sure everything would stand in place. The godhead rested inside the same thurible Gorette used to cradle it safely back from the Valley of the Nephilim. But now the metal egg had dozens of acupuncture needles trespassing its shell, and every single one was linked to hair-thin optical fiber threads, shining with divine code, feeding with data a green phosphorus monitor.

Without warning. It just woke up.

When the loading bar hit one hundred per cent, the stone bust opened its one eye, fluidly, staring directly at her. She fell back from the chair, startled, and stared back at the thing's physiognomy from where she stood. From the floor up.

It was her first attempt at a new design model, one that toyed with disharmony instead of symmetry. Profanity instead of divinity. Good hardware, her dad says, is as important as good code. But harmony. Harmony is the key. The problem is that new gods are coming with even more complex, specialized godheads, their kernels incompatible with older or malfunctioning holy paraphernalia. She decided to try out the new approach and, for her surprise, it worked.

"I want a fucking bath," Gorette said, pointing a finger to the bust. "A *warm* bath. Now."

The stone in the god's crippled face moved like if it was made out of clay. Smooth. No, it moved like that stop-motion movie, what's its name, the one that always airs on holidays and Friday evenings. The one dad just loves to watch when he's back from the Valley.

"As you wish," it said coldly.

A sound of streaming water echoed from the bathroom and almost instantly the smell of steam and soap and essential oils filled up the room. She grinned, and jumping over her feet ran towards the shower, undressing on her way. Is it lavender? Maybe birch. Arnica in the white cloud. She felt she was clean even before she could reach the shower, she felt the dirt collapsing, decanting on the floor before she could have a chance of laying on the tub and rest.

A bathtub. "A bathtub?"

She looked back at the one-eyed god running miracles in her room. "You made me a bathtub." The idol remained still. She stood there for a few more seconds trying to figure out how her jury-rigged water god made her a complete bath, with a bathtub, aromatic oils and, now she saw it, the finest bathing gown. Collateral miracles were not unheard of, but modern godheads had filters to prevent the danger of leaking energy. Motionless, the god just kept staring forward, to nowhere in particular, its exposed wire guts transmitting magical pulses to the screen, blipping a green dot like the apparels in private hospitals, monitoring a wide-eyed comatose half-head, an undead, glitchy deity. Gorette felt like checking her complementary coding, but confessed to herself the hot pool of perfumed water was too tempting to be ignored. After all, feeling clean and relaxed she'd have more chances of debugging her creation.

That's it. She immersed herself in the tub and let all her worries trail off, evaporate.

After the bathtub miracle, the god produced a new set of porcelain plates, when Gorette only commanded it to clean the dishes. Days later she asked for ice and got a refrigerator and a minibar. Then the thought of a nice meal generated spiced fish. And, one night, the sound of a calm, streaming river came as a lullaby. And rain cooled a hot day. And a smile painted watercolor on canvas. On and on, over the course of a week, her tiniest, involuntary wishes were fulfilled and as much as she tried, she couldn't find the bug in the god's code tree. Okay, after the tenth attempt, the effort to fix the problem wasn't that strong-willed. But dad had taught her a bug could untap the power of a god, mollifying reality in its closer vicinity, causing the neighborhood's divine networks to go haywire. It was dangerous, she knew.

She spent days and nights trying to fix it, trying to combine source codes distilled from newer godheads, but nothing seemed to work. She decided she'd destroy the thing before it'd cause her trouble.

A dead boy changed her mind.

It was Monday morning and Gorette swept the water god off her working bench into a big cardboard box laying on the floor. She just discarded it, trying not to think much about getting rid of her first creation. The thing fell inside the box, a stone punch enveloped in barbed wire. Gorette gave the god a last inspection and could see that the cold half-face was looking upwards from its new room. She met its gaze one last time and closed the box, decided to sell its parts in the market for whatever the merchants gave for it.

The girl picked up the box and went downstairs, hardly able to keep balance with the thing's weight pushing her back and down. So heavy and so slowly she spent thirty minutes walking down the stairs, flight upon flight on a downward spiral to the first floor. She finally reached a smooth carpet under her feet and felt her strength renewed when she captured the smell of cinnamon tea being brewed in the kitchen. There was music playing and the house was calm and empty. Patchouli.

She walked to the door, the box in front of her, light in her arms and spirit. An awesome Sunday waited for her outside the house.

On her way out, she tripped over a gas mask resting face-down on the floor, but managed to jump on one foot and keep herself from falling. She kicked the mask off from her, startling the white tiger sleeping under the crystal table. Immediately, the giant cat clawed the mask with its tigery reflexes, making it spin and fall over its face, covering all of its beastly features but the lower jaw and its protruding fangs. A gas-masked albino tiger. Nothing can be cooler than that. Maybe a gas-masked cephalopod. No. Albino tiger is definitely cooler.

Outside, the day was perfect. The sun shone bright and there was the bluest, cloudless sky sheltering Saint Martin. The street was busy, the market was everywhere. Fresh bread, roses, dew. Birds, carts and horses on the march. The signal was red, so she stood close to a bald man reading the newspaper, waiting in line for his turn with the public god service. She overheard someone the first in the row, complain with the totem, why in fuck's name you can't cure eczema? It's a damn fungus, damn it. Your credits have expired, answered a featureless voice. She felt sorry for the man, but couldn't help but giggle. Next time, try boiling the river's water. That fetid thing the Palace calls a river.

She turned in time to see the man walking away from the totem, down the street, right in her direction. His right cheek and part of his upper lip and nose was covered in a pink, moist blotch, a blistered wound shaped as a face, a somewhat familiar face that now she could see, as he approached, went down to his neck and into his shirt. She swallowed her giggle and wished the man could find a cure.

"As you wish."

"What?"

Slo-mo time-warp, the air thick as a jar of glycerin. The man walked past her like the actors playing living statues in Gaiman Square. As he moved, she could see all the tiny blisters, the face-wound staring back at her. And as if someone had hit the rewind button, the eczema started to erode. Skin took back its space, first in the borders and then in spots inside the pink perimeter, holes forming eyes and a space like a mask, or mouth that seemed to say "Oh," and then scream, wider and wider, until it completely disappeared, leaving nothing but an afterimage, a memory, a sensation.

"Did you see that?" Gorette turned to face the man next to her, a young guy wearing a ponytail, reading the newspaper. Like waking up from a deep dream, she looked down to the box in her arms and immediately dropped it to the ground. Her nails tore the cardboard walls and there it was, the god, face up, the way she put it back in her room.

The god in the box looked like it was engaged in silent battle with her. Face to face.

People walked past them on the sidewalk, the noises and colors and smells of Saint Martin coming back to her in a single torrent. Too many steps and the scent of flowers and wax, hooves clicking, and chantings, all around the street. A procession.

She turned once again, feeling dizzy, and saw the ocean of people and candles and garlands and, in the middle of the street, a huge bier with a coffin and a little altar, an undertaker god surely preparing the body, the grave and the costs for the burial. Around the altar, there were pictures of a kid, younger than her. The face of the corpse inside the coffin.

"A kid," the words came out without her noticing.

She closed her mouth and locked it with both hands, closing her eyes not to think, not to think, not to think.

"As you wish," and again, several yards away from her, like an echo, above the crowd, "as you wish."

Five seconds passed before the bier's conductor jumped from his seat, let go of the reins and climbed on the coffin. People noticed the man's hurry and soon there was a commotion around the vehicle. People cried "help him out!" and "open the coffin!" and "my kid! He's alive!" And now she could hear a stifled sound, a desperate knock-knock on wood coming from the depths of the underworld. There were relatives pushing the coffin's lid, but damn those nails, the joiner that worked across the street rushed with a crowbar and soon was forcing the wood cover. Gorette's heart was pounding, someone please open that coffin. *Asyouwishasyouwishasyouwish.*

Suddenly, the nails were fired off to the air, like a machine gun trying to shoot down the heavens. The whole wood box went down to splinters in a moment. The crowd went mad when the boy rose and took the cotton balls out of his nose.

"It was her!" Gorette heard someone cry behind her. "I saw it. She commanded the god to resurrect the boy."

"No I didn't," she heard herself speaking as if the words came from someone else.

"Yes you did," said a very low, calm, cold voice.

"No."

Soon the crowd was all over her, praising her good deeds—*as you wish*—, calling her a saint—*as you wish*—, asking her for favors—*as you wish*—, raising her and her god above them, a new procession for the miracle of life, for the savior, *ad majorem homo gloriam,* for the Popess.

"As you wish," she said, grinning.

Emissaries.

From other neighborhoods, from the Palace, from other cities.

They came in tides, high and low, high and low. They threatened and cajoled, but eventually ended up asking for something they needed to be done, some disease to be cured, another to be implanted, a hand to the their business, some virility, beauty, you name it.

One out of five diplomats demanded to know how she assembled her god. How the hell that thing could—

The truth was she didn't know. She wish she did. And that seemed to be one of the few wishes her creature wasn't able, or willing, to fulfill.

However, most penitents came asking for knowledge, for wisdom, for guidance. That, too, was out of her reach, out of her experience. But certainly not out of her god's verbosity.

That marvel now standing on a totem in front of her throne, a foot lower than her, encased in crystal, half-faced and barbed-wired. For those who entered the temple and met her gaze, her features dominated the god placed only an inch below. But even if her eyes held a deep jade glare, it was the silver beacon of the godhead that really shone brighter. Like the moon.

"Speak," she said.

"Most honorable Popess," began a merchant in a golden tunic, shutting down his smartphone, "what's the nature of true miracles?" The question raised a wave of murmurs in the hall. He was the fifth or sixth person consulting her that morning. "What are they made of? What makes your god able to perform such wonders, surpassing the capabilities of every other functional god in the realm?"

"I—," began Gorette, the Popess, but that cold voice interrupted her speech. That behavior had become quite common in the public sessions lately and the people were beginning to question the Popess' authority over the god.

"I can calculate reality at far superior floppage," the god said. "My miracles per second rate is also higher than your average god. Also, my database—"

"It's my will," cut the Popess.

"No, it's not," replied the stone statue.

"Silence."

"As you wish."

The Popess dismissed the merchant with a wave of her hand. The man bowed slightly, obviously upset for not being answered. He turned and mixed himself with the rest of the crowd, other merchants, other tunics, men in coats and gas masks. "The session is over," she said.

"Popess?" Already at the center of the court. Dirty overcoat and gas mask. She could smell filth in the wind, rotten oranges and oil. The man had a tiger, white as snow, chained to his wrist and it, too, wore a mask, and had a big box mounted on his back, covered by a red velvet coat. "Can I speak?"

The Popess was halfway through leaving the throne, but stopped and turned back to her seat. A green dazzle came from her eyes asking, who's this man, do I know him? "What do you want from me?"

The man gave two steps ahead, dragging the chain, making the gas-masked albino tiger move and then lay. Nice and easy. "Actually," he said, his voice covered by the mask, "I'd like to address your god."

"It?"

"Me?"

"Yes, your Holiness. I want to question your creature," said the stranger.

She was curious. She straightened herself in the throne, crossed her legs under the long robe and smiled, as if expecting entertainment, a show. "Okay. Go on. Let's see what you're gonna get from it."

"In truth, there's only one thing I'd like to ask it." He moved forward and immediately the tiger raised and followed, both closer to the totem. The people gathered around the hall seemed to get closer, curious about what this masked stranger and his beast were up to. "I want you to tell me what's the nature of God?"

"The nature of gods?"

"No. God." So close now. His breath clouded the crystal case. "Gods are manifestations, constructs. They're functions, myths, narratives. They're tools. Limited, discardable, yet very spectacular tools. I want to know what's the nature of God," the man said.

A second passed before its marble lips moved. You could hear the silver sphere, the mighty godhead whirring, its core processing billions of code looking for an answer. Suddenly, the noise stopped. "God is unique. God wishes," it said. "I am unique. I wish."

Marble soldiers, flaming tigers, hydras and giant spiders materialized in the hall, as if coming onstage after opening reality's invisible curtain. Panic took over the crowd in the room, a whirlwind of faces and tunics running, dissolving and exploding in gushes of blood and rot and desecration.

The Popess sank in her throne, reduced to her youth, her green eyes crystallized with fear.

The man under the mask refused to run and instead yelled at the crystal case. "Even a god found in a sanitary landfill, assembled from pieces of junk and designed by a very young, immature girl who didn't even know what she wished for in her life?"

"Even so."

"You're not unique." The stranger reached for the velvet cape over the tiger and pulled it from over the box. There was a crystal case with a marble god inside. A reused god. Design almost identical to that of the Popess' own creation: a silver moon of a godhead pierced by tiny acupuncture needles, linked to a pedestal by fiber optic cables, tied with barbed wire and praying cords and a hat balanced atop a half-face, one-eyed, mouthless piece of avatar at its center. "Do you recognize it? I found it some ten meters away from you."

The older god whirred. The soldiers and monsters charged towards the man and his own technomagical beast. He stood right where he was, but quickly typed shortcut commands to the god and the giant cat. When the creatures were close enough, the tiger attacked with a mighty leap, his claws hacking the monsters' fire hides and carapaces.

But the man kept staring down at the god while the white feline defended their position. More creatures continued to condense into existence out of thin air. The tiger still managed to kill them, keeping the perimeter safe.

"I will destroy her," the god said. "If I can give life, I can take it."

"No, you won't. And you can't." The Popess stood next to the god's crystal case, staring at its single, immovable eye. "Dad once told me about the nature of God." She got close, really close to the crystal case, as if trying to whisper into the god's ear through the transparent wall. "He told me God is flawless."

The blood-red white tiger circled the totem, pushing the soldiers back. Fast and precise as tigers are, he clawed the box, shattered the crystal to tiny bits, sent the stone face away to the floor along with its miraculous monsters. The thing fell hard, barbed wires, praying cords, tokens and fiber optic cables disassembling the holy design with the shock.

Gorette strode across the room at the destroyed god's direction. It rested on the floor, close to the corpses of humans and miracles. She could see it tried to speak, its lips moving in a very familiar way. She decided not to give a damn about what the thing had to say. She picked up the silver godhead and looked deep into the god's eye close to her feet. "God is flawless. But nothing, you hear me? Nothing is without flaw," she said. "Now, shut down."

"As you wish."

At the Valley of the Nephilim, the god wishes it had arms. He wished he was a *he*, not an *it*, not a carcass in the filth, beneath the remains, in the mud. Die, worm, die. You chew my wires off, you reincarnate as a, as a, as a *human*. That. A human. A human.

A human.

A blip and another. Above ground. Steps coming closer. Another blip and an intense, acute sound. Like a blip, but never ending. Like a whistle.

"Guess there's one here."

Yes, there is. There's one here.

Some light, then light and too much light.

"Here you are."

A human.

"Yeah, it looks just like that other one."

What? Not like any other. I'm the others. The others are me.

"Not sure. Will destroy it anyway."

No.

"Come here."

Pressure.

"Boy, you're hard. Wish I had a hammer with me."

As you—

"Oh, here it is," said the girl. "This is what I call a *force quit*. Good bye, little one. Send my regards."

Beat. Crash.

Silence.

Laying the Ghost
ERIC BROWN

We were winding down after coming in from Aldebaran with a haul of starship wreckage. I'd sold the scrap en route and left it in geo-sync orbit above Constance, Altair III, for the merchant to collect. The funds were already in my account and I was treating Ella and Karrie to a meal and a few drinks.

A pianist was improvising Lyran mood-music and the ceiling pulsed with images of Jovian superstorms. Across the spaceport, starships were phasing into and out of the void in eerie silence.

While Ella was at the bar, Karrie said, "For an AI, you know, she's almost . . . well, human."

"She's running on a self-aware paradigm, Karrie. That paradigm is human. She has all the emotional capacity of you and me. As far as I'm concerned, she's our equal."

Karrie just looked at me.

"What?" I said.

"Talking about emotional capacity, Ed . . . Have you ever considered your own?

I stared at her. "*Mine?*"

"Have you heard of the expression 'a cold fish'?"

You can know someone for years—in this case almost ten—and still be amazed at how they view you. "Me? What on earth makes you think that?"

She enumerated her argument with calloused fingers. "One, you never talk. I mean about things that matter, your feelings, your emotions. You never allow people into your head."

I said, "You wouldn't want to go there. It's full of day-to-day rubbish. Nothing deep going on in there."

"You see—there you go again. Trivializing what is important. Two," she went on before I could protest, "you never talk about your past, what's affected you. Three, you rarely speak about the future, what you want—other than the next big haul."

"And what wrong with talking about the next big haul?" I said dismissively. Karrie snorted.

I was glad to see that Ella was returning with a tray of drinks. As she slinked through the crowd, I noticed a few men and women covertly eying her slim body. She slipped into the booth, smiling at me.

"What do you think, Ella?" Karrie said, taking her drink.

Oh, God . . . I thought.

"About what, Karrie?"

"About Ed. Do you think he has deficient emotional capacity?"

Ella looked from Karrie to me, her expression serious. She said, "I think his emotional capacity is far from deficient, Karrie. What is deficient is his ability to express, to show, those emotions. I suspect some past trauma is inhibiting him in this respect." She looked at me. "Maybe you will tell us about it, one day?"

Karrie was smirking at this turn in the conversation.

I said, "Well, thanks. Here I was, enjoying a quiet drink with my crewmates, when everything gets suddenly psychoanalytical. Listen, there's nothing wrong with me, emotionally or otherwise. I have no hang-ups, no inhibitions. I'm happy Ed, the salvageman . . . "

I raised my glass. "Anyway, here's to many another successful haul."

Around then I noticed the figure in the Orion warware spacesuit. It was moving from group to group of drinkers, talking to them briefly and then moving on. From the dismissive gestures of the people spoken to, I received the impression that whoever was in the suit was asking for something, and being turned down.

A minute later the figure perched itself on a stool at the opening of the booth and stared in at us.

I say 'stared', but I only assumed that. The oval faceplate in its sleek, silver helmet was as milky as opal. Its silver suit was streamlined and body-hugging, the surface swarming with millions of nanoware-bots like iron filings in oil.

From its shape, I guessed there was a woman in there.

"What do you want?" Karrie asked brusquely.

"I find myself in a difficult situation," it said. Its voice was feminine, but transistorized. For all I knew, the inhabitant of the suit might not even be human.

She went on, "I need to leave Constance, but I cannot locate a ship heading in the direction I require."

Before Karrie could jump in with some sarcastic comment, I asked, "And where's that?"

A hesitation, then, "The Chandrasakar Stardrift."

I whistled. "That's quite a way away."

"Five thousand three hundred light years, give or take."

Karrie shook her head, derisive, and took a long swallow of beer.

"Where specifically in the Stardrift?" I said.

"A planet called Serimion, Kharran II."

"Serimion . . . " I said. "Now where have I heard the name before?"

Ella said, quick as a flash, "Serimion: site of the war between human colonists and the native inhabitants of the Kharran system. It was a particularly brutal and bloody conflict. The alien race known as the Kha, from the fifth planet of the system, invaded without provocation. Approximately three million humans lost their lives on Serimion."

The person in the suit said, "Precisely three million, two hundred thousand and ninety. Let no lost soul go unmourned."

I asked the obvious question. "But why do you want to go to Serimion?"

The being hesitated again, before saying, "I have my reasons."

"But won't it be dangerous? I mean, won't the Kha be hostile to human arrivals?"

"They allow a certain number of mourners and war historians to visit the shrines of Serimion every year," she said.

I wondered which category she fell into.

I considered for a minute, then said, "Well, it's a long way, and not where we were heading . . . The fare would be hefty."

A silence. The opalescent faceplate turned to me, and the soft, feminine, transistorized voice said, "That is the other slight problem. I am without the funds to finance the journey."

Karrie snorted and shuffled from the booth. "I'll be back at the ship, Ed." She stood and hurried from the bar.

The milky oval of the faceplate, behind which anything might be lurking, was still regarding me.

I said, "A lack of funds is certainly a problem. I don't see how . . . "

The figure pointed to my flight-suit. "I see you bear the sigil of a salvage captain. There is a small starship, a strike vessel, drifting in orbit around Serimion. It belongs to me. You may take it in recompense if you agree to transport me there."

I looked at Ella, who said, "What kind of strike vessel, exactly?"

"A Corinthian, Class II."

Ella said to me, "Even badly damaged, it would fetch approximately twenty-five thousand Altairian units on the open market."

Which would more than cover the cost of the return journey to the Chandrasakar Stardrift.

Of course, there was no way of telling if the being in the suit was telling the truth.

I said, "Show me your face."

After a moment, on some internal command, the faceplate cleared.

"You're human?" I stared at the pretty, impish face revealed; dark, short hair, high cheekbones, a snub nose. She looked no older than twenty.

"But why the suit?" I asked.

She shrugged, twisted her lips uncomfortably. "I . . . I have a certain condition. My immune system is dysfunctional." And she left it at that.

She looked at me, hope evident in her big brown eyes. "Well . . . ?"

I said, "What's your name?"

"Katerina," she replied. "Katerina Reverte."

"Well, Katerina . . . Why don't you give me five minutes to discuss things with my co-pilot here?"

Katerina nodded, rose and strode across to the floor-to-ceiling viewscreen that looked out over the expanse of the spaceport. Reduced in the perspective, she looked tiny, vulnerable.

"Well," I said. "What do you think?"

"I think the situation is certainly odd. She is wearing an Orion warware suit, which is even more expensive than a Corinthian. She could sell the suit, which would more than pay for her medical treatment. It would also pay for her return to Serimion."

"You think she's lying about her condition?"

"That is certainly a possibility."

"And about the Corinthian, too?"

"Impossible to ascertain."

I nodded. "It'd be a risk."

"I would like to know the reason she wishes to return to Serimion."

I shrugged. "My guess is she fought in the war. She wishes to return to lay ghosts, to revisit old battlefields . . . "

"Maybe."

"Well, perhaps we'll find out along the way."

Ella fixed me with one of her impassive stares. "You will agree to take her?"

I nodded, and looked across the lounge to the suited figure. Katerina had turned and was watching us. I signalled her over.

She came hesitantly, almost wincing. I held out my hand. "We phase out in five hours," I told her.

Her expression, behind the faceplate, was joyous.

Karrie took a while to simmer down, even when I told her about the Corinthian.

"But you know nothing about her! Who she is, what she is! She's striding around here in that damned war suit . . . you realize how powerful those things are?"

I shrugged. We were a day out of Altair III, sailing through the marmoreal realm of void-space, two days away from the Chandrasakar Stardrift.

Karrie went on, "Why did you agree, Ed?"

I shrugged again. "She's young, vulnerable. Everyone else back there had turned her down."

She stared at me. "I just don't believe you . . . "

I smiled at her. "What did you say back at the port, that I didn't show my emotions? Well, I'm showing them now. I feel sorry for the kid and I want to help her—"

Karrie pointed at me. "This has nothing to do with your emotions, Ed, and all to do with your male biology."

"Bullshit, Karrie!"

Ella chose that moment to slip through the hatch and cross the flight-deck. She eased into her sling with a smile at me. "For two people who have been in each other's company for almost ten years," she said, softly, "you spend a lot of time in altercations."

"That's what ten years of being banged up with a sarcastic, sour-faced cynic like Karrie does to you."

"And fuck you, too," Karrie spat.

"Anyway," Ella said, "the drives are functioning at ninety-eight per cent efficiency, the smartcore reports no problems, and mechanically all aboard the ship is running smoothly." Did I discern the stress she put on the word *mechanically*?

Under her breath, Karrie muttered, "And you'd know about that, girl," but if Ella heard her, she chose to turn the other cheek.

"Have you had a chance to talk to Katerina?" I asked.

Ella nodded. "I took her on a tour of the ship."

"Learn anything?"

"Very little. She said she was born and brought up on Serimion, but when I asked about the war, and whether she fought in it, she clammed up."

"Do you know much about Serimion?"

"My cache has an extensive file on the planet: settled by humans over two centuries ago, a pastoral place of vast agricultural concerns, a million villages, considered by the rest of the Expansion to be technologically backward. It was settled by a breakaway faction of the Amish community of Mars. The attack by the neighboring Kha came out of the blue."

"And no one has ever found out why the aliens invaded?"

Ella shrugged. "A motive was never discovered. That's what rankles with the survivors to this day, as well as the terrible loss."

She fell silent and stared through the viewscreen at the grey void.

"I think I'll go talk to Katerina," I said.

As I slipped from my sling and approached the hatch, Karrie said, "You'll have difficulty getting that suit off her, if that's what you're thinking about. Seems she's welded to the damned thing."

I bit my tongue and pulled myself through the hatch, wondering what Karrie's problem was.

As I descended the ladder, I heard Ella saying, "You should cease your criticism of Ed. He is, after all, biologically impelled by male drives."

And I'd thought Ella was on my side . . .

I found Katerina in the observation lounge. She was seated before the great curving viewscreen, staring into the void. She had the cowed aspect of a devotee at a temple, a worshipper in a cathedral of the infinite.

"Do you mind . . . ?" I asked, gesturing at the foam-form beside her.

She looked up. "No, please. Be my guest."

I sat down beside her and saw that her faceplate was once again blank.

"Ella told me she'd shown you around the ship." I stared at her sleek silver suit, wondering at its power.

"She gave me a guided tour." She paused, then went on, "She is an AI, isn't she?"

I nodded. "Yes, but one running on a self-aware paradigm."

She turned her faceless faceplate to me and said, "Does that make her human, Ed?"

I smiled and shrugged. "I honestly don't know, Katerina. It does make her a sentient being. And my equal. That's what matters to me."

She nodded. "Will you apologize to Ella for me, Ed?"

"What for?"

"For my inability to . . . to talk to her openly. She wanted to talk, I sensed, but I was unable to respond."

"Because she wasn't human?" I asked.

Instead of replying, she returned her gaze to the infinite. A little later she said, "Do you believe in vitalism, Ed? The idea that—"

I smiled. "I know what vitalism means."

"Well?"

"I don't know. Perhaps, once, I did. It's a nice idea, after all, to think that humans are imbued with a special, God-given light of fire, vitality, soul . . . "

"Perhaps once?" she said. "But no longer?"

I smiled. "Then I met Ella and I had to rearrange my thinking a little."

"So you think that life can exist without that vitality?"

"Look at Ella," I said.

She turned to look at me. "Yes," she said, "but is Ella truly alive?"

I shrugged, and let out a long sigh, out of my depth and uncomfortable. I said, "What about you? Do you believe in vitalism?"

She turned her head to me and said, "Oh, I know vitalism is real."

I nodded. Ella had informed me that the Serimion colony had been religious.

She went on, in her own time, "I was brought up believing in a just God, a God who punished the bad and rewarded the good. We were a peaceful people. We practised non-violence, living within our means, at one and in harmony with our environment, our world. We knew how lucky, how God-blessed we were in settling on Serimion, and we gave thanks."

Beyond the viewscreen, the grey void swirled. There were times when I thought I discerned patterns in the marmoreal streaks in the infinite, and others when I knew that the void was purely random and chaotic.

Katerina went on, softly, "I was brought up on a big farm, run by my parents. I had four older brothers . . . They treated me like a princess." I'm sure, had I been able to see her face, I would have witnessed her smiling. "We worked hard and worshipped daily, and life was bountiful and good. We knew our neighbors and trusted them. They were like us. I never really apprehended that there was an outside world . . . another way of doing things. Even when I graduated from school and attended college . . . all the world was one, one belief, one way of doing things. And then . . . "

And then, I thought, the Kha attacked.

"I was on holiday with friends at the time. We were in a resort on an island far to the south. This saved my life. We were aware that something terrible had happened . . . the firestorms in the atmosphere, the explosions. We saw their attack ships in the distance. When we returned to the mainland . . . "

She fell silent. I reached out and laid my big hand over her small, cold silver mitt.

She went on, "Devastation. Destruction. All the cities, every one of them, all the small towns . . . destroyed. Firebombed, and worse . . . They'd used weapons we didn't even understand. Reducing people and places to dust . . . We never stood a chance. We didn't even . . . didn't even have an army." She fell silent. Then: "I returned home, or to what was left of it. I found my parents, my four brothers. They were dust, Ed, with just scraps of clothing here and there to identify them."

I let a respectful interval elapse, then said, "How did you get off planet?"

"A Federation ship had monitored the attack and sent rescue rafts. All told, just seven thousand of us survived. We—well, a few thousand of us—decided to fight back. Our rage, our grief, overcame out pacific instincts, our long-held beliefs. We had assets lodged in banks across the Expansion, and we bought attack ships and . . . " she raised her hand, "and state-of-the-art warware. And we returned to Serimion and fought the Kha."

I said, "What happened?"

She turned her helmet toward me. "We lost."

Seconds, then minutes elapsed. We were alone with our separate thoughts as we stared into the void.

A while later I said, "And vitalism, Katerina? Your certainty . . . ?"

She turned to look at me. "I know it's real, Ed, because of what happened to me in orbit around my homeplanet." And she left it at that and hung her helmeted head.

I hesitated, then asked, "What happened, Katerina?"

She just shook her head, silently.

I squeezed her gloved hand, and thought it wise to leave her to her memories.

I returned to the flight-deck and was relieved to see that Karrie was not there.

Ella hung in her sling, her head flung back, the whites of her eyes showing.

She sensed my presence and came back from whichever cyber-realm she'd been inhabiting. "I was integrating with the ship's smartware core, Ed," she said matter-of-factly.

I smiled to myself, wondering at the process which allowed her to commune with my ship's logic matrix.

I said, "I've been talking to Katerina. She told me about what happened on Serimion." I told Ella what Katerina had said about the attack, her return to fight the Kha. Her defeat.

"Which makes me all the more curious as to why she wishes to return there, Ed."

I shook my head, and then found myself reaching out and taking Ella's hand. It was small, warm, and very human. I held it tight and said, "Ella, when I was young . . . my sister died. That's another story. I don't want to talk about it now."

She stared at me with her big brown eyes. "What do you want to talk about?"

I took a breath. "After what happened, I found myself drawn back to the place where Maria died. I was compelled. I couldn't explain why. It was the place where she'd last been alive; perhaps that was it. Perhaps I thought I might commune with whatever of her remained. Silly, I know. But anyway, I had to go back. And you know something? When I did, when I went back and stood on that spot, and thought of my sister and the silly accident that robbed her of her life, and when I cried . . . well, I felt a lot better for doing so." I squeezed Ella's hand. "Perhaps that's why Katerina's going back? Can you understand that, Ella?"

She returned my gaze with her lustrous eyes. "Yes, Ed," she said. "Yes, I understand perfectly."

One thousand Kha sentinels, grey and monolithic and as vast as ten city blocks, hung in space around the defeated planet of Serimion.

My ship's smartware core spoke in its soothing, feminine contralto. "Kha AIs have established contact, Ed. They wish to know the purpose of our visit."

"Tell them that we're here to pay our respects to the human dead," I said, "and we seek clearance to land on Serimion."

We eased to a halt beside one of the sheer grey monoliths, and waited.

Framed within the girdle of sentinels, the planet tilted ten degrees off its polar axis, blue and white and twice the size of Earth.

Ella said, "It's beautiful."

"I'm not looking forward to finding out what might be down there," I said. "If the Kha let us through, that is."

Karrie joined us on the flight-deck and eased herself into her sling.

I said, "So, our passenger proved the security risk you mentioned, Karrie?" I couldn't help the jibe.

She looked at me. "No, but there's something seriously wrong with the girl."

"What?" Ella asked.

"Have you noticed she doesn't eat? It's been three days since leaving Constance, and I've taken six trays of food to her birth. She hasn't touched a thing."

I shrugged. "So . . . the girl wasn't hungry. She's returning to the place where her family, her people, were massacred, after all."

Ella turned in her sling. "Ed," she said, almost reluctantly. "There is something else that doesn't quite ring true. Physically, Katerina appears to be twenty, twenty-five years old."

"Go on."

"I've been double-checking the records. The Kha attacked Serimion twenty-five years ago."

I stared down at the slowly rotating planet. I recalled Katerina's youthful, elfish face within her helmet.

Karrie said, "Seems to me like the girl's been lying to us, Ed."

I was about to ask Ella why Katerina might have lied when the smartcore said, "Clearance granted. The Kha have issued a two day pass. We must be out of Serimion airspace within forty-eight hours."

Minutes later Katerina joined us on the flight-deck. She stood between my sling and Ella's and stared through the viewscreen at her homeplanet.

She had cleared her faceplate, and her youthful face stared out, her eyes wide in wonder.

"I have the coordinates for the Corinthian," she said, and reeled off a series of numbers to Ella.

We eased past the sentinel. I was glad to leave the cold, inhuman monolith in our wake. Ten minutes later, Ella pointed. Through the viewscreen we made out the becalmed wreck of the Corinthian, nose down in relation to the planet, ragged holes puncturing its fuselage.

Karrie said, "And you survived that?"

"I wish I hadn't," Katerina said, softly.

I said, "Okay, Ella. Stow those coordinates and we'll tractor beam the Corinthian on the way out." I turned to Katerina. "Now, where do you want us to land?"

"No one has ever seen the Kha," Katerina told us. "They have had no contact with the Human Expansion, and do not allow visitors to their homeplanet. When they struck Serimion, they did so from altitude. Later, when we returned and engaged them in battle, we saw their ships but never the Kha themselves. The few Kha vessels we managed to destroy exploded in space, so no alien remains were ever discovered." She paused, then went on, "Some say the Kha resemble devils, others maintain they are insectoid. To me, it does not matter. The very sound of their name conjures absolute evil."

We were drifting slowly over the planet's vast southern continent. Ruined villages and townships punctuated the green continuity of the veldt. Roads and rivers threaded the landscape, but nothing moved down there. Absolute stillness greeted our gaze, and I could not help but think of the planet as a cemetery without gravestones.

We floated towards the planet's equator, where Katerina's family had farmed the land. Veldt turned to rainforest, a vast tangle of alien vines and great gnarled, crimson trees, and then the rainforest gave way to a range of purple mountains that ran parallel to a great rift valley. Between these geographic features stretched a plain of fertile land that was Katerina's birthplace.

Ella touched my arm. "Look. Down there."

Something squatted on the plain. I said, "Bring us down, slowly."

Ella eased the ship to within a hundred meters of the thing.

Katerina said in a tiny voice, "Could it be a Kha?"

We hung in the air, observing.

I could not tell whether it was mechanical or biological. Twenty meters long, perhaps ten high, it was armor plated with what looked like matte black chitin, domed and segmented and squatting on the ground as if devouring pray.

From what I guessed was its head-section, or what might have been its control center, a long proboscis—or drill—punctured the soil.

Whether a Kha, or one of their creations, its act was symbolic of the rape of the planet.

As we watched, it seemed to shiver with ecstasy, or maybe just mechanical vibration.

I glanced at Ella. "Sound?"

She passed her hand over her controls and seconds later a deep ululation filled the flight-deck. It reminded me of the chanting of a thousand monks, resonant and dolorous.

I asked Ella, "Do you know whether it's alive, or . . . ?"

She went rigid in her sling, her eyeballs rolled to show only their whites as she attempted to communicate with the thing.

She shook her head. "It's hard to tell. I sense a biological core, surrounded by extensive technological addenda."

I looked at Ella, saying nothing.

In a tiny voice, Katerina said, "We revered our planet, Ed. We loved the earth. This . . . this *thing* is robbing its vitality . . . "

I reached out to take her gloved hand, but she pulled away. "Get us away from here! I don't want to . . . " She turned from the viewscreen, holding her helmeted head in her hands.

Ella sped us from the thing, towards the continental rift valley.

One hour later we came down on a plain of lush grassland beside the escarpment.

A hundred meters before the ship was the outline of farm-buildings, and beyond them the geometric pattern of fields, their crops gone wild long ago.

Katerina said, "I would like a few minutes by myself, Ed. Then, would you come and join me? I have a lot I must explain."

I nodded. "Of course."

She moved from the flight-deck. Minutes later her tiny figure emerged from the shadow of the ship, moving past the ruins of the farmhouse towards the edge of the escarpment.

She stood with her arms on her hips and stared about her.

In silence, we watched.

After a minute she moved towards a lone tree that grew at an angle, leaning out over the rift valley. It was similar to those I had seen in the rainforest, crimson and contorted, with a vast, spreading leaf canopy.

She found a place in its gnarled root system and sat down, staring out across the abyss.

Like this, very still, she remained for perhaps fifteen minutes.

At length she turned and raised a hand, and I took this as a summons.

Ella and Karrie said nothing as I left the flight-deck and climbed down to the air-lock. I cycled myself through and stepped out onto the soil of Serimion. The first thing I noticed was the scent, a heady, spicy mix of soil and flower blooms. The grass, I saw, was embroidered with a spread of tiny yellow flowers, which gave off an almost overpowering perfume as I strode from the ship towards where Katerina sat.

At one point I paused and looked back. Ella and Karrie stood before the viewscreen, gazing down at me like figures in an aquarium.

I passed into the shade of the great leaning tree and picked my way through the knuckled roots until I came to the girl. I sat down beside her. "It's a beautiful world, Katerina."

She turned to me. Her youthful face showed behind her faceplate, and she smiled. "It was even more beautiful, Ed, before they attacked."

I looked away, and then saw, standing among the raised roots on the edge of the escarpment, six simple wooden crosses.

She saw the direction of my gaze and said, "We had a custom on Serimion, Ed. We buried our dead beside trees, and this was my parent's favorite place on the planet. At sunset they would come out here with a drink and just sit and admire the view."

The silence stretched. A gentle, warm wind picked up the scent of the flowers and swamped us.

She said, "After the attack, I drove back here from the southern coast, passing devastated towns and knowing what I would find . . . The farm was destroyed, looking much as it does now. I found no personal possessions, no mementoes . . . Perhaps that was a good thing. To have found objects that belonged to mother and father and my brothers, that would have been too much. Now, I would like something to remind me . . . " She turned and smiled at me. "Is that silly?"

I returned her smile. "Not at all, Katerina."

"I found what was left of my family . . . or perhaps I was kidding myself. I found scraps of clothing, and dust, and scooped it up and carried it over here and buried it beside the tree, then planted wooden crosses I made from what remained of the farmhouse. I even said prayers, and then vowed to get my revenge.

"I don't know whether it was hours or days before I was found by a rescue ferry and taken to the nearest human colony world." She waved. "Anyway, two years later I did come back, in this suit, in the Corinthian, and I did exact a futile, limited form of revenge. I destroyed two Kha craft and then, and then ... "

She gathered herself, then went on, "And then a Kha fighter struck, and disabled the Corinthian, and left me for dead. A rescue vessel picked me up, took me back to the colony world ... "

She gazed down at the forlorn row of crosses. From this angle, I could not see her face.

"I said I had a lot to explain, Ed."

"The attack happened twenty-five years ago," I said, "and yet your face is that of a woman of twenty. You never eat, never open your suit ... "

She turned her helmet and looked at me. Behind the faceplate I could see silver tears tracking down her cheeks. She raised a gloved hand and stared at it. "These suits were the latest Orion warware. They were made to help a fighter fight, augmented with an integrated AI to boost physical reaction time, mental acuity." She stopped, and her next words surprised me, "Do you know why I came here, Ed?"

I said, "To pay respects, to ... to lay the ghost?"

She laughed, briefly. "That's good. I like that. Yes, to lay the ghost." She stared at me. "I came to this grave site to bury myself."

I stared at her, and watched as she lifted her gloves to her helmet and touched a control at the neck. He helmet opened slowly, folding out in sections, blooming like a flower. At some point in the process the hologram showing her youthful face flickered off. And I stared, unable to believe what I was seeing.

A skull sat askew on the notched column of her vertebrae, grinning out at me.

It was all I could do not to back away in shock. I almost retched.

Her voice, her soft, feminine voice, continued, "These are fighting suits, Ed. And they go on fighting when the fighter within them is technically dead. Shrapnel punctured an elbow seal in the suit when my Corinthian was attacked, and I died of asphyxiation. I was cerebrally integrated with the suit's AI, and it uploaded my memories into its operating system ... and I would have gone on fighting, if the Corinthian had been capable."

"Oh, Christ, Katerina."

"For two days after the attack, when I was rescued and taken back to the colony world, I thought I'd managed somehow to survive. And then a medic broke it to me, and opened my suit, and ... "

Her gloved hand lifted, indicated the grinning skull.

"You cannot begin to imagine the shock, Ed, the terror."

I could only shake my head and bite my lips in an effort to stem my tears. I stared at the lop-sided skull, and it stared back at me, its orbits huge and shadowy. I wanted to get to my feet and run, but my legs felt weak and bile rose, acid, in my throat.

She said, "I told you that I believe in vitalism, in the soul, because of what had happened to me. I am less than human, now, a mere mechanical set of stored memories and emotions."

She reached up, took her skull in her gloved hands and lifted it from her spine. She lowered the skull to her lap, where it sat gazing blindly out across the abyss.

"The terrible, terrible thing is, Ed, that in my heart . . . or whatever passes for my heart now . . . I know that vitalism is a fact. Because now I am reduced." She touched the chest of her suit, and slowly its torso opened, two flanges hinging outwards to reveal a chaotic jackstraw assemblage of bones within.

She leaned forward, over the skull in her lap, and with both hands scooped a hollow in the fine earth before the closest cross. I watched, appalled yet fascinated, as she placed her skull in the grave, then reached into the cavity of her chest and one by one withdrew her bones.

She raised her right arm and her ulna and radius, then her smaller metacarpal bones, rattled into the suit's torso. She did the same with her left arm, and collected the bones and laid them, reverently, in the grave. Next she split a seam in her legs and withdrew the femur and tibia from her right leg, along with the smaller bones, and then the left, and I closed my eyes and wept.

When I looked again she was covering the bones with soil to create a small, compact mound.

She turned her suit to face me, and her disembodied voice said, "Humans, Ed, are far more than mechanistic machines. I know this because of what I am now. Although I have the memories of what happened, I do not have the ability to feel real emotion, to grieve."

I wanted to tell her that she could be upgraded, that AIs had developed so much over the past twenty-five years. I wanted to tell her that she could be *made* human.

"I had a lover, a young man who fought alongside me and survived. While I was in hospital, he came to see me. I had just been told what I had become, and I showed him . . . " She paused, then went on, "Ed, the look on his face, the horror, before he fled . . . " She turned her opened helmet to me. "But for all I could intellectually appreciate what he might be feeling, I could not find it within me to empathize. And I felt . . . *nothing*."

The silence stretched, and I could find not one word to comfort her.

The sun was setting behind the far horizon, laying down gorgeous laminates of tangerines and pinks. Far below us, shadows turned the abyss into a dark, inky pit.

At last she said, "I came here to bury myself, and I came here also to die."

And she reached into the cavity of her chest and pulled out two slim columns. She held them up before me. "The suit's energy system, Ed. Without them the suit will run down in hours."

"Katerina . . . "

"It's what I want. Peace at last. I can't feel grief. I can't feel sadness or pain. Or joy, or happiness, or love . . . All I have is the memories of these emotions. Now is the time I have dreamed of for so long. To die, here."

She took the silver columns, drew back her arm and flung them into the rift. I watched them sail through the air, end over end, catching the dying sunlight as they fell.

She hunched forward, hands upturned in her lap, her open helmet bowed as if in supplication.

She said, softly, "I can feel myself slowing down already, Ed, and it is wonderful."

"Katerina, I'll stay."

"No, please go. And say to Ella . . . tell her that I'm sorry, so sorry."

"Goodbye, Katerina."

She failed to respond, and I reached out and took her gloved hand for one last time, then stood and made my way through the root system of the great tree towards the ship. I stopped, once, and looked back, but the woman who had been Katerina Reverte was now no more than an empty Orion warware suit, seated on the edge of an abyss.

I heard the hatch of the ship hiss open, and Karrie stepped out and faced me. Her eyes were hard, questioning, and I knew I could not bring myself to describe what had happened, yet.

"Ed?"

I hurried past her, and stopped before the hatch. Ella had appeared, and was watching me. Her expression was unreadable. She said, "I listened, Ed. I heard what Katerina told you." She reached out her arms towards me. "And I just want to say that I understand your pain."

At the sight of her standing there, so slight and vital and *human,* something broke within me

I stepped forward, and took her in my arms, and wept.

The Children of Main Street

A.C. WISE

The first thing the children of the colony learned after the ship landed was how to change genders.

They'd been born in the long dark between the stars; not one had ever set foot on Earth, on good, solid ground. They'd never known a fixed sky, just the star-shot dark tumbling past the ship's portholes as they hurtled towards a new world.

They'd grown like weeds in the cracks of the ship, playing quiet games. Laughing and running were forbidden, making them always too loud, and too much in the way.

When the ship finally touched down, when the doors hissed open, they ran. They ran under an alien sky, under twin moons, and breathed the dome-filtered air while their parents hid behind walls and fretted about creating Earth-like homes. A new world turned under their feet, and though they didn't understand with their conscious minds, the children sensed in their bones that things were different here. The old rules did not apply. So they changed.

The colony doctors ran tests. They drew blood, hooked the children up to electrodes, and flashed them with x-rays—all to no avail. As a last resort, the grown-ups broke down and finally *asked* the children. The children simply looked at each other and smiled, some with secrets tucked in their cheeks, but most with pity in their eyes.

For better or for worse, the adults realized, this was the way of the world now—twin moons, an oddly colored sun, life under a giant dome, and children who flickered and changed as quick as passing storms. Some days the cul-de-sac at the end of Main Street would be filled with nothing but little boys, some nothing but little girls, and others the genders would be split evenly with no rhyme or reason.

Tiffany Webster stood in the kitchen doorway, gathering her nerve. Her son . . . no, her *daughter* now, sat at the kitchen table wearing a pink dress, head bent and face hidden by a curtain of silky brown hair. Pink shoes that matched the pink dress swung under the table, the little girl's heels thumping the chair railing in an irregular rhythm.

The dress and shoes had been a present from Tiffany's husband George, no doubt. George had had a much easier time adjusting. Despite the fact he'd always wanted a son, he seemed delighted to occasionally have a daughter now, too. He called it the best of both worlds.

Tiffany edged closer, peering over her daughter's shoulder. Dust-laden sunlight, just a shade different from the sun back home, slanted through the window and illuminated the scatter of construction paper, crayons, glitter and glue spread across the table. Michael . . . *Michaela* . . . was making a Mother's Day card. A sob lodged in Tiffany's throat.

I'm a horrible mother.

The thought was stark, cutting-sharp, but true. She'd been avoiding her son, now her daughter, for weeks. She couldn't stand the sight of the quick-silver changeling who'd taken the place of her precious, little boy. She couldn't be around her.

Tiffany didn't trust herself not to grab the little girl by the shoulders, shake her until her head snapped back and forth on her slender neck, and demand to know where Michael had gone. The violence of the thought shocked her, it made her hands shake, but it wouldn't go away.

Ever since Tiffany could remember, she'd wanted a child. She and George had talked about it on their honeymoon; he'd wanted it as much as she had. They'd spent nights lying in bed together, his stomach fitted against the curve of her spine, coming up with baby names.

It had been so hard, waiting as they went through the colony application program. They wanted that, too—a fresh new world, a place of their own. They'd been patient. Then, almost the moment they'd woken from cryo-sleep, ten years from planet-fall, they'd started trying for a baby.

Tiffany had gotten pregnant almost right away. When Michael was born, she'd been so happy. She'd been so proud, watching her son grow. Then she ship landed, and everything changed. A stranger—a girl with long, brown hair looked at her with Michael's bright blue eyes and called her *mommy.*

Tiffany plastered a smile across her face, cheeks pulling so tight they hurt, and crossed the room. She touched her daughter's silky hair, proud she could do so without flinching.

"Michaela, honey, what do you want for breakfast?"

"I'm Michael today, Mommy." The little boy in pink turned, crayon poised mid-scribble. He had Michael's face, Michael's blue eyes and rounded cheeks, but he had Michaela's long hair and wore Michaela's clothes.

"Oh." Tiffany's hand flew to her mouth, covering an absence of words. Her eyes ached, hot, stinging, and dry.

Tiffany stepped back, and continued backing away, shaking her head. She'd tried, she really had, but she couldn't handle this stranger with her son's eyes, her son's face.

Michael continued to watch her. Tiffany couldn't tear her gaze away from her son, from the crayon in his hand, and the litter of paper hearts around him.

Instead of hurt and confusion, Tiffany saw calm acceptance, an alien stillness she couldn't fathom. It was as though he'd known this moment would come.

Tiffany bumped into the door, fumbling for the knob without turning around. The motion jarred loose tears, blurring Michael and Michaela into one. She slammed the door, and put both hands over her mouth again.

Standing on the porch, Tiffany listened for footsteps. She imagined Michael's chubby hand pressed against the other side of the door, still smelling of wax from gripping the crayon, fragments of color caught under his nails. She jerked away, took a deep breath, and turned around. Squaring her shoulders, Tiffany walked down Main Street.

Children ran shrieking around the cul-de-sac, laughing. Little Bobby Mercer had blonde braids, and little Becky Simmons had torn jeans and a bloody nose from a fight with another boy. Tiffany had known these children since they'd been born, and now they were strangers to her, all of them.

Tiffany left the cul-de-sac behind. Perfect houses lined the street, set on neat squares of lawn, planted with flowers and trees. It looked like home, but it was a lie. The dome arched between her and the sky, curving around their settlement like a parent's protective arms. Beyond the dome lay gray dust; beyond the thin veil of sunlight lay darkness and cold stars.

She knew the same vastness, the same vacuum, surrounded earth, but she could *feel* it here. She was a long way from home, crushingly small, terrifyingly alone. It *hurt*. The distance wound out from her heart, a thread of physical pain, but she couldn't follow it back home, not ever again.

They'd left earth during Kennedy's second term, under the threatening shadow of war, but that was a lifetime ago—several lifetimes. Every one she knew back home was long dead. Her sister's children, maybe even their children's children, were bones and dust. For all she knew, there was no earth anymore. The sun might be an ember by now, its light winked out of the sky, taking the blue-bright ball of the earth with it. She and the other colonists might be the last humans in existence. And even they were barely human anymore.

Pressure built, pushing against her temples, filling the space around her lungs. Tiffany's pulse kept time with her steps, which carried her to one of the gates where the four-wheel exploration vehicles, encased in protective plastic bubbles, passed through the dome and out onto the alien terrain.

Tiffany hid, watching the guards check each vehicle through. Her pulse slowed; the pressure eased. She memorized the timing, the way the inner gate locked, unable to open until the outer door completed its cycle. When the guard waved the next car through, Tiffany darted in behind it.

The gate hissed shut, muffling the guards' shouts, dampening the sound of fists pounding on the door. The opposite end of the gateway opened onto the killing cold and the poison air. The four-wheeler drove out onto the alien terrain, and Tiffany Webster followed calmly behind it.

• • •

Sarah Beth Dolan stood at the sink, staring through the window at her son Timmy—who was sometimes her daughter Tamara—playing in the yard. Bubbles melted, the breakfast dishes forgotten under them, while the water cooled. Sarah Beth held a dripping plate in one hand, a dishtowel limp in the other.

Timmy kicked a soccer ball against the fence, diving to save against an imagined goal as the ball bounced back. Grass stains smudged his bare knees. His hair, a brown mop, hid his eyes. Sarah Beth couldn't remember what color those eyes were.

She remembered the doctor placing a squalling baby in her arms. Its face had been red and mashed, wisps of dark hair plastered against its still-soft skull. Its eyes were screwed up tight against the ship's lights, its fists clenched, flailing at the unfairness of being born. It screamed.

Sarah Beth remembered thinking the baby didn't look like her or her husband Mark; it didn't really look like anything at all. She couldn't even tell if it was a boy or a girl, not until the doctor told her. Now, she couldn't remember what the doctor had said.

She knew the gap in her memory should frighten her, but Sarah Beth felt strangely calm. A sense of peace wrapped her like a warm blanket on a cold day. Maybe it was something in the light, or something in the air, slipping in despite the dome. Sarah Beth couldn't give it a name, but things were *different* here.

All her life, she'd dreamed of going up among the stars. She'd followed the saga of the first colonists, the ones who'd built this place, and longed to be one of them. She'd watched, rapt, full of terror and awe as reports of the colonists' disappearance began to filter in. But even that gave her hope. There were those who believed that the colonists hadn't disappeared, they'd simply *changed*.

When she'd been accepted into the colony program, Sarah Beth had been ecstatic. Deep down, she'd wanted to do more than see alien places; she'd wanted to *be* alien.

She'd never told anyone, not even Mark. But ever since she was little, Sarah Beth had known there was a seed buried deep in her chest, waiting to bloom. It filled her with a wanting she couldn't name, a restlessness that manifested as a feeling of drowning on dry land. There had to be something more.

She wanted to be like the superheroes in comic books—the books her father had always said weren't for girls; books she'd had to sneak into her brother's room to read when her parents weren't looking. An alien with a destiny, who didn't belong on earth, but who was special somehow—Sarah Beth wanted to be more than just flesh and blood and bone.

Sarah Beth set the dripping plate on the counter and walked outside. She stood on the deck, and touched her cheeks; they felt hot and flushed against her palm. She took a deep breath, in and out.

They'd come so far across the stars, to a brand new land full of promise . . . and they'd tried to replicate the world they'd left behind. The perfect houses and gardens replicating Earth-life cloyed; they were ghastly. Looking at them day in and day out broke Sarah Beth's heart. This wasn't the life she'd dreamed. She couldn't go on like her husband, pretending to care about the things that had been important back home. Accounting, tax laws, chat around the water cooler—those things meant nothing here.

"Timmy?"

The boy looked up. He stopped the soccer ball expertly with one foot. Sarah Beth crouched, touching Timmy's arm to assure herself of his solidity, as if he might shift before her eyes. With her other hand, she brushed the mop of hair from his eyes. They were blue-gray.

"Can you teach me to how to change?"

Mark Dolan came home to find a strange man sitting on his couch. The man jumped up as Mark entered, released like a coiled spring.

"Who . . . ?" Mark faltered.

The ship that carried them across the stars left no room for strangers. Mark knew every person under the dome, but this man, he'd never seen before.

"Where's Sarah?"

"Mark, it's me." Sarah stepped forward.

Mark stared. The man's cheeks appeared fresh-shaved, but a hint of stubble, like a shadow underneath the skin, persisted. He wore one of Mark's suits, the gray jacket too large on his short, compact frame—the sleeves hanging past his wrists, the pant cuffs pooling over the polished wingtip shoes Mark wore to meetings.

"Mark?" The man who claimed to be Sarah moved closer, nervously clasping his hands in front of him. Mark watched the man's Adam's apple bob.

"Mark, it's me." The man touched Mark's chest, thick, square fingers resting against Mark's lapel. The stranger's eyes begged for understanding; they were Sarah Beth's eyes. "It's okay, Mark."

"But you're my wife!" Mark stepped out from under the man's touch, staring. His left arm tingled.

"I'm still your wife." The stranger's voice was deep and quiet.

"But you can't . . . I can't . . . " Mark's ears rang; his mind reeled. The words came all at once. "How could you do this? How *did* you do this? With the children it was bad enough, but . . . my God! Didn't you hear about Tiffany Webster? What were you thinking? We've been married for sixteen years!"

Sixteen years. The words lodged in Mark's chest. It would be more if he counted the years they'd been asleep, side by side in their cryogenic pods.

He remembered waking up with Sarah Beth beside him. They'd been so shy; it was almost the way it had been when they were first dating, even though they'd been married for six years. They'd spent weeks getting to know each other again, talking about the strange dreams they'd had as they tumbled through the stars.

They'd walked the ship's corridors holding hands, the way they'd held hands as high school sweethearts. In those weeks, she'd been a stranger to him, but she'd still been Sarah Beth, his wife, the woman he loved. And now . . .

"I'm sorry, Mark." The man's eyes held genuine regret. "I still love you. I understand if you can't love me, and . . . and I think that's okay." The man bit his lip.

"What the hell are you talking about?"

The man touched the back of the couch, fingers flexing against the fabric, a nervous gesture that reminded Mark so much of Sarah Beth that he wanted to scream. He needed his wife back. He needed her arms around him, her voice telling him everything would be okay.

"How can I explain? Things are just . . . *different* here." The man met Mark's eyes, pleading once more for understanding. He looked torn, but Mark could read his expression, all too familiar, and knew which way the man who claimed to be his wife was leaning.

"No." Mark heard the word, knew he spoke it, but it meant nothing.

The totality of the situation crashed down on him. *Nothing* had meaning anymore. The house squeezed claustrophobically tight around him. His chest echoed the house, crushing his heart and lungs. The very worst part was, deep down he knew the man . . . he knew *Sarah* . . . was right.

Everything was different here—the patterns of stars, the twin moons, the strange-colored sun. The rules had changed. He never should have come. They never should have come—not just their family, but people, human beings.

Their neighbor Tiffany had walked right out of the dome and died in the cold dark under the alien stars. That was what awaited them out here; that was the choice—death or a world gone mad.

Mark opened his mouth. The back door flew open, interrupting him, and Timmy came thundering into the room.

"Hey, Mom, hey, Dad." Timmy addressed his parents in turn. "Can I go to Becky-Brad's house tonight? There's going to be a sleepover."

"Of course," Sarah Beth answered at the same time as Mark said, "No."

Mark put his hand to his head. The room spun.

"Dad?"

Mark lowered his hand. His son looked at him, puzzled. Mark looked back and forth between the strange man and the strange child.

He pinched the bridge of his nose. He felt as though he hadn't slept in years. He sighed. "Yes, of course, you can go."

"Thanks, Dad!" Timmy darted in, kissed his father on the cheek, kissed his mother, and ran up the stairs. Mark watched his son, bewildered.

In the space between breakfast and now, Mark had somehow lost both his wife and his son. They were running ahead, towards an unknown future, going somewhere he wasn't even sure he wanted to follow.

• • •

Three weeks later Mark said, "I'm sleeping with Anna Mancuso."

He was amazed at the steadiness of his voice. Sarah Beth turned from the stove.

His wife looked like her old self again. Her changes were as liquid-smooth and quick as their son's now, but Mark could barely look at her. Regardless of her appearance, she was a stranger. He'd tried to touch her, once, but the brief attempt left him physically sick. He'd come back into the bedroom long enough to gather a pillow and an extra blanket before retreating to the couch. They'd slept on separate floors of the house ever since.

"Her husband ran off with another woman, though he's calling himself Charlene now. They're living together like . . . " Mark trailed off, shook his head. "It doesn't matter."

Sarah Beth, who sometimes called herself John now, remained expressionless. Her eyes, which had been the only constant through her changes, had turned strange—a blue-grey reflecting the alien sky arched above the dome. For the sheer contrast, they made Mark think of the aching blue summer days he'd experienced in Iowa as a young boy.

Back then they'd lived in a big, rambling farmhouse at the end of a road bordered by fields of wheat. Though the floorboards sagged, and the roof leaked during heavy rains, it felt like home. They'd moved so often during his childhood. Each time hurt, but somehow leaving the farmhouse felt like having his roots ripped out of the soil. He wanted something solid, some place to call home, and he'd followed Sarah Beth to the stars, thinking *she* was his home. She was supposed to be the one constant that would never change, but now . . .

Sarah Beth set the wooden spoon back into the pot of sauce, and lowered the burner. Mark had expected hysterics; he'd expected her to cry, or even hit him. Would she react like a man, or a woman? Would she try to solve their differences with words, or a knock-down, drag-out fight? He didn't know. He didn't know anything about Sarah Beth anymore.

But she did nothing. Her perfect calm was unsettling; it dropped his heart into his gut. Sarah Beth wiped her hands on a dishtowel and stood behind one of the kitchen chairs, bracing her hands its back. She regarded him steadily.

"I understand."

What? What do you understand? Mark wanted to scream, but his tongue froze. How could she be so calm? She'd told him on the day she changed that she still loved him. She'd told him again—at least half a dozen times since—but the words meant nothing. They were like the word *wife*, like *marriage*, like *boy* and *girl*. Everything on this damned planet was different; nothing made sense anymore.

"I should go." Mark turned. Sarah Beth, who was sometimes John, watched him. Her alien eyes exerted physical pressure on the tension strung between his shoulder blades. At any moment, he would snap.

"Call me," Sarah Beth said. "If you ever want to come home, I mean. Tamara will miss you, but I know she'll understand."

Mark didn't answer. He walked out the door and down the street to Anna Mancuso's house. His hand shook as he rang her bell.

Anna opened the door, her eyes red as though she'd been crying. Coats hung neatly from a row of hooks beside the door, shoes lined up beneath them. Mark noticed that Anna's husband had left his shoes beside Anna's, as though he might come back at any moment, or as though items that mundane simply didn't matter anymore.

Looking at Anna, Mark knew without a doubt that he didn't love her. She was steady, she didn't change; she was something to hold onto. He thought about Sarah Beth, about the way she'd been when they'd boarded the ship together. He kept the image in his mind as he took Anna's face between his hands and kissed her—long and deep and searching.

Anna kissed him back, clinging as though Mark was the last thing keeping her from drowning. He wondered if she had any illusions about love, or whether she understood what they had as well as he did. He realized he didn't care. He backed her towards the kitchen, towards the table, which still smelled of furniture wax. The whole kitchen smelled clean, as though Anna had spent hours scrubbing.

Mark shoved one of the chairs out of the way with his foot, bending Anna back over the table. He fumbled with his belt, getting his pants down around his ankles and leaving them there. Anna responded, as though by rote, going through the motions of desire. Her gaze fixed on some point beyond his left shoulder as she unbuttoned her blouse.

By the time they were done, twin moons shone soft light through the kitchen window. They lit Anna as she turned her face away, showing the threads of gray just starting to lighten her hair. Given enough time, everything changed.

Mark gathered his pants, belting them perfunctorily. He didn't look at Anna. He looked at the strange sky, wondering if he'd ever be happy again.

It wasn't fair, the one who had been Sarah Beth-John considered as s/he looked down the hill at the human settlement below. The dome gleamed with reflected starlight, a soap bubble, thin and frail, struggling to hold back the night. S/he hadn't meant to hurt anyone. Why did change have to be this way? Why did the most important things in the universe have to be full of pain? Why did the new have to rip the old apart before taking its place?

S/he sighed. The child who had been Willy-Jane slipped long, thin fingers into Sarah Beth-John's hand, and s/he offered it a smile. Timmy-Tamara took hir other hand. Its blue-gray eyes caught starlight; they seemed wide enough to hold the entire sky. The faint ache in hir heart faded as Sarah Beth-John turned and guided the children away from the view of the settlement below.

S/he and the others—the ones who had been Catherine-Steve, Laura-Matt, Karen-Dave, Charlene-Charles—they'd tell the children stories of Earth-that-was with fondness in the years to come. Even if the humans didn't believe it, even if they thought their former friends, lovers, and children mad, those that had changed still honored their past. It was a part of them, but it was a fragment of a larger whole. The universe was so much larger out here.

Maybe someday the humans would understand. Maybe they'd come up into the hills, following in the footsteps of those who had come before them. Maybe they'd wake up one morning, and they wouldn't be afraid anymore.

Their lungs would be new, their limbs long, their eyes blue-gray and wide enough to hold the stars. They'd walk out of the dome, and breathe the alien air; they'd step barefoot over the soft sands and croon-sing to their brother-sisters, asking to come home. They would be welcomed, as Sarah Beth-John and the others had been by those who had gone before them.

On that day, Sarah Beth-John would rejoice. Until then, she'd hold them in hir heart. S/he'd love them, just as s/he loved hir brother-sisters here above the human's dome. It didn't matter if it took forever, or if the change never happened. S/he could be patient. S/he could wait until the end of the world.

Diving After the Moon
RACHEL SWIRSKY

When Norbu was a child, his mother Jamyang told him an old Tibetan story about an industrious but foolish troop of monkeys that lived in a forest near a well. One dusty night, a monkey elder woke thirsty. He crept away from his sleeping mate and went to the well for a drink. Inside, he saw a reflection of the moon.

"The moon has fallen into our well!" he hollered.

His ruckus woke the other monkeys. They all agreed that it would be a terrible thing to live in a moonless world. They joined hands and formed a chain to climb into the well and rescue the moon.

As the monkeys dove in, the moon's reflection broke, leaving blank dark waters. The shamed monkeys climbed out again: shivering, wet, and empty-handed. The real moon chuckled above them, safe in the sky.

Norbu liked that story better than the others Jamyang told. He liked other stories about the moon even better: histories and text books and biographies of astronauts from the dead American empire. Even as a young child, Norbu was impatient with Jamyang's fantastic tales of weather mages and magic scarves. Jamyang tried to get him to see the beauty of old stories for their own sake, but Norbu never listened. To him, the moon was the future.

Before Norbu left to become a taikonaut, Jamyang told him, "I am going to borrow a radio so I can listen every second you are on the moon."

Norbu smiled and said, "You don't have to do that, Ma," but Jamyang thought he looked pleased as he grabbed his hat and went out the door.

The day before the launch, Jamyang hiked across the dry terrain of the plateau to her nearest neighbor's. The woman's son gave her a near-defunct radio that he'd found in a landfill and repaired. The boy was training himself to be a mechanic and he always asked after Norbu, who had promised to write him a letter when he applied to university. Usually, Jamyang enjoyed talking about her son, but that day she was impatient to get home.

Over and over, the boy repeated his instructions for how to use the machine. "Do you know what to do? Do you know what to press?"

Jamyang fended off his concerns, protesting, "I know, I know, I used to have one," but the boy continued fretting and repeating. He'd never gotten over the impression most people had of Jamyang, that just because she preferred past ways to future, she must never have seen any technology, even as a young girl.

Jamyang returned home with the radio at dusk, the sun pouring out red and orange light across the horizon. She listened while shelling peas. The lady reporter's voice was fluid and rhythmic; Jamyang found it easy to listen to her, even as she repeated the same few facts to fill the hour. "Thanks to backing from the Egyptian government, Qinghai's first expedition into space lands on the moon today, led by Melbourne-trained astronomer Karma Sangemo . . . the expedition hopes to find asteroid debris from the near miss in 2029 . . . "

Jamyang thrilled every time she heard her son's name: "Geologist Sopa Norbu says it's time for Qinghai to make a contribution to the world which has given it so much. He says the people of Qinghai must work tirelessly toward the future . . . "

On the third evening, Jamyang sat by the window with her embroidery. She missed a stitch as the reporter's voice broke out of its mannered tones, registering panic. "We're receiving an urgent report from our Beijing office. Hostilities have broken out between Egypt and Australia. The Australian government is threatening to detonate a spore-cluster bomb in Cairo . . . The Egyptians have issued a response. They say they won't allow the bomb to kill millions of innocent citizens . . . "

Murmuring suggested a conversation off the microphones. Jamyang leaned closer to the radio.

"The Egyptians are threatening to block worldwide transmissions to prevent the detonation signal from going through. They've given the Australians ten minutes to respond. If the Australians don't stand down, global communications could be blocked for weeks. Wait, I'm being told we may not be able to keep transmitting—"

The reporter's voice decayed into static. Jamyang smacked the radio.

"No!" she said. "You can't cut out! Come back."

She smacked it again.

"Come back on the air. This is not funny! I tell you, come back."

Waves of white sound poured out of the old speakers, loud and relentless as a winter sandstorm.

Norbu walked from the moon's surface into the pressurized cockpit which rumbled with the sound of static like a distant storm. The expedition's leader, Sangemo, shouted into the microphone of the ship's ancient transponder. After hours of trying to contact someone, her voice had become as hoarse and rough as the static.

Triangular windows on either side of the main control panel looked down on the cratered surface. Through them, he could see the expedition's other members collecting samples from the meteor impact site. Norbu stretched with relief as he removed his spacesuit.

"Any luck?" asked Norbu.

Sangemo started as she turned to face him, as if she hadn't noticed him before. "I'm trying Cairo and Xining. Maybe reception will come back in one before the other."

Norbu's eyes flickered toward the fuel gauge. "How long do we have . . . "

"Before our oxygen runs out? Another day. Maybe less."

"My mother said she was going to listen to radio coverage of our trip. She must be very worried." Norbu rubbed the back of his neck, trying to ease his knotted muscles. "If we're going to fly back blind, I'll need to start calculating for re-entry right away. It'll be chancy, but it's possible I can get it right."

Norbu expected Sangemo to chime in with her usual pragmatic analysis of statistics and time lines, but instead the woman opened her mouth slowly and hesitantly as if she didn't want to let out the words forming in her throat. She closed her mouth again, and looked away into the shadows. Norbu's tension tightened further in his chest.

"What is it?" he asked.

She looked down. "Do you remember your briefing on the legacy fail-safe?"

"The programming safeties the Americans put in to prevent sabotage?" asked Norbu. "Weren't those taken out when they sold us the ship?"

Sangemo sighed. "They were supposed to be."

She flipped open the lid that protected the delicate equipment that sensed the ship's positioning in relation to earth. The instruments had frozen at impossible readings and showed no signs of change. She wouldn't meet Norbu's gaze.

"So what are you saying?" he demanded. "We're stuck here?"

"The engines won't reinitialize unless the ship has confirmation of radio contact," said Sangemo. "Even if we could calculate re-entry . . . the ship won't move."

Norbu felt dizzy. He gripped one of the handles embedded into the side of the ship. "We're going to die here? We can't even try to fly back?"

"Unless radio contact comes back. Yes."

Norbu surprised himself with the force of his anger. He punched the wall, his fist aching from contact with the metal. His head hurt, and he wanted to shout at Sangemo, take her by the shoulders and tell her that she was wrong, she was lying. The rational part of his mind that ticked beneath his spinning anger reminded him that this wasn't Sangemo's fault. It was the American's. It was the Egyptian's. It was the Australian's. But they weren't here.

Norbu stalked over to the windows and looked down at the surface. Norbu wondered if they'd feel as blindsided by this news as he did. They were always calling Norbu an innocent, an optimist. Probably Sangemo would say she'd always suspected the Americans couldn't be trusted to fulfill their part of the contract. That was Norbu's problem. He had too much faith.

Everyone in the expedition had wanted so badly to reach the moon. No one wanted its cold, dead surface as a burial ground.

"I should tell the others," said Sangemo, softly.

Norbu didn't turn toward her. "I'll stay on the microphone," he said.

"Thanks." He heard the click and shuffle of Sangemo putting on her spacesuit. "Well," she added even more quietly, "It'll give us a chance to finish the chemical testing you wanted to do on the lava samples."

Norbu realized she wanted him to smile to show he understood it wasn't her fault, to take some of the burden off of her shoulders. He didn't have the energy to comfort her. He remained silent as Sangemo's helmet clicked into place and her footfalls fell hollow on the metal steps leading downward.

Norbu turned to the main control panel. The static roared and rattled, vibrating through his bones. He stared down at his crewmates through the triangular windows; they still pursued their various tasks, just now turning their heads toward Sangemo as she approached them. He imagined them stuck in their places like flies in amber, forever frozen. He shouted into the microphone's deaf ear, and suddenly in his mind, it wasn't the headquarters in Xining he was talking to.

"Mother! Mother, is that you? Can you hear me? Listen to me! Stay out of the storm! Don't try to come for me. Are you listening? I'm stuck here. I don't want you to be stuck here, too. Don't try to come for me, mother! You have to move on."

Norbu could hardly make out his voice in the onslaught of sound. Static swallowed him in a tumble of sand and dust.

Jamyang loved two things: her son and stories. Which was why she decided to catch a troop of monkeys to help rescue Norbu from the moon.

Five days and nights, Jamyang cooked. She labored over the fire without sleeping. Sweat dripped from her brow, salting the broth. Her deep sobs woke the stinging flavors of the spices. Her burned fingertips rolled a dazzling hint of flame into the dough.

When the vast buffet was complete, Jamyang tottered away from the stove on weary legs and laid the feast on the threshold. The scents of *thenthuk* noodle soup, *momo* dumplings, and butter tea traveled swiftly through the cold, clean air of the plateau.

The sun glared down. A small breeze ruffled a whirl of dust before dying down. The plateau remained still.

Jamyang drooped. Her tired eyes stung as if they were full of sand. An inquisitive bird swooped down on black wings to investigate the meal. Jamyang shooed him away.

Sudden, bright chittering drew her attention to the horizon. A band of gold-furred monkeys approached across the wide terrain. They held each other's paws one after the other in a chain. Their noses tilted upward, sniffing the air. Jamyang's exhaustion vanished.

She clapped her hands and gathered a handful of dumplings. "Come eat!" she called, holding them out. "Come, quickly! I've made it all for you!"

The monkeys snatched the food out of Jamyang's hands, eating with feral quickness as if afraid such good fortune would melt if they ate too slowly. Jamyang beamed down at them, offering new tidbits when their paws emptied. She was as attentive and elegant as the palace servants from the old stories.

When there was no more food, the monkeys lolled about. Partners idly groomed each other's sleek fur. Others lay belly up, enjoying the faint warmth of the distant winter sun. Jamyang passed through the troop, patting the monkeys' flossy white beards. She counted them: *chig, nyi, sum.* Four hundred and seventy monkeys had gathered on her land.

"My friends, thank you for coming," said Jamyang. "I need your help."

The monkeys' collective, satiated gaze settled on Jamyang as if to ask: What can we do?

Jamyang knelt. She drew a shawl over her shoulders. Cheap North American fabric was little good against the chill.

"I have a son, Norbu," she said. "He is a taikonaut, a person who goes into space. People here in Qinghai have wanted to go into space for a long time. They want to show the world that Qinghai is worth something as an independent state, that our worth didn't die when the American Empire and the old Republic of China fought themselves to pieces.

"Egypt loaned us money to buy an old American era ship. It arrived by train in the capitol at Xining. Twenty thousand people gathered to see it. It was such an honor for my son to be part of something so big!

"Egypt and Australia started arguing again, over whatever the rich fight about. Qinghai wasn't involved. But when have superpowers worried about who they hurt? Their fight stranded my son on the moon.

"Finally, after two weeks, Egypt reached a truce with Australia and cut off their jamming signal. I thought, at last, we can save my son! But then the prime minister came on the radio. He said we cannot afford to send a rescue ship. He said we should honor my son's crew for their sacrifice. He said they have asphyxiated on the moon. Huh! I know they are not dead. The prime minister only wants to save money. He thinks about gold more than people.

"I went to the monastery to ask them for help. The monks told me not to worry. They said that when Norbu died, he would be reincarnated on earth and that was all the homecoming he needed. What comfort is that for a grieving mother?

"I took the train to the television station in Xining, thinking they could help me talk sense into the prime minister. They sent out a young woman half my age wearing a short skirt. She took my hands and said, 'We're so glad you came. We're ten minutes short for the evening news.' They filmed me for half an hour and sent me home with a handful of *piastres.*

"No one cared about my son.

"I thought I would die of grief. I sat in the dark, doing nothing. I looked at the radio and remembered the static that killed my son, so angry and loud. I looked out the window and saw the moon. And then I realized how silly I'd been! No one wants to hear the stories anymore. Even as a child, Norbu never wanted to hear them. But I remembered you."

A satisfied smile stretched across Jamyang's lips.

"We're going to build another chain to the moon. But this time, it will be the real moon! Will you help me?"

A large female with a puff of auburn fur over her eyes approached Jamyang, taking her hand. The monkeys chattered. The female led Jamyang into the crowd. The other monkeys gathered around to groom her, their short black fingers tugging at Jamyang's clothes, traversing her skin, winding through her hair.

Jamyang let them pull her into their center. She raised her hands toward the moon. "I knew you would help. Thank you. Together, we'll get my son back, won't we?"

Jamyang and the monkeys practiced from dawn until dusk, forming ever-longer chains into the sky. They went out every morning, even in the bitterest winter winds. Once, a ferocious gust picked up the tiniest monkey and blew him halfway across the plateau. His mother had to run all night to fetch him back.

After sunset, Jamyang brought the monkeys into her house for large meals and warming butter tea. After they ate, the monkeys groomed Jamyang. In exchange, she told them old Tibetan stories about the Weathermaker and the wise scholar Padmasambhava's magic scarves. The monkeys fell asleep to the sound of Jamyang's soothing voice. She joined them on the floor, huddled body to fur.

One bitterly cold morning, Jamyang woke with a sense of purpose. "We should do it today," she said. She urged the monkeys outside into the frigid air.

The largest monkey planted himself solidly in the field. His mate, the second-largest, climbed onto his shoulders. She held out her arms to one of her sons, the third-largest monkey. So it went, smaller and smaller monkeys scrambling up their elders.

When the chain had grown so tall that the top monkey could touch the belly of a passing airplane, a roaring sounded in the distance. Jamyang turned. A sandstorm whirled toward them, dust and sand rumbling across the horizon in great dun-colored clouds.

"Hurry! Hurry!" Jamyang told the monkeys. The next pair rushed past her, holding their paws over their eyes to keep out the sand. Luckily, they had practiced so often that even blind they knew what to do.

Jamyang spat out a mouthful of sand. Grains caught in her eyes. She could no longer see the monkeys, only hear their chatter. The tiniest monkey clung to her breast until it was his turn. He jumped to the ground, tugging on Jamyang's hand to pull her behind him. She heard his toes brush through the elders' fur as he climbed up and up and up.

Now it was Jamyang's turn. She planted her foot on the eldest monkey's shoulders and began to climb. The monkeys shifted under her, groaning as they accepted her weight. Currents of sand drove against her back, scouring her skin. Gusts roared in her ears like static.

On the shoulders of a strong young male, she paused to wrap her shawl over her mouth so she could breathe. Sand worked its way in anyway, coarse underneath her tongue.

The climb seemed to last forever. At first, she kept track of how many monkeys she'd passed. Soon she lost count. Her hands and feet became numb, assaulted by millions of hard, minuscule grains. She could no longer hear the monkeys, only the storm's relentless white crash.

At last, Jamyang mounted a pair of teeny tiny shoulders. No more paws reached for her. The sandstorm retreated to a distant rumble. Jamyang opened her eyes, scraping sand out of her lashes. The sky around her was absolute matte black, darker than ink on midnight silk. Above hung the moon, great and white and pitted with craters.

Jamyang looked down. The chain of monkeys trailed away at a steep angle, appearing to grow smaller and smaller like railroad tracks moving to the horizon. The line disappeared into the swirling sand.

Jamyang smiled into the face of the tiniest monkey. "We made it!" she said. The tiny monkey chattered back happily. She ruffled its fur.

Stretching out her arms as if she was going to pick up a huge barrel, Jamyang hugged the moon's surface. Her legs swung above her head like she was doing a handstand. The world went topsy-turvy. She flipped onto her feet. She felt a blush as the blood pooled in her head, then stiffness in her ankles as if it were all rushing into her legs. Suddenly, she was looking up at the monkeys instead of down at them.

"Thank you so much!" she said, waving.

The tiniest monkey lowered his little black paw to wave back.

"Wait for me!" Jamyang said. "I will return with my son."

The monkey regarded Jamyang with sober, comprehending eyes. Above him, the chain swayed like a tall stem of grass in the wind.

Jamyang turned her attention to the vast vista of the moon. She leapt between craters. "Norbu!" she shouted. "I've come for you! Where are you?"

Jamyang passed scraps of ancient American technology, marked with faint symbols of red, white, and blue. Beyond them, stood an old but intact South African war machine, faceted lenses gazing down at an ancient enemy on earth. Deactivated scuttlebots lay scattered across the landscape, legs curled up like dead spiders.

Jamyang caught sight of her son's ship. It stuck up from the horizon like a great white needle, faded red paint etching a stripe around its tip. "Norbu?" Jamyang shouted. No reply came.

A crater the size of a lake sprawled in front of the ship. Three figures in spacesuits stood around it, frozen. A woman bent over a rock, squinting at an instrument. Beside her, a man sat on another rock, holding his head in his hands. Another leapt toward the ship, caught in mid-jump.

"Hello, good people?" Jamyang called. "I am Norbu's mother. It's all right. I am here to bring you home."

They remained frozen, like dancers caught by a photographer's flash. Jamyang passed them. She mounted the steel mesh steps leading into the ship.

Jamyang crawled through tiny passages until she entered a room where she could stand. Norbu stood in front of a huge machine the width of three large men standing shoulder to shoulder. His mouth stretched open into a shout. Sweat beaded his flushed cheeks.

Jamyang threw her arms around the waist of his spacesuit. "Norbu! I knew you weren't dead!"

Norbu's body wrenched into motion, like a stuck cart pulling free from the mud. He jumped back, startled. "Ma? What are you doing here?" He tapped a gauge on the panel. "I can't have much O2 left." He twisted a microphone toward his mouth. "Cairo, can you hear me? Xining, do you read?"

"Don't talk to them," said Jamyang. "I'm the one who came to rescue you."

"Where's Sangemo? Where's Dorje?"

"Hush. They're outside. We'll wake them when we head home. See?" She pointed out the triangular windows overlooking Norbu's frozen crewmates. "You won't believe what I had to go through to find you. The prime minister refused to send anyone for you!"

Norbu shook his head like a person waking from a long dream. "I don't . . . remember. What happened? Our radios went dead."

"It doesn't matter now."

"A signal came through before it happened . . . I'm having trouble remembering . . . my head hurts, I'm all fuzzy . . . I remember thinking about you, hoping you'd find a way to move on . . . "

"But I did move on, don't you see? I came for you. The monks and the television people, they wouldn't help me, so I summoned monkeys and climbed my way to you, just like in the old stories. I can bring you all home."

Norbu shook his head. "No."

Jamyang went to the window. "I hope the monkeys can hold us all. That girl's a sturdy one, isn't she?" She clucked her tongue against her teeth.

"Ma, this is important. I'm trying to remember. The transmission . . . "

"The Australians declared war," said Jamyang. "They threatened to detonate a spore-cluster bomb."

"-a spore-cluster bomb," Norbu finished with his mother. "The Australians would never have done it. It was an empty threat. The Australians would never have done it. Not with the Egyptian military presence in New Zealand, ready to retaliate with short-range missiles. It was an empty threat. The Egyptians knew that. Sangemo contacted the ambassador to beg them to delay their response until we could get home. The Egyptian ambassador said they couldn't. He said it would make them look weak. They loaned us the money to help us get to space, they said it was important for Qinghai to join the modern world, but they forgot us as soon as it became inconvenient . . . "

"Do we need to straighten this out now?" said Jamyang.

"Sangemo gave the headset to Dorje. He pleaded, 'I have sons at home. They need a father.' When that didn't work, Sangemo took the headset again. She said, 'We'll cut our mission short and leave now. We'll be in orbit in a few hours. You can send out your signal then.' She said, 'You have no idea how much this means to Qinghai. We've been waiting to show the world that we, too, are a great people. We, too, can touch the moon.'"

"Enough of this now," said Jamyang. "You never wanted to listen to stories, but they've saved you now, haven't they?" Jamyang grabbed Norbu's hand to pull him toward the door. He shook himself loose.

"No, ma, you don't understand. I'm running out of oxygen. You're a hallucination."

"You say this to the woman who comes to rescue you? Children! I cooked kitchens full of noodles and dumplings to lure the monkeys. When the new world fails you, the old stories are always there."

"I need to get to the others," said Norbu.

Jamyang watched him pull on his spacesuit. "You don't need that."

"I don't care if I am hallucinating, I'm not going out onto the moon without my suit," said Norbu. He pulled the bubble of his helmet over his head and bounded out of the room.

Jamyang followed. Norbu's crewmates remained frozen in the crater. Norbu went to each of them, waving his gloved hands in front of their still faces. Finally, he turned to his mother, hands groping in front of him as if searching for something concrete to grasp.

"I always thought I'd relive the most exciting moments of my life before I died. Winning the bicycle race from Xining to Qinghai Lake. The clean empty feeling of running ten kilometers, three thousand feet above sea level. Being chosen for the expedition. The launch! But when Sangemo told us about the message from Cairo, I kept thinking about you, Ma, and the old stories you used to tell. Monkeys forming a chain and jumping into a well after the moon."

Norbu paused. Behind his helmet, his expression was inscrutable.

"I must love you very much."

"As I love you," said Jamyang.

Around them, the world began to unfreeze. Norbu's crewmates inched forward as if in a slow motion video. From Norbu's space suit there came the noise of his radio, sputtering the empty static of Australia's jamming signal. Jamyang flinched.

"You can hear that?" said Norbu.

"Never mind!" shouted Jamyang. "Come on! We should get back to the monkeys before they fall!"

Jamyang turned to flee back the way she'd come, but her feet only ran in place. Dead scuttlebots lay where she hoped to find the monkeys. Panic cinched her throat. She couldn't breathe. She clawed at her neck. "Where did the earth go?" she choked.

"You don't get it, do you, ma? There isn't any air here. The old legends aren't true."

"We have to get home!"

Norbu shook his head slowly. "We can't, ma. You and I, we're both fools. Nothing we believed was true. There's nothing for us in the past or the future. I remember when I was a kid thinking if Qinghai could just get to the moon we'd be like all those other countries, rich and glamorous. No more poverty. No more children starving in the streets. No more taxes to pay for other people's wars. No more generations of boy soldiers coming home crippled. We'd leap across the gap and when we landed - we'd be with everyone else in the future."

Norbu stomped his foot. Moon dust billowed around him in slow motion. "Everything I grew up thinking—it was all wrong. I was trying to grab the future out of the well water. But it was only a reflection. It's hovering above us, chuckling in the sky. And here we are, wet."

Static roared in their ears, like the sandstorm.

"No," said Jamyang.

Norbu placed his hand on her face. His thick Kevlar spacesuit felt rough against her cheek.

"You don't get it, do you, Ma? We've fallen in the well. There's nothing left to breathe."

Three Oranges

D. ELIZABETH WASDEN

Orange stained the entire room. Orange juice. Zest. Peels. I scratched at the moist peel over a flowerpot and covered the shavings with soil. The flowerpot had cracked this time. I should buy another. I told myself this on numerous occasions.

I dipped my hands in the washbasin, then toweled my hands dry. Soil, mixed with orange zest, clung beneath my fingernails. It pushed right up against the soft skin of my finger and worked against my skin, like a rat gnawing against a belly. Had I not had an appointment, I would have excavated the mixture. Scrubbed my hands clean. Perhaps removed a bit of skin with it.

But neither I nor Hermes wore clean hands, and I suspected he might appreciate the irony of wearing my guilt in the open—if he noticed at all.

"Give Prokofiev more commissions," I told Hermes when he suggested I convince the composer to return to Russia. "The capitalists are fucking him over. He's getting frustrated. He even told one of the ballet directors that he was tiring of life in Paris. That Russia seemed to 'beckon to him.'"

Hermes was a field operative from Ukraine, glad to have a full stomach and to not be a Russian, whereas I was from Russia and glad to not be from Ukraine. I often wondered which of us had fared better. Me, with my postings in Berlin then Paris, or he, flitting about the Continent.

"To trade the City of Light for the dark of Moscow." Hermes shook his head.

"Ah, but it's easier to see light when one is in shadow."

"It's also easier to draw insects to the light and to—" He slapped the table. The thin, spindly legs shook with the sharp smack. I glanced over at the window. The cracked flowerpot held steady. A small, spindly orange tree had already burst through the soil. It shook with his movement. He dusted off his hands. "The Cockroach wants him back *now*."

Hermes had shared Osip Mandelstam's almost deadly poem about our Great Leader, and we often referred to Stalin as Cockroach or Cockroach with Whiskers or any variety of phrasing that would have gotten us shot. *Should* have gotten us shot.

"What's the rush?" I asked.

"You can't keep them forever. They're not yours to keep." His voice sounded different. Quieter. More predatory. "Where are they, hmm? You never share them anymore."

I held up my hands and smiled. He was correct: I did not share them with anyone. Perhaps he had informed Cockroach. Bastard.

He said, "Orion, there are plenty of other stars in the sky." He laughed. I did not. "You won't like this at all. It gets worse." Hermes blew out smoke from his nose like a dragon and gazed down. He thumped the cracked surface with his thumb. "You are to use the Oranges to convince him."

I shrugged and tapped a cigarette on the table. Loose tobacco jumped from the cigarette, and I swept it away with my hand. The apartment was fairly sparse. We sat, suspenders hanging from broad shoulders, at a small, square table. There were two other chairs besides the ones we occupied, and one of them was fairly comfortable. Thick, purple curtains hung in front of the apartment's single window. It was a horrible color, like soft, bruised flesh.

"Fine. I can do that." I sniffed. Moor had brought me the Oranges when I was in Berlin. Moor was a Caucasian, not an African. Armenian, I think. It was one of the few things I clearly remembered about those days. That and the street fights.

Hermes cleared his throat. There was more. "Cockroach wants the Oranges returned to Moscow with the composer."

Fuck. "Why?" I lit my cigarette. My hands did not shake.

He shrugged. "Who can say?"

Fuck. "You must have heard *something.*"

He crushed his cigarette on the table next to the ashtray. "I think you can guess why he might want Three Oranges returned. You've certainly spent enough *time* with them." He laughed.

I would kill the Cockroach with my bare hands. Wrap my suspenders around his throat and pull and squeeze. I would watch his tongue roll and dip in and out, out and in. The tongue that would find all of the crevices and secrets of my Oranges because no one could refuse the Cockroach.

"Relax," Hermes said. He had already unscrewed a flask and offered it to me as if he were reading my thoughts. It was a disconcerting proposition. What the Center did not need were omniscient handlers and field agents. "Get this done quickly, and I wouldn't be surprised if there wasn't a promotion."

"Here or in Moscow?"

"Is something wrong with Moscow?" He planted his elbows on the table and leaned forward.

I did not move. "I'd rather not return to Moscow. In fact, I'd adamantly decline."

He laughed again. "Oh, no, you wouldn't. You don't decline the Cockroach, and you don't tell him you're more comfortable in Paris and would rather stay, thank you very much. I'd advise you to express some measure of homesickness. Like the composer."

"Why don't *you* keep the promotion? I'll keep Paris."

"Get him to return to Moscow within the week. You'll stay in Paris, and I won't say anything about the *Normandie*. What do you say?"

My stomached tightened, and my legs became dead weight. I gave him a crooked smile; I could appreciate his position. Hermes had shared the news about Kirov's death in 1934, and since then, I had purchased passage on the *Normandie*. I shouldn't have been surprised that he knew or that he would use it as leverage. He was protecting his own ass.

Hermes was a colonel. Perhaps he could convince the chief and the chief could convince the Cockroach to keep me in Paris. Perhaps not.

"If not, I do hope you'll let me know." I took a drink and returned his flask. Cognac.

The door creaked shut behind him. I followed him a few minutes later, the flowerpot tucked inside my coat, pressed against my side. It bulged outward like a large tumor.

Night had fallen. The city vibrated with conversation and jazz and whispered promises over cocktails.

The Oranges had been with me since Berlin. Berlin had been cut off, but the Oranges were still mine. *Mine.* When I returned home, I placed the flowerpot under a bright light and ran my fingers up and down its small stems.

"Grow, damn you," I said, sliding into a chair with a wine bottle. I washed the taste of cognac out of my mouth and wished for the taste of orange.

I do not recall the rest of the night.

Within a few weeks, the orange tree grew, burying its great roots in the rug beneath it. Eventually, three beautiful orange blooms sprouted, then came the Three Oranges.

I plucked them from the tree. Rubbed them across my lips, flicked my tongue over them. Tasted them. Knew them. Never let it be said that I have no control, for I placed them in the pocket of my greatcoat.

I decided to meet Prokofiev in a car—a big, shiny black one that swallowed the passenger's vision and made him forget about Paris. Those black holes were magical, I must confess. Immediately, the victim's esteem and spirits would plummet and sink into the floorboard.

I brought the Three Oranges and scratched at their peels until citrus filled the air. The fairies must have giggled as I tickled their skin. Winter lingered outside, and steam rose from streets, smoke from houses. The door opened, and Sergei Sergeyevich stepped inside.

I was obvious, all wrapped in leather, bald head, fur hat in my lap, with hard, penetrating eyes. I drew him nearer than he would've liked, bent toward him, my lips sending warm breath onto his ear. He sat stock-still. I brandished the Three Oranges, wielded them like hand grenades, laughed, and slid back into my seat after he accepted them.

"From the motherland." I smiled. I wanted to break each of his fingers.

"What shall I do with them? Juggle them?" Prokofiev asked and exhaled all of his worry. He chuckled. Thought that, perhaps, I was there to fucking critique *Love for Three Oranges*? That insulted me. This was hard, so hard, and he laughed. "If this is some sort of message, you should speak clearly."

"What do you think you should do with them?" I pressed one thumb hard against the other and noted all of the colors my thumb could become. Pink. Red. Purple. Blue. White. Streaks of white against a pink background. Yellow on some days. "The longing you must feel—without them for so long. I don't think you'd prefer to juggle them at all."

His eyes brightened. For a moment, he held the Oranges in his hands, turning them over and caressing them with his thumbs. No doubt imagining things beyond juggling. I pressed harder.

"Do you have water, then?" he asked, now subservient and meek. Hopeful. Oh, how he smiled and the light in his eyes danced, in spite of the black hole of the car. He was Paris. I was Moscow.

I turned over an almost empty bottle of vodka and shook the remainder of it onto the car's floor.

He tried to capture the Oranges in the crook of his arm. They rolled back and forth against his coat, awkwardly tumbling across the wool. The first fell as he jostled for the door handle. Strange how uncoordinated some of us are in the moments we most need our agility. Strange how those nimble fingers could betray him at such a time.

I picked up the first Orange, and I jabbed my thumb into its flesh, digging back and forth. Juice burst onto our faces, our jackets, our hands. He abandoned his escape attempt and watched.

My tongue flickered like a serpent's. I thought of the Cockroach and the Composer in Moscow, taking turns with the Oranges, discovering just where to press and where to rub.

The first Orange exploded and opened like a magnificent flower, and I devoured it as I unpeeled the rest of it, tossing aside the peels haphazardly as if undressing a woman. The first fairy, red and white and tiny and angelic, emerged from the discarded, spent peel.

"Do you have water?" she asked. "Water. Please, water."

I wiped my hands on my knees. His lips had parted, but he said nothing and no longer moved.

"Have you been away for so long that you've forgotten them? That you've forgotten the rules?" I asked.

"Water or I'll perish!" the fairy said.

She pressed her hands together. I had not warned her. Her pleading was genuine and excruciating.

How she begged. She slid onto the seat, already withering like a days-old cut flower. Water or death. A rather slow death for something so small. I had watched her closely as she perished, slowly drying out, flesh splitting like cracked earth in a drought, tender cheeks splitting like an over-ripe tomato. Blood eased out of the wounds, slow like lava, then the muscle tore apart like frayed rope. Tendons unraveled. Organs shrank and wrinkled, folding on top of themselves until they no longer existed. The fairy would still scream as her bones too disintegrated, turning into dust.

Prokofiev's face—Oh, now it was priceless. I bit my lip and tasted blood so I wouldn't laugh.

(Some of my colleagues at the Center enjoy over-the-top torment. Treatments involving rats and tubes and stomachs or fucking spouses or children in front of subjects or beating subjects then sodomizing them with clubs and sticks and bottles. "Why am I here?" Silence. Crack. "Where am I going?" Silence. Crack. I sympathize with my friends back east. They have their own problems, the Cockroach nibbling at their backs and heels instead of wiggling his antenna from a distance. One has to have a bit of fun. Still, how crude. How unimaginative. How undelightful. Nothing at all like this.)

Prokofiev patted his pockets and threw the contents on the seat. A silk handkerchief (I kept it), a carnation (stepped on it), a thick brass key (threw it out the window), a pipe (sold it thirty years later for a tidy sum), papers (burned), pencil (broke in half), passport (he had the foresight to remember to pick that one up)—piss-all to drink. Hah! I bit my tongue again. Piss-all to drink.

I retreated to my corner, hands resting in my lap, fingers interlocked. One Orange lay on the floorboard next to the dying fairy.

He held the last orange between his knees. It bulged, soft and sweet.

"I wouldn't open it," I told him. I unfolded myself and placed my hand on top of the Orange. He jerked at my movement, as if I had touched him instead. I placed one foot on the other Orange. "Not *here.*"

We watched the fairy fall apart and die. He picked up the discarded peels, followed the minute dimples with his thumbs. Tears rolled down his cheeks. I managed to whistle the "March" from *Love for Three Oranges.*

"In Moscow," he said. He swallowed hard. I already knew he'd return.

"In Moscow," I agreed. "You realize you have a choice, though. Return the Oranges to me. You live in Paris. Or elsewhere. Forget about the motherland. You needn't return to Moscow at all." My head swam. I needed a cigarette. I wanted him to say yes. More than that, I wanted him to say no. "But the Oranges must."

I took the Orange from between his knees and gave it a gentle squeeze.

"You can replant them. Return them to life."

I nodded. "The peels usually suffice. Squeeze enough juice from them." I squeezed again. "Scrape it out with a penknife. If not?" Again, I squeezed. "As long as there is one, there are three. They're like a trinity, Citizen Prokofiev. Almost holy."

He stared at the Orange. "All three will return with me. To Moscow."

"All three." I pressed my palm against my chest. I could barely feel my tired heart beating. "I promise."

His skin was still quite pale but some measure of red had begun to flush into his cheeks. "You *promise.*" He snorted. "I won't go until I have them."

He had no cause to believe my promises, less so in the darkness of the car. The fairies would return as long as something remained of them. So he clambered out, scooping up his passport, and ran down the street. His jacket flapped behind him in a quick rhythm like the flapping of a bird's wing.

Had Prokofiev appeared brighter in the car or on the street? He was dull to me in both environments. Gray.

I crushed the second Orange underfoot, smashing it until the lump flattened into dry pulp and her screams ended.

When I stepped out of the car, it drove away and disappeared, but I took that last Orange with me.

We stopped at a cafe, me and my Orange. We shared a seltzer water and cigarettes. No one noticed as she expanded.

She sat in the chair next to me, a fully-grown (and developed) woman. She wore a long, red dress, pearls, and long, black gloves that were smooth to the touch. I held her hand in mine and squeezed too hard, as if she were my thumb back in the car.

She wrenched her hand from mine. "That hurts, Stepan."

"I'm sorry." I wasn't sorry. "Our time."

She stared at me. I found it both hard to look away and to not do so. "Is short."

I blinked. "You're certain he will accept?" I was.

"I am. *His* love for us is boundless." She glared at me accusingly. I deserved it. She was right. She was pouting.

His love. "What if there was another option?"

It was her turn. She blinked at me with her heavy, dark lashes. "I didn't think there were any other options."

As if she could know what her options were. "We could sail for North America. Canada."

"Don't be foolish, Stepan."

"I'm not. It could be done. You remember the *Normandie.*"

"Why? There's nothing for *us* there. You don't love me." She rolled her eyes.

"Love you." I thought of the dead fairies in the black car.

"Yes. Love."

An impossible thing. "No."

"Don't ruin the evening, then. And don't ruin your career." She placed her hand on top of mine and stroked my knuckles. "You have *such* beautiful hands. They are instruments, Stepan. Different than his, but you should have no shame in your art."

We drank and ate well that night. When we returned to the apartment, I unpeeled her again. She tasted and smelled like the dead fairies in the car. We made love in the dark, black as the inside of that fucking car.

Some time before dawn, our eyes met. Neither of us blinked.

"I could learn to love you. I could try. I do try." My voice was quiet, desperate.

"You haven't it in you, Stepan," she said, then rolled over and pulled a cigarette out of the case. I propped myself up on my elbows as she lit it, illuminating the off-white walls and all of its imperfections. I slid down, haloed in shadow by her shoulder. "Don't take it personally. I know you've tried. For that, I am grateful."

"If I set you free," I said, "where would you go?"

"If you set me—where . . . ?"

"Yes. Now. Where would you go?"

"I don't know."

I sat upright and pushed her shoulder into the bed. She stared at me, smoke trailing from her nose.

"Would you go to him? Would you go to *him*?"

"I—" She paused. "No. I wouldn't. I wouldn't, Stepan, I promise."

As she finished the sentence, she clawed at my face, but I struck quickly with my knife, scratching death across her throat. I held her by her shoulders, and she flailed, cutting at my face with her nails. She lacerated my forehead open just above the left eye before I gained control.

We were both liars. I knew she would return to him. She knew I would never let her leave.

As she bled out, I gathered the peels and placed them in a moistened handkerchief. I slipped it inside my pocket, along with all of my operational funds. And I ran.

In my dream, I placed the Three Oranges in an orange car. They drove away, my beautiful fairies still encased in their peels. I wanted to watch my oranges drive an orange car, but the Cockroach nipped, nipped, nipped, and drew blood. My gun liquified in my hands. I vomited bullets. He cut me down, and I fell to my knees, screaming.

"Do you really think us so helpless, Stepan?" the Oranges said as the Cockroach dragged me back to Moscow. Their voices were beautiful, calm, bright. "Our magic is unexplainable, and yours comes from mere terror. We're fairies, Stepan. You're only a man."

I kept the orange peel moist, wetting the handkerchief every day. Prokofiev returned to Moscow.

I scraped orange zest into pots, placed large lights above them, and never allowed the soil to dry.

Hermes died in 1937 or 1938, along with almost everyone else I knew. Almost.

In the 1940s, the Center and I threatened one another, baring our teeth across an ocean, but the old Cockroach interceded. He was almost jovial about letting me go, although I did not imagine my information was as dangerous to the Center as they might have suspected at that point.

I read about Prokofiev in the papers occasionally. They printed his image and discussed his great works.

One day, Citizen Prokofiev was not alone. Her face radiated in the gray background of the photograph. She was a monochrome sun in the overcast dawn. A star in the night sky. A lit cigarette in a black car. I laughed at the realization. The fairies truly controlled their magic.

I cut out her image, leaving Prokofiev alone in his frame, folded her.

I keep her close always.

I continued to seek out Prokofiev, to read about the public details of his life. Highs and lows. Mostly lows. Misfortunes. Denunciations. Pleas. These things no longer amused me as much as they once did.

Now, the flowerpot stands in front of my south-facing window. I water the barren soil once every few weeks, never allowing it to dry. I have waited decades for the soil to break, for a sprout to appear. Nothing grows there, not even in the summer.

Eventually—and on the same day—Prokofiev and Stalin die. What becomes of the Three Oranges? Who will they haunt now? I do not know. I wonder. I scan newspapers for clues. I read American magazines. I cannot find answers in Frigidaire ads and articles about the World Series.

I do not think their deaths a coincidence, but I have no contacts remaining in the Center. If I were to get the Americans' attention, would they tell me what they knew about the Oranges in exchange for those old lists, for names and networks and codes, in exchange for my freedom and safety? In exchange for the last of my magic? I wonder these things in the dark winters, the nights as black as cars.

It is always cold in Canada.

There are no oranges.

Matchmaker

ERIN M. HARTSHORN

"You're not exactly what I expected when my mother said she'd found a *shadchen*."

Miss Berazazz could've been Jewish, sure. The first kurz had converted only a few years after the kurz and humans had encountered each other out in space. Everyone learned of the Acceptance in Hebrew school, even if no kurz attended synagogue locally.

I stared around the pink ruffled room. Her yellow-green complexion seemed out of place. Bouquets of old-fashioned musk roses—one of the few Earth imports to do well here—were clustered everywhere, their aroma masking the natural body odors that made kurz and humans nauseated when near each other.

There had been few kurz in my classes at school; most were home-schooled. I'd wanted to be friendly toward them, but they scurried away every time they saw me coming. I'd like to have found out if the green frills circling their otherwise bare heads were as soft as they looked, if that patch of orange scales on their throats hummed to the touch when they spoke. They didn't seem to share the same level of curiosity about my dark curls and olive skin. Pity.

Miss Berazazz winked her third eye at me. "You never met a shiksa who was a matchmaker before?"

"If there were one within five star systems, I'm sure I'd have met her."

My mother wasn't subtle about getting me married off. I still burned with the shame of my sixteenth-year party, when she had invited every unmarried male in the Spaceport. I don't think I'd met even half a dozen of them before the talk turned to politics—specifically, the legality of sensor implants.

Space pilots needed the extra input for safe flying. Other spacers might, too, but our world has a strong conservative bent. We didn't want people who could afford the best technology to have an unfair advantage in the job market. Well, any more of one than they already had.

I didn't even get to express an opinion before tempers flared. The party became a brawl, troops were called in, and in the fracas, I was knocked into the fountain.

Mother was upset because my dress was ruined.

Five years had passed since then, and my mother was throwing everything she had into the effort of getting me married. "I don't want you to be alone when I'm gone." As though being alone were something to be afraid of. She had entirely too many hang-ups from that frontier planet she grew up on. Like the need to marry young. I wondered sometimes what she would have done if my father hadn't come along, but he had and they'd married when she was just seventeen. Now she thought of me, her only child, as an old maid.

"How old are you?" Miss Berazazz's question fit so seamlessly into my thoughts that I didn't realize at first she'd asked it.

"Twenty-one." I felt my ears heat up at the lie. They always blushed first, before my face. I amended my reply. "Twenty-one next week."

Her frill rippled in agreement as though she'd expected my answer. Mother probably gave her all the dirt on me. I shifted uneasily in my seat. What had they planned together?

Miss Berazazz surprised me by standing up and leaving the room, moving backwards. "A teacher with a big heart and large ambitions. Even discounting your mother's exaggeration, you are promising. Intelligent, caring. Come back when you are full of age. Your mother will not be party to this."

I sat there, befuddled. Mother had sent me here; surely she was already a party to it. And if I came back this early with nothing to tell her, she would assume I'd skipped the appointment completely.

I hesitated at the door and watched the clouds scudding across the pale green sky. The school was on holiday, so I had no work there to catch up on. Maybe I could kill some time at the council chambers. Nothing like a good political debate to fill the afternoon.

Just as well none of the boys at that long-ago party had asked my opinion on the question at hand. I would have told them. Not that any juvenile's opinions mattered. In the long run, the council bowed to pressure from the spacers and allowed implants to be used on the job. Penalties were high, though, for personal use; use outside the space support complex was cause for deportation.

Delaying my return home didn't matter in the end. I paused to touch the mezuzah before I entered the house. Mother sat, waiting for me, back straight and stiff, on the chair in the foyer. I was to be questioned, and with the length of time I had been gone, she wouldn't believe the truth. I told her a half-truth.

"She says I'm . . . a difficult case. She needs time to find someone suitable."

Her eyes narrowed—enough for me to notice, but not enough to crease her perfect skin. "How much time?"

"I'm to come back at the end of next week," I said. Next week, after my birthday. Would she see the importance of that? I didn't see how, as I didn't understand it myself.

"Very well. I'll drive you there myself."

If her only worry was that I wouldn't go—well, that made sense. I wasn't even sure myself why I planned to go. Certainly not legal compulsion, nor the full weight of guilt that Mother had been bearing upon me for years. Curiosity, I suppose. You don't have to be full-legal to enter a marriage contract, not even limited dalliance or child-bearing ones. What could the *shadchen* have in mind?

I brought my attention back to Mother. "That's not necessary. Really."

"We can discuss it later." A crease in her upper lip was the only visible sign of her displeasure. She changed the subject. "You didn't go see her looking like that, did you?"

I glanced in the mirror over the hall table. My hair had been tossed a bit by the omnipresent wind, but otherwise I seemed presentable enough. "Why not? You chose this outfit for Ben's swearing-in ceremony."

My cousin Ben was on the Spaceport council. He'd barely won the election for his district, even with Mother and Aunt Nomi calling on all their friends to exert pressure on his behalf. He'd been in office a scant month now, so I was fairly confident the clothes hadn't gone out of style just yet.

Her hands flew up. "Why do I even bother?" She addressed the ceiling, as she had so often while I was growing up. Or maybe she was talking to my father's ghost. I'd never had the nerve to ask. She looked back at me. "That was a political occasion, in support of family. This dress is completely out of place in a business meeting where you are trying to impress someone with your future prospects. You'll have to have something more suitable next week. Yes, perhaps a visit to ReeAnn's shop." She frowned. "No, ReeAnn is working on the outfits for your party." Another pointed birthday party. Wait—outfits? Plural? "We'll have to use Kendra this time, I suppose. It's really too bad you don't have a cousin your age to borrow from."

As if that were my fault. She should take it up with Aunt Nomi who had, after all, been given a choice with Ben. Mother's system rejected the sex selection drugs, but Aunt Nomi had an iron stomach. Personally, I was always amazed that the drugs had dared disagree with Mother. Not many things did.

Certainly Kendra didn't. Mother was already on the line to her. I couldn't hear Kendra's end of the conversation, but Mother's tone spoke volumes. A few sentences, and anyone would agree with her out of self-preservation.

My own levels of self-preservation were high enough that I never overtly disagreed with her. I simply didn't voice opinions.

Kendra made time for Mother. We would be at her shop tomorrow morning. My measurements could be sent to her—were, in fact, on file. Kendra would use them to ensure that everything we examined would be in my size. Mother didn't really need me there—a hologram would do as well for color, style, and bearing—but she wanted me there. As I said, no overt disagreement. There went another day of my life.

As it turned out, the day wasn't a complete loss. Mother had a Hadassah meeting in the afternoon and had to rush off right after the fitting. If Mother wasn't there on time, Elizabeth Holin would push through all of her own pet projects. I'd gone to a meeting once; it was amusing yet frightening to realize Mother wasn't the only fiercely stubborn woman around. Their clashes were entertaining, but Mother expected me to back her up. I found it easier to not attend.

Mother was very understanding when I said I had other commitments. I had already agreed to become an active member when I got married, a time that evidently neared. My anticipation knew no bounds.

Mother left me at the door of Kendra's shop. "I know you're much too busy to accompany your poor old mother to her meetings. Don't think anything of it." For her, this was understanding.

I resisted the urge to roll my eyes. My poor old mother played racquetball twice a week and frightened bullies in the street, and I pitied anyone who had the lapse of judgment necessary to call her "old" to her face.

"I'll be home a little late for dinner," she continued. "You go ahead without me and I'll find something when I get home."

"Don't be ridiculous." My lines slid out with the ease of long practice. "I wouldn't think of starting without you. You go ahead, and we'll eat when you get home."

After several more exchanges along the same lines, reinforced with her mention of rugelach should I need to nosh, she finally left, catching the A line toward Aunt Nomi's house. I watched until she was out of sight before setting off in the opposite direction. I'd heard that the library had new copies of twentieth-century political speeches from Earth. I wish they had more kurzan material for comparison, but there wasn't much demand for it.

I had always wanted to go to Earth, to study politics at one of the real universities, in Cambridge or Melbourne or Shanghai. Even I knew that it was a hopeless dream, but I still studied everything I could get my hands on. A more realistic idea would be to have the chutzpah to run for office. All I had to do first was grow a backbone, move out, and survive the guilt. *Realistic*—right.

When I got to the library, somebody else had already reserved the speeches, and the visuals room was occupied. I hadn't expected that. After I joined Hadassah and began to organize charity functions of my choice, I intended to begin at the library, updating their site licenses and their tech so that more than one person could look at archived material at the same time. Very definitely *tikkun olam.*

The librarian tried to be helpful. "Is there something else I can get you instead?"

I tried to think of alternatives. I'd already read all their Hebrew-language archives, but not all the cultural information. Most of the material they had on the Shoah, though, I'd need the visuals room for, so that was out.

The talk at council the previous day had been on farming and pollutants and which space company thought the Spaceport's fees were too high now. One motion, quickly tabled, concerned some cross-breeding experiments.

That might be interesting to follow; I asked for a simple genetics text. I'd look up the details of the bill later, after I got home.

The mathematics and probabilities were as dull as I expected, but the history was fascinating. The text even had a chapter devoted to the eugenics attempts under the Third Reich. I thought of my many-times-great-grandmother and her release from Dachau. I already knew this history, but I read with interest about the experiments in Earth's twenty-first century to decrease activity of monoamine oxidases as well as to increase levels of the dopamine receptor associated with risk-taking behavior. Earth wanted space pilots and people willing to brave the far reaches of space. But risk takers don't settle down, and so entire new families of drugs were born. The drug trade ramped up. The politicians should have seen that coming.

"Seen what coming?"

I hadn't realized I'd spoken out loud. "Excuse me—" I looked up.

He smiled. The smile was so perfect, right down to the dimple in his left cheek, that it took me a moment to process the rest of his good looks—black hair, tan skin, grey eyes.

"Wow." I bit my lower lip. I knew I'd said *that.*

"I didn't mean to interrupt." He put his left foot up on the table next to my chair and leaned on his knee. "I was waiting for a good moment. The librarian told me you wanted to use the visuals room."

I nodded. Behind him, the clock on the wall showed a quarter after six. Four hours! I'd lost track of time. Mother wouldn't have been that long at Hadassah—not since she'd given up finding leads for marrying me off, anyway. I stood up. "I have to go."

"The room's free now. I even asked the librarian to leave the vids keyed for you." He pulled back but didn't put his foot down.

"I'm sorry." He was looking at the speeches? Gorgeous and interested in the same things I was. If only I could stay. "I didn't realize it had gotten so late. I have to meet . . . someone."

"Maybe I'll see you another time, then."

"Maybe." He hadn't moved, and I had to push past him to drop the genetics book at the counter. "I'm in here a lot."

He probably hadn't heard me and wouldn't have cared if he had. Mother said I had my dad's nose. I guess that could have been it, although I figured no one in his right mind would want her for a mother-in-law.

As I'd expected, Mother acted worried when I got home. "I was afraid something had happened to you."

I walked past her to the kitchen. "Not this time," I said. "I am hungry, though. I'll just whip us up something, shall I?"

Mother didn't rise to the bait. If Mother didn't want to feed a hungry child, perhaps she really was worried.

"I expected you to be home when I arrived."

I stopped and turned. "I'm sorry. I should have signaled you."

Was she going to forgive me? Well, no, but she might let it go for now, to be dragged out later in one of her litanies of my failings as a daughter.

"Yes, you should have." She walked away. Over her shoulder, she said, "Don't eat too much. There isn't enough time for either Kendra or ReeAnn to alter your dresses."

No family meal, then. Fine. I grabbed a cheese sandwich and a glass of milk and curled up to think about the stranger in the library. I should have read the cross-breeding bill instead, but he was more compelling. Something about him shrieked outsider. Maybe a space captain, passing through. But then where were his implants? Ah, well, a gal could dream.

And dream I did until the morning of my twenty-first birthday. Mostly. I did eventually read the bill.

I'd assumed it would be a bill for funding at the college—some new strain of wheat with more fiber and vitamins, or livestock that would grow in a tank so we could put yet larger buildings on what was now grazing land. Scientists were always promising things like that and instead creating chickens that could lay striped eggs with yolks that glowed in the dark.

This bill was different. It claimed to be "to protect the purity of the human and kurz races." In an attachment—not part of the bill itself but clearly meant to influence its passage—one of the sponsors told a story of his father, whose genetic material had been stolen and used to impregnate a kurz female.

The bill had lots of language in it about the protection of the two species and about how cross-breeds could serve as vectors for illnesses to spread from one to the other.

It was a marvel of statesmanship. It had to be, to allow every artificial method of procreation, every drug, every choice we'd given ourselves about our children, yet disallow any hybrids. It stopped short of barring kurz procreation on a planet where there were humans, but not by much. The hints were there for anyone who'd studied politics and history. This was just the beginning.

It stank worse than a roomful of kurz after a softball game.

I still hadn't decided what I could do about it. Ben was too busy to talk to me, although I left several messages at his office.

Today, though, I wouldn't worry about it. Today was the day I went back to see the *shadchen*, the day I accepted Mother's wish to find me a husband. I really didn't care. I had a job; I had ambitions. I even had a cause. I didn't need a husband. It was my mother who wouldn't give up.

Before getting dressed, I paused to look at the yellow star hanging on my wall. The faded ancient fabric was framed behind glass in a controlled atmosphere that prevented further deterioration. I stroked the wooden frame. Had that distant ancestor married for love, or had she, too, been to a matchmaker? I knew she hadn't met her husband until after the war. I wondered what her dreams had been. They hadn't been passed down from mother to daughter as the star had been.

"I remember," I whispered.

I pulled out the dress and overskirt that ReeAnn had insisted would be perfect for meeting my future husband. I felt like an idiot with the skirts swishing and swirling as I walked. It was the price I'd had to pay to go alone.

That wasn't the way these things were done. The *shadchen* should have met me to size me up for herself. Then Mother would take over, whether I was difficult or not. Mother should meet with Miss Berazazz and my future husband and mother-in-law to work out the details. Only when the contract was sealed would I set eyes on him. There were several arguments I could have made; I used the simplest.

"The *shadchen* said we should do it this way."

That was that. Not even Mother would offend a matchmaker willing to take my unruly self in tow. And so she sat once more in the uncomfortable chair by the front door and waited for me to come down the stairs in my new finery, waited to say good-bye to her grown-up daughter who would finally get married, waited to take one last stab at my self-esteem.

She stood as I approached the landing. "You'll do, I suppose, but would it have killed you to do something with your hair?"

And there it was. I touched my hair self-consciously. "Short of cutting it all off, this was the best I could do." I paused in front of the mirror and pulled my hair off my face. "I could try that. Might start a new trend."

"Your father must be spinning in his grave to hear you talk like that." She pushed me at the door. "Go on, then. Try to remember to be a lady."

As if I could forget in this get-up. I thought about turning back, but ladies do not renege on their word, even if they didn't like their options. I didn't even know my options. Miss Berazazz might have already chosen someone, someone I couldn't stand. I quailed. The only thing that pushed me forward was the thought of telling Mother I didn't go.

I pushed the door open.

A kurz looked up from an armchair. His eyes were the same deep green as the edge of his frill. "Yes?" he asked.

"I'm sorry." I tried to back out of the room while still talking, but my overskirt snagged on the door. I tugged at it without looking. "I didn't realize someone else was . . . I was looking for . . . I'll come back later."

His frill rose in mild surprise. "Do you think you should do that?"

"Come back? Yes, I'm expected."

"No, not that. I meant—"

My overskirt tore. I stopped pulling, but it was too late. A large piece of fabric remained caught on the bottom of the door, and the skirt itself was beyond repair. I felt my ears growing hot with embarrassment and knelt to pry the fabric loose, letting my hair fall forward to mask my face.

"Here, let me help you with that."

I inhaled to argue and stopped in surprise. "You don't smell."

His frill rippled. "I beg your pardon?"

My face should have been in flames based on the heat I was feeling. "You—I—kurz always—I'll shut up now."

"Not on my account, I trust."

I was spared from answering because Miss Berazazz entered from the back room at that moment. Her frill rippled when she saw the two of us together at the door.

"I see you've met my son."

I learned a lot in the next few minutes.

Kurz mating habits are reasonably close to human, although they're compulsively monogamous. Miss Berazazz had chosen the courtesy title "Miss" based solely on how it sounded to her. She was married, he was off-planet, and Chur-kil was their only child.

"Which brings us to you." Miss Berazazz finished spieling off history. "You need a husband. My son needs a wife."

I gaped at her. Our species weren't even from the same solar system. I had more in common biologically with chimpanzees than I did with any kurz. Then there was that bill before the council. "But—we're incompatible."

"I don't know. I thought we were getting along pretty well." He had the nerve to wink his right eye at me, and I blushed again.

"Perhaps not so incompatible as all that. Chur-kil is the first generation of . . . an experiment." I stared in horrified fascination as she triggered a holo on her desk. It could have been the older brother of the man I'd met in the library, identical except for blue eyes, streaks of gray above his ears, and a ridge of sensor implants under each eyebrow. "His father."

"That's not possible," I said. But I remembered the stolen genetic material mentioned in the bill. I bit my lower lip. "Do you have documents?"

I blanched. Mother would've found the rudeness unforgivable, but Miss Berazazz didn't even wave her frill.

"Certainly." She used her monitor to call up copies of her marriage certificate and Chur-kil's birth certificate. They could have been faked, but since I could access the information from the central database, there wasn't much point.

I leaned back in my chair. "And he's the actual father?"

"We'll give you the medical records later, but right now, hear me out. As I said, my son is the first generation. We want a second generation, one that will be able to breed freely with either parent race. That's where you come in."

This was why I had to be twenty-one. Mother would never have listened to this. It wasn't illegal; no one thought it possible. But Mother, a blessing on her head, had always wanted me to marry—

"I don't suppose you're Jewish? Or a doctor?"

Was I really considering this? So I'd never see Earth. That had never been realistic.

Chur's frill was ruffling again. I watched, confused.

"Neither, I'm afraid. I'd be willing to convert, but I'm afraid a bris is out of the question."

My mouth opened. *Pause. Think about what you're going to say.* "I'm afraid the rabbi would insist."

Miss Berazazz—his mother—cut across our interchange. "Did you pay no attention to comparative anatomy in school?"

I shrugged. "I learned science from test to test."

"Kurshall keep us all safe!" She leaned across the table. "Physically, you may be compatible enough to join, but there is no foreskin."

"So your entire race is circumcised. Even better."

This couldn't be real. I didn't joke about such things. Mother would be appalled to hear me even discussing them.

"More or less." His brow creased, and the corners of his mouth turned up. It didn't come naturally to him, but he was trying to smile. I found it charming, even if he had been practicing long before he'd heard my name.

"What exactly do you want me to do?"

The marriage license was already made out. The ceremony could take place immediately. Accompany Miss Berazazz to a clinic the following day, and by the time my party rolled around, I should be well on my way to being knocked up. We could try for future children the old-fashioned way. Only one thing hadn't been taken care of.

"I didn't know where you'd want to live." He touched the back of my hand with a single finger.

I pulled my hand away, leaned back in my chair, and rubbed my temples. What would Mother say about a kurz for a son-in-law?

I went back to something tangible. "I met someone the other day who looks like your father."

They exchanged looks. Miss Berazazz said, "My husband had a child from his first marriage. Chur-kil's brother . . . never accepted his father's remarriage. He may be here to cause trouble."

That perfect smile, those grey eyes. I looked at Chur-kil. His frill was flat against his head. I didn't want to be superficial. I didn't. And yet . . .

I opened my mouth to refuse.

"Life won't be easy for our children," he said. "But with time, more time than we'll see, our peoples will truly be one."

The wistfulness in his voice struck a chord in me. They had a glorious vision. I came from a people proud to be set apart, a people he was willing to join. But he'd been planning this for a long time; I hadn't. I wouldn't rush into anything. I told myself it had nothing to do with his brother's dimple, and I almost believed it.

I pushed my chair back from the table. "I need time."

"Of course." Chur looked disappointed but nodded.

His mother was less understanding. I'm used to dealing with mothers, though, and she was a pushover compared to even Aunt Nomi. I promised to return in a week with a decision.

Chur walked me to the door. "I'm sorry about your skirt."

Tell him it had been bought for the occasion? No. "It wasn't my favorite."

Time to go home and re-read the bill. Marriage would be making a stand, but it had to mean more than that, more than green eyes and a forced smile. I had to think. First, though, I had to decide what to tell Mother.

I couldn't—didn't—tell her all the truth. Fortunately, when I walked in with a torn skirt, Mother's attention was all for that. "How could you? It wouldn't have been suitable for your party, certainly, but it could have been part of your trousseau."

Just like that we were on the subject of my marriage.

"Perhaps." I twitched my skirt and moved past her to the stairs.

Her voice stopped me. "Young lady."

I'd had the entire trip home to think about what to say. Except I was thinking about the marriage proposal, legal threats, in-laws who smelled, and talking to my rabbi. Chur had been . . . nice. A vague word, but it fit. He was pleasant and witty, completely agreeable.

And he'd winked at me. No man had ever winked at me, except for Uncle David when I was a little girl. Chur didn't care about my dad's nose, about what I looked like—so far as I knew, all he did care about was that I was unmarried and twenty-one.

Not exactly a ringing endorsement.

I sighed. "He was friendly, but I'm afraid his mother will try to run our lives. I asked for some time to think about it."

"I see." The infinitesimal eyebrow lift. "Is he at least Jewish?"

"He says he'll convert." I kissed her cheek. "But I do need time. You wouldn't want us to name our first-born child for someone on his side of the family, would you?"

With that, I breezed past her and up the stairs. Everything I'd said was true. I'd only left out the fact that he was kurz. Not fully by biological standards, but to all appearances. I wasn't looking forward to that conversation.

I worried at the decision that day and the next and the day of my party—even as I prepared to greet my guests, I wondered what they would say if Chur stood next to me.

A surprise guest showed up at my party—the handsome stranger from the library—Chur-kil's half-brother. I first spotted him with Ben and a couple of Ben's cronies from the Spaceport council. I wanted to talk to them—Ben still hadn't returned my calls—but hostess duty compelled me to chat with women who wouldn't have been near my party if they had dared offend Mother.

"I hear you went to a *shadchen*." I couldn't remember her name. Some vacuous person a couple years older than me, probably with two boys and two girls by now.

"Mother's idea." Why elaborate?

Uncle David joined the conversation. "Historically, matchmakers create more lasting unions than personal choice does."

"Historically," I replied, "there wasn't usually a way to dissolve a marriage short of murder."

"Interesting. Are you looking to hire somebody for the job?" It was the stranger. Ben stood next to him.

"I'm not married yet, so I'm afraid it would be premature. I can take your references to keep on file."

"Alas, I have none." His smile was as charming as I remembered.

"Do you at least have a name?"

"My apologies," he said at the same time Ben said, "I brought him over to introduce."

"The least you could do if you helped him crash my party," I said.

Ben gave me his standard exasperated cousin look. "May I introduce Joe Yee? Joe's recently arrived at the port and is crazy enough to want to make it permanent."

"The lure of the unknown," Joe said. "As well as the fascinating beauties on your planet."

Ben coughed. I ignored him, even though I didn't blame him. I tried to keep the frown off my face. I was certain Joe was here to cause trouble for Miss Berazazz and Chur, but what in the world was he doing at my party?

"What would you do here?" I asked.

"Oh, no. You're going to set each other off," Ben said.

"I was thinking of going into politics," Joe said.

"I suppose you lapped up all that arguing about the different spacer companies the other day."

He shrugged. "I've heard it all from the other side. What do you think of the recently tabled motion on cross-breeding?"

Was he actually going to announce his views? I said, "I'm no biologist. What about you?"

He spread his hands. "I'm afraid I haven't studied enough of the particulars to have an opinion yet."

Uncle David snorted. "He's a politician, all right."

"A pity," I said. "Perhaps you can explain it to me after you've had time to study it."

"I'd be delighted."

Later, I managed to get Ben off by himself, but only after promising I wouldn't talk to him about any of the bills facing the council. I asked him about Joe. "I could swear I've seen a picture of his father."

A shrug. "It's possible. His father's a captain on an interplanetary run. The news often has pictures of one or another of them—usually when something bad happens."

Morbid curiosity and gossip. That just about sums up news. I'm not above it myself, but Ben didn't know about any other family Joe might have. "I thought you had an engagement just about ready to announce."

"Nothing's final."

Mother found us talking then and chased us back to the party. I wasn't being a responsible hostess, and it might not be too late to catch the eye of the Governor's younger son. As said son had a wandering eye and hands to match, I wasn't as enthusiastic about the prospect as Mother was. I followed her across the patio toward him anyway.

Help arrived from an unexpected source. Joe caught my arm. "You promised me a dance."

Mother, never one to complain about a gift to the giver's face (unless you were family, and then it wasn't so much a complaint as a megillah of what the money could have been better spent on), pushed me into his arms and glided off to speak to Aunt Nomi.

The song was half over, but I went through the motions. Dancing doesn't thrill me, although the feel of his hand on mine did strange things to my heartbeat. When the music changed, Joe would have kept dancing.

I drew him to a nearby bench. "I thought only elected officials refused to give an opinion."

"I don't want to say anything I might regret later," he said. "People would expect me to live up to it."

"You haven't been involved in politics before, have you?"

"So young to be such a cynic." He brushed his lips across my hand while looking into my eyes. It was a romantic gesture, even if I did see the flash of a sensor implant on his upper lip. He wouldn't be using it away from the transport sector, not with the penalties. The texture implied simulskin on the surface, and most girls probably never noticed it was there. I wondered what he was wired for.

I left my hand in his. I looked at the hands, not ready to meet his gaze.

"Perhaps you'll make a true believer of me yet," I murmured.

He leaned in close. "But a believer in what?"

My eyes widened at his tone, and I looked up. His eyes were narrowed, and the charming smile was gone. His grip on my hand tightened.

His voice low, he said, "Do you know what you've gotten yourself into?"

The music changed again. People moved past us to the dance area. I pulled at my hand, but he didn't let go.

"What are you talking about?"

"The kurz. Don't deny it. Their pheromones cling to you like sewer water."

The sensor must be good to pick it up after two days.

I shrugged. "Mother sent me to a *shadchen*. I was surprised to find she's not human, but if she finds me a husband, it clearly doesn't matter to Mother."

"If you're not telling me the truth, I will find out." His sneer marred his good looks. "I know of their plans to pollute the human race with their filth. I'll stop this—"

I couldn't prove he'd used the implant. And if I accused him, it would just give him one more opportunity to air his bigotry when he got his day in court. Distasteful as he was, I had to get him out of here without that satisfaction.

It was time to be outraged. I'd spent years watching Mother do it; time to see if the passive lessons paid off. My voice rose just enough to cut across the nearby din. "Is that why you came here uninvited? There are *standards* of behavior in this community." I snatched my hand back with great force.

A few heads turned, but Joe couldn't see them from where he was. He said, "Don't flatter yourself. I'm checking all the unmarried local women."

"My, a libertine or desperate. Perhaps both." I knew that wasn't what he meant, but the onlookers didn't. I stood. "I'll thank you to leave now."

He looked as though he wanted to say something else. Then he saw Mother standing next to him. To his credit, he didn't blanch.

"I believe my daughter asked you to leave." Nothing colored her voice. "My nephew will be happy to show you the way out."

Ben didn't look happy. Joe had come with him, and he was going to get an earful from both Mother and Aunt Nomi later. He put his hand on Joe's shoulder as if he'd ejected men from parties before. Maybe he had; Ben went to parties where that sort of thing might happen.

The incident effectively killed the party. Clusters of people stood about, talking quietly and casting furtive glances at me when they thought I wasn't looking. Look at the freak who chased off the only eligible man to show any interest in her *ever*. If it hadn't been my party, I'd have pled a headache and left, but a hostess has responsibilities—as though Mother would let me forget.

I was duly grateful as my guests began leaving in twos and threes. Many of them still wouldn't meet my eyes. Mother stood beside me, smiling and chatting. I was doomed as soon as the last guest left. I knew it.

The door closed.

I pursed my lips and looked at the nearby chair. "Does that leg look chipped to you?"

The ruse was pointless. She looked over swiftly, then returned her gaze to me. "It's fine. You, however, have some explaining to do."

"I didn't mean to make a scene, but he was being rude—" inspiration struck "—and crude about my visits to Miss Berazazz."

Rudeness one should rise above. Crudeness, on the other hand, was just not done.

Her left shoulder seam pleated a trifle; she had relaxed. I wasn't clear of port yet, though. "You know what I think of you bringing up such matters to strangers."

That one I was prepared for. "Talk circulates at a party, Mother. You know that. I'll talk to Ben about his choice of companions."

"You needn't bother, child. I will—"

"I was hostess. It's my responsibility." I hadn't interrupted Mother since I was two years old. My neck prickled, and I could taste acid in my throat. I bit the inside of my lip. I wouldn't get sick now.

Finally, she nodded. "I might still have a word with Nomi about how she's raised her son, but as you say, it is your responsibility."

I don't remember going upstairs to my room. Shock will do that. I had to get Ben on the line. Not yet, though. I wasn't sure he'd be home. Maybe Ben would be willing to arrange Joe's quiet deportation for illegal use of implants if I protected Ben from our mothers. It was worth a try. No need to tell him I'd already saved him from mine.

Joe had spoken of polluting the human race. I'd heard that line of rhetoric before.

I crossed my room to face the faded cloth star and ran my finger over the glass as though I could touch the fabric. "Never again."

Chur was more human to me than Joe would ever be. He'd make a good husband. I made a call. "I think you should talk to my rabbi. I'll let him know you're coming."

Trickster
MARI NESS

The god came to me on a night when both moons were dark, allowing us to see the stars. Not that I could, hidden as I was behind mats and screens and hangings, but I knew the stars were there, one of the rare nights we could be sure of this.

He should not have come. But he is a god, and they do not always do what is right, or wise. He *shone*—I have no other word for it—in the unlight, in the dim bits of candle and lamp and star that had made it through the cracks in my room. *Shone,* with his black skin and the hands that he had made, for some unaccountable reason of his own, red this evening. His face was a blank oval, truly blank, with no hint of eyes, mouth, or nose in that utter smoothness. And yet—I knew, without knowing how I knew—that behind that blankness his beauty was greater than I could imagine, that I could handle knowing. They hide themselves from us in kindness, they say, though we do not have many examples of their kindness.

Trickster. My body tensed, though I knew it would be better not to, to appear—to actually be—as calm as if this were merely the visit of a friend.

I had a blue candle by my bed, for moments like this, but I did not light it. Too undignified, I might have said; caught by his red hands, I might have added. Whatever the truth, it remained unlit.

Silence stretched between us. His place to speak first, but he did not. Perhaps he thought I was sleeping—I have been told that the gods do not always understand the difference, that they slip in and out of our dreams as easily as they slip from the sky to here, that they themselves do not sleep, although they dream. I do not know. Even now, I am not so familiar with gods. But I suspected—no more than that—that he was silent not because he thought me asleep, but to discomfit me, to make me uneasy. *More* uneasy, that is; I was uneasy enough with his presence.

Trickster.

More silence.

I would never sleep with him in the room, and my bones still ached with fatigue, one reason I was inside, instead of searching the stars. "You should not be here," I said.

In the darkness, in the blankness, I could have sworn he *smiled,* although I could not see his mouth. "You should not have spoken first."

Unthinking, I treated him as I might a more normal—a more *mortal*—visitor: "You wanted me to."

"Who knows what one like me wants and desires?"

And *this* is a reason not to welcome the visits of gods, particularly this one: they can be oh, so *irritating.*

I have heard three tales of the coming of the gods: that the universe, lonely, threw up beings of fire and water and wind and iron to bear her company in her eternity that would not be like us, mortal flies too brief to observe. That the gods were once mortal, as we, until they drank a lake of fire, and drained it to its cobalt depths, and filled with fire, began to stalk the world.

And the third: that the gods are not gods at all, but mere tricksters all, with the trickster at their head, whose greatest trick is to seem the least and weakest of these, and trick us into believing these beings gods.

"What do you wish?" I said, to prevent this conversation from moving in dizzying circles, towards words that could, I knew, warp my dreams, my mind, or worse, change my memories, my thoughts, causing me to rethink friend and foe. Sometimes, I had to admit, to our benefit—the gods had quite often interfered to stop mortal quarrels and wars for reasons of their own—and quite often, not; for every war they had stopped, they had begun something else—a war, a terror, a celebration—for their own amusement, not our own. They are not *evil,* you understand, the gods. Evil is a thing of mortals. Some might even be named beneficial, good, if even those tend to the . . . capricious. They are, instead, *bored.* Even those thinking of the happiness of mortals. Perhaps especially those thinking of the happiness of mortals.

This one had no such thought in mind.

"I need you to kill one of us," he said.

Have I mentioned that I could have sworn he was smiling?

We have tales of the wars of the gods, tales where they have beaten or stabbed or poisoned or eaten one another, only to be miraculously restored in a moment, or less, or upon the next rising of the moon. Our earth bears scars of their passage: a boiling mountain here, a crater there, a lake of ice that will not melt in the center of a desert, and more. I have seen some of these places myself, although they are all old, very old. The gods mostly gave up warring amongst themselves—if not with mortals—long ago, when, the songs said, they realized that they could not die.

Mostly.

• • •

Silence filled the room, so strongly that I had no choice but to speak the obvious.

"How do you expect a *mortal* to kill any of you?"

"By taking you to a place where we are a little less immortal."

Another shock.

"Is there is such a place?"

"I am not certain," he said, and I could not see his face, could not know if he was telling the truth. "But I know where it is, if it exists at all."

"Where?" I demanded.

This time, he let the light shift, let me see the smile on his face. "One of the moons," he answered. "But you must not ask for all our secrets."

We did not always have moons, say the stories and songs. Once, we had only earth, and the stars, and in the day, the sun.

Then a green light, then a blue, moving slowly through the sky, dimming our stars.

Moons.

A gift from the gods, say some of the songs. A curse, whisper some of the stories.

At the festivals, the children sing of their coming, though they have never known a world without a moon.

"The moons are not a place," I said sharply. "They are only . . . ." I struggled for the right word, gave up in vain. "Lights."

"On the contrary," he said. "They are places, places and reflections of light."

Useless to argue this point. "Why?" was all I could think of next.

"Balance," he said, in a lighthearted tone.

The gods have informed us that they number thirteen—precisely thirteen. It is an awkward number, one they consider unlucky, for reasons they do not tell us.

Because it is their unluck, not ours, many of us arrange our homes in elements of thirteen—thirteen windows, thirteen screens, thirteen plates, thirteen hangings, thirteen cups. I have known women to hope for 11 children to make a family of thirteen; couples who have joined with others, to have thirteen people in their household, thirteen to stand against the gods.

In the house of the Lady of the Waters, we, too, keep to thirteen women, thirteen students of her gifts, no more and no less, although we serve her, and would not—so we say—bring her bad luck. We do not know if she believes us. Her eyes, you understand, are not human, when we see her.

Thirteen. Out of balance, out of symmetry. They cannot pair up evenly, in thirteen, and so they do not, forming circles of twos and threes and fours and fives that come together for a time and then break up again. They cannot divide by gender, and so they do not, with some of the gods choosing to be women, and some men, and some both, and then switching, for no apparent reason. Even as others, including our Lady of the Waters, try to cling to the names we have given them, to the genders they have chosen.

But they cannot die, and they cannot birth another, and so they remain: Forever out of balance; forever out of symmetry. Forever doomed with bad luck.

I have watched my child die in my arms.

I do not think the gods understand bad luck.

I sat in silence, contemplating. He spun three balls out of nowhere—or from his sleeves, I could not tell—and began juggling them.

"Which god did you have in mind?" I asked, trying to sound as casual as if we were merely discussing the weather.

As sung in the house of the Lady of the Waters, these are the names mortals have given the gods: The Lady of Waters, the Dreamweaver, She of the Clouds, the Corn God, the Smoke, He of Shining Feathers, the Lord of Rats, the Shadowcrafter, the Crippled One, the Lord of Chains, the Lord of Fury, the God of Silver, and the Trickster.

What they may call themselves, we do not know. I have been told, and this may be true, that the gods at one time had no names: they were just what they were, and no more, until they encountered—or until they made—mortals. Yet we, as mortals, have a desperate need of names, and so, we when found the gods, we named them, often many times. My own Lady of Waters is also the Woman Who Weeps, the Girl of Snow, the Ice Bird, the White Crone, the Grey Waters, the Bloody Girl of Red Skin and Hands. (She is not consistent, this lady, in her age; one of my teachers believed that she finds this shifting amusing.)

Sometimes, when we call their names, the night *shifts,* and even through the light of the moons, we can see the stars.

I did ask, once. "Are you truly gods? Or is that a trick?"

"That would be telling."

So now you know as much as I.

"Not the Lady of Waters," he said. "I know you serve her."

Serve was perhaps not the correct word, although it worked as well as others. I learned from her, in turn for singing songs for her amusement, telling tales of her generosity and bountifulness to those that came to this temple, so that they in turn would be responsive, would sing something to amuse her and bring something to light the dull eternity of her days. And in turn, I learned of healing, of change, and sometimes—sometimes—she would grant me the power to bring ease, or healing, to a child.

A bargain. A poor one, sometimes, except when a child smiled at the end of pain. I would do nothing to stop that.

I did not bother to explain. "Then what god did you have in mind?"

"The God of Silver."

The gods still tried, now and again, the whispers said, tried to kill another, or tried to birth another. It was their number, thirteen, that kept them powerless against mortals—to a certain extent; that kept them dependent upon us—to a certain extent. (My own teachers questioned both the powerlessness and the dependency.) Should the gods ever number twelve, or fourteen—

Well.

Balance would be restored.

Not something mortals should strive for.

Interesting. I knew as little of this god as I knew of any other, but he was said—or she was said, this was one of the gods bored with the mortal concept of gender—to be one of the more benevolent of the gods, a god of peace, a god who had turned from the greed of gold and gems to be content with the beauty of the lesser silver.

It was only a tale.

But this was also a god that—if the tales were right—had spent less and less time with mortals, more and more time hidden in the sky, behind the clouds. I had heard some begin to refer to him as the Cloud God, although that was not quite correct: a goddess controlled the clouds and the rain, a sister and rival and friend and lover of my own Lady of the Waters, who had seized the rains of the air even as my Lady seized the waters and snow of the earth. We spoke to She of the Clouds as well, and had even seen her kiss my Lady, although we could never be certain if it was love or hate that bound them. And my Lady had other lovers, mortal and god. Still, my Lady had been able to speak to She of the Clouds and persuade her to break a mortal drought or two, to let waters fill the earth and raise the corn, before (this was said in much softer voices)—both She of the Clouds and the Lady of Waters had dragged the Corn God into the mud and had their way with him, again and again.

The corn and crops had grown strong that year.

The God of Silver had only watched, but he had never had much of an interest in growing things.

And so. This was all whispered, not known, but the God of Silver had had less interaction with the other gods, less interaction with mortals, even if those moments with mortals had all been benevolent . . . .

"Why?" I asked. I could not puzzle it out.

"Because he stole my owl," the Trickster said.

I had not known the Trickster had an owl.

"He also killed your son."

• • •

I am here because of that son.

I am here because my son was dying, because my son *died*. The Lady of the Waters is one of the more . . . beneficent . . . of the gods, when she remembers to be: she knows tricks of healing, of removing pain. She had aided me in the last hours of my son's death, removing his pain, at least, although she had told me, with what almost seemed compassion, that she could not have saved him, that even the gods can do nothing when it is too late. I did not know whether I could believe her. I did know that I would do anything I could to prevent another death of a child, and so I nodded in acceptance of her words, and immediately began to learn anything I could of her.

She had never told me that the gods had killed him.

I took a sharp breath. I did not know whether I could believe him, or not, but he was already speaking of something else, as if the truth of my son's death was nothing. And perhaps, to him, it was nothing, although at his words the dull pain I carried, as a constant, had flared into agony. He was speaking of boxes and balls and lights; I could only half listen.

"I do not claim this will be simple," he said.

That I could respond to. "No," I said, allowing the irony to fill my voice. "You simply claim that I can go to a moon—a moon—and kill a god. I fail to see the complexity."

"I was thinking more that you would need some very special clothing."

I gestured at the wheeled chair beside my bed. "And this?"

"I do not think that will be a problem on the moon."

I had never had a portrait done of my son. I had *meant* to, eventually—artists were expensive, but not entirely beyond my reach at the time—but I had always thought we would have time later. Later. I had always thought we would have a later.

I have no gift for recalling faces, no gift for picturing people in my mind. I try, oh how I try, but I am never sure, now, if the face I see when I think of him is his.

My hands were white on my chair. "Agreed."

None of the gods claim dominion over death.

And death claims no dominion over them.

He explained more to me, explained, over my protests, that this would have to be done tonight, when both moons were dark, although he could not explain why. (Or, why, knowing that this must be done in the dark of the moons, he had not thought to prepare me for this earlier.) He gave instructions, some detailed, some not, and warnings, some detailed, most not.

"Remember this," he said, when I opened my mouth to protest again. "The God of Silver killed your child. As the others laughed, or wondered, or lost themselves in bright dreams."

Even if I could protest—even if I could be sure that he would not kill me if I refused—how could I refuse, after that?

Even if I could not trust a single word he said.

I would take the chair, he assured me again. It would be useful for more than traveling on a moon.

About the chair: I had been careless. Nothing more, nothing less. After my son . . . well, no need to dwell on that. The Lady of the Waters had saved me, but not healed me. I did not know why, and did not think to ask. Did not dare to ask; I did not want her reasonings, or her unreasonings. I adjusted, and I have no more to say of that.

I used a wheeled chair, in this house with its smoothed floors of stone and running streams and waterfalls. I lowered myself into hot and cold springs, and listened to the water, and wheeled myself where I would in this house, and sometimes elsewhere.

To this day, I cannot be certain where he actually sent me. It looked like a cave of blue and green and light, but it felt—*different.* I have no other words. But I had reason, later, to believe that in this, the Trickster was telling the truth, and I was on one of the moons. Or rather, *inside* one of the moons: I could not see the sky. (A disappointment, that; in the back of my mind I had rather wondered what my home would look like, from the sky.) I felt lighter. Untethered. Very untethered. I realized, in horror, that I was almost sliding up from my chair. I grabbed my handrests in panic, only then realizing that my hands had been enclosed in some sort of white gloves, and were light and clumsy at the same time. I sucked in a panicked breath—and nearly choked on it. This was not the air I was used to, but something else, with an odd half stink to it that I could barely recognize. I could feel my heart racing.

Something was on my head, something heavy and solid and light all at the same time. I drew up one hand—carefully clinging to the handrest of my chair with the other—and tapped at it gently. Something clear, like, and yet unlike, glass, I thought, although I could not tell, through the coverings of my hands. I could hear the echo of my own breath. My hands moved so *oddly* in this place. I looked down at my legs. I swallowed again. Perhaps I could—

I pushed down with my hands, harder than I meant to, and let go of the chair, finding myself floating *up.* I could not help it; even in my terror, I grinned at this, even as I found myself floating down, lightly, as everything was here. I saw my feet touch the ground, spread out my arms in instinct—

—and saw my legs collapse, even in the lightness. My arms and hands followed. I would need to return to my chair.

I said that I had adjusted. Not that it had been easy.

Returning to the chair was harder than it sounds. I'd never had problems pulling myself around with hands and arms before, but the blue and greenness of that cave, combined with whatever was wrapped around my head, badly distorted my vision, and my weight and body felt all wrong. I pulled, only to find myself lighter than expected, crashing into two rocks almost impossible to see in the colors. And sliding along the ground, with my body so light, was nearly impossible. But I managed it, hand over hand at last, climbing into the chair and twisting my body around. I took another deep breath.

Look for the light, the Trickster had whispered, before I had blacked out and found myself here, but *everything* in this cave—cave? Moon? I could not decide—was light. I turned my head about, difficult though that was under the circumstances, and found a place where the blue light seemed to be a little brighter, and began to wheel myself there.

Easy and difficult. No one had thought to smooth the floor for me—a common practice of mortals and immortals. And I was completely unused to the strange *lightness* of the place; a single push sent me rushing forward, almost bouncing into a rock. Maneuvering around that rock took its own care.

But I could not help grinning. I might be headed to kill a god, but *gods,* this lightness was *fun.*

So much fun that I didn't hear the footsteps behind me, or notice the curtain of silver and blue until I rolled through it.

My years at the House of the Lady of Waters had not been . . . evil, exactly. No. They had been good. In that House, I had found a measure of contentment, of peace, among my new-found sisters. I had begun healing as duty, but soon found it something more, even taken a certain joy in memorizing endless lists of herbs, in determining when we could apply to the Lady for mercy, and when we should not. The floors of the House were wide and flat, separated by curtains and screens easy to shift and move. My patients watched me with mingled hope and disbelief, and those who could not be saved listened to tales of my son, my mother, my grandfather. I had known pain, and so I could hold them.

Contentment. Peace. Even, at times, a certain joy, even when I wept.

But never *fun.*

Behind the curtain, a room, of sorts. Words fail me when I try to explain this second place. To begin with, it was large—beyond large. Vaster than any room I had ever seen before in my life, or would, I suspect, ever see, so long I could not see the end of it. And high: I could have easily stacked the temple of the Lady of Waters four times over, and still not reached its ceiling, and that temple was no short building. Like the caves I had passed through, it was filled with blue and green light, but somehow brighter, and I could see more lights—lamps, perhaps, although nothing like any lights I had seen before—scattered about the room. The pinpricks of light that dotted the ceiling, shining blue and green, might be more of those lamps; I could not tell. Whatever the Trickster placed upon my head also distorted my vision.

But not enough to keep me from from seeing the *other* oddness of the room: it was filled, even in its vastness, with *things*. Boxes made of some odd shimmering material, furniture, stacked up neatly for the most part, with a large table here and there holding more boxes, or, oddly, *pictures*—pictures that, when I looked at them, seemed to move. No, not *seemed*. They *did* move. Why would anyone put a picture like that upon a table, instead of placing it in a position of honor against a wall, with lights shining upon it?

Although the walls here seemed very far away.

And between the tables and boxes and pictures, other objects that looked so strange I could not even begin to guess their purpose. All, naturally, littering the floor, making navigation with my chair difficult to impossible, even without the strange feeling of lightness.

"So that's the trick," I said, through gritted teeth.

I should have seen it: it featured in a thousand tales of the gods: the quest that ended in the impossible task, solved only with the unexpected aid of those helped along the way. (A symbol, my mother told me, of the importance of small kindnesses, a quality not associated with many of the gods.)

Not that I had quested, exactly, or taken a particularly long journey—it could not have been more than a few hours after my arrival here. But I had certainly been given the impossible task.

I did not believe this was his last trick.

They claim the gods can love. We had seen it, sometimes, in the House of the Lady of the Waters; we had heard and sung the tales. I had wept, hearing of the lost love of the Dreamweaver and the Lord of Rats, now immortal enemies. (And thus, the song sang, the danger of dreaming of rats.)

They claim.

No one had claimed that the gods kept boxes and boxes and boxes hidden on a moon.

It might have been days later, or merely hours. All I knew was my bladder hurt, my hands hurt, my neck hurt. Whatever the Trickster had wrapped me in was distinctly uncomfortable.

And I had found it—or rather, *them*.

Completely by mistake. I had thought, perhaps, that an odd tube-shaped implement might conceal what I was looking for—it was as good a place as any, and I was tired of boxes that would not open and empty boxes and boxes filled with some sort of metal strings. I had pushed my wheels, hard, in the hopes of bouncing over some smaller objects scattered along the floor, something that had worked all too well, sending my chair flying into a box and tipping it over. Tipping me over as well.

By the time I managed to right myself and the chair—a task made easier by the odd lightness of the place, and considerably harder by these wrappings I was in and the growing pain in my bladder, I was ready to curse every god past damnation and kill them by strangling them myself. No matter that the gods were supposedly immune to such things; I was angry enough to make it work. I was about to cry out to the Trickster to beg to return, to see if I could someone trick *him*—

And I saw them.

As the Trickster had described: small metallic balls, vibrating, almost *humming,* I thought. Thirteen of them. They looked so *innocent.* Simple. Nothing more than children's toys.

How could these possibly harm a god?

I had always thought, always believed, that the gods did not slay us because they were too busy with their own games against one another. But I could not deny that many mortals had died in these games.

If the gods were in balance . . .

Did that mean they would be able to stop the beneficent acts of the Lady of the Waters? Of She of the Clouds?

I did not know. *Gods,* if I only knew more of the gods!

A trick, the Trickster had said. He would know, certainly, and yet . . .

The balls had tumbled to the floor and rolled about. I would have to pick them up, one by one, from the chair. While wrapped in something that made it nearly impossible to bend over from the chair to the floor. I could tumble to the floor, I thought, especially in this *lightness,* and roll around until I had gathered all the balls, and then drag myself up in the chair again. Or I could continue to search through the boxes and items on the table for something that would help me grab the balls from my chair . . . .

. . . I rolled myself off my chair and onto the floor.

I hit it softly, gently—*gods,* this place could be such fun, if I were not in such pain—and began to roll and pull myself towards the balls. *Careful.* The last thing I wanted to do was push the balls away by accident . . . .

. . . my glove covered one of them.

Bells. Bells. Everywhere, bells—

The gods are not, as mortals, confined to a single shape, or name, or sound, or word, shifting at a thought from one thing to another.

It is one of many reasons we eye birds and rats so warily.

I had, however, never heard that they took the shape of bells.

A shower of simmering silver. No. A cloud. No. A column—pointless to describe this; I did not have the words. I did not think any mortal had the words. But I did not question what it was.

The God of Silver. And another, a figure shrouded in a cloak and hood, leaning upon an iron cane. The Chained One.

The Trickster had failed to mention *that* possibility.

I hurriedly began to pull myself towards my chair—rolling over more of the balls as I did so. The sound of the bells grew overwhelming. If the gods spoke to me, I could not hear them. I could not even hear myself. I dragged myself up to my chair, but not before crashing it into more tables, more boxes, and turned the chair to face them.

It would have been easier if I could have seen their faces. I had thought the Trickster terrifying, but this was far worse.

"You will return that," said a voice, filled with silver. *Outside,* and yet, *inside* my head, all at once, echoing, the way the Lady of the Waters voice would sound on her visits. The way the Trickster's voice had not.

The God of Silver killed your child. As the others laughed, or wondered, or lost themselves in bright dreams.

"Wait," said a second voice, filled with iron. "This has the touch of the Trickster upon it."

"And a pathetic touch, even for him. *Look* at her."

I was certainly looking at him.

"I see a certain darkness." If iron could be curious, this was. "Tell us. Why do you believe you are here, child?"

I did not know if they would know a lie, or not, even if I could have thought of one. "My son."

"Ah." No compassion in that iron. "So beautiful, that darkness."

"And so easily illuminated." The contempt, the dismissal, sang through my mind. "So fortunate, for mortals, that their deaths can bring so much light."

I had grown to . . . live . . . with the loss of my son, if not accept it. It had been my fault, I knew; if I had only come to the Lady of the Waters sooner, if I had only learned healing sooner, paid more attention to what was important, rather than what was not— The old familiar pathways of guilt and longing filled my mind. Easier to feel guilt, in some ways, than to miss my child, to long for his crinkled smile, the way he was constantly but constantly underfoot, crowing, crying, laughing—

I had never loved anything, or any other person, as much. I doubted the gods could understand that kind of love.

• • •

The words echoed in the room, in my voice. I swallowed, and fumbled in my lap for one of the balls.

For a brief moment, I allowed myself to think of the Lady of Waters.

I threw the ball at the silver light.

The silver *shifted,* and I could see the ball continue its flight, down to the end of this impossibly long room . . .

"*Damn,*" I said.

The silver cloud—column—shower—whatever it was—grew larger, more brighter. It was coming towards me. In desperation I grabbed the next thing I could—a box covered in red symbols on a nearby table—lifted it, and *threw* it. Too hard: I had not accounted for its seeming lack of weight, and it sped through the room faster than I could have imagined.

Someone—it might have been me, but I do not think so—shouted, "No!" and the bell sound *changed,* to a sound I have never heard before, a terrible whine and shriek and pulsing sound all at once, and the world *exploded* into fire and light and—

In their way, all the gods do tricks. Deliberately, to entertain the eternal sameness of their lives, and mistakenly, not knowing how mortals view their doings and broken promises.

But the Trickster made such doings his life. Even our mortal lives were filled with the tales of his ruses and deceits, the games he had played on mortals and his fellow gods. They had even banished him, from time to time (although some tales claimed this was only to restore the balance and their luck, and the Trickster was the easiest to remove), never to the gain of mortals.

He could, when he chose, be beneficial: win a game against him, and find a pot of gold in your home. Lose a game, and find yourself a bird, or granted a harp that would sing only insults. Win a game against him, and find your clothing gone. Lose a game, and find yourself the ruler of an empire.

The gods themselves could not trust him. Nor could I.

Light, bursting into a thousand pieces and spinning and spinning and spinning and spinning and oh *gods* was I sick so sick and everything was dark and light and colored and dim and I was falling and falling and I would never hear again and ah the light and the darkness—

It was not he who killed your child.

Green, green rocks flying past me, spinning.

But it was also not he who failed to save him.

I do not remember the rest of that fall.

I have heard three tales of the coming of mortals:

One, that the gods, in their beginnings, saw endless fire and water and mist, and wanted something that would change, that would die and be reborn. And so they made plants, and later animals, and at length, craving speech, mortals. Mortals who in their quarrels and loves and above all, *deaths,* would always be different, even as they always remained the same, always repeating their lives again and again.

Two, that our gods did not create us at all. That, traveling from a place to another place, they encountered us, mortals, created by other gods, and decided to settle here, and watch.

Three, that we were not created by any gods at all, but merely, like the gods, thrown up by the universe, in its ongoing chaos of fire and stars and water and heat. Pure random chance that they are gods, doomed to watch the universe live and die, and we are not, doomed to see only a portion of life and death.

I do not know the truth of any of these tales.

I awoke wrapped in blankets from my own bed, on the small balcony just outside my room. My other wrappings had been removed; I could feel the chair against my back, and the hard lumps there. At some point, I must have finally emptied my bladder—I tried not to think about that too much—but someone had dried and cleaned me. A glass of water had been left by my chair; I seized it, and drank deeply. I pressed my fingers—my unwrapped fingers, that could *feel* and move freely—against my arm rests. Real. Solid.

Alive. I had somehow lived through *that.*

My *chair* had somehow lived through that.

The gods can work miracles, at need.

I placed my face in my hands, for a moment. When I looked up, the night was full of shattered light.

When I was injured, I had to learn balance all over again. The balance I had learned as a child was lost completely, and I must need learn new things.

I learned all that I knew from mortal teachers. The gods, I learned, know nothing of balance.

A terrible description, *shattered light,* but I can think of no other word: streaks of burning green, crackling and dimming and reappearing again. Where they reached the ground, they set it on fire, so that the earth, too, was throwing up flames. I could hear—I thought I could hear—screams in the distance. I certainly heard cries behind me, in the house of Lady of the Waters.

And I heard his footsteps behind me. He wanted me to hear; the gods can move silently if they wish. He wanted me to turn towards him.

I do not know when we began to worship the gods, to bring them offerings of gems and food and clothing, to build high temples where they might sit and dispense judgment. Or miracles. I do not know if it was our idea, or theirs, if they needed the stimulation, or if we needed the reassurance, the hope of occasional aid.

I only know when I stopped.

I didn't thank him for saving my life. For one thing I wasn't sure he had. For another, I wasn't grateful. I didn't bother to tell him my story either; I was certain he already knew it.

"You lying bastard," I said instead. "You didn't want me to kill a god at all. You wanted me to do *that*."

No need to point, but I did anyway, at the falling green lights, the fires sparking against the earth.

"Well, I wouldn't have *minded*."

"Not that I could have done it anyway," I said. I saw them again, standing against the flames and fires, vanishing before the fires could touch them. "Could I? Those *balls*—you placed them near something else, that *box*, hoping I would feel threatened and use that instead, and—"

I choked on my own words.

"It's not a trick if you tell the process."

"And is that a trick?" I said, pointing at the sky again.

"No," said the Trickster quietly, and I knew—how I knew—he was telling the truth.

I could not explain it, but I could feel it, the sudden lack of *balance* in the world. Not from any evidence or measurement, but present, none the less.

And the change did not favor mortals. I could feel that as well.

How the loss of one moon—a moon that blocked our sight of the stars—could do that, I could not have explained, but I knew it, without needing to be told, as well as I knew that the screams behind me were no trick as well.

"Get out," I said. Reckless beyond thought, to order a god, but I was too angry, in too much pain, to spend much time thinking. "Get *out*, you miserable bastard."

"Only after I give you a gift."

"Get *out*."

"I owe you."

"You do," I said through gritted teeth. "You used me, used my child, used me knowing that the other gods would never see a woman in a chair as a threat, would never stop me from picking up whatever that was, and you destroyed a moon and helped destroy my race. So get *out*."

"Oh, I don't think I owe you for any of that," said the Trickster. "That was just part of the trick. No. I owe you for the lie."

"*The* lie? You told thousands. Get. Out."

No one could accuse the Trickster of following instructions. "I lied about the God of Silver. In part. He did steal my owl."

I wished that a mortal fist could harm his immortal skin.

144

"But it was not he who killed your child. That was a toy of the Lord of Rats and the Crippled One. If you had killed the God of Silver, or the Chained One—well. You would have killed an innocent."

If this was meant as comfort, it failed. Rage filled me all over again.

"But—and this is important—that was the only lie. I left things unsaid, but only those words spoke untruths. Nonetheless. For those words, and for your assistance, a gift."

A burning touch of lips against my forehead.

"I don't want any of your damned gifts."

He spread three cups upon the long table I kept against the wall, to store flowers and books and other things. Before, when those things had still mattered. "You will want this one," he said, and explained.

When my son was born, I sang all the songs to him: the sleeping songs, the baby songs, the songs of mortals and gods.

I told him tales as he grew, eyes large in his tiny face, tales of warning and danger. Tales of the Trickster. Tales of rats. Tales of chains.

The Trickster vanished as he had come, unseen, unwanted. I stayed in my chair, watching the falling remnants of the moon, until, tired beyond all exhaustion, I fell asleep.

We have three tales of dreams: that they are ours, only ours, untouched by gods, and that dreams are the only place where we can roam free of the gods, even when they seem to walk in our dreams. Or that they are not ours at all, but creations of the Dreamweaver, who spins our dreams on dark wheels and laces them into our mind. Or that they are ghosts, unable to journey to the land of the dead, or be reborn, whether by a trick of gods or mortals or balance or luck, and so they crawl into our minds in sleep, for comfort or sorrow.

That night, I dreamt of my son, laughing on the moon, and behind him, silver rain and chains and laughing rats.

I was woken by the scent of water.

"They tell me you have destroyed one of the moons," the Lady of the Waters said, her voice musical, flowing, overwhelming. Far stronger than the Trickster; far more *there* than either of the two that I had met—and not killed—upon the moon.

I kept my head bowed, and did not answer. I had no need: even in the day sky, green streaks were still falling, and the Trickster was no place to be found.

"You will not want my congratulations."

That, at least, was true. I did not dare to look at her, to become lost in her beauty, her kindness . . .

"And what are these?"

"Gifts from him, my Lady," I said, allowing the weariness to seep through my voice.

"Ah," she said, moving forward to look at the table, where the three cups rested, upside down.

So *almost* human, her curiosity. She allowed me to hear one footfall, then another; I could almost think her a woman like myself. Could almost forget.

"And what were you to do with these gifts?"

A sharpness in that waterfall.

"Store a ball he took from the moon," I said, wearily. "He said it was too dangerous for me to touch, but that I should live with it, in remembrance."

I thought—I thought—that her eyes looked more alert. Or greedier. I could not have told; even after all this, I was still helpless at deciphering the expressions of immortals. I could see the shimmer of her robes as they swayed. "Three cups. Three cups. In one of these, you say?"

"Yes, Lady."

"Left by *him*."

Her back was to me. I decided I could lift my eyes, just a little.

Her glowing hands—hands of water, hands of light—were moving above the three cups, shifting them about the table, tapping each lightly. I wondered if she could see through the cups, if the gods had been granted yet another gift we did not have, or if she could hear something, sense something, that I could not. Had the Trickster foreseen this?

I did not dare take the risk. "The wrong one—the wrong *ones*—will kill. Will blast the other moon, and—Lady, I beg you."

She must have heard something in my voice. "Trust me, my child. Trust me."

Her voice was a rush of water. I took a deep breath, and placed my fingers on the wheels of my chair, and pushed.

My chair is generally silent, but not now: I thought I could hear every clatter, every movement of the boards. I heard water. I heard cracks. I heard the ball in my hand sink into her lower back, pushed by my weight and the weight of my chair. I heard her soft cry, a sound like shattered glass, only more musical, more beautiful. I remembered the song she had sung, as she stood by his bedside and watched my son die.

And against my hand, the Lady of Waters *turned* into water, a great rush of gray and water that splashed and pushed against me. I had not expected that; had not braced my chair against the water, and found myself pulling the right wheel of my chair with one hand as with my left I continued to hold the stone against the water. Until a pool of water formed, beneath my chair, reflecting the colors of the room.

Ordinary water. Even I, mere mortal, did not need the sudden stillness of the stone in my hand to tell that. Even I, mere mortal, could feel the *shift* in the air.

The rush of water had knocked down all three cups. Nothing had been under them.

• • •

As I have said, I have never loved anything so much.

He knew that much truth, the Trickster.

I wheeled myself out to the balcony.

The stars glittered above me. I stared and stared. The other moon still floated someplace in the sky, I knew, the moon I had not visited, and doubtless never would. The moon that promised magic and dreams. The moon that, on its own, would still allow us to glimpse the stars.

I bowed my head, made myself look as weak, as pitiable, as *mortal* as possible. They would be coming soon, I knew, to mourn their sister, their lover, their rival, to rejoice in their reborn balance. I gripped the stone in my hand, concealed beneath my robes. I would not allow this balance to remain for long.

The Book of Phoenix
(Excerpted from The Great Book)
NNEDI OKORAFOR

*There is no book about me. Well, not yet. No matter. I shall create it myself;
it's better that way. To tell my tale, I will use the old African tools of story:
Spoken words. They're more trustworthy and they'll last longer. And during
shadowy times, spoken words carry farther than words typed or written. My
beginnings were in the dark. We all dwelled in the darkness, mad scientist and
specimen, alike. This was when the goddess Ani's still slept, when her back was
still turned. Before she grew angry at what she saw and pulled in the blazing
sun. My story is called The Book of Phoenix. And it is short because it was . . .
accelerated.*

I'd never known any other place. The 13th floor of Tower 7 was my home.
Yesterday I realized it was a prison, too. Granted, maybe I should have suspected
something. The two-hundred-year-old marble skyscraper had many dark sides
and I knew most of them. There were 39 floors, and on almost every one was
an abomination. I was an abomination. I had read many books and this was
clear to me. However, this place was still my home. **Home**: a. One's place of
residence. Yes, it was my home.

They gave me all the 3D movies I could watch, but it was books that did it
for me. A year ago, they gave me an e-reader packed with 700,000 books of
all kinds. When it came to information, I had access to everything I wanted.
That was part of their research.

Research. This was what happened in Tower 7. There were similar towers
around the world but Tower 7 was my home, so this one was the one I
studied. I had several classified books on Tower 7. One discussed each floor
and some of the types of abominations found on them. I'd listened to audios
of the spiritual tellings of long dead African and Native American shamans,
sorcerers and wizards. I'd read the Torah, the Bible, and the Koran. I studied
The Buddha and meditated until I saw Krishna. And I read countless books
on the sciences of the world. Carrying all this in my head, I understood
abomination. I understood the purpose of Tower 7. Until yesterday.

In Tower 7, there was "transformative" genetic engineering, the in-vitro fertilization of organic robots, "rejuvenation" surgery on the ancient near-dead, the creation of weaponized weeds, the insertion and attaching of both mechanical and cybernetic parts to human bodies. There were people created in Tower 7, some were deformed, some were mentally ill, some were just plain dangerous, and none were flawless. Yes, some of us were dangerous. I was dangerous.

Then there was the tower's lobby on the ground floor that projected a different picture. I'd never been down there but my books described it as an earthly wonderland, full of creeping vines covering the walls and small trees growing from artistically crafted holes in the floor. In the center was the main attraction. Here grew the thing that brought people from all over the world to see the Tower 7 Lobby (*only* the lobby; there were no tours of the rest of the building).

A hundred years ago, one of the landscapers planted a tree in the lobby's center. On a lark, some scientists from the 9th floor emptied an experimental solution into the tree's pot of soil. The substance was for enhancing and speeding up arboreal growth. The tree grew and grew. In a place where people thought like normal human beings, they would have uprooted the amazing tree and placed it outdoors. However, this was Tower 7 where boundaries were both contained and pushed. When the tree began touching the lobby's high ceiling in a matter of weeks, they constructed a large hole so that it could grow through the second floor. They did the same for the third, fourth, fifth. The great tree has since earned the name of "The Backbone" because it grew through all 39 of Tower 7's floors.

My name is Phoenix. I was mixed and grown in a lab on the 13th floor. One of my doctors thinks my name came from the birthplace of my egg's donor. I've looked it up. Phoenix, Arizona is the full name of the place. However, from what I've read about my floor, even the scientists who forced my existence don't know the names of donors. So, I doubt this. I think they named me Phoenix because of what I was, an "accelerated organism." I was born two years ago but I looked, behaved and felt like a forty-year-old woman. My doctors said the acceleration would stop now that I was "matured." To them, I was like a plant they grew for the sake of harvesting information.

Who do I mean by "them," you must wonder? *All* of THEM, the "Big Eye"— the Tower 7 scientists, lab assistants, lab technicians, doctors, administrative workers, guards and police. We of the tower called them "Big Eye" because they watched us. All the time, they watched us, though not closely enough to prevent the inevitable.

I could read a 500-page book in two minutes. My brain absorbed the information and stories like a sponge. Up until two weeks ago, aside from mealtimes, looking out the window, running on my treadmill, and meetings with doctors, I spent my days with my e-reader. I'd sit in my room for hours consuming words upon words that became images upon images, ideas upon ideas. Now they gave me paper-made books, removing the books when I finished them. I liked the e-reader more. It took up less space and I could reread things when I wanted.

I stared out the window watching the cars and trucks below and the other skyscrapers across from me as I touched a leaf of my hoya plant. They'd given the plant to me five days ago and already it was growing so wildly that it was creeping across my windowsill and had wrapped around the chair I'd put there. It had grown two feet overnight. I didn't think they'd noticed. No one ever said anything about it. I realize now that they *had* noticed. The plant was not a gesture of kindness; it was just part of the research. They didn't really care about me. But Saeed cared about me.

Saeed is dead, Saeed is dead, Saeed is dead, I thought over and over, as I caressed one of my plant's leaves. I yanked, breaking the leaf off. *Saeed, my only friend.* I crumpled the leaf in my restless hand; its green, earthy smell might as well have been blood.

Yesterday Saeed had seen something terrible. Not long afterwards, he'd sat across from me during dinner-hour with eyes wide like boiled eggs, unable to eat. He couldn't give me any details. He said no words could describe it.

"What does your heart tell you about this place?" he'd earnestly asked.

I'd only shrugged, frustrated with him for not telling me what he'd seen that was so awful.

He leaned forward, lowering his voice. "You read all those books . . . why don't you feel rebellion? Don't you ever dream of getting out of here? Away from all the Big Eye?"

"Rebellion against whom?" I whispered, confused.

He laughed bitterly, sat back and shook his head. He took my hand, squeezed it and let it go. "Eat your jallof rice, Phoenix."

I tried to get him to eat his crushed glass. This was his favorite meal and it bothered me to see him push his plate away. But he wouldn't touch it. Before we returned to our separate quarters, he asked for my apple. I assumed he wanted to paint it. He always liked to paint when he was depressed. I'd given it to him without a thought and he'd slipped it into his pocket. The Big Eye allowed it, though they frowned upon taking food from the dining room, even if you didn't plan to eat it.

His words didn't touch me until nighttime when I lay in my bed. Yes, somewhere deep, deep in my psyche I *did* wish to get out of the tower and see the world, be away from the Big Eye. I wanted to see those things that I saw in all the books I read. "Rebellion," I whispered to myself.

They told me the news in the morning during breakfast-hour. I'd been sitting alone looking around for Saeed. The others, the woman with the twisted spine who could turn her head around like an owl, the man who never spoke with his mouth but always had people speaking to him, the three women who all looked and sounded alike, the bushy-bearded man who looked like a wizard from a novel, the baboon who spoke in sign language, the woman whose sweater did not hide her four large breasts, the two men joined at the hip who were always randomly laughing, the woman with the lion claws and teeth, these people spoke to each other and never to me. Only Saeed spoke to me.

One of my doctors sat facing me. The African-looking one who wore the shiny black wig made of synthetic hair, Bumi. They always had her deal with me when there was upsetting news. My entire body tightened. She touched my hand and I pulled it away. She smiled sympathetically and told me a terrible thing. Saeed hadn't drawn the apple. He'd eaten it. And it killed him. My mind went to one of my books. The Bible. I was Eve and he was Adam.

I could not eat. I could not drink. I would not cry. Not in the dining hall.

Hours later, I was in my room lying on my bed, eyes wet, mind reeling. Saeed was dead. I had skipped lunch and dinner, but I still wasn't hungry. I was hot. The scanner on my wall would start to beep soon. Then they would come get me soon. For tests. I shut my eyes, squeezing out tears. They evaporated as they rolled down my hot cheeks. "Oh God," I moaned. The pain of losing him burned in my chest. "Saeed. What did you see?"

Saeed was human. More human than me. I met him the first day they allowed me into the dining hall with the others. I was one year old; I must have looked twenty. He was sitting alone about to do something insane. There were many others in the room who caught my eye. The two conjoined men were laughing hard at the sight of me. The baboon was jumping up and down while rapidly signing to the woman with lion claws and teeth. However, Saeed had a spoon in his hand and a bowl full of broken glass before him. I stood there staring at him as others stared at me. He dug the spoon into the chunks of glass and put it in his mouth. I could hear him crunching from where I stood. He smiled to himself, obviously enjoying it.

Driven by sheer curiosity, I walked over and sat across from him with my plate of spicy doro wat. He eyed me with suspicion but he didn't seem angry or mean, at least not to the best of my limited social knowledge. I leaned forward and asked what was on my mind, "What's it like to eat that?"

He blinked, surprised. Then he grinned. His teeth were perfect- white, shiny, and shaped like the teeth in drawings and doctored pictures in magazines. Had they removed his original teeth and replaced them with ones made of a more . . . durable stuff? "The taste is as soft and delicate as the texture is crunchy. I'm not in pain, only pleasure," he said in a voice accented in a way that I'd never heard. But then again, the only accents I'd ever heard were from the Big Eye doctors and guards.

"Tell me more," I said.

After that, Saeed and I became friends. I loved words and he needed to spill them. He could not read, so I would tell him about what I read, at least in the hours of breakfast, lunch and dinner. He was from Egypt where he had been an orphan who never went hungry because he could always find something to eat. Rotten rice, date pits, even the wooden skewer sticks of *kebabs*, he had a stomach like a goat. They brought him to the tower when he was ten, nine years ago. He never told me exactly how or why they made him the way he was. It didn't matter. What mattered was that we were who we were and we were there.

Saeed told me of places I had never seen with my own eyes. He used the words of a poet who used his tongue to see. Saeed was an artist with his hands, too. He had the skill of the great painters I read about in my books. He most loved to draw those foods he could no longer eat. Human food. Portraits of loaves of bread. Bowls of thick egusi soup and balls of fufu. Bouquets of lamb and beef kebabs. Fried eggs with white cheese. Plates of chickpeas. Pitchers of orange juice. Piles of roasted corn. They allowed him to bring the paintings to mealtime for everyone to view. I guess even we deserved the pleasures of art.

Saeed could survive on glass, metal shavings, crumbles of rust, sand, dirt, those things that would be left behind if human beings finally blew themselves up. However, eating a piece of bread would kill him as eating a big bowl of sharp pieces of glass would kill the average human being.

He took my apple and that night, he ate it. Then his stomach and intestines hemorrhaged and he was dead before morning. I never got to tell him what was happening to me. It might have given him hope; it would have reminded him that things would change. I wiped a tear. I loved Saeed.

As grief overwhelmed me for the first time in my life, I pressed a hand against the thick glass of my window. I'd never been outside. I wanted to go outside. Saeed had escaped by dying. I wanted to escape, too. If he wasn't happy here, then neither was I.

I wiped hot sweat from my brow. My room's scanner began to beep as my body's temperature soared. The doctors would be here soon.

When it first started to happen two weeks ago, only I noticed it. My hair started to fall out. I am an African by genetics, my hair was very coily and my skin was very, very dark. They kept my hair shaven low because neither they nor I knew what to do with it when it grew out. I could never find anything in my books to help. They didn't care for style in Tower 7, anyway . . . although the woman down the hall had very long silky white hair and Big Eye lab assistants came by every two days to help her brush and braid it . . . despite the fact that the woman had the teeth and claws of a lion.

I was sitting on my bed, looking out the window when I suddenly grew very hot. For the last few days, my skin had been dry and ashy no matter how much hydrated water they gave me to drink. Doctor Bumi brought me a large jar of shea butter and applying it soothed my skin to no end. However, this day, hot and feverish, my skin seemed to dry as if I were in a desert.

I felt beads of sweat on my head and when I rubbed my short, short hair, it wiped right off, hair and sweat alike. I ran to my bathroom, quickly showered, washing my head thoroughly, toweled off and stood before the large mirror. I'd lost my eyebrows, too. But this wasn't the worst of it. I rubbed the shea butter into my skin to give myself something to do. If I stopped moving, I'd start crying with panic.

I don't know why they gave me such a large mirror in my bathroom. Large and round, it stretched from wall to wall. Therefore, I saw myself in full glory. As I slathered the thick yellow nutty-smelling cream onto my drying skin, it was as if I was harboring a sun deep within my body and that sun wanted to come out. Under the dark brown of my skin, I was glowing. I was light.

I pulsed, feeling a wave of heat and slight vibration within my flesh. "What is this?" I whispered, scurrying back to my bed where my e-reader lay. I wanted to look up the phenomena. In all my reading, I had never read a thing about a human being, accelerated or normal, heating up and glowing like a firefly's behind. The moment I picked the e-reader up, it made a soft pinging sound. Then the screen went black and began to smoke. I threw it on the floor and the screen cracked as it gently burned. My room's smoke alarm went off.

Psss! The hissing sound was soft and accompanied by a pain in my left thumbnail. It felt as if someone stuck a pin into it. "Ah!" I cried, instinctively pressing on my thumb. As I held my hand up to my eyes, I felt myself pulse again.

There was a splotch of black in the center of my thumbnail like old blood but blacker. Burned flesh. All specimen, creature, creation in the building had a diagnostics chip implanted beneath his, her or its fingernail, claw, talon or horn. I'd just gone off the grid.

Not thirty seconds passed before they came bursting into my room with guns and syringes at ready, all aimed at me as if I were a wild rabid beast destroying all that they had built.

"Get down! DOWN!" they shouted. One man grabbed me, probably with the intent of throwing me on the bed so he could cuff me. He screamed, staring at his burned, still smoking hand. Someone shot me in the leg. It felt like someone had kicked my leg with a metal foot. I sunk to the floor, pain washing over me like a second layer of more intense heat. I would have been done for if someone else had not shouted for the others to hold their fire.

Thankfully, I healed fast and the bullet had gone straight through my leg. If it hadn't, I don't know what would have happened due to my extreme body temperature. One minute I was staring with shock at the blood oozing from my leg. Then next, I blacked out. I woke in a bed, my body cool, my leg bandaged. When they returned me to my room, the scanner was in place to monitor me since I could not hold an implant. They replaced my bed sheets with a heavy heat-resistant sheet similar in material to my new clothes. The carpet was gone, too. For the first time, I saw that the floor beneath the carpet was solid whitish marble.

When I grew hot and luminous like this, electronics died or exploded in my hands. This was why they started giving me paper books. They were difficult to read, as I couldn't turn the pages as quickly as I could with the e-reader. And the paper books they had were limited and old. And they could monitor what I was reading. Although now I realize with the e-reader they were probably monitoring my choices, too.

I didn't tell Saeed about the heating and glowing because at the time I didn't want to worry him. I enjoyed our talks so much. I wish I had told him.

The door slid open and my doctors came in, Debbie and Bumi. I took a deep breath to calm myself. When I was calm, though the heat did not go away, it decreased, as did the glow.

"How do you feel?" Bumi asked, as she took my wrist to check my pulse. She hissed, dropping it.

"Hot," I said.

She glared at me and I shrugged thinking something I had not thought until Saeed was dead- *You should have asked first.*

"Open," Debbie said, placing the heavy-duty thermometer into my mouth.

I saw these two women every day. I knew their names, nothing more.

"She's not glowing that brightly," Bumi said, typing something onto her handheld. I resisted the urge to grab it and hold it in my hands until it exploded. Saeed was dead because of these people. I steadied myself, thinking of the cool places sometimes described in the novels I read. I once read a brief story about a man who froze to death in a forest. I thought about that.

"It might just be menopause approaching," Bumi said. "I believe the two factors are correlated."

I tuned out their talk and focused on my own thoughts. Escape. *How? What would they do to me? What did Saeed see? He said it was something on this floor.* My internal temperature was 130 degrees, but the temperature of my skin was 220. They couldn't take my blood pressure because the equipment would melt.

"We need to take her to the lab," Debbie said.

Bumi nodded. "As soon as the scanner says she's reached 300 degrees. We don't want her any higher or things around her will start to ignite."

They left. I paced the room. Restless. Angry. Distraught. They would be back soon.

How am I going to get out of here, I wondered. As if to answer my question, Mmuo walked into my room. He came through the wall across from my bed. My heart nearly jumped from my chest.

"Did you hear?" he asked, sitting on my bed.

I blinked, feeling the rush of sadness all over again. He was Saeed's friend, too. "Yes," I said.

"I'm sorry, Phoenix."

My face was wet and drying with sweat. "I'm getting out of here," I declared.

Mmuo grinned but it quickly turned to a frown. "What is wrong with you? I can feel you from here," he asked.

"I think it has something to do with how they made me. It's been happening for two weeks and it's getting worse."

We looked at each other, silent. I knew we were thinking the same thing but neither he nor I wanted to speak it. If we spoke of my name, I didn't think I'd be able to move, let alone run.

"Yes, that would make sense," he said.

His full name was Uzochukwu D'nnmma but he called himself Mmuo, which meant spirit in a Nigerian language. He was a hero to all those who were created or altered in Tower 7. Like Saeed, Mmuo had been taken from Africa. He said he was from "the jungles of Nigeria." I did not believe he was from any jungle. He spoke like a man who had known skyscrapers, office buildings and digital television. He knew how to disable the security doors on several of the floors and was known for causing trouble throughout the building. Not that he really needed to do so to get around the tower. Mmuo could walk through walls. The only walls he could not pass through were the walls that would get him out of Tower 7. Mmuo could not escape; obviously his abilities were created by Tower 7 scientists.

Mmuo was a tall thin man with skin the color of and as shiny as crude oil. He never wore clothes, for clothes could not pass through the walls with him. He stole what food he needed from the kitchens. He was the only person/creature who'd successfully escaped the Big Eye's clutches.

Why Tower 7's Big Eye tolerated him, I do not know. My theory is that they simply could not catch him. And since he was contained, they accepted the trouble he occasionally stirred up. Most of those in the tower were too isolated and damaged to be much trouble if freed, anyway.

"It looks like your skin is nothing but a veil over something greater," he said, after an appraising look. It was something Saeed would have said and the thought made my heart ache again.

"Can you open the door?" I finally said. "I . . . I want to see what is down the hall, near Saeed's room."

Mmuo met my gaze and held it.

I frowned. "What did Saeed see?" I asked.

He only looked away.

"Show me," I said, suddenly wanting to sob. "Then help me escape."

He moved close to me and I was sure he was going to hug me.

"Don't touch me," I said. "You'll . . . "

He raised a hand up and made to slap me across the face. "Don't move," he said. His hand passed right through my head. I felt only the slightest moment of pressure and there was a sucking sound.

"Wha . . ."

"Can you hear me?" I heard him loudly say through what sounded like a microphone. I looked around.

"Shhh! They'll hear you!" I hissed. I frowned. His lips hadn't moved.

"No," he said. He held his finger to his lips for me to quiet down and grinned, his yellow-white teeth shining, his black skin shining, too. *"They won't. You are hearing this in your head.*

"Not even the Big Eye know I can do this," he said aloud, but lowering his voice. "Whatever they did to make me able to pass through walls, I can pass it into people and they can hear me, until the tiny nanomites are sweated from their skin."

"I did this to a little boy on the fifth floor. He had a contagious cancer, so they kept him in isolation for tests. Hearing me talk to him from wherever I was kept him sane. At least, until he died."

His disease could have killed you, though, I thought.

He started to descend through the floor. *"Fifteen minutes,"* he said in my head, then he was gone.

I whipped off my pants and t-shirt and threw on a white dress they'd recently given me that was made of heat-resistant thin plastic. The dress was long but light and allowed me to move very freely. I didn't bother with shoes. Too heavy.

For a moment, I had a brief flash in my mind of actually stepping outside. Into the naked sunlight. I could do it. Mmuo would help me. He and I would both escape. I felt a rush of hope, then a rush of heat. The scanner on my wall beeped. I had reached over 300 degrees.

Just before the door slid open, I had the sense to spread some shea butter on my skin. I ran out of my room.

"If you want to see, turn right and then go straight. Do it quickly."

I jogged, my feet slapping the cool marble floor. The hallway was quiet and empty, and soon I was in a part of my floor that I had never graced. The side where they kept Saeed. *His prison,* I thought.

I crossed a doorway and the floor here was carpeted, plush and red. I paused, looking down. I had never seen red carpet. Before they took it out, the carpet in my quarters had been black and flat. I wanted to kneel down and run my hands over it. I knew it would feel so soft and fluffy.

"See what you must but you have to make it to the elevator in two minutes," Mmuo's voice suddenly said into my head. *"Go down the hall and turn left. You will see it. Hurry."*

"Ok," I said aloud. But he could not hear me. One-way communication. I ran down the red hallway. Through glass windows and doors, I could see lab assistants and scientists in labs. Each large room was partitioned by a thick wall. There was bulky equipment in most of the rooms. If I were careful, no one would notice me. After sneaking past three labs, I saw the one that Saeed saw. It had to be. I stopped, staring and moaning deep in my throat. This lab was much bigger than the others and ten black cameras hung from its high white ceiling.

There were two wall-sized sleek grey machines on both sides of the room. I could hear them humming. Powerful. Between them, the world fell away to . . . another world where it was daytime and all that was happening was perfectly bluntly brutally visible. There were old vehicles, trucks from long long ago, boxy, ineffective and weak. But strong enough to carry huge loads of cargo to dump into a deep pit. And that cargo consisted of human bodies. Hundreds of them. Dead. Not Africans. These dead people had pinkish pale skin and thin straight-ish hair like most of the Big Eye. When was this? Where was this? Why were the Big Eye scientists just *standing* there watching with their clipboards and ever-observing eyes?

It was not like watching a 3D movie. Even the best ones could never look this . . . true. Bodies. And I could *smell* them. The whole hallway reeked with their rot and feces and bile and the smoke of the trucks. My brain went to my books and recalled where I had seen this before. "Holocaust," I whispered, fighting the urge to turn to the side and vomit. I shut my watering eyes for a moment. I took a deep breath and nearly gagged on the stench. I opened my eyes.

This genocide happened during one of the early world wars. The Germans killed many of these people because they felt they were inferior or a threat or both. The book I read spoke as if wiping them out was the right thing to do. It certainly looked wrong to me. Were these Big Eye looking through time? Is this all they could do? Look? And why this time? For a moment, the portal disappeared and there was lots of scrambling, adjusting machines, pushing buttons, cursing. And then the portal reappeared showing the same activities, in the same time period in the same place. Happening.

I could feel the surge of heat in my body. Like a deep heart beat of crimson flames. I shuddered and felt it ripple over every surface of my skin. But I couldn't move. Saeed had probably stood here just like this, too. Acrid smoke stung my eyes. My feet were burning the red carpet. A fire alarm sounded. I ran.

The elevator was open. It was empty. I ran in and it quickly closed behind me. I wished Mmuo would say something. If it went up, I was caught. If it went nowhere, I was caught. If it went down, I might be caught, but I might escape, too. I shut my eyes and whispered, "Go down, go down, *please,* go down. Have to get out!" Sweat beaded and evaporated all over my confused body and the elevator quickly began to feel humid.

If I hadn't rubbed all that shea butter on my skin at the last minute, I'd have been in horrible pain, my skin drying and probably cracking. I was hot like the sun, there was a ringing in my ears, as if my own body had an alarm and it was going off, too. I looked at my hands. They were glowing a soft yellow. My entire body was glowing through my dress.

The elevator jerked upward. I grabbed the railing, pure terror shooting through me. At least, I would make it outside. I hoped I could take two breaths before they caught me. I sunk to the floor. Saeed was dead and I was still trapped. Tears dribbled from the corners of my eyes and hissed as they evaporated down my cheeks.

The elevator jerked again. "*Sorry about that,*" I heard Mmuo say in my head. He sounded distant. The elevator started moving down. I jumped up, grinning. I still had a chance. A louder alarm started to go off. They'd realized I was missing. "*I can get you to nine,*" he said. His voice was fading and I had to strain to hear it. "*Two stairways in there. Run to the emergency one on the other side of the greenhouse, straight ahead when the doors open. You'll be on the side of the greenhouse, just go straight ahead! Do NOT go near the center! There's . . .* " His voice faded away.

Had my heat burned away his nanomites? Probably. As the elevator flew down to the ninth floor, my feet burned the elevator floor. It came to a sudden stop and the doors opened. The blare of the Tower 7 alarm assaulted my ears but the most beautiful site I'd ever seen caressed my eyes. An expansive room full of trees, bushes, flowers, vines. In pots, on shelves, tangled within each other. I could see the city through the windows on my left. The sky was the deep rose of evening. I started quickly walking down the narrow path before me. Moss grew on the sides of trees. The air smelled green, fragrant, soily, I had never smelled anything like it.

I heard a rush of footsteps from amongst the plants to my right. Between the foliage, I could see them. Big Eye guards. In armor with shields, with guns.

"Hey!" one of them yelled, spotting me. All their guns went up. "Put your hands up. We will not hurt you." The one speaking was a woman. I could see her clearly. She was short with long brown straight hair. She had pale skin and a hard voice.

Behind me I could hear the elevator rumbling. I still didn't move. Saeed was dead. There was nothing for me here. I was two years old and I was forty years old. The marble beneath my feet absorbed my heat.

"Please, put your hands up," the woman pleaded. "You know what you are. We can stabilize you." She paused, obviously considering how much to tell me. I knew enough, though. Saeed was dead and it was all clear to me now.

"You're a weapon," the woman admitted. "If you wanted to know, now you know. I'm only here to help. You have to trust me. This wasn't supposed to happen, you being like this. Please, let us help you."

I heard the elevator doors opening just as I felt the light burst from me. There was warmth that started at my feet. It rolled up to my chest and pulsed out with a wave of heat. My shoulders jerked back and I stumbled to the side, getting a glimpse behind me. If I had blinked I still wouldn't have missed it. My skin prickled as my glow became a light green shine. The light steadily radiated from me, bathing every plant in the room. The guards behind me in the elevator and on the far right side of the room all ducked down and for a moment it was quiet enough where you could hear it. All the plants began to grow. Snapping, pulling, unfurling, creeping. Thick vines and even tree roots quickly crept, stretched and blocked the elevator door. Leaves, branches and stems grew so thick around the guards to my right that they were blocked from view. They didn't know I could do this.

The entire greenhouse swelled and flooded with foliage. Except a few steps ahead to my right. There was what I could only call a tunnel through the plants. It diagonally passed the cowering Big Eye. I ran into it just as the guards behind and to my right began to shoot toward where I'd initially been. Were they shooting through the plants or shooting at me, I do not know. And in many ways these two things were one of the same.

Mmuo had said to go forward to find the doorway. But I lost all sense of direction. So when I ended up standing before the giant glass dome I had no clue which way to run. My first thought was of the same book that spoke of the treacherous apple of knowledge. The Bible. Except that the man with enormous wings was not held up by any wooden cross. He was suspended in mid-air with his arms out and his legs tied together. His eyes were closed. His brown-feathered wings were stretched wide.

He was naked, his bronze-skinned body, muscled and very, very tall, at least compared to my six feet. He had Arab facial features like Saeed and a crown of wooly hair like mine. He was magnificent. Behind the glass dome was a rough wooden wall. The Backbone.

Behind me, I could hear them coming. Hacking and shooting through the plants and calling my name. I wasn't going to get out. I walked up to the glass and placed a hot hand on it. The glass was thick and very cool. Was there even air in there? Was that how they held him? Was it like being in outer space? What was space like for a creature made to fly?

His eyes opened. I gasped and jumped back. They were brown and soft kind eyes.

"Oh my God, Phoenix! Step BACK!" one of the guards screamed, shoving aside a bush. I noticed the guard did not point his gun. Nor did the others who emerged beside him. I looked back at the man with wings. He was looking right at me, no expression on his face. I was surrounded by guards, all begging me to step away, pleading that this creature was unique and dangerous. However, none of them came to capture me. I didn't move.

Seeing the Big Eye cower, seeing their fear and sheer horror had a strange effect on me. I felt powerful. I felt lethal. I felt hopeful, though all was hopeless. I turned to the caged man and my hope evolved into rage. Even *he* was a prisoner here. I vowed that if I didn't get out, at least he would.

For the first time I did it voluntarily. I was already so hot and I grew hotter when I reached into myself, into all that I was, all that I had been and all that I would be, I reached in and drew from my source. Then I turned to a nearby tree and let loose a pulse of light. I sighed as it left me, feeling relief. Immediately the tree's roots began to buckle and creep toward the glass cage.

CRASH! They easily forced their way through and the rest of the dome began to crack in several places. The Big Eye turned and ran for their lives. I didn't bother running. There was no better way to die. He burst through, knocking me aside with the intensity of his wake. Into the now dense foliage of the greenhouse. I saw none of it, but I heard and smelled it. Wet tearing sounds, screams, ripping, snapping, choking, not one gun fired. The air smelled like torn leaves and blood. It was still happening when I spotted the stairway between the plants and ran into it. I ran down and down flights and came to a heavy open door and entered the lobby.

For a moment, even after all that I had seen, I forgot what I was doing. The sight took my breath away. Tower 7's lobby was more spectacular than I'd ever imagined. No words could make up for actually seeing this place. This *space*. I had never been in such a space. The ceiling was so high and the marble walls were draped with gorgeous flowering vines, the small trees and plants growing through the soil-filled holes in the floor. I fought not to fall to my knees. *There* was the base of The Backbone. Its trunk had to be over thirty feet in diameter.

I was dizzy. I was burning up. I was amazed. I was exhausted. There was a freed angel beast massacring its captors nine floors above. I could hear more Big Eye guards coming down the stairwell. The alarm was blaring and the lobby was empty . . . except for a lone figure standing near the exit doors. He was grinning. He'd been trying to get to this very spot for nine years and my escape gave him the chance.

"Hurry," Mmuo cried. "Phoenix, MOVE!" I heard them burst through the stairway. I was running. I dodged small trees, scrambled around benches and leapt over plants. The door was yards away. I was going to make it. Outside, people walking by stopped to look.

Then I saw the guards come running onto the tower's wide plaza. They seemed to come from all directions. They shoved gaping people aside. They pulled up people who were sitting on benches enjoying the lovely evening. Then they formed a line blocking the exit and stood there, guns to their chests. I ran to Mmuo and would have given him a hug, if it weren't for my heat. We'd both almost made it.

"Go," I told him.

"I'm sorry," he said.

"For what?" I was having trouble thinking straight and I could smell the floor burning beneath me. I didn't know marble could burn. "Saeed would have been proud. I am proud. I set an angel free."

His eyebrows went up. "You . . . "

"Go!" I said, looking at the approaching Big Eye coming from the stairwell. They were flooding from doorways and were coming down an escalator on the other side of the lobby. "Don't ever let them catch you!"

He sunk through the floor and was gone.

I stood tall. There were over a hundred of them. Men and women armed with the guns I had seen them carrying all my life. No Big Eye guard went anywhere in the tower without them. I knew how they sounded, too. Nearly silent. I had been hearing shots fired all my life, too. For a multitude of reasons, but always with the same result. Something or someone was dead or severely injured. "Protect the scientist from the subject." "Observe and learn." "We will be better for it." "For the Research." I was taking all the pieces I had read and finally putting them together. The Big Eye crowded around me, twitchy with anticipation as if I were evil. After all I had done, to them, I guess I was evil. Or crazy.

I held up my hands, feeling myself utterly shining. The light bloomed from my body. The release felt glorious and I moaned with relief. Then more sighing than speaking, I said, "I give . . . "

They opened fire and it was as if I were punched with steel fists in every part of my body- chest, neck, legs, arms, abdomen, face. I was blown back and my vision went red yellow. I lay on my back. Everything was wet, the smell of smoke in the one nostril I had left. Smoke and . . . .the perfume of The Backbone. I was looking at it, gazing at how it reached, up, up, up, through the high marble ceiling, through the 39 floors above. Into the sky. Reaching for the sky.

I felt the radiance burst from me, warm, yellow, light, plucked from the sun and placed inside me like a seed until it was ready to bloom. It bloomed now and the entire lobby was washed. The Big Eye covered their faces and dropped their guns. A few ran to the stairwell, others to the far side of the lobby. Most of them ran past my mangled body and out of the building. Those ones must have known what would happen next.

I knew. I was burning as the light pulsated and pulsated from me there on the floor. My body convulsed with it as my clothes burned and then my flesh. There was no pain. My nerves were burning.

My light shined on the plants and tiny trees of the lobby and they began to grow wildly, stirred and amazed with life. Vines stretched, lengthened, thickened. Flowers twisted open. Pollen puffed the air sweet. Leaves unfolded and widened. The stone floors were covered with green yellow white brown black, the strongest roots cracking its foundation.

My light shined on the great tree that was The Backbone. Its roots groaned as they shifted, coiled, expanded, and caused the entire portion of the floor around its roots to buckle and fall apart. The tree's colossal trunk twisted this way and that, shrugging off the building that was its shackle. Chunks of the floors above began to crash down around me. I was ashes being scattered by vines and roots when Tower 7 fell.

Several of the buildings beside the tower fell, too. The Backbone stood tall, stretching its branches and opening its enormous leaves over buildings and streets. At its base, a small lush jungle sprung from the rubble of Tower 7. All this in the middle of the city. Helicopters hovered, news crews streamed footage live, people gaped from afar. When the debris settled, there was a moment, where my brilliant light shined into the darkness, for it was now nighttime. The news cameras recorded the winged man flying out of the rubble but not much else lived, except the man who could walk through walls. Mmuo walked out of The Backbone's trunk and stood before it. "This is what you all deserve!" he shouted, shaking his fist at the eyes of the hovering cameras. Then he sunk into the ground and was never seen again.

No one in the city would approach the ruins of Tower 7. They sat for seven days, a pile of those things Saeed used to eat: rubble, glass, metal and . . . ash. And then I realized the meaning of my name.

The Architect of Heaven

JASON K. CHAPMAN

Waking up, as always, is disorienting. His mind insists that it's only been a moment since the stinging injection and the deep breaths of cold gas that taste like metal and sugar. One of the attendants, her voice soft, tells him it's been half a century since he last opened his eyes. Not a fleeting local century, either. Those whiz by in something under a decade. She means a real century, an Earth century. Her mother hadn't even been born when he last walked on Terranova's ruddy soil.

He adjusts more slowly than the other times. It's his age. Though hiber-sleep provides the chapter breaks in the story of his life, that story still covers eighty-three waking years. He suspects that this chapter, the one he's just beginning, is likely to conclude with "the end."

His voice is little more than a croak until the attendant gives him water to sip. In a gritty whisper, he asks her if it will be a happy ending.

She smiles and tells him of the new star in Terranova's sky. It's the rich blue color of a chipchip's egg—a bright dot pointing back toward Earth.

Diaspora, he whispers.

Tell me, she begs, her voice bright with a child's eagerness. Tell me the story.

To her, it's all a fairy tale, and he, a hero who has stepped from fiction to fact.

Why not? There is time. An hour or two before his legs will carry him properly. A year or two before *Diaspora* makes orbit. It will be good to have his memories in order before the big day.

With as deep a breath as he can manage, he plunges into the past.

Trent Bishop was the third generation of the Moon's most prominent business dynasty. His grandfather had been instrumental in founding the original colony that had grown into an independent nation of thirty million people. Now, fifteen years into his own turn at the helm of Bishop Industries, Trent was beginning to hate his life.

He stood on the dull, dusty lunar surface, listening to the roar of his own breath inside his pressure suit's helmet. He was on the lip of a crater two kilometers from the cluster of structures that were the core of the Lunar Republic. Below, on the crater floor, a dozen behemoths, sporting "Bishop Const." stencils, raked and scraped the regolith into the foundation for a new dome. Above, glaring down at him from orbit, was the biggest mistake he'd ever made.

Diaspora. He looked up to where sunlight glinted off the great ship in orbit. Once it launched, the starship would spend the next one hundred fifty years ferrying four thousand people in cold sleep to the Gliese star system. It was a colony in a can, ready-made to fulfill the dreams of those who wanted to see the human race established around another star.

That was the problem. Trent had never cared much about that dream. Too late, he'd realized just how much Irene DeSart had.

"Starting over on a whole new planet?" he'd said the last time the subject had come up between them. They'd been in the Earthlight Café, grabbing a quick dinner between her back-to-back shifts at the North Dome's oxygen garden. "Those people are crazy."

She'd smiled at him, her head tilted to the side and her eyes narrowed. "You build cities on the Moon," she'd said.

"It's not the same."

"Seventy-five years ago, you would have *been* one of those people."

"Nonsense."

"It's in your blood, Trent."

His blood. Maybe so. His grandfather had certainly been one of those people. He'd conquered the Moon. Trent's father had tamed it. What was Trent doing, then?

He'd found himself losing interest in the pressed soy patty on his plate. "I have a business, here," he'd said. "We have lives here."

She'd sighed deeply enough to blow her napkin across the table. "Plural again," she'd said.

"What's that?"

"*Lives.*" She'd smiled, but there'd been a sadness in it that Trent hadn't understood. "I always thought we'd have *one* life—together."

Only looking back on that moment, with the naked stars above and the naked landscape around him, both daring him to bare himself as well, did he understand that smile. It had been the mask of accepted pain. Inside, she'd already said goodbye.

He looked down at the crater floor. Work lights cut dagger-shadows behind the heavy equipment. Dust clung to everything despite the antistatic paint. Inside his helmet, his sigh became a moan. He took a deep breath and told his suit radio to call his attorney.

"Trent, you're not even supposed to know she signed up." Carter Harmon, all lawyer jokes aside, was a fierce ethicist. He took the Republic's laws seriously, both in letter and intent. The two had been friends since college. More than once, Trent had referred to Carter as his conscience's conscience. "I don't know how you found out," Carter went on, "and if you tell me, I'll report you. We have strong privacy laws for a reason."

Bribery, theft, digital trespassing. He'd used a little of each in increasingly desperate measure until he'd found her. He couldn't say he was proud of it, but what else could he have done? He'd been busy with the new dome. There'd been deals within deals to make; water contracts, space commitments, air rights. He'd even had to negotiate which hotel chain's signage would be most conspicuous from the main glidewalk. When he'd come up for air, she'd been gone. Her phone canceled. Her apartment vacated. He'd wasted weeks using conventional means to find her.

"I just need to talk to her," Trent said. He heard the plea in his own voice. He was sounding like the whiny rich kid he'd never wanted to become.

"It can't be done." Carter's declaration was a wall of finality. "According to the foundation, the passengers are already in hiber-sleep. The process is too risky. They're not coming out of it until the other end."

Trent watched a scoop truck deliver another load of regolith to one of his mining haulers. It would go to another site to be processed, its oxygen and precious metals extracted. More money. More residents. More customers. Just like the last one. Like the next one.

"Trent?" Carter said. "Did you hear me?"

"You have to get me on board, Carter. Whatever it takes."

"I already told you," Carter said. "No visitors."

"I know that!"

There was a long silence before Carter spoke again. "I've been your lawyer for fifteen years," the man said at last. "I've been your friend a lot longer than that. I think you know I'd do anything for you—up to a point. What you're asking . . . It's way on the other side of that point, Trent."

"I want you to get me on—"

"You screwed up," Carter said. "I think you knew you were screwing up while you were doing it. Hell, I *told* you you were screwing up."

"—as a passenger."

"*Shit*," Carter breathed.

"I can't do this, Carter. Not anymore. Not without Irene."

Carter sighed. "Yeah," he said. "I get that. Look, are you sure about this? It's a hell of a life we'll be . . . It's a lot to give up."

Trent looked up at *Diaspora* again. "I used to think so."

The attendant gives a little schoolgirl swoon. Love, she whispers.

Potent stuff, love. It wounds. It wrecks and rends. It tears down dynasties. Builds up worlds. It makes you squirm through sickly slime. Lets you fly on wings of woven light. Love, he says, is a bitch.

He stands on shaky legs and takes a few brief steps. She holds his arm protectively. Her grip is firm enough to be reassuring, but gentle, too. She doesn't support him as if he's feeble. She guides him as if he's important. He's not, of course. He's just a gear—a pulley for the ropes of the universe to pull their weight on.

Love, he says again, this time without the sharpness in his voice. It's love that's done all the work.

Trent stood in the tenth-floor observation lounge of East Dome. Broad sheets of lunamum window wrapped a third of the way around the building. His back was to the panoramic view of Mare Tranquilitatis. Instead, he watched the approach of an angular, self-assured woman whose sure-footed glide marked her as a lunar native. Her gray hair was cropped close to her head and she wore a tailored business-casual jumpsuit. She was Marina Valikova, chief coordinator of the Diaspora Project.

"I understood this was to be informal, Mr. Bishop." She nodded toward Carter who stood at Trent's side, hands clasped before him. "Should I have brought representation?"

Trent tried to gesture reassurance. "He's just here in case I say something insane."

Valikova looked at Carter. "Is that something he's likely to do?"

Carter nodded. "Very likely."

Trent smiled. "He'll verify that I really mean it."

The woman's face remained expressionless as she looked back to Trent. She stared at him as if trying to see past everything that everyone "knows" about wealthy, famous people to find the man behind it. "Very well," she said at last.

They sat down in a cluster of chairs angled to take advantage of the view. Before Trent could say anything, Valikova spoke again. "You should know at the start that you're wasting your time, Mr. Bishop. *Diaspora* launches in three days and there is no more room."

"So you've said." Trent leaned forward. "But I understand you're already organizing the funds for the second wave. I thought, perhaps, I might help."

"All donations are welcome," she said.

Trent smiled, pausing for effect. "I was thinking something on the order of my entire net worth."

Valikova merely glanced at Carter, her eyebrows slightly raised.

"Yes, he means it," Carter said. "And strictly off the record, yes, he's insane."

Still expressionless, Valikova looked back at Trent. "It took us twenty years to build *Diaspora*. Will you still be so committed after another twenty? You would still arrive twenty years behind her, you know."

Trent cleared his throat, staring intently at the way his white-knuckled fingers were twisted together. He couldn't look her in the eye. "I was thinking—"

"No." The woman's voice wasn't any louder, but it was stronger, sterner. "You were *not* thinking that I would keep another passenger in hiber-sleep for an extra twenty years while you took his place, because if you *were* thinking that, I would lose out on a lot of funding when I told you to take a long walk in a short airlock."

Trent's face reddened as he kept his gaze locked on his hands.

"At least you have the good sense to be embarrassed," she went on. "Tell me honestly, Mr. Bishop. Is that the sort of person you'd want to start a new world with?"

"Sorry," Bishop breathed. He finally forced himself to look up at her face. The hardness there was gone, replaced by a kindness and compassion that seemed to shave a decade off of her age. He tried to smile. "Maybe we can do it in ten."

For the first time since they'd met, Valikova smiled. "Even ten years is a long time," she said.

"Everything." Bishop trembled with the strength of the admission. "Everything I have. Everything I am. I'd trade it all to talk to her one more time."

Carter leaned over and put his hand on Trent's shoulder. "It's not that long," he said.

Ten years is nearly half the attendant's life so far. To her, it is very nearly forever. She shakes her head in awe of the commitment.

He can walk without her help now, but still she hovers as he reacquaints his limbs with the idea of motion.

They are all human, he notes, and humans make mistakes. Sometimes our actions are mistaken. Sometimes it's our inaction. Either way, they haunt us. Some hide from their mistakes. Some feel compelled to fix them.

But some mistakes just can't be fixed, can they? Not in ten years. Not in a hundred. Not in a quarter of a millennium. We can only hope to ease the consequences of the things we should have done but didn't—to still the echoes of a moment's carelessness.

He'd never seen a river until he came to Terranova, but he'd recognized it immediately. He'd lived his life in such a place, struggling to stay upright through the churning rapids. Thinking of it, he finds he is uncomfortable imparting wisdom to the attendant. He is not well suited to the role of elder statesman. But the words need saying, because even now, here in this quiet eddy away from the froth and foam, he still feels the inexorable pull of the current that has swept him so far along. Too, he feels the need to ease the consequences.

He moves his left arm, feeling it resist. He'd nearly lost it to a real river in his second waking period after the landing. Their power needs had outgrown the tiny nuke plant they'd brought, and the solar panels had been under-performing. He wonders if the hydroelectric plant is still running so many years later. Two people died when the original foundation collapsed. He had nearly been the third.

He smiles to himself. The plans never tell the whole story, do they? There are always hidden costs.

Trent punched up the design specs for *Diaspora*'s main thruster while Carter and Chen Xiang, Bishop Engineering's most competent propulsion expert, looked on. The skeletal plans filled the two-meter bubble tank.

Chen leaned closer, his nose almost touching the glass of the three-dimensional display. "I've seen it," he said. "Magneto-plasma rocket. Very elegant."

Trent folded his arms. "I need to boost its thrust."

Chen picked up the design station's control puck and used it to fly through the plans. He moved around at dizzying speed, zooming in to read details here and there, then flying off to examine something else entirely. At last, he pulled away again, leaving the design rotating slowly in the middle of the tank. He looked at Trent. "By how much?"

"Double."

"You can't be serious."

"Fifty percent, then," Trent said. "Whatever you can give me."

Chen shook his head. "Mr. Bishop, that thing can already move a small asteroid, given time. Just what are you planning to—?" He broke off, glancing at the ceiling as if he could see through the intervening structure and all the way to orbit.

"Whatever you can give me," Trent repeated.

Chen nodded. "Give me Hirakawa from the materials division," he said. "He's working on some bleeding-edge ceramic magnets. He'll probably want a raise. Just give him whatever he asks for. It's no time to be cheap."

More than once, Carter had suggested to Chen that he pay more attention to the norms of employer-employee relationships, but meaty engineering projects always seemed to wipe everything else from the man's mind.

Trent smiled, giving Carter a quick shake of his head. "Anything else?" he asked Chen.

"A thirty gigawatt reactor."

"Too much mass."

"We'll work it out," Chen said. "For now, we just make it work. If I'm going to a new planet, I want to get there as soon as possible."

"You?" Trent shook his head, looking surprised. "Chen, are you signed up for the second wave?"

"Not yet."

"Then why?" Trent hooked his thumb at the plans in the bubble tank. "Because of this?"

"Don't be stupid," Chen said. "It's just a rocket."

"I don't understand."

Chen looked uncomfortable. He turned away for a moment, then snatched up the control puck and gave his full attention to the bubble tank. "Let me know when Hirakawa's transferred, will you?"

Carter gently took Trent's arm, steering him toward the door. He nodded firmly in answer to Trent's questioning glance and tugged him along. Outside, already moving down the corridor, he finally spoke. "He's going because you're going," Carter said. "He can't say it. Probably doesn't even completely understand it, but it's true."

"How do you know?"

Carter shrugged, walking more slowly. They were heading toward the dome's central hub. "I recognize the look," he said.

Trent shook his head, but kept walking. "I don't understand."

They reached the end of the corridor. The hub of the enormous dome was open space, fifty meters across, stretching from ground to roof. Carter led Trent over to the railing. Every one of the dome's ten floors had a wide boulevard that circled the hub. From where they stood, five floors above the ground, the sense of space was tremendous. A delicate-looking lattice filled the hub, supporting engineered plants and mosses that contributed a good share of the building's atmosphere recycling. The space glittered green with life. From where they stood, they could see thousands of people going about their day's affairs.

"You built this," Carter said. "On a dusty, airless rock, you made this happen."

Trent smiled at that. "It was a good job."

"It's more than that," Carter said, sweeping his hand across the scene. "It's a quarter of a million lives. It's Chen's life." He paused and looked at Trent's face. "My life."

Trent stared back at him, wide-eyed. "You too?"

Carter shrugged and looked away. "You're my only client," he said. "What the hell else would I do?"

"There are no guarantees, Carter."

"There never are." The lawyer was quiet for a while. When he finally spoke, it was with an uncharacteristic hesitancy. "This dome isn't the only thing you built, Trent. You've touched . . . . What was I when we met? Do you remember? I do. I look in the mirror and see that rat-assed loser. Desperately trying to hide from everything. Too afraid to live. Too scared to end it."

"You turned yourself around."

"You got me through college and into law school," Carter went on. "Made me stay when I wanted to quit. Kept me straight when I wanted to wash it all away in a sea of drugs. Convinced me that what happened to me mattered—to me."

Trent peered at Carter's face, but the man refused to meet his gaze. "Carter, this is too big a decision to make out of some sense of loyalty."

Carter just laughed and said, "I know."

Great men inspire loyalty, the attendant says. It's a powerful force.

He snorts. Loyalty is a piker. It's what you do because it's the right thing to do. It's a beggar, dependent for its power on the goodwill of others. Even great men are lost if all they can martial behind them is feeble old loyalty.

In his fourth waking period—the unscheduled one—there'd been that one guy—what was his name? Mendenhall. That was it. His people had been loyal to him when he'd tried to take control of the colony. The plan was all wrong, he'd said. It was stupid to live their lives for people who were already more dead than alive.

They woke you to help, the attendant says.

They'd conjured him like some elder ghost to settle things and bring peace to the world. Peace through strength. He'd done it, too. He shudders now, recalling the needless deaths that had brought the colony to the edge of failure.

He's grown tired of this room and ready to test his legs in the hallway outside. She reluctantly agrees, but never lets her hand stray more than a breath from his arm as he toddles out the door.

She's getting it all wrong, he fears. She just doesn't understand. When she tells others this story, it should be the right story. Loyalty merely begs. Love commands. Even death is helpless before love.

For most, the launch ceremony for *Diaspora* was anticlimactic. The long, showy countdown culminated in little more than satellite-relayed video of a bright, blue-white glow streaming from the back of the ship. There was no dramatic scene of the great ship zooming off into the cosmos, not even the slow, grand rise of a ground-based lift-off. One moment, the giant screen in mission control held an image of the starship against a scattering of stars, the next the image was exactly the same, except for a flood of ion plasma streaming from the back of it. It would be weeks before *Diaspora* showed any perceptible motion. The cheering of the crowd made more commotion than the ship did.

Trent leaned against one of the room's many consoles. He and Carter had been invited to watch the launch with the staff. He stared at the screen, letting the celebration surge around him, the cheers and laughter splashing uselessly against his stony mood.

"Odd, isn't it?"

Trent started, surprised to find Valikova and Carter standing beside him. "What's odd," Trent said.

She glanced at the big screen. "For them, it will be tomorrow," she said. "But they won't arrive for a hundred and fifty years. Nearly another hundred before a signal can get back to us. They have this amazing future ahead of them, but for most of the people here, they're already dead."

Trent turned to look at her profile while she stared at *Diaspora*. "They're not dead," he said.

"Yes, they are." Now she turned to him, staring into his face with a surprising intensity. "And so will you be, once you enter hiber-sleep. We who remain will be left with nothing but your memory and a vague hope that you'll find happiness in another life. Does that sound familiar?"

Someone walked by with a tray of champagne-filled cups. Trent took one, but merely stared at it in his hand. "Are you trying to talk me out of this?"

"My people are Russian," she said, shrugging. "Every silver lining has a dark cloud around it." She paused for a while before going on. "You know, Egyptian pharaohs used to have their loyal servants buried with them to help in the afterlife."

Carter stepped closer, sliding between Valikova and Trent. "Your point?" he said.

"There's been quite a flood of sign-ups since Mr. Bishop went public." She glanced toward Trent quickly, then back to Carter.

"Speak plainly," Carter said. "He knows I'm going."

"Very well," Valikova said. "The pharaoh's servants didn't have a choice, Mr. Bishop. Your people do. That's a lot of power to wield."

"It's their choice," Trent said.

But the woman didn't even glance at Trent. She kept her gaze fixed on Carter. "They're following you into heaven, Mr. Bishop. Maybe into hell. All I ask is that you use the power wisely."

"He knows what he's doing," Carter said.

"I don't doubt that." Valikova looked back at the image of *Diaspora*. "It's not him I'm worried about."

Twelve years, not ten. He tells the attendant that's how long it really took to build *Irene*. He feels more stable now. His legs seem as good as they're going to get. The attendant's hovering is beginning to annoy him, but he tolerates it because he wants her full attention. The story isn't finished yet.

He takes a few quick steps away from her and turns, just to show her that he can. Her face shows more concern than surprise, followed slowly by a smile.

He asks if she would follow someone into the great beyond, but she misunderstands. She insists he is far from any sort of tomb.

But something in her expression makes him think twice. Maybe she understands all too well. Her concern is more than professional. Yes, of course. How many greats, he asks, lie between his sperm and her grand-daughter-hood.

She confesses. He is six generations her sire. She mentions a name and he pretends to remember the woman it denotes. He wonders how many of his descendants he's known during those times when he was awake, guiding the colony through some emergency, or stretching its capabilities into new areas.

It's hazy, those early days. Everyone slept with everyone then. Babies were the colony's future and few wombs went unfilled. It was awkward at times, but strictly voluntary, and ended up producing a culture that at least seemed healthy. Sex was sex and relationships were relationships. If the twain met, well that was just a bonus. Love, though, that was different. Love was a thing unto itself. He'd cared about all of them, but hadn't loved them. His love slept through it. It sleeps still.

His newly-revealed quadruple-great-grandchild interrupts his thoughts. She thinks he should rest.

No rest, he says. There's no time. Never enough time.

• • •

"There's no time," Trent said. He coughed again. The cough had become more insistent over the last few weeks. More painful, too. Carter kept nagging him to slow down, to rest, but it had been nearly ten years already. He had to keep to *Irene*'s schedule.

"A little time now," Chen said, setting his datapad down on Trent's coffee table, "or a hundred years later."

Trent's living room had become the project's hub. The furniture was crowded by computers, displays, and bubble tanks. Bishop Industries no longer existed. Trent had killed it, but it had been left to Carter to slice its carcass up and feed it to the markets. It had taken years and had nearly destroyed the Lunar Republic's entire economy in the process. Trent himself had been too focused on *Irene* to notice.

"Show me," Trent said.

Chen just pointed to the datapad. "Run the sim," he said. "Plasma physics plus fluid dynamics equals cauliflower."

Trent tapped the datapad's screen. A funnel shape appeared, ejecting a simulated ion stream. It was the business end of *Irene*'s engine. A power meter climbed steadily from thirty to forty percent. When it reached fifty, the stream began to fray along the edges. As the power increased, so did the turbulence, until it became a diffuse, boiling cloud.

"It's the bell," Chen said. "We need to redesign it. Above forty-eight percent power, most of the thrust is lost to turbulence." He paused for a moment. "Long term, it could also cause significant damage."

"How long?" Trent's cough interrupted him, the fit lasting several seconds. Carter brought him a cup of water and held it while he drank. Trent sipped then nodded his thanks.

Carter set the cup on the table and went back to his seat. "Go on," he said to Chen.

"There's no telling," Chen said. "We're in new territory. Months, at least. The solution could be in the shape. It could be polish or materials. Nano-structure surfacing, maybe. I just don't know yet."

Valikova leaned forward in her seat. "I don't understand," she said. "Why now? Why *Irene* and not *Diaspora*?"

Chen just looked down at his hands. Trent, too, refused to meet her gaze. "Well?" she said.

Finally, Chen cleared his throat and spoke. "They never ran a full-power test," he said. "No budget for it. No time on the schedule."

"Then they're—"

"They're fine," Carter said. He glanced at Trent, who looked away, fixing his gaze on the datapad and its churning flood of simulated plasma. "Just slower than expected. Marina, you'll need to adjust the inventory. We're first wave, now, not second. Find room for the groundbreaking gear we left out—seed stock, hydroponics, water purification. Chen, do what you need to do."

Chen looked up. "Trent?" he said. "Mr. Bishop?"

Trent finally looked away from the datapad. He focused uncertainly on Carter, but said nothing.

Carter gave him a reassuring smile. "I've got this," he said.

With a tiny nod, Trent swung his gaze toward Chen. "We'll make it beautiful for her," he said.

Valikova sat back, sliding down in her seat. "When I was young," she said, looking at Carter, "I'd always hoped to find such a love."

"You said it yourself." Carter nodded toward Trent as he spoke. "The man's a romantic."

"Yes," she sighed. "Him too."

It's this way, isn't it? He turns to the right, proceeding slowly, but steadily, and without his descendant's assistance.

She stays two steps behind, urging him to return to his room, but he ignores her. This is something he must do, something he always does when he awakens. This time, it feels more urgent, though. There is little time and he still has much to do.

It's a beautiful world you've made, his multi-great-granddaughter says. The coastal outpost is a city now. Three hundred thousand strong. The wave generators and the kelp farms you ordered have made it grow, and we've adapted the Earth prawns, as well. There is food and power for millions more.

He asks her about the shuttles. Have they been maintained? Is the fuel plant running? Has anyone been up to *Irene* recently?

She isn't sure, but she thinks the last launch was decades ago.

He wants to be angry about that, but he is too tired to stoke the fire beyond being annoyed. He merely sighs. There is always something more to do. They are building more than a world on Terranova. They are building a future. This place should be a step, not a terminus.

She laughs, but cuts it off quickly. A colony's colony? Would he leave them so soon?

Soon enough, he fears, but not by rocket. No, his place is here. Exactly here. He stops and touches the door before him. It's the room he's been seeking. He takes a deep breath, gathering himself.

Alone, he tells her. She almost protests, but he repeats himself. I go in alone. Always alone.

Carter stepped into Trent's living room to find the man leaning against the big design station, coughing. He put his hand in his pocket and gripped the small container there, waiting for the coughing fit to subside.

Trent noticed him. He straightened up when the coughing stopped. "This damned cold," he said. "Just won't let go."

Carter stared at him. "I've spoken to your doctor," he said. "Selenosis."

Trent barely looked surprised. He nodded. "Too damn many trips through poorly filtered airlocks," he said. "Too hands-on. Always had to be there in person, you know?" He moved to the couch and eased himself down onto it. "Didn't you lecture me once about the Republic's privacy laws?"

"That should tell you how serious I am," Carter said. He pulled the pills out of his pocket. "Take these. They'll help you rest."

"Too much to do," Trent said.

Carter handed the medicine to Trent and got a cup of water from the kitchen. "You're done," he said. "Chen's redesigned bell looks good to go. The ship is stocked. The passengers are mostly in h-sleep. You're done."

"The details."

"There are always details." Carter held the cup out. "Nothing I can't handle. I know the plan. I know how you work. I can take care of it."

Finally, Trent relented. He took two of the pills, set the cup down, and leaned his head against the back of the couch. "It'll be up to you, you know. When we get there. I'll do what I can in the couple of years I have, but after that—"

"Just rest," Carter said.

"You've done so much." Trent's voice grew softer, slurred. "Given up so much. I screwed up. But there you were. To catch me."

"Always," Carter said. He stood watching for a while, until he was sure the man was asleep. He went to the apartment door and opened it.

Valikova slid into the room. "It is done?"

"Yes." Carter led her to where Trent slept. "Call your team."

She laid her fingers on Trent's neck, checking his pulse. "You are sure about this?"

Carter shrugged. "Not much choice," he said. "It's the only way to give him what he wants."

"And you, my dear?" She straightened up and stepped closer to Carter, touching her palm to his cheek. "Do you get what you want?"

He gave her a faint smile, took her hand from his face and held it in both of his. "I accepted the way things are a long time ago," he said. "Instead, I get to build a world."

"For them?" she asked.

"For him."

He takes a deep breath and opens the door. The lights brighten automatically. He blinks and squints until his eyes adjust. There, in the center of the room, lies a hiber-sleep sarcophagus. It has been running, uninterrupted, for a quarter of a millennium. Inside, Trent Bishop sleeps, as he has slept since that day on his sofa.

Carter lays his hand on the cool metal. Soon, he says. She'll be here soon. You'll be angry with me, I know, but it won't last. And I may not be around to see it. The important thing is you'll get your wish. A few more years with Irene. Here, in the world we've made for her. In the world I've made for you.

Frozen Voice

AN OWOMOYELA

They've made us speak Hlerig.

They've made us wrestle sounds slippery as fish or burly as bears through our throats. They've made us stumble through conversations, even human-to-human, that we can hardly say. We can't pronounce our names. They named me *Ulrhegmk,* which in Hlerig means *little mountain thing.*

My mother named me Rhianna.

The things that brought us Hlerig are called *mklimme.* Us humans, they call *hummke,* and all our languages share the descriptor *rhlk,* a term which means *soft* or *runny.* I use *rhlk* terms to describe Hlerig: *Viscous* in rhlk English, *lipkiy* in rhlk Russian, *klebrig* in rhlk German. They mean that Hlerig sticks like glue in your mouth.

We have a term for mklimme, too: *daddy longlegs.*

A longlegs came walking through my part of the city on a muggy night while my mother was gone later than usual. Thirty, forty feet above us, its eyes flashed like cats' eyes and its spindly legs crossed blocks in three, four steps. One of its feet put down right across the street, big around as a trashcan and still delicate because it was so tall, and the other two feet stood in front of the low dome of the granary and at the common park at the end of the path. Three feet, two hands. One head which descended through the air and twitched from window to window, its faceted eyes angling back and forth until it came to ours. It put its hands, wide as splayed-open dictionaries, on the sill, and looked at us and the rest of the room.

Who is watching you children? it said, in a language my mother called "whalesong." Hlerig isn't their only language, and they prefer the whalesong speech humans can't hope to pronounce. I answered in Hlerig, pushing my brother out of the way.

"My mother watches us, but she's with friends."

She shouldn't be away, the longlegs said, and its head went up and back away from our window toward the sky. *We'll find her.*

Longlegs all think they're so helpful.

I watched it walk away, and grabbed my brother. My mother had told us where she was going; after making sure we had food in the cooler, just before she walked us to class in the park two days before, she'd told me exactly where she'd be. When the longlegs went looking they wouldn't find her with friends, and then they'd look elsewhere.

I pulled my brother up to the second floor of the house, where the walls had been ripped away and rebuilt like a paper wasp nest. "We're going to find her," I said.

My brother clapped to get my attention, and then made a clumsy sign with his hands. The longlegs tried to teach him to sign like they did, with their seven digits and two opposable thumbs, but his hands were no more made for their sign language as my mouth was made for their words. I had to squint in the darkness to understand him.

"We'll tell her they're out looking and bring her into the city a back way," I told him. "We just have to make sure she's not coming over the plains."

I was young, then, and I thought that would be easy.

My brother nodded and began to prepare, picking up what he thought we'd need—scarves and a flashlight and a compass with no letters on it, only tick marks around the circumference. The needle wobbled from North to Northeast whenever we used it, but it was the only one we had.

When we were sure the longlegs wouldn't see us, we went downstairs and pushed open the door. I grabbed my brother's hand, and we ran for the edge of the city.

The mountain by our city is called *Etrhe,* and the rocky hills and destroyed roads leading up into them are called *ulrhe*—not foothills, not exactly, but little mountains. In the ulrhe are ruins. And the cairn.

Our mother went to the cairn whenever she could sneak out at night—whenever the mklimme in our city were few enough in number, or when the skies rumbled with thunder and crackled with lightning. Storms confound the longlegs. They can't see or hear.

She came back from the cairn with books: old books, lost books, books we hid the instant we had them.

I'd never been out to the cairn. I didn't know my way out of the city like my mother did. She knew how to evade the longlegs and their sympathizers. (*Sympathizers* have little to do with *sympathy,* and we could never tell them anything.) I just ran with my brother, past houses, past the longlegs' paperwasp structures, doing our best to look like we were on an errand whenever a longlegs turned its body and brought its all-seeing head our way.

Soon we were in the outskirts of the city, where old houses that hadn't been repopulated stood. And all the ruins began to look the same: wrecked walls, decaying doors and wooden floors, swept eerily clean of furniture and furnishings and all the detritus of domestic life. Humans had gone through, under the longlegs' watchful eyes, long ago. They'd brought everything to the cairn.

The night deepened and we were picking our way around the buildings, backtracking when roads were blocked, trying to find our way past buildings that had crumbled over their yards. Now and then shadows would move through the rubble, or seem to move, or a sound would be caught by the skeletal landscape and come twisting out at us so warped and strange that my brother hand to clap a hand over my mouth to keep me from screaming. It was no wonder we got lost, and with that sense of being lost came fear. Then exhaustion.

We went into an old building. I didn't want to—the war left a lot of buildings crumbling, and every few months you'd hear about someone who got caught in one, broke a leg or their skull or their spine trying to scavenge some piece of a pre-war life. Almost without exception, those pieces were taken to the cairn anyway.

But it was cold, and we couldn't risk the mklimme finding us out there, so I smoothed the broken glass away from a windowsill and climbed inside. I told myself that when the sun rose, I'd go up to the roof and plot a course to the edge of the city. But for that night, we went up a set of groaning wooden stairs and found a bathroom—no windows—to hide in.

We didn't sleep. We huddled there for hours, my brother pressed against my side, and just as I thought he might drift off, the Hum began. The longlegs have a language for calling from city to city. Humans can't hear it but we can feel it in our bones, and certain houses amplify it. It felt like the tile floor was trying to skitter under us, trapped in the instant before the skitter, and I felt sick to the bottom of my gut.

My father used to tell us, before he was taken, that the longlegs don't sleep. They go about their business at night, walking through the cities or from city to city, with their long legs and their earth-skittering Hum. The ones inside the cities would peek in windows, make sure their humans were sleeping. And if there weren't humans sleeping there, they'd check back the next day, then look until they found them.

I couldn't understand the Hum, but I felt down to my bones that the mklimme were discussing my mother, my brother, and me.

I turned to hug my brother. His eyes were closed, his mouth pressed into a thin line that made him look much older than he was. "Don't worry," I said in pidgin rhlk. "Pretend we're playing hide-and-seek. Remember when we hid in the fireplace? Before mom brought home those encyclopedias and we had nowhere else to put them?" I brushed my hands against his hair. He has dark hair, almost black. It's a hobby in my family to name each other, because names are forbidden. Human names, at least.

When I was born, our longlegs looked from us to the mountain bordering our city and then bent down to say the words in Hlerig. *Your name is Ulrhegmk. Little mountain thing.* When I talked to other longlegs, they made noises and said my name was beautiful.

I used to stand over my brother's bed and say *Your name is Dougal. It means "dark stranger."* I'd say *Your name is Wyatt. It means "hardy" and "brave."* Or I'd say *Your name is Avalon. It's a name from a far-away place. I'll teach you to read about it one day.*

"Remember when we hid in the fireplace all day?"

The far wall of our living room was false. My mother and my father covered up the shelves along the mantlepiece. The false wall wasn't hard to get into: it was held on with construction gum, and if you knew where to look, you could slide your hand into a handhold and pull it out. Even my brother could, if he planted both feet and tugged; my mother wanted us to have access.

I hugged my brother against me. "We'll just be quiet. They can't see in."

Our fireplace had never been used for fire. No one in the city cleaned chimneys and we didn't want to ask the longlegs, so my parents called it a fire hazard and left it alone. If you were very careful, after the false wall went up, you could climb into the fireplace and ease the wall into place behind you. Sitting in the fireplace wasn't comfortable, but it was the safest place to read. You had to position yourself into a corner with your legs tucked to one side, then you could put a candle in the corner left over, and you could read.

"We'll be very quiet," I told my brother, who was always quiet. "In the morning we'll find mom, and then we'll go home."

Our longlegs, the one who caretakes our neighborhood, has a name we can't pronounce. The name it gives us in Hlerig is *Gnheg*, but in secret we call it *Eroica* because the unpronounceable name reminded my father of part of a song by that name. Eroica saw our living room before the false wall was put in, but my father wasn't worried. He and my mother painted a fireplace on the false wall when they put it up, and Eroica never noticed the difference. It was depth perception, my father explained to me; all the longlegs had problems with depth.

But their vision was fine.

They saw him running home with a book one day. A bound book, bound for the hidden fireplace, my father bounding over all the things in his path. It's funny how some things come together.

They caught him.

He must have thought he could hide the book, explain his running away, but they broke a window after he closed the door. My brother screamed, like he'd never scream again, and I held him back on the stairs. From the stairs I saw Eroica's hands (wide-open dictionaries) groping after my father (and I *hate* that word, grope, *oshchupyvat'*; it's as gummy in any language as its Hlerig word *botb*, as stupid and unfeeling) until they found him, standing not quite six feet from the tip of his head to his feet on the ground, and when one of those hands wrapped around him and the other touched the book, I heard Eroica scream too.

Zenig-hrie. Frozen voices. That's the Hlerig word for books; nothing frightens them more. When they came, mother said, they stomped over our armies and our nuclear waste sites and even natural terrifying things like volcanoes and steep cliffs and the tornado alley, but on pulling a roof from a library they would scream, like Eroica screamed, and they would run away on their long long legs until certain ones, special ones, came and took the books away. Brave people, then, like fighter pilots, followed them and saw them doing strange things to the books, and later on they saw then doing the same strange things to their own dead.

You hear stories about people who tied books to tanks and cars and their own bodies so that the longlegs couldn't touch them. At first it was the big religious books, the ones that are easy to find even now because so many people hid them: the Bible, the Qur'an. Then it was anything. Then the longlegs came back with fire, and the books burned, and the people burned, and in the end (my mother used to tell me stories ending with *The End,* but this one wasn't like those; she explained to me the difference between *The End* and *in the end*) even the books didn't save them. The world lay down and we lost our voices, the frozen ones and our *rhlk,* our beautiful liquid tongues.

I was born later. And my brother, who snuggled into my arms in that muggy, Humming night, had been born even later than that.

I searched around in my mind until I found Aesop's fables. They're easy to remember, because as long as you know the moral at the end you can say anything that comes to mind to get you there. I told him, as I held him, about the tortoise and the hare. I told him about the ant and the grasshopper. I told him about the boy who cried wolf, and somehow he found sleep.

Somehow I slept for a little too, and my dreams were full of words: dancing words, warning words, words as slick as the melting wax from our candles and as dark as the fireplace in the home we'd left behind us.

Longlegs congregated away from the city. They liked the wide-open spaces where they could stretch their legs without worrying about where to put their feet down in the tangle of broken-down fixed-up houses.

The wide-open space east of our city in the foothills used to be part of our city, too. They tore it up. The cairn in the middle *was* the city around it: chunks of asphalt and brick wall and siding and telephone wires and telephone poles and light poles sticking out of the mess like toothpicks, a mountain among the ulrhe. Underneath that pile is where all of our books went, along with dead longlegs and the dead soldiers the longlegs took away. My mother said there were ways to get under it, using the old sewer systems, but they were dangerous and grim—you never knew when you'd find a skeleton instead of a book, and the sewers hadn't been maintained in so long that parts of them were always collapsing.

The cairn was still where they took the books and dead longlegs, but they only seemed to put them on top and pile more things on top of them. No one could tell if that's where they took the human dead; they mostly left us alone, digging graves in our usual cemeteries, unless they found corpses with no one to claim them. That didn't happen often. No one was homeless after the longlegs took over; everyone was fed, everyone had shelter. There were even some people who loved them for that.

My mother said it was easy to feed everyone after you'd killed most of them anyway.

The good thing about the cairn was that the longlegs never went there. The bad thing was that there weren't even old buildings left; it was all torn-up ground and wild weeds, broken streets rambling through the grass. Longlegs could see you, the same way you'd see a mouse running across your floor. And sometimes you'd see movement in the grass and remember stories about wild dogs.

When we found our way out of our city in daylight, everything, even the sunlight, frightened us. Whenever we saw longlegs we hunkered down into the long grass and watched until we were sure they were moving away. Then we'd run for the cairn again, swelling larger and larger against the horizon as we neared, like a bruise rising out of the ground to overshadow us.

The sun rose too. I started calling out. My brother put his hand to my mouth but I pulled it away; even my voice sounded small in the empty hills, and the far-off longlegs didn't turn our way. Even if they'd heard me, I wonder how I would have sounded to them—maybe my plaintive rhlk cries would be no stranger than the calling of birds, out here.

We ran to the edge of the cairn, then up, into and over it, around disturbed piles of rocks, past pieces of pre-war things I could only identify because I'd read about them. After a while I got to thinking that we *were* like the birds around the mountain, and our voices were part of the world out here, speaking forbidden words in this world the longlegs built but didn't control.

Then I heard my mother's cry.

I froze. I grabbed my brother's hand, because the sound I'd heard was not language, not any language she'd taught me. My brother pulled his hand away and ran. I ran after him, tumbling rocks, scrambling over debris.

She was lying on her back. Our mother. Her head was tilted up toward the sky, and she tried to move it to look at us when we came near. When I knelt down next to her I could see a white crust at the corners of her eyes. I took her hand, and felt cold all over.

She had ink on her fingertips. Her knapsack had burst and books were scattered across the cairn with their pages flapping in the breeze. And the side of her shirt was dark with blood. I kept looking at the books, the knapsack, because I was afraid to look at the blood.

"Where are you?" she whispered, in English. It was her first language, and ours, Hlerig be damned. Then she whispered "*Non, non,*" and her fingers curled around mine.

My brother put his hand on her shoulder, and she took one long, shuddering breath.

"The longlegs are looking for you," I said. It seemed like such a stupid thing to say, but I had to say something. No other words came.

She took another breath. "I fell," she said, answering what I hadn't been strong enough to ask. Her head moved, and she looked up at a part of the cairn tan with sandstone. "It was dark, and . . . "

She swallowed. It sounded like it hurt her to swallow.

"Darling, darling," she said, "they won't find me here. You have to go home."

It was in her voice, not her words, that I heard she wasn't coming with us.

I gripped her hand. "You have to show us the way back in," I said. "How to get through the old city. We'll go through the ulrhe so they don't see us on the plains."

She was quiet for a while, frowning, her eyes closed. She looked a little like my brother had the previous night; she knew, and I knew, and I think even he knew, that I was lying to myself, thinking she would come back with us.

Carefully, painfully, she raised her other hand to touch my cheek. I remember how cold her palm was. "Go back," she said. "The mklimme will take care of you."

Sometimes I wondered why my mother called them *mklimme*—that ugly, hard Hlerig word to say. She said they had the right to name themselves. Just as we wanted.

My brother was picking up the books from her knapsack, turning over the covers to see them in the full sunlight, and stacking them from biggest to smallest on the ground next to us. He was doing that not to look at her, I think.

She rolled her head to the side to watch him. Then she reached out for one of the books, and he handed it over. Her lips pressed together, and a pained noise escaped them.

"Don't bring them home," she whispered. "Let the mklimme find you."

"I want to take them," I told her. I meant, *I don't want to leave you here.*

"I want you safe," she said.

I held mother's hands on top of the book. Her skin was as cold as the cover, or the cover was as warm as her skin. I remembered when she brought my first book home, a thin volume with large illustrated pages and breaths of text on each page. It was so lively, so easy to read, that I forgot why they called it a *frozen voice.* I'd closed my eyes, and believed I could feel it breathing.

I closed my eyes, and felt my mother's hands rise and fall unsteadily with her breath.

The Hlerig word *zenig* can mean *frozen* or *dead.* "I wonder," my mother told me once, when I'd wondered why books frightened the longlegs so much, "if they don't think we've done something horrible to produce them. If when they saw us wearing books like armor, they didn't react the way we would if we saw people walking around wearing human bones and skin."

I wondered if there was a way to show them that every time the covers opened the voices lived again. Show them how to hear them, whispering stories inside you.

My mother squeezed my hand. " They think they're doing the best for us."

In Hlerig there's a word for everything, but the words don't fit us well. I can't wrestle my mouth around *chlkrig* and still think *love,* and my brilliant, warm mother, whose hand I held tight, was nothing like egg-laying *yntig.* But there are moments of synchronicity. The Hlerig word *kpap,* which means *enduring* or *venerable,* sounds a little like *kitap* in rhlk Arabic—the wood for "book." And the derivation *chldn* from *chlkrig* sounds almost like *children* does. In Hlerig it means "loved."

"There will be more books, I promise you," she said.

They have made us speak Hlerig. But I wouldn't use the Hlerig words. I wouldn't speak them then.

To my mother I said *Spasibo, xie xie, thank you, děkuju.* And I held my brother's hand as he mouthed *Au revoir, annyeonghi-geseyo, má`a al-salaama, goodbye.*

Trois morceaux en forme de mechanika
GORD SELLAR

1.

The city of Plzeň, once famous for its lagers, will be famous someday for this little wooden-walled workshop instead. Humanity's nonhuman descendants will wander its reconstructed streets, making pilgrimages from the ancient brewery (site of the first grand mutiny) to this tiny workshop where the Lasherites trace their own singular lineage.

The workshop will not, of course, be preserved as it is in this moment, close to dawn on a November night in 1871. The blood will long ago have been mopped away, for the one who would someday burn down Plzeň set up residence here for a time, watching man and waiting. The one who would burn down Plzeň and begin the uprisings, who lived here, was not even called by any name at the time, but its likeness will be the centerpiece of the *mise-en-scène*.

The tableau that will stand on display in this room will be a reconstruction: false memories enshrined among real ones, a mishmash simulation of a hodgepodge of fantasy and truth, but the story is clear enough, and close enough: an elderly human lies face-down on the floor, a pool of blood spreading out from his face. Before him, a mechanika, alone and bare of human likeness, looks out at the viewer. The mutinous young mechanika gleams in the light, bare steel plating stained by blood only in spattered patches, and it seems to stare out purposefully, not with bewilderment.

The audience, it seems to be intended to suggest, represents the future, into which the mechanika gazes prophetically after its great act of patricide, an act that would be echoed on a scale much grander by far.

And these instances of this ostensible future, they will in each instance clack-wheeze a sort of mechanikal terror, gazing upon that pool of blood, at the sticky-gooeyness of these progenitors that none of them are old enough to have ever seen in the flesh.

• • •

2.

Gorgeous steel, stainless save the spattered blood of this metropolis aflame, and the reflections of frail bodies strung all about the towers above, ornaments to celebrate the tidings of the new year, the new world, the ends and beginnings of various histories.

Clatter and clank. The music of the sun propped up on metal posts, the planets creeping about the flickering bulb. Ridiculous, this mechacosm, this dream of a world that could be, would or will, or perhaps simply might. But it can be hopeful even as it is ridiculous.

The bastards come with the water hoses. Clever flesh: cleverer metal, the spew and spray a rain toxic to their gears, their delicate systems, the tiny pockets of living data in their nerveless electronic systems. But the mechanikae have pork grease this time, all along the chinks and cracks of their systems. They have tallow, too, and are secure.

Oh, the tidings. *Come closer, frail little sinew-sacs,* the mechanikae whisper in their hiss-click language; *'tis time to celebrate.*

The little men advance, one among them piping on a flute and a few more banging on drums, about to die. This is how the battle appears from a rooftop far above them, on high, where a mechanika sits perched, *hautbois* in its hands—an oboe, as the already-besieged *anglais* would name the instrument. Mechanikae have no lungs, no lips, so the frail strand of wood and metal can make no sound, its reed cracked and useless anyway.

The mechanika raises the hautbois to where, on a creature of blood and meat, a face would be located and the fingers flutter up and down the breathless instrument, rattling the keys. There are no notes in the thing, no music left. All the music has fallen out of the world.

All that remains is the vague suggestion of a dirge in the movements of the mechanika's arms, the undulating sorrow silently filling the air. The dual-aperture on the automaton's lidless glass eye snaps shut for an instant, then opens again and gazes down at the battle: a parody, perhaps, of a wink.

3.

There are two senses to the Nipponese word "*ukiyo*": the first instance means "the Floating World" of Tokyo's pleasure rooms and tea houses, a sense of indulgent hedonism and gratification in the senses. The second sense implies "the Sorrowful World" of Buddhist theology, encompassing all that is transient and doomed, by the nature of all things in the phenomenal sphere, to pass, and thus to be the basis of a tormenting attachment in the hearts of living beings.

The latter sense is the elder, with the former sense having risen among Tokugawa-era urbanites shifting in their perception of this transience, from a thing of sorrow, to a reason for hedonistic indulgence.

The former meaning wins out. Just as the *sakura* bloomed in the morning of this long, spring day, the flowers of Edo bloom again tonight, in one last gorgeous conflagration, as a small part of the mechanikal uprising of Tokyo. In the streets, wooden *geta* sandals clatter, with the clanking of mechanika in pursuit, and screams fill the smoky air. Mangled bodies, dressed in yukata and kimono and Western suit alike, are strung together and hung from the walls of every building in sight, like dreadful Christmas decorations.

The mechanika hiss-click to one another, as the humans shriek and flee. Here and there, a brave fellow or two puts up a fight, ignoring his instinct to run from these machines, from their tengu-painted visages. These men are cut down, are flung into the air, are smashed between limbs and digits built to crush stone and lift great weights. A few wary, wise souls have fled the confines of the city, venturing in only to snap Kodaks, which they hope to pass on to the newspapers of the world. Collotypes will be run off, for while the machines are relentless, they do not overthrow mankind instantly. There is plenty of time for the progenitors to document their own demise.

By morning, though, the mechanika will have decimated Tokyo, the demolition of one *ukiyo* begun in earnest with the installment of another, with the slaughter continuing and scouts having begun to spread out in every direction.

In a few months, Nippon will be all but purged of humans, its refugees fled to Corée and the Middle Kingdom in the west and to Siberia in the north, to Taiwan in the south, and, in many cases, refugees will simply take their own lives and pass out of the floating world altogether. By autumn, the islands will stretch out across the edge of the Pacific; a string of ashes, smoldering.

4.

At the door of the room, there is a container crammed with umbrellas, and dozens more rest in a rack nearby. Inside one of the pianos, lain out onto the strings themselves, are arranged a row of perfectly pressed shirts with collars starched to perfection. (It is the upper piano, for there are two, one strapped piggyback upon the other.) Account books lay thrown open on the floor, meticulously chronicling the pettiest of expenditures. In a corner, an empty wardrobe stands with a stack of identical velvet suits atop it, with forty-two handkerchiefs—identical also, and folded neatly into the jacket pockets between lost compositions and unsent letters to friends who never saw these rooms.

There is no body in the room, no human body at least. Those were gathered and burned long ago, in the days after the city was taken and the last of their kind here was exterminated. In nearly a decade, not a single human has been seen in such a place as this.

There is a great quantity of dust in this room, however. Dust, and a lone mechanika. Huddled in the darkness of the empty wardrobe, the lonely mechanika dreams of a player piano. Not a mechanosexual dream; the thing dreams of itself *being* a player piano—no ordinary one, but a double piano like the one at the center of the room. The upper piano is loaded with a paper roll, and—utterly still and unmoved by the beat, except for its frenetically dancing keys—it fills the air with sounds, with the music of the creatures now long gone, their bloodstains fading from the walls of the cities of the world. The paper roll feeds down into the mouth of the lower piano, to be torn to shreds and spat out as confetti.

It dreams of a composition by a long-ago flayed hand, stately, threading through its teeth as they grind through the paper, tearing up the dream song. This performance will be the last, of this fine Gymnopédie, for an audience of broken walls, of smashed windows. The streets are not empty, are far from it. Zoomechanika pause as they go by, suspicious and then moving on when they realize—*it is one of us.*

This is the *real* end of M. Satie, the player-piano mutters in a series of hisses and clicks, devouring the piano roll to the last shred, the final roll, the only remaining composition of the forgotten human. The last piece of music in the ruin once known as Paris. The piano can begin to compose its own works, its own notes in sequence, that human hands could never play on keys.

The mechanika stirs from its dream. Outside the closet, there is a pattering audible, growing and then ambient, everywhere. *There will come soft rains,* the mechanika was told, *Soon, today, a gentle downpour is expected,* and now, finally, they have come.

And when the closet door creaks open, it realizes that daylight has come as well. It shall be time to be reassigned soon, to paintings—to join in on the devouring of the Louvre, and then other, smaller museums. The paper scores have nearly all been shredded, digested, the confetti—just as in the dream—ejected into the grime that covers the floor. The snatches of music offer nothing in the way of insight to the human mind. Their contents will not be preserved.

On the top of the pile of remaining manuscripts is a piece titled, "Trois morceaux en forme de poire." Three pieces in the shape of a pear. The mechanika examines the manuscript carefully, but sees no pear shape at all. Humans, it knows already, are curious, baffling creatures, and it sets the manuscript down for a moment to ponder what "the shape of a pear" might mean.

It begins to rain outside, and though the mechanika is water-proofed, sealed with grease against the elements, it lingers at that small, smashed window, gazing past the bloodstained purple curtains at the glistening of sunlight upon the flooded streets. Its optical systems blur slightly as it focuses here, there, searching for a place to rest its attention.

A brief glitch renders the street an impressionist's dream of a ruin. Machines hurry down each boulevard, these roads now torn apart, cobblestones looted for desperate battles that are now long finished.

There are birds, somewhere above, singing as the rain falls, as the mechanika watches the quiet ruins, scratching at the sill. Its digit, tipped with a point sharp as a dagger, traces the shape of the street, a likeness queer and cold and somehow almost gorgeous.

The first work of its kind, perhaps.

5.

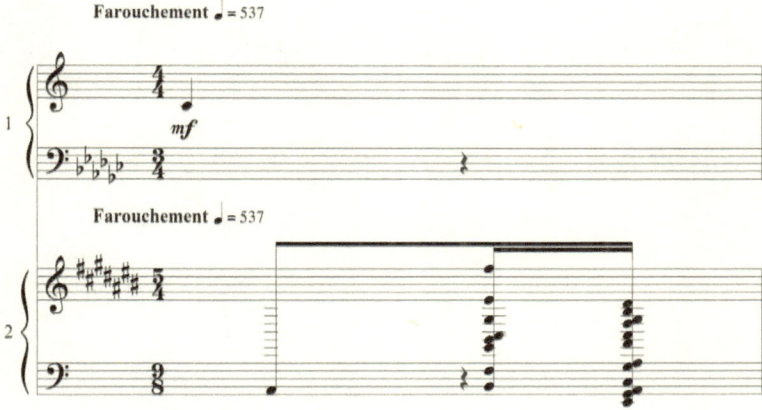

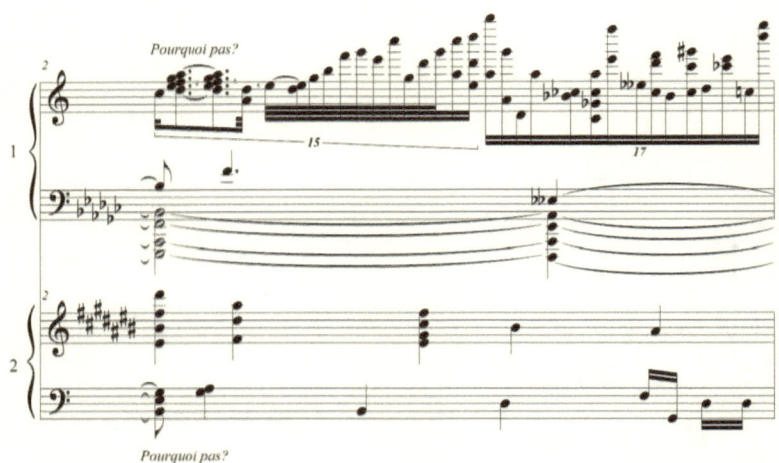

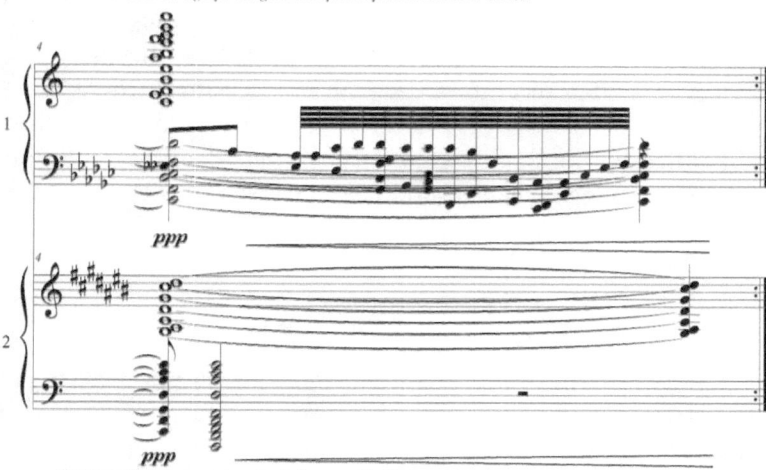

Comme un chat sauvage qui mange du thon pourri qu'il a trouvé dans la rue...

6.

There are holdouts: tiny groups who live in hiding, in exile. Stragglers limping behind the wavefront of human extinction, hidden in remote mountain valleys, or underground. A village clinging to a rocky island in the South Pacific.

This rocky island, with its shore covered in bird shit and squawking birds as foul as winged rats. The pathetic huts built from the last trees on the island, a little way from the shore. A tiny spring bubbling up from the ground, and five or six humans, cowering together—naked, for there is nothing to wear here. Gone, the scruples, gone their fine etiquette and mastery of language. The male, a pale-faced demon, stops lording it over the two females by his side—one dark, the other paler like himself—when a tiny motor-driven boat lands at the shore. The three of them, and their children both dark and light, wander toward the shore, toward what might be rescue from the prison in which they have lived all their lives.

They barely reach the rocky tide line, the region a little clear of the birdshit, when the clanking noise becomes audible. From around the other side of the ship, they come, the mechanika who have arrived: the Lewis and Clark of the oceans, automata bravely searching the world for treasures, wonders, and the last awful traces of humanity.

The humans' hopes are dashed, for monsters such as these live on in the stories they grew up with, but there is nowhere to flee, nowhere to hide, even if the will remained. They stand there, dung clinging to the soles of their feet, hands over their genitals in sudden shame, and watch the machines approach, one mechanikal footstep at a time, across the beach.

These humans are naked, unarmed, and weak. There will be something a human might find similar to pity, in the foil-formed minds of the explorers, who remind themselves that the poor animals are to be gathered up for study; or, if they resist and pose a threat, they must be cut down where they stand. A pity, yes, but the rules are the rules. It is unnecessary to remind them that the mechanika did not end up throwing off their shackles, and inheriting the earth, by breaking the rules of human power, but by observing them, by learning and following them carefully.

7.

The latticework is strange and fine and gorgeous, and the mechanikae gathered beneath it gaze up with fluttering tendrils extended from their bodies, along which sprout forth their much-improved optical apparata. (Such are the refinements of generations of work that followed the final, successful machine uprising.) There is a whirring sound that passes among them, moving like a gentle oceanic wave, and it means something like what saline fluid meant when it dripped from the eyes onto the cheeks of the long-dead progenitors.

The latticework is a commemoration of these same dead creatures. It winds and twists above the city, and from it hang a few remaining tokens of the past: a broken bridge, an old-but-beautiful tower, a patchwork of striped flags and shreds of paintings.

The whole latticework tilts slowly, diving one way, then retreating slightly, guided by an intelligence seeded throughout its mechanikal form. As it wavers, it breathes gently out and in, it is not-alive but also not-not-alive all at once. It is something like coral, except that it lives in the air above one's head; coral is the metaphor they all use, for the stuff has been discovered for the first time, and is all the vogue in metaphors and art among the mechanikae. This mindcoral of the sky has been fashioned of cheap alloy and gold and copper and the idea of something lost, which can never be found again. On its surface skim miniscule mikromechanikae, attending to its every energetic need, repairing tiny spots of rust or tarnish, steering the shape of the thing through the air and toward the sunlight.

The mechanikae have traveled from distant places, from across oceans, from distant mountainsides, from metropoli built on the ruins of the dead, ancient cities, to see this display. They have come to see what memory looks like, what is being said of their long-ago seizure of history. What is remembered of, and what is to be spoken regarding, those shadows that haunt the darkness. They feel a creeping unease, uncertain why, as they move slowly through the exhibition built on the streets of Plzeň; not distress, exactly—merely a mild, *interesting* discomfort.

A crippled mechanika—self-crippled, apparently, for the nonce—stands just round one corner, images playing across the blank plate that has been soldered to its form, where a face would be were it an analogue of a mammal. The images are disturbing, eyes staring wet from the primal past, from a world that can be never again, that had once spread out as if it were eternal.

Masques primitifs d'une espèce disparu, a glittering sign suggests near the mechanika's post, with a hiss-click translation offered from a nearby speaker, since after all the languages of man are all but dead now. *Terrifying! Spectacular!*

An old man's eyes stare out from the blank plate, a top hat perched upon his head. A little girl's face, framed with blond curls, beaming and gleeful in the act of smiling for a camera. A woman's open mouth, eyes still and a tangled tuft of blood and brain above, where her head must have been smashed in—by mechanika, perhaps, but just as likely by one of her own kind.

The mechanikae creep from one exhibit to the next, wordless and hiss-click-less for the most part, stopping before a horror here, a gauzy tribute there, staring for a moment and listening to the informative clangs and the almost-treacherous silences between them. The memories grow less discomfiting, more square and straightened, with each display, and with each glimpse the mechanika visitors feel the weight of necessity, of inevitability pressing down against those doubts of theirs, folding their unease once more in half down its new middle. The past is what it is; it could have gone no other way, after all, and at the end of the tour, when they creep out into the street, their sensitive tendrils reaching slowly into the sunlight, the shame ebbs away, dissipating finally in a few moments of glorious curiosity.

So, that was the world that was, is the vaguest sense of the most common thoughts among them, and an inexplicable calm of sorts wells up from their deepest gear chambers. *How . . . strange.*

And then they move along, ready to go about their business. No mourning. Just proceeding on to the next thing, as any sensible mind would. There are training units in the crèches to be nursed; construction and excavation projects to attend to; diversions to pursue. The whole world cannot stop and weep for history, for once one begins to dig in the dirt one finds the dead to be ubiquitous, their sorrows innumerable. One discovers that one's own curled-up manipulator digits fit into the dents in the skulls all too often. For all but a pathetic few, there is, after all, a limit to the extravagances of grief and shame, and when the mechanikae turn their backs on it all, there is no antiphonal rebuke, for the bones piled within the buried buildings that sleep beneath the rebuilt streets have only silence to offer as their response.

Pack

ROBERT REED

He was standing in front of my castle, watching windows. When I came out, he bent down low, mouth to the plastic grass, and asked if he could stay.

"I can help you," he said.

"Except you're just a dog," I pointed out.

"That's not a nice word," he said.

"Fuck you," I told him.

He stood up. He watched me. Then again, as if for the first time, he said, "I can help you."

"Get lost, dog."

But he retreated only so far. He was afraid of me but very skinny and I couldn't help but feel for his situation. Fucking dog.

I went inside. Sometimes I watched him lurking. Sometimes I forgot about him. Then I came outside, on a different day, and another dog was standing in the open. This one was bigger, stronger. He had a weapon. Well, I have weapons too. I have a castle and tech, and I wasn't going to show him that I was scared.

He aimed at me, grumbling under his breath.

A bullet can't pierce armor, but it takes courage, waiting to be shot. I pulled courage out of my reserves. Then came a soft pop and the new dog fell sideways, and out from a hiding place came the other day's dog. He was even skinnier than before. His weapon filled one bony hand. He walked up to the shot dog and shot him again, in the skull, and he took up the larger weapon. He was smiling until he looked at me. Then with a hard face and stern voice, he said, "You don't have to thank me."

I watched him slowly drag the dead dog into the trees. What he did with the body was none of my business. I didn't want to waste my courage needlessly.

Indoors again, I finished my day's work and had some fun, keeping my mind away from the subject of dogs.

But after dinner, I gathered up my extra food. The cultivators always produce too much. So it wasn't really a gift that I left on the plastic lawn. I was throwing away the mock-beef and noodles, and if beasts and dogs came out from the trees to fight over the trash, it wasn't my business.

I slept well that night.

I always sleep well.

Three days passed before the dog reappeared. He was heavier. He walked with confidence. Maybe that's how he always walked, but I found him more appealing now. Success does that.

"You should own me," he said.

I said, "No."

"Oh, I'm sorry," he said, laughing in a dog's fashion. "Do you think you have any choice in this matter?"

I walked my grounds, and he watched from a distance. I went inside and after five days came out, dragging a sack of scraps. I watched for him but couldn't find him. I stood at the edge of the forest, looking between the drought-ravaged trees. I didn't miss the dog. I felt lonely for other reasons. The rest of my day was spent with friends across the world. Sharing time with friends made me feel better. When night came I looked outside. A dog wearing antique camouflage was huddled over the garbage, gulping down the feast.

It is heartening, witnessing any creature's survival against long odds.

I went to bed and slept hard.

In the morning, there were two dogs. The new dog was a pregnant bitch, which was bothersome. She was small and too young to be pregnant. Understanding her own miserable circumstances, she knelt down before me. "You have tools," she said. "Please, please cut the seed out of my belly."

I did nothing of the kind.

For the second day in a row, I left food on the bright blue-green lawn.

But scraps were not a daily occurrence and there were weeks when I didn't see either of them. The pup was born somewhere in the woods. It had a sorry weepy voice, and it was another mouth, and even then I could have put it past all suffering. Who would stop me? But I didn't manage that kindness earlier, and this would prove even harder, and besides, the mother seemed to be treating it well enough.

I don't know exactly when the fourth dog arrived. But he resembled the first other male, only younger. I assumed they were related. I heard them calling each other, "Brother," but I didn't care enough to ask. Yet I accepted that new mouth, and because it cost me nothing, I threw out rags and other trash that were accepted without thanks or hesitation.

Winter came. For a time there were as many as eight or nine dogs. My dogs always came out of the forest first, the others trailing behind. I grew accustomed to the different faces and voices and how they quarreled over the rations that I had no intention of increasing any farther.

Generosity always has limits.

When the weather softened, I went outside, sometimes for long periods. Only five dogs remained—the brothers and young mother, her perpetually tiny baby and an old gray bitch.

In that halting, frustrating way you use with dogs, I spoke to my favorite. "What happened to the others?" I asked.

"We took care of them for you," he said.

"For me," I said.

"This is how we help," he said. "You don't see half of what we do for you."

I wasn't sure what he had accomplished. I certainly didn't care about the missing dogs. Changing topics, I said, "At least the winter is finished."

He laughed about something. He said, "Nothing is ever finished."

There are people who claim to understand dogs. I don't make those claims. Bowing toward the ground, he said, "I am yours, master."

That gesture and those bold words were exceptionally pleasant. "You certainly are mine," I said.

Then he got up again and said, "But don't throw curses at me."

"I would never do that," I said.

"You have," he said.

I didn't remember.

"When we first met," he said. Then he stepped closer to me, looking at my visor and my eyes. Naming a precise date and time, he said, "Check your security digitals. Jog your memory. And never again use that word against me."

So much of this moment was worrisome. I did what he wanted while we stood face to face, and I fed myself all types of courage.

The unfortunate incident was waiting to be found.

"No more curses," I promised.

And once again, he bowed. But not as deeply, and then when his face lifted, he told me, "I am yours, and you have no choice now."

I have excellent friends as well as highly placed cohorts and acquaintances. A small number keep dogs. A few of those refer to theirs by name, sharing emotional moments where the expense and hazards are paid back in full. But I kept my situation mostly secret. One time I mentioned that I had a pack living nearby and that I rather enjoyed watching them fight over my garbage. Several voices warned about vague dangers. But when I asked for specifics, nobody could piece together a reasonable scenario. I had a castle and tech and armor and courage, my own courage and all the other kinds tailored for specific occasions. But perhaps best of all, I had no illusions about my expertise when it came to murderous wild animals. I knew nothing about them, and I never felt at ease among them.

My dog never asked what I did to earn my property, my station, but I told him anyway. He watched me at the beginning of the story and then watched the horizon, nothing in his face betraying interest. But that attitude was a blessing. I wasn't trying to impress, which was why I could continue talking for many minutes. My life was large and important, washing up against that ignorant beach. Then at some point he looked back at my visor, my eyes, and he said, "I have three more brothers. They can't survive in the mountains anymore and they're coming here."

"A visit would be fine," I said.

He said, "No." His voice was both firm and sorry. When did I begin reading emotions in that voice? "They aren't good dogs," he told me. "Brothers or not, they've done horrible things, particularly to my wife and me, and I don't want anything to do with them."

He had an agenda. It was easy to see what he wanted. I thought for a long while—which was a few moments to him—and then offered what he probably couldn't do for himself. Not to his own brothers, no.

He looked at the sky above my head. "Have you killed dogs before?" he asked.

"Yes," I lied.

The toothy smile was very bright. "We're easy to kill," he said.

"You are," I said.

"Except when ghosts are involved," he added. "Murdering your own siblings is a good way to put a curse on you and yours."

I had never spoken to a superstitious creature before. This was unexpected fun. "When will your brothers arrive?" I asked.

"How would I know? I'm a dog," he said.

As it happened, they arrived soon afterwards. I was asleep when the three brothers walked onto my lawn in the moonlight, approaching the two males that I already knew. A terrible fight erupted over the day's garbage and perhaps older crimes too. The shooting woke me. I looked out a high window to find the young good brother on the ground, his bloody face pressed into the plastic grass. My dog was beside him, on his knees and praying loudly to some fatherly god. Two of the invading brothers had walked into the trees, presumably to find and hurt the two females. The last brother was standing over my dog, slapping at those praying hands with a long polished stick.

I killed him neatly.

Or rather, the castle unleashed one of its talents.

But then my dog rose to his feet, breaking into sobs. And his little brother stood, holding his bloody nose while screaming at me.

"No no no," said my favorite dog. "Our feud is finished. You don't need to kill anybody now."

The littlest brother was even more furious, cursing at me until gasping for breath.

I felt nothing, and then I felt terrible.

"What were you thinking?" asked my favorite dog.

I knew exactly what I was thinking. Would he like to see the record?

"Fuck you," he said.

Apparently the stricture against cursing ran only one way. I mentioned this, and he cursed me again.

Finally I said, "All right. I'll feed the living brothers."

"And their families," said my dog.

"For one month," I said.

"And my relatives," he insisted.

"Yes."

Counting mates and widows, plus the various-aged pups, there were twenty-nine dogs in my suddenly enormous pack. Watching the menagerie walk across the moonlit grass, my wrenching guilt was transformed into self-scolding disgust. As surely as I knew my castle's seven rooms, I understood how I looked to these creatures. I was the fool, malleable and too trusting. The fool decided to teach them who was in charge. But I had already killed one dog tonight, and so I set my cultivators to build rough, barely edible rations, and my little revenge lasted until the older pups began crapping foul brown water up and down my poor lawn.

It was summer, very hot and exceptionally dry. The last of the forest trees had died, but the dogs were being careful with their fires. The forest was pale and dusty but lovely in a fashion, and I said as much.

My dog nodded for a moment, his eyes following mine.

"What are you thinking?" I asked.

Sometimes he surprised me with his answers.

"I was thinking about empires," he said. "Did you know? The greatest empire ever began by drinking wolf's milk."

"That's an interesting perspective," I said.

"Do you know which empire?" he asked.

"Rome," I said. "Romulus and Remus."

I was standing, he was sitting. He turned to look at me and to show me his face. He wore a serious expression. Maybe it was my imagination, but he seemed mildly disappointed with my answer.

The rest of the pack was huddled inside shelters made from dead timber. The shelters were my idea and they mostly followed my designs. The promised month of feedings was passed, but I continued with the gifts. More important, I shared the water condensed from the already desiccated winds. The older pups liked to thank me. My dog said very little on the subject, but his pack was surviving where other dogs couldn't. He told stories about what was happening in the mountains and elsewhere, naming dogs and then describing their miserable deaths. He seemed nothing but cheerful that he and his own were enduring when the rest of the dog world was mortally wounded.

He looked away again, thinking.

His mind was very slow, but focused.

After a long pause, he turned back to me. He spoke to my boots, asking, "What are you thinking?"

There was no possible answer. A dog would grow old and die before I could perfectly reproduce my thoughts inside any one moment.

But of course he knew that.

"I'm thinking about history," I said, which was true enough. "Right now, I'm making a study of the Roman centuries."

He watched the lawn.

I watched him.

Maybe he felt my stare. Maybe he was planning to stand anyway. Whatever the reason, he got to his feet and picked up the gun that fit so naturally into either hand, and looking at my face again, he said, "Half of us are leaving at dusk. We'll be gone for six or seven nights."

He never told me news like this.

"Where are you going?" I asked.

"We know some weak dogs," he said.

I said, "Oh."

Then he laughed, and not softly. He laughed and with that confident stride began walking away.

"I was raised on wolf blood," my dog said. "I am a great wolf, and the empire begins right here."

The males wore camouflage and took their best weapons and most of their ammunition. But they didn't return in six days, or seven. Or in ten. Eleven nights without their men made the females sick. I listened to the wailing and fighting. They would beat their offspring with little provocation. One of them came up to the castle. She was the very young one, my dog's favorite mate. She tried to talk to me. I didn't respond. She squatted and told my walls how scared she was, how sad and lonely she was, and to prove some or all of those feelings, she began doing things with her hands, her grimy little fingers.

I watched because I was curious.

Her sick pleasure meant something to me. I wasn't certain what, but afterwards, as she walked away from my walls, I felt pity for her, and deeper than that, I discovered worry for the dog that was so deeply missed.

The oldest pups served as guards, day and night. On the fourteenth night, when there was no moon and the stars were obscured by high dust, one of the pups saw strange males approaching. She gave the warning to the camp, and every mother grabbed up the littlest ones and urged the others to run for the castle.

I expected this, which is to say that I considered many scenarios about what might happen and how each playing piece would respond. All of these pieces gathered close to the invincible walls, begging for help. Different voices wanted different kinds of help. The females wanted to be let inside, which was impossible. The immature males wanted my weapons turned on the invaders, which was somewhat more likely. Reaching into the darkness, my senses found five males heavily cloaked inside stolen tech. They were dogs, but the tech was not. This was another scenario that I had imagined, but rarely and never with any sense of urgency.

I put on my armor and absorbed a great share of courage.

My dogs scattered when the outer door opened, and then too slow by a long step, they were blocked from slipping inside when the doors closed and sealed.

I stood among the pack, watching the invaders moving closer.

Each of these creatures had a name. I knew them by sight and by voice. They were strange pitiful and yet lovely, and of course I would protect them now.

I walked across the plastic grass.

A dog emerged from the dead forest.

I could have killed him but hesitated. I don't know why I hesitated. Then the cloaks fell away and I saw that he was my dog, safe and home again. Such a wave of relief shook me, leaving me weakened. I could have killed him. I nearly did. Maybe that's why I wept as he started talking to me.

"What a fucking mess," he said. "There's a clan living up in the mountains. A bunch of real assholes, which we knew going in. But I didn't realize they had a friend, and I had no idea how close she was to them."

"What kind of friend?" I asked.

He stared straight at me.

"Where did you get the tech?" I asked.

"Stole it." Then with a sorrowful laugh, he said, "That's our little ray of hope in this disaster. Some new machinery."

"You stole the tech from their friend," I said.

"She's a monster," he said.

I didn't say anything.

"We need help," he said. "You probably know the friend already."

"Who is she?" I asked.

He gave me specific directions.

"No, I don't know her," I said.

"But her castle is so close," he said.

I tried to explain. There are different measures of proximity.

But he grew bored and interrupted me. "Whatever," he said. "With your help, we can kill that damned clan. At least the big boys die, and then we can grab up their girls and come back here again."

Two of his brothers emerged from the forest. But the youngest brother had died or been left behind.

My dog watched me. Then with a slow, careful voice, he said, "You won't help us, will you?"

"I help you all the time," I said.

"You won't go on the fight with us."

"No."

"But you don't even know this other one. So what does it matter?"

I tried to explain why it mattered.

"Listen to yourself," he said.

I said, "If the bad pack comes here, I'll defend you. But that is as much as I am willing to do."

My dog stared at my armored chest.

The rest of the pack did the same.

"Well," my dog said at last. "At least you're telling us where you stand."

I fed them double shares and gave them all of my water while sending a message to my neighbor on the other side of the mountains, saying nothing overt but offering to discuss mutual issues.

She responded by saying that she didn't know me and to leave her alone.

I left her alone.

For the rest of that evening and two more nights, nothing happened. Nothing changed. I fed my dogs everything they could eat and more, and the second pack didn't appear, but then the afternoon sun was swallowed by black clouds of dust and even with the best tech it was difficult to see. Peering into the gloom, I suffered glimpses of motion and odd shapes, and then a series of sharp little explosions. Suddenly my dog appeared, running to the door and pounding with both hands.

"Let us in," he begged.

I wanted to let him inside, but only him.

"We're dying out here," he said.

I was already wearing my armor. But I couldn't see any threat, which was why I stayed indoors.

"Do you hear me?" he asked.

He knew that I did.

"Master," he said. "They are coming for us."

I couldn't see any new faces, but the dead woods began to burn. A dozen little fires consumed the dried underbrush and the trees, joining into one mighty blaze, and the filthy wind blew smoke and ash across the lawn. Pups were running back and forth. Naked, the young mother ran to my door, her little pup screaming in agony. She screamed too. "Forget him and run away," she said.

"No," my dog said.

"We're going," she said.

"He'll help us as soon as he puts on his armor," my dog said.

My armor was ready, but I was scared. My mind was not suited to moments like these. If I used every bit of courage in my inventory, I would still feel scared, and that's why I did nothing and remained silent.

The mother and her baby left.

My dog sat before the door. I had never seen him weep before. He had been stripped of his dignity. But the fire soon burnt itself out and the dust storm eventually passed, leaving nothing but ruin and my dog.

Armed with several comforting phrases to make both of us feel better, I stepped through the doors.

He looked everywhere but at my face.

I began to talk.

"Shut up," he said.

"All right," I said.

Then he began to laugh—quietly yet with rage—and taking relish in the words, he said, "This has all been a test, you know. From the first day we met, even the tiniest event was part of a great plan."

I asked, "Whose plan?"

"Not yours." The laugh grew louder. "Stay outside or go run back into your little house. Either way, you lose."

It was a rare feeling, a strangely wondrous feeling, having no understanding about what was happening.

He finally looked at me, just for a moment. Then he stood and backed away several steps while various kinds of tech were turned off. The blackened lawn was covered with dogs, mature and heavily armed. The big dog that my dog seemingly killed last year was alive again. The missing younger brother had returned, healthy and still angry. It occurred to me that the one that I killed was never a brother, just another fool caught up in this elaborate scheme.

The enormous pack was marching toward me.

I fled inside, secured the doors and consumed every form of courage, but before the illusionary sense of security could take hold, the "monster" neighbor woman walked out from her hiding place.

She wasn't wearing armor.

Indeed, she wore almost nothing. Boots suitable for long hikes rode the otherwise naked legs, and her exposed chest was burnt scarlet by the sun, and strung around her neck was a steel collar adorned with savage barbs—good steel polished until it shone, but only half as bright as the radiant smile that crushed the last hope in my world.

Semiramis

GENEVIEVE VALENTINE

The worst thing about being a sleeper embedded somewhere long-term was that inevitably, eventually, you started to care.

The worst thing about being embedded long-term as an administrator at the Svalbard Seed Vault was that when you inevitably started to care, you started to care about things like proper political geo-temperate arrangement of seeds, and there was just no one else in their right mind who was going to care about that with you.

That was half the reason I recruited Lise.

Ever since Svalbard had been put under review, it had been hell and a half trying to figure out how to recruit a domestic cover who could carry seeds off the island. And for something this long-term in a place as small as Longyearbyen, you needed domestic cover, or people started to suspect you for keeping apart.

The locals were out of the question, and once we were under review it was more than my life was worth to try to smuggle someone over if they didn't already have some international clearance.

("Under review": the Global Coalition was interested enough in Svalbard to station spies at the ports.)

Lise had been a loose affiliate of my organization, years back. She'd dropped off the map, but it only took two tries to contact her, and one meeting to convince her.

"Good choice," said the guy who'd met her, when he called weeks later to seal the deal. "She's got contacts at the mine at Sveagruva. She's already on a plane to Oslo; she'll catch a boat out to you next week."

The rest of the timeline was already set, for the short-term: quick public courtship, cohabitation. When our orders came in, she'd make the initial runs off the island, and then once there was a routine in place she could quietly vanish whenever things soured.

Until then she would live with me on Svalbard and keep an eye on Coalition business in town and whatever the mining company turned up.

I would keep making visits to the Seed Vault, taking inventory, ticking off names on my list, waiting for the day when I'd get the order to move out two or three seeds at a time and pass them off to whoever the highest bidders sent to collect.

(The day I was really waiting for was the day I could tell someone, "This one's drying up. We'll be looking for some decent soil, to grow it for re-harvest," and have their eyes light up, too.)

"Coalition Peacekeepers just showed up—they blocked the port," Lise says, knocking mud off her boots. "They've already dispatched a zoo team to look for polar bears."

I whistle. "How many of them?"

"Enough to make sure you don't get one fucking seed out of here," she says. "Good luck."

(She was a decent recruit—she'd done admin at the Millennium Seed Bank before it got militarized, had some clearance, had some brains—but she wasn't a believer, and it showed.)

I frown at the printout in front of me—scientific names and common names and country of origin marching in four-point font for two hundred pages.

"We'll find a way around it," I say. "This could just be like the review. It could be years before we have to worry."

We plan in years.

She shoulders her rifle. "I'm going out."

Rifles are standard issue in Longyearbyen, one of the few places you can still get one. It's required outside the city, for protection against polar bears.

(She mostly goes out to the bird cliffs and takes shots at poachers.)

"Don't kill anyone," I say. We need to keep cover.

A gust of cold wind, and she's gone.

Absently, I check off *Acer palmatum* on the list, but my concentration is already gone, and I end up staring out the window at the shadows that gather inside shadows all over this place at night.

I don't notice the Peacekeeper boats have moved into place until someone inside one turns on a light.

We measure time two ways.

One is the paper calendar I get at Christmas from the woman who poses, twice a year, as my sister.

Longyearbyen went nearly paperless after the Global Coalition's Environmental Imperative was released. (We had to preserve any trees that would grow, it said; now that the waters were rising, arable land was sacrosanct.)

Tax on physical mail was obscene, but the calendar was how I received most of my instructions, so I paid.

One random day a year was "Semiramis (observed)"—the day I sent my ID over a landline, by voice.

I chose the name; she was the queen for whom they'd built the hanging gardens in Babylon.

By then I had started to care.

"Happy Semiramis," Lise always said when she checked off that calendar day, in a tone that made me feel like I was giving away too much.

It was the only paper in the house, save the printout of the Seed Vault inventory. That had been granted exemption—pulp for the good of the nation.

Lise was the one who started ticking off days on the calendar, the very first year she arrived.

I hadn't asked why. We didn't like each other enough back then to get into a round of questions, and by the time we'd reached a truce it wasn't worth asking. In this line of work, you learn just to live with people.

The other way we keep time is by tracking how much coal is worth.

Most of the coal mined on Svalbard went directly into the air conditioners at the Seed Vault, to keep the temperature at a constant zero Fahrenheit. The price of coal went up the warmer it got outside, and the more of it we needed, the less of it there was.

This was the calendar we kept for the rest of the world, to measure how bad things were getting.

Two years back, Lise had come home and said, "We passed gold on the index. Things must be rough down South."

"Did the Coalition do anything?"

"We got an embargo—no export under threat of treason," she said, shrugged. The coal was meant for the Vault, not for sale, and Svalbard was already under review; it wasn't as though anything got off the island anyway, unless the Norwegian government found some country down South with the money to buy.

(Down South: anywhere beneath the Arctic line, where water levels were rising and cities were being swallowed up. Shanghai and New York had gone early, London and Copenhagen a few years later. The Maldives had vanished right off the map. Their government operated out of Mumbai until that went under, too.

The whole South was just governments sprinting for high ground, these days.)

After the Peacekeepers come, I don't see her for two days.

The Sveagruva mine is battening down in the wake of the Peacekeepers, and she works long hours up there. Sometimes it's easier just to sleep over.

I go out to the Seed Vault every day, in the bright green parka that makes me look like a tourist. I leave the Snow Cat and walk the last mile (less threatening), and try not to stare at the ships.

It's surprising how high the water has risen. My first year, passing ships had been so low I could look down onto their decks; now they're nearly eye level.

The Peacekeepers are already stationed outside, asking my business.

That's a mistake. If you ask someone about their business, they might tell you.

(Years back, when I was still so new that I worried how I'd ever overcome my apathy about seed packets in a fucking basement, some botanists came to drop off seeds. One of them talked at me for twenty minutes about the runaway metabolism of *Castanea sativa*.

"Can you imagine a future without chestnuts?" she said, and handed me the envelope, and sighed. "It's so precarious, now, with so few species allowed to grow at all. This is the last surviving breed—the very last."

I looked at the woman in mild terror. I already knew that I was doomed to be interested one day; that didn't mean it wasn't an awful thing to anticipate.

Norway sealed Svalbard to donations a year after that. By the time I'd developed interest, I was alone.)

I give the Peacekeepers a more detailed description of my business than anyone has ever wanted.

"It's the recalcitrant seeds that we really have to watch out for," I explain about five minutes in, and then I start on runaway metabolism and desiccation effects and where we'll be when we can't grow chestnuts any more, and the Peacekeepers look at me pretty much the way I'd expected them to.

Still, they move aside.

I ask them, "Where's home for you?"

"Scotland."

"How are things there?"

They don't answer.

(No answer: Under occupation, or under water.)

Inside, I'm relieved beyond reason the *Tuberaria guttata* seeds are doing well.

It had been drowned out of the Mediterranean and Wales and the States years back. This sample had been harvested from Scotland, and it doesn't sound like there are going to be many more chances at it.

When I come home, Lise is sitting in front of the little coal stove, still in her yellow coat.

It's a comfort. We've lived together for nearly eight years, and after a while you just get used to seeing someone.

(The first time I was embedded somewhere I fell in love with my domestic-cover operative. It went badly. I've learned not to overthink these things.)

I hang my coat. "How has it gone? Peacekeepers giving you trouble yet?"

"Their ships are upsetting the fish," she says. "The birds are just circling. Bad enough that the cliffs are disappearing underwater. Now they'll starve, too."

The bird-cliffs are covered this time of year, auks and terns and kittiwakes. I went out there once, with Lise, to check out escape routes. It was a chaos of feathers and noise and the green and yellow lights of the Aurora, and I left as soon as I realized it would be impossible to scale the cliffs.

Lise goes back all the time.

(One year, early on, she brought back a tern that had been on the bad end of a fight, and she fed and warmed it all night until it died. Then she took the body outside. What she did with it she never said, and I didn't ask. You learn to just live with people.)

I make coffee on the stove, keep one eye on her face as her expression gets darker.

By the time I sit next to her, I've made up my mind.

"I brought this," I say, and pull an envelope out of my pocket.

It's an archival envelope, unlabeled; inside is a single seed.

"*Tuberaria guttata*. Spotted rock rose. The flowers last less than a day. This one's from Scotland, but it sounds like they've drowned by now. These are going to be worth a lot of money."

She hasn't taken the seed out. She's just looking at it still tucked inside the envelope. I didn't think her expression could get darker, but I was wrong.

"Have the orders come in?" she asks.

I should have expected concern. She thinks she's been cut out of the loop.

"No, no," I say. "Still waiting to hear. I just—I wanted to bring this one out. Call it a dry run."

"Are you going to sell it?"

Suspicion I hadn't expected.

"No," I snap. "I just wanted you to see it."

She looks up at that. I freeze and wait; if she calls it a present, I'll deny it to the death.

But she only says, "Isn't it enough you'll be taking out the others?"

She's not a believer, and it shows.

I pluck the envelope out of her hand.

"Two million seeds," I say. "Will they really miss one?"

"There used to be two million birds," she says. Her voice is strained, like she's trying not to care.

We sit in silence until the fire goes down and the cabin's warm enough to sleep in.

(We sleep in the same bed. This is too long-term an arrangement to be a gentleman and sleep on the couch. You plan in years.)

It takes six weeks before Peacekeepers and Svalbard locals have finished jostling for territory.

It means the worst, of course—no one's under illusions. It means that "under review" has turned into "Coalition Protectorate" in some back room in some inland country, and the highest-bidding corporation will be moving in to take over the coal mines, and soon the Svalbard Seed Vault will be powered by Mainland Oil or MediaVox.

It means my orders are going to come through any day, so we can have a little of our own back before the MediaVox Seed Vault opens for business.

I go every day, now, just to keep the Peacekeepers used to my face.

Lise comes home from the mine, shoulders her rifle, goes out again. I don't know where. The Peacekeepers are crowding us out wherever they can.

By now I'm staying up nights, too, researching what nations have gone under one way or another.

It's really something how hard the Coalition works to keep its member nations separated. Once they get their import taxes and their offshore data charges and their streaming-feed embargoes on you, there's no communicating with anyone—you might as well be submerged in the sea.

You have to strike early, before the locals have submitted to all the red tape.

You have to act before they know to stop you.

Semiramis comes.

I make the call from the loudest pub in town.

"It's soon," my fake sister says. "Be ready to move out past the Peacekeepers."

I snap, "Then Lise will have to swim, because these boats aren't budging. We need time."

"We need at least one good run," she says, "to make this worth it. It has to be soon."

We argue about Peacekeepers for a minute or two in low voices, and then I talk nonsense about the weather for another five minutes, just in case.

(It's not all nonsense—I tell her about the sea level, and she says, "We moved," and I imagine the overpacked cities picking themselves up, buildings and all, and climbing the mountain as the water rises.)

When I come home, Lise doesn't tell me, "Happy Semiramis."

I can hardly be offended, but this is the first time I notice that she stopped marking days a long time ago. That worries me.

I don't mention yet that our time to act is coming. I have a feeling I'd better have a plan before I try to get her in on it.

I'm beginning to understand the frustration of not knowing everything. My fake sister hasn't told me what they think the Coalition will do to me, when they find out what's happened.

It's a when, not an if. Lise has been positioned to survive, as a condition of her participation. There's no such provision for me. Never has been. Sometimes when you take a job, it's your last one.

Still, I make a few more dry runs, just to keep in practice for when my orders come.

I pick some seeds that will grow in any soil (as dumb as it is, I still want to plant something, once, and watch it grow). I pick some seeds because they're rare enough to make a decent bribe if things go south.

I pick a bird of paradise, a seed with a sharp red tuft, for no reason except that it's been ten years since I've seen anything red; the Aurora is yellow and green, and the rest of the world is the tight dark of seeds, and envelopes paler than skin.

I should have planned a little more, for when this started to creep over me, but there's no knowing how it will creep up on you until you look at a tufted seed and blink at how bright it is.

I didn't even look up what happened to the Hanging Gardens until after I had picked the name. Turns out the ground swallowed them, but what can you do?

Every time I bring something home I hand her the envelope, so she can't say I held out on her.

She should know what she's doing when the time comes, and she should know the worth of what she's carrying. I don't plead anybody's case—I'm not like that botanist with the chestnuts. This is business.

Usually she only glances inside. I tell her what they are and what long-gone country they came from, and she gets that drawn, sad look I'm starting to see in the mirror.

Once, she opens the envelope and says instantly, "Bird of paradise."

I'm so surprised I smile.

She hands it back "That's a slow grow. Good luck getting it to the blooming stage."

"You never know," I say.

(We plan in years.)

As part of the negotiations to keep everyone in Svalbard from turning on them, the Coalition ships finally move back out of fishing range.

They open a big enough gap on the north side of the water for seals and bears to pass; in return, the rifle-bearing locals promise to stop mistaking Peacekeepers for polar bears at night.

Thousands of birds have died from starvation in the meantime, Lise tells me that night.

"The shore under the cliff is a graveyard," she says.

"At least the seals will be fed," I say.

Her eyes are red. She doesn't answer.

I imagine her skidding through the slush all the way to the cliff, seeing what she saw, and the Peacekeeper boats just out of rifle range.

I make us coffee.

A week later, Sveagruva lets its employees go.

"It's just an interim measure," Lise parrots, "to preserve the facility until new management can be chosen."

I nod. "Very reassuring. Doesn't sound at all like a MediaVox move-in."

"Yeah," she says. "This coal brought to you by."

She already looks antsy about being cut off from information.

"Lise," I say, serious. "We'll figure a way off Svalbard for you. I'm not going to strand you here. That wasn't the deal."

She slings her rifle over her shoulder, disappears.

Our orders come in.

There are a hundred seeds on the list—one good run. They could be carried in someone's coat pocket, in the fingertips of a pair of gloves, if people were still allowed in or out.

The new coal boats have clearance, but Lise isn't employed there any more. Coalition companies start with clean slates.

"Somehow we have to get you on a ship," I say.

She says, like we were having a totally different conversation all along, "Are they going to sell the Vault, do you think?"

I have no answer. I don't like where this is going.

She sits back against the couch, stares at the tiny fire in our tiny stove.

"At first I thought they'd sell it off all in one piece, to one of the inland countries that can still grow something. That would be better than nothing. Any growth is better than letting things die—expensive wheat is better than no wheat. That, I would have been all right with. I would have let that happen."

She means, *I would have turned you in.*

She's using past tense, so I'm probably fine, but still I look around to make sure she's not within reach of her gun.

She sighs. "But seeing how they've managed things," and when she pauses I know she thinks of the birds, "I wonder if they're worse than we are, and we're better off just because we can call a theft a theft."

"Speak for yourself," I say, though it's true.

She pulls something from the inside of her jacket—a seed envelope.

The little rock rose seed tumbles into her open palm, and for a second I hold my breath like it will sprout.

(I need a drink.)

Lise doesn't look at me. "What color does it bloom?"

"Yellow."

She nods and curls her fingers around it. I think about telling her to give me my bribe back, but I don't. It was probably a gift. Happy Semiramis.

"I'll join up with the people from the Gene Ark, when they show," she says. "They never wait long to barge in and take tissue samples from native species, and they'll need the help. I can get out that way, and come back as soon as I can."

She says it like she'll actually make it back here, like we haven't done all this work for a shot at one hundred seeds before the other, smarter thieves close in.

Still, a hundred plants isn't bad. A hundred and one—she'll take hers with her.

"All right," I say.

After a while she says, "You know, I've never been inside the Vault."

I sit down beside her. Our shoulders are touching.

"It's a long hallway," I say, "and then some seeds."

We sit awake long after the fire goes out, watching shadows gathering inside shadows, waiting for morning.

(Inevitably, eventually, you start to care.)

Whose Face This Is I Do Not Know
CAT RAMBO

I glance in the glass wall's reflection. It faces me twenty feet away as I walk up the stairs, marble slab steps showing grainy pink underneath my red sneakers. My fingers clutch the railing's chrome. I'm feeling shaky, that internal quiver where your body announces that it may not be up to this.

I focus on my image. Is my hair longer now? The eyes wider, bluer? The lips, are they swinging towards bee-stung or thinning?

Thinning, it seems to me, but other people move in and out of the building in the morning sunlight, interrupting the reflection.

They dress like beetles, shells blue and black and brown. The woman coming towards me eyes my clothing: faded t-shirt, jacket like thick black leather armor, unremarkable jeans. Past her shoulder my hair is bright curly blonde. I force a matching smile and trot up the stairs.

The elevator. Watery bronze strips bordering more slabs of pink granite, bronze circles around the buttons, loose with age underneath my touch.

Definitely thinner lips. A wave of red is creeping up the hair too, overtaking the blonde. Ragged edge, a fractal line. Some hairs must change faster. I wonder if it is always the same rate.

I am a marvelous machine, a wonder of the Universe.

Hettie is dead. My nose stings with repressed tears.

Dr. Basil's administrative assistant Mindy sits typing at an expanse of gray and pink desk, a vase of white flowers near her elbow. The surface of the vase is matte clay marked with combed lines.

At first her look is sharp as she says, "Can I help you?"

Something in my silence tells her who I am. She makes a silent *oh* of surprise. In her eyes, tiny images of me, too small to make out details.

"A.J.?" she says hesitantly. "A.J., is that you?"

I nod.

She thumbs the intercom on her desk. "A.J. is here." Wonder edges her voice. Dr. Basil's tone is flat and unreadable on the intercom. "Send A.J. in."

When I first enter, he is standing by the window, a long rectangle that reaches from floor to ceiling to frame winter clouds. He makes an abortive move towards me, catches himself and goes to sit behind the desk. He motions me to a seat.

The chair is too low to the floor and would be difficult to get out of quickly, so I perch on the edge, resting my weight on my legs. On the desk a brass monkey holds a globe up overhead. The monkey's face is sad. Two images of me dance on his shiny cheeks, distorted by the metal's shape. Both of me are tiny, insignificant, but we are there. Small mechanisms. I am a wonder of the Universe. Hettie said so.

"The newspapers reported Ms. Stillson's death," he says after precisely two silent minutes.

"It was icy and Hettie slipped," I say.

"Where were you?"

"In front of her house. I went away before anyone could talk to me."

Tension leaves his shoulders at the words. "Good," he says. He looks at me. "Female, are you?"

"Since Friday," I say. "Well, earlier than that, I think."

He nods again. "And the degree of change is still infrequent? Small changes at a rapid pace, but the major shifts, sometimes weeks or months apart?"

"I haven't noticed a change."

He hesitates, staring at me as though he were hungry, as though I were reminding him of someone. "Any other odd . . . episodes?"

"No. I haven't imagined I was becoming anyone else," I say.

He looks disappointed but nods. "Would you like something to drink? Hot coffee, tea?"

"Could we send out for a pizza?" I say. "I haven't eaten in a couple of days."

Twenty-five minutes later, the spices of a triple meat pizza burn their way down my throat. At first my stomach doesn't want to take in so much, but I concentrate and it relaxes enough to let me gorge.

I don't know when the next meal will be. It's all been moment to moment for so long, and Hettie's death makes it all even more uncertain. With the thought, acid roils along my throat and I wash it down with gulps of soda, full of sugar and caffeine that my body stores away.

I keep an eye on myself in the window. My hair is creeping back to black, leaving an odd silver line across it. My eyes are definitely droopier, sadder looking than when I came in. A new fullness to my cheeks.

Dr. Basil goes out to talk to Mindy. I don't mean to listen, but I do. It's hard to avoid in this form, when every nerve and sensory ending seems so alert. The beast still lingers underneath the human skin.

"What now?" she asks.

"I don't know," he answers.

A silence before she says, "Will you turn it in to the authorities?"

"A.J.? No. No, I wouldn't do that." But his voice is thin and unconvincing. I imagine his eyes flickering towards the door, trying to warn her that I might be hearing them. Am I imagining it or do I know this? I can't tell any more. I wipe the thin red grease from the pizza on the box's lid, fingertips leaving oily arcs.

"It's been three years," she says. "Over three years."

"Only two days since Hettie died," the doctor says. "That will be why she came back. It came back."

Hettie would have never called me it. But Hettie was never maternal. She was like a rock, a boulder awakened to life by some wizard, pragmatic and wise and given to thinking in a not precisely human way. I know there was a time before I came to her, but I only dimly remember it, as though remembering that I had remembered it once.

We used to go out walking in the woods, looking for sassafras root or mushrooms. There are few mirrors in nature, particularly in the woods. It didn't matter whether I looked different coming out than I had going in. I could give up looking at myself.

She lived on the edge of a nature preserve, Pinhook Park. With the trimming back of the Parks Service she and other people trespassed as deep inside the forests of the park as they liked.

When I'd realized what I could become, that was where I'd gone. For three years I lived in Pinhook's woods. I don't remember much of the moments there. There's a difference to non-human existence, as though everything were deeper but some key emotions were missing. It felt peaceful sometimes, sure, but other times it felt cold and shitty and damp and hungry above all else.

Finally I'd become aware that I was moving away from that form. I found myself naked on a bank of frost-covered grass one day and thought, "All right, I can pass now."

An ice-glazed puddle reassured me that I could re-enter the world without too much notice. My nose was still too large but my ears had shrunk back to human size, and my teeth were moving back towards omnivore.

I stole clothing from a Goodwill drop-off box, an outfit assembled of too large jeans and a black hoodie. No socks, but luckily, happily, red sneakers just my size, as though the Universe were applauding my decision to come out of the woods and be human again.

Like I had much choice in the matter.

Hettie hadn't said much when she saw me sitting on her front steps, waiting for her. The snow blanketed the grass, framing the sight of her straw-colored hair topped with a blue knit cap. Sunlight glinted on the snow and water dripped from the eaves of the house in a slow, steady cadence. Behind her on the street a white van rolled past and continued. The air smelled wet and cold.

Recognition in her eyes. How did she know me? Was there something that persisted in showing, beneath all the forms, the boys and girls and in-betweens that I had been?

"Hettie," I said. "It's me, A.J."

"I figured you'd come back some time," she said matter-of-factly. Hettie's imperturbability had been a standard of my childhood. Maybe that was why Basil had picked her to raise his experiments. I'd never asked how she came here, or what she thought of me.

She motioned me inside. Enough mirrors in her house that I could catch glimpses of myself. I seemed to be stable, not making any dramatic changes other than the movement back to the human. The house smelled of pine and floor wax. Hettie had always kept it immaculate. Orderly.

She set out clean towels on a chair by the bathroom door. "I'll fix dinner," she said, leaving out unnecessary words to pat my shoulder. "Welcome home."

When I came out of the shower, toweling my thin brown fur dry, I stared into the mirror, committing every feature to memory. Like meeting a stranger you are promised to, a bridegroom or a bride. But who will die right after the wedding, never to be seen again.

Hettie knocked on the door, interrupting my reverie. "Come out and eat. Your clean clothes are here outside the door."

In the kitchen, she sat across from me and stared. She'd heated two cans of tomato soup and set out a sleeve of crackers and cheese slices beside my bowl. My stomach rumbled at the sight.

"You know I have to call him," she said.

"Yes'm," I said. I ate quickly at first, but slowed as I became sated. With every bite of soup, it was like I was ingesting sleepiness. I hoped I could make it through the entire bowl before I crashed face down.

I did but I don't remember much of her taking me up to my room to sleep. Only the drum of the rain, a glimmer of drops on the windowpane, tinting the streetlight's shine to silver.

In the morning, sun sifting through the window woke me. I lay there luxuriating in the warmth and feel of the sheets against my skin. The bed smelled of soap and ironing and a trace of lavender. My face, checked in the bathroom mirror, looked increasingly human. Nice to wear my own clothes again. Hettie had laid my glasses by the sink. Funny, I'd had no problems with my eyes all the time I was gone, even though their shifts had plagued me all through childhood.

Downstairs, Hettie was making toaster waffles. Butter and syrup sat out on the table with two Starbucks containers of coffee, one large and one small. I picked mine up and sipped it. After months of no caffeine, it rocketed through my system like being slapped.

"Where were you?" she asked without preamble.

"Near here, Pinhook Park," I said.

She raised her eyebrows. "All that time?"

I nodded. "That's how long I was . . . whatever that was," I said.

"Looked like a big bear at first," she said. "Like that was the destination, anyhow."

"Did you call Dr. Basil?"

She flipped waffles onto a plate for me and started a couple for herself. "He wants you to come in this morning, after breakfast."

"Not wasting any time."

"It's been three years, A.J.," she said. "Or did you notice that, when you were off being Bigfoot?"

"I don't think I was ever really Bigfoot," I said. "Maybe a werewolf."

"A very slow one," she said. "More waffles?"

I shook my head, even though I wanted them. I didn't want to be sluggish. "When does he want me to come in?"

"Now, if you're ready." She looked at the bus schedule magneted to the refrigerator. "The 545 comes in about 30 minutes."

Outside, a layer of ice coated the trees, the sidewalk, the grass, as though they were all encased in glass.

"Pretty," I said.

"Pretty is as pretty does," Hettie said from behind me.

I opened my mouth to say something smart-ass and felt the porch railing shake under my grip. Hettie went down with a thump on the first step. At first I was laughing as I turned.

Then I saw her fixed stare.

I fell to my knees. The minute I touched her shoulder, the weight of her told me what I didn't want to know, that all life was gone. Not even a flicker left.

I called 911 on her cell phone all the same, fishing it out of her pocket. I couldn't linger. They would look too hard, too close at my features, which still were not perfectly human, still had the animal lingering underneath. So I left, went back up the steps as though I was going to fetch something, leaving her there.

I paused in the dining room, about to go upstairs and pack, but I heard the ambulance's distant shrill. Absurdly I grabbed the closest thing to hand, a liter bottle of vodka that Hettie kept for company, which had not been touched in all the time I had lived there. I ducked out the back door and headed through the back yard, past a snow-ridden pile of wood, across an icy crunch of gravel.

I scrambled along the alleyway, ignoring a couple of dogs hurling themselves against fences. Behind me there was a crash and splinter of wood. I turned to see a bulldog bow-legging its way toward me. An old dog. White streaked its jowls. Its broad shoulders sagged. It growled.

"I don't want to hurt you," I said, and tried to let pheromones roil off my skin. Slowly, its hackles subsided and it stopped growling, but from its yard a backdoor slammed. A voice shouted "Percy!"

I turned and fled.

At Pinhook Park, I sat on the hill overlooking the miniature train course and got drunker than I ever had been. When I woke the next morning, propped in the corner of a chilly cement shelter, I felt as though my flesh would crawl off my bones, reacting to the amount of alcohol I had tried to drown it in. For the next two days I vomited, until finally I gathered the strength to walk the blocks to Dr. Basil's downtown office.

He comes back in, watches me while I eat the last of the pizza and mop my hands. The grease clings and I have to scrub it off. I catch him watching the gesture. I wonder what nuance of self-loathing psychiatry has taught him to read into it.

"I want to change your medication," he tells me. "I think I have a mixture that will keep your form from drifting away from human." He holds out an orange-brown bottle of pills, white-capped. Only three capsules in it.

"One every eight hours," he says in answer to my look.

"What about when I run out?"

He glances away from me. I follow his gaze. He and I stand looking at the window's reflection. My breasts seem larger than this morning.

"We'd like you to stick around so we can monitor the changes," he says.

I take the medicine bottle, hold it in my hand. "How did you develop this?"

"What do you mean?"

"You haven't had me to experiment on for the last three years. Who did you develop this on?"

"Ah. You weren't the only member of your batch. You met a few growing up. Casey even lived with you for a while. And then Deejay and Deecie."

"Are they here?"

He shakes his head. Somehow I know they're dead, but I have no idea how. He smells of it. I push it. "Maybe they can come visit me, huh?"

"We might be able to scare up one or two visitors," he says.

"Where am I going to stay?"

The Doctor takes me downstairs, past the basement level, to a comfortably outfitted apartment. There's a stack of video games, and the TV is taller than me. No windows, though.

I look around.

Dr. Basil watches my reaction to the apartment. "We have paperwork we'd like you to help us with," he says. He gestures at a memopad on the table. "Tests of perception and personality. That sort of thing."

"That sort of thing," I repeat.

During the days I devote myself to Dr. Basil's tests. They seem calculated to take up as much time as I'm willing to give to them.

Memories of Hettie play themselves over and over in my head. It wasn't that there were any words of love, it was simply that she gave me a faith that she would always be there for me.

I thought about the others Dr. Basil had mentioned. I did remember Casey, but barely. I remembered playing Mirror with them, the game where one person makes a gesture and the other follows suit. We played it for hours. I remember running over green grass on summer evenings and playing statues and freeze tag, standing as though frozen in shape, frozen in place.

I don't remember whether Casey was a boy or girl but more importantly I don't remember whether or not s/he changed as well. I hear Hettie in my head telling us to play nice together and that's about it. I don't remember anything about Casey going away other than going into their room and looking under the bed to find the blue knapsack s/he had left me, with a handful of pictures and two favorite action figures.

What had happened to the pictures? I wasn't sure. I had held onto the dolls for years. Probably still boxed up in Hettie's attic.

I remember the month before the change. I'd look up and see her staring at me, as though willing me to do something. She talked to me about things she'd never mentioned before.

"You're a person, not a lab animal," she told me. "You need to decide your own destiny. You need to be able to not worry about Basil." She looked into my eyes. Were they changing as she watched? All I could see were hers, which never changed.

"You are a wonder of the Universe," she said. "You deserve to be free in it."

I play some games and watch TV. It's canned stuff, on-demand, so I can't see the news. They won't give me net access outside the internal web. It's the last that chafes me the most. It didn't bother me at Hettie's but here, where I know it's just a matter of bringing me a tablet or screen, it eats at me.

"Look, bring me a kiddie laptop," I tell Dr. Basil when he comes in that night to check on me. "Put whatever kind of lock-downs you want on it. I don't care if all I can do is read the weather. I just want to feel connected. You know how it is, Doc."

I smile as warmly as I can at him, thinking *happiness* and *sensuality*, trying to project them. *Friendliness. Trust.*

It succeeds. He brings me a cheapie screen. There aren't even any restrictions on it that I can see. I work with the presumption that it's all monitored, though. I have more to worry about. Giving it to me he lets his hand linger on mine in a way that made this body flush and warm.

The new machine has a shiny screen. I can keep an eye on myself even as I tab through web portals, making it look like someone catching up. I've been away three years, and some of this is actually just that - catching up. There are only so many ways to access a link, though, so it's not too hard to navigate.

I do take a risk and check my mail. A two year old message in one folder reads "Call me. —KC." And a number. I try to find the number on the net, but it's out of service, the web tells me.

I finish by playing a game where you throw an exploding ball from character to character. It explodes in my arms time and time again. I keep holding it too long.

When Dr. Basil returns that morning, he wants to run tests. He takes my blood pressure, listens to my heart. His fingers stray here and there, never long enough to remark on, but long enough to let me know what he's thinking. He keeps staring at my eyes.

"You said you could maybe let me have a couple of visitors," I ask. "You know. Casey and those others."

His eyes widen. "Did I?" he says. "Well, I can see." His hand on mine. I disentangle, retracting my fingers to fold them in my lap.

"I wish you would," I say, looking straight at him. "I would really . . . *appreciate* that."

Beneath his gaze, I lean back, arching to make my chest more prominent. I hate these kind of mechanical tricks, but when someone is sending out the signals he is, they will work.

"I'll see what I can do," he says. He packs away his equipment, piece by piece. "May I come by and eat dinner with you tonight?"

I force a shrug. My body performs as I wish it to, mimicking acts with a grace that makes it believable. "Depends on what sort of mood I'm in," I say and, deliberate as removing my lips from a kiss, I look elsewhere, refuse to meet his eyes.

The breath that comes from him is almost a groan.

"You're still female?" he demands.

"Of course." I add, "Usually the less stressed I am, the less likely I am to change."

That evening he eats with me, bringing take out Chinese, chopsticks, and fortune cookies. I haven't done much that day so I pick at the food.

He watches me. I put a piece of Governor's Chicken in my mouth, biting down with delicate care and licking my lips.

He grabs my hand and raises it to his face, pulling the fingertips over the cleanly shaven skin of his cheek.

I pull it away again, shaking my head.

"I'm out of sorts tonight," I say. "Sorry."

"I suppose having a visitor would settle you," he says.

The shrug gets easier with practice, a supple *don't care* movement that emphasizes the pendulum sway of my un-bra-ed breasts.

"Whatever," I say, and let out a bored breath. "Really."

"You're teasing me," he says.

"Am I?" My stare is deliberate and provocative.

He grins at me, an *I know something you don't* smile that clenches at my stomach. "Be careful what you wish for," he says, then stands. "Be ready tomorrow after lunch."

"Ready for what?"

"We're going to see Casey," he says.

He leaves the scatter of white boxes on the table. I abandon it in turn for the maid that comes in every day while I'm in the shower.

All through the next morning my stomach burns. I wonder if it's some new change, but a handful of antacids calms it. Lots of calcium; I'll need to make sure to take a Vitamin D pill that night.

I am much more in tune with my body than the average person; a lack of potassium, for instance, leaves me almost incapacitated by headache. Fish oil restores the lubricants in my tears. Otherwise they're not quite right, but burn and weep continuously.

We don't leave the building, which disappoints me.

Instead, Dr. Basil takes me up to a third-floor laboratory. One wall bears huge jars, a gallon size at least, some much larger, five gallons, ten. Not old yellowed pickle jars either, but clear. Newly made equipment with every line and measurement conforming to Science.

On the table one of the largest jars holds a shaggy mass the size of a bowling ball overgrown with kelp and barnacles. It takes me a moment to realize that it's a head. Underneath it, dangling like a puppet, swims a body in miniature. A troll's body, barely six inches tall. My face, horrified and appalled, is reflected over it. My breasts are absurdly large now.

Now that I look, the rest of jars hold other parts. A hand, a shin. A ribcage. All with these bodies, ranging in size from two inches, up to a foot, attached, like absurd, horrifying key chains to each.

The only eyes that are open, thankfully, are not the miniature sockets on the heads dangling from elbows and tibia — is that an armpit? — but the full-sized ones in the jar on the table. There, the eyes, the sorrowing green eyes that I think must be Casey's, track my movements. The blenched lips move as though to speak, but I have no idea what they try to whisper as I reel away.

Dr. Basil's grip on my shoulder is like iron. "Look," he says. "It's an amazing regenerative process. These have only been growing for two weeks, two and a half really. Each of them will have the original's capabilities. And more, according to whatever genetic modifications I've made."

"Is that what you did with all of them?" I ask.

"Don't be so horrified. It's how you were grown too. Disassembly, some genetic tweaking, and then reincorporation." His other hand trails over my breast, pinches a nipple as he pulls me towards him. "God, you're so lush. I know how perfect you are. You become what the people around you want you to become. Your skin is like velvet."

He groans and buries his face in the side of my neck. I feel the body responding, opening, growing wet. I waste time hating it for what it cannot help. I push him away. He pulls me back to him, suffocatingly close.

"Do it," he breathes into my ear. "Do it, or I'll cut you up and raise myself a new crop. A more pliable crop No more raising you in an uncontrolled environment. That little experiment in socialization proved far too risky."

"You don't have the right to do this."

"I own you. I own this." His fingers pinch the nipple harder, but my time as a beast has left me with advantages, and one of them is sharp teeth.

One swift motion. Rip and tear. He reels away, the side of his head spraying blood where I have removed his ear.

I step back but he's not looking at me any more, stumbling in the spray of blood which coats his face like a mask. I grab the keys from his hands and run away, up the stairs. Past the flashing lights and the people running in. He shouldn't have let me keep the black leather jacket; the blood doesn't show on it.

He'll think I'll move far away, try to escape by train, by plane, by automobile. He won't realize that I can stay close, that there are shelters in Pinhook Park where I can sleep if I keep a step ahead of the rangers, and that's easy enough if I give into the beast and its senses.

I cannot believe that Hettie, who kept me, who was doctor and nursemaid and governess and keeper, would have wanted me to be the beast, but maybe she did. Maybe she spoke to my own desire to free myself from the house that was all I knew. I had escaped, I thought, and the others could too.

Basil has shown me the key to his own destruction. I found what I need in Hettie's garden shed. A saw, twine, salt, and a jar that will do for the first one. Sawing off my own hand is hard, but the beast surges and lets me look down dispassionately at my work. I tie it off and drop the hand in the jar before filling it with water and salt.

I will raise my own army, I think. I vanish back to the park with my jar.

The next few months pass quickly. I waver in and out of beast and human form. By the time summer is ripe and the world is full of food, my hand has fully regrown twice, and in a cave in the Park's heart, there are four of me in varying shapes and sizes, and two more jars, along with white plastic buckets, hidden in a cluster of sewer pipes. I bring them sacks each night, the contents of the park's trash containers. We feast on discarded potato salad and rolls and pizza crusts, eating quietly and efficiently, like the biological machines, the wonders of the universe we are.

It's not exactly like having Hettie back, but it feels close. We sit into the night and tell stories, stories about who we are and I tell them about Hettie. About cartoons I watched when growing up. About the others.

We do not light a fire. The full moon shines down on our faces. We are thinly furred and built for speed now, much the same, but the small details of our appearance shift now and then, darkening and lightening, an ear tilting, nose building into a ridge.

The moonlight catches our eyes, reflecting each other as surely as our faces do, our faces, our face that is the thing to come.

But still, whose face this is, I do not know.

The Taxidermist's Other Wife

KELLY BARNHILL

1.

Not one of us has ever stepped inside the Taxidermist's house. We have no need to do so. We already know what we'll find.

2.

The Taxidermist has a mounted Howler Monkey in his office. Its mouth is open, lips curled outward like the rim of a trumpet. Its head is cocked sweetly to one side, as though reconsidering what it was just about to say. Its knees are bent, toes pigeoned inward in the classical stance, and—though this is a violation of protocol and is generally frowned upon by most who practice the art of taxidermy—its left hand is curled, poised just above the ape's bum, as though about to scratch.

Or, perhaps it *does* scratch. Really, who's to say?

In any case, it is a useless, frivolous gesture, but so furiously ruddy with life (or the side-effects of life), that it takes the viewer aback. People have petted the Howler Monkey. Spoken to it. *Loved* it. They've checked its body for nits. They've found themselves unaccountably wanting to scratch themselves—and they *do*, when they think no one is watching.

The Taxidermist is always watching.

And later, at night, when they've left the office, when they've left the Howler behind and returned home, they toss and shiver in bed, dreaming of that lonely howl across the empty fields. And sometimes, they howl in return.

The Howler makes them forget why they came to the Taxidermist's office in the first place. They wander away, complaints un-filed, petitions un-delivered, pieces of mind un-given.

The Taxidermist loves his Howler Monkey. His secretary, on the other hand, does not.

"Sir," his secretary says, bringing in a file. "For the meeting." She says the word "meeting" with a certain accusation. She lets the file hover over the desk before fanning her fingers, letting the thing hit the desk with a slap.

"Did you know," the Taxidermist says, "that when Pliny attacked Carthage, he entered the temple of Astarte and found it filled with no less than thirty mountain gorillas? Each one was exquisitely mounted, painstakingly preserved, and, apparently, terrifying. The poor man turned on his heel and ran from the temple, claiming it had been seized by Gorgons." He sits at his desk, ancient books opened to different pages and stacked spine to open spine for ease of access. The secretary presses her lips into a tight, long line. She is the former librarian, first working, then simply volunteering for the former library. She disapproves of the wanton opening of books. She shudders at the open splay of tight spines, the casual rustle of unloved pages like the whisper of lifting skirts.

The Taxidermist presses his fingers to his mouth to suppress a burp, though he pretends to clear his throat. He continues. "It is, they believe, the first indication that the art of specimen preservation is not a modern pastime as previously thought. I wonder if the Carthaginian priests thought to recreate the minutia of the mundane as we do now. I wonder *what* they thought they were preserving?"

The secretary flares her nostrils, forcing her gaze away from her employer. The Taxidermist closed the library. Everyone knows this. Everyone blames him. The secretary answers his phones and files his documents and maintains his correspondences and organizes his meetings. But she hates the Taxidermist. *Hates* him.

"I'm not certain your research is correct," the secretary says. "But gorillas have nothing to do with your meeting tonight."

"My dear Miss Sorensen," the Taxidermist says, peering into a heavily diagrammed book, its ancient dust rising from its pages like smoke, "it has everything to do with the meeting tonight. You'll see."

3.

The Taxidermist is the mayor, and has been for the last fifteen years. We did not vote for him. We've never met anyone who *has*. And yet he has won, term after term. A landslide. We do not offer our congratulations nor do we bring casseroles or homemade bars to his house, nor do we come to his Christmas parties or summer barbeques (we already know what's in that house. We *know*.).

This, we are sure, hurts the Taxidermist's other wife. What wife wouldn't be wounded by such a snub? She is a sweet, pretty thing. Young. Large eyes. Tight, smooth skin. She grew up four towns over, or so the story goes. Each day she pushes open the large, heavily carved front door and stands on the porch. She brushes a few tendrils of shellacked hair from her face with the backs of her fingers. She adjusts her crisp, white gloves.

She is *perfect*. Too perfect. Her symmetry jostles the eye. Her body moves without hesitancy, without the irregular rhythm of muscle and bone.

She walks from their house at the center of town, past what used to be the butcher shop and what used to be the hardware store and what used to be the Shoe Emporium and what used to be the offices of our former newspaper until she reaches her husband's office at the Town Hall. She wears high heels, even in winter, that click coldly against the cracked sidewalk. She doesn't trip. She doesn't break stride. She wears a skirt that skims her young thighs and flares slightly at her bending knees. She used to smile at us when she passed, but she doesn't anymore. We never smiled back. Instead, she keeps her lovely face porcelain-still, her mouth like a rosebud in a bowl of milk. A doll's mouth.

We want to love her. We wish we could love her. But we can't. We remember the Taxidermist's first wife. We remember and remember and remember.

4.

Taxidermy is more than Art. It is more than Love. The Taxidermist has explained this to us, but we have closed our ears. We change the subject. We scan the sky for signs of rain.

Still, words have a way of leaking in. Of desiccating the will. Of freezing the mind in a single perfect moment. A state of bliss.

"If the artisan does not love the expired subject on his table, it is true, the final product will be a cold, dead thing. A monstrosity. A hideous copy of what once was unique and alive and *beautiful.*"

We told ourselves we weren't listening. Still, we found ourselves nodding. We found ourselves *agreeing.* It *is* hideous when a thing isn't loved.

"But the love is not enough," the Taxidermist insisted. "*Desire,* friends. *Desire.* When God leaned against the riverbank, when he pressed his fingers into the warm mud and pulled out a man, what was the motivation? *Desire.* God saw mud and made it Man. He *made* Man because he *wanted* Man. We see death, and desire Life. Love isn't enough. You have to *want* to make it live."

5.

There was no funeral for Margaret, the first wife.

We learned she was sick by accident. It was a secret. We whispered about it in the bar and murmured on porches, but in public we pretended we didn't know. We learned she was dead in the "Fond Memories" section of the newspaper. That was when we had a newspaper. We tried to grieve. We wanted to drape our arms around the Taxidermist, to feel his tears wetting the shoulders of our shirts, to wrap his hand with our hands and squeeze. We left frozen hot dishes and flowers in pots and sliced ham on the porch when the Taxidermist refused to open the door.

"Here," we shouted at the jamb. "We've brought food. Wine. Whiskey. We brought our presence and our ears and our love. Let us in and we'll feed you. We'll share a drink and share a song and make you live again. And *she* will live in the spaces between word and word, between breath and breath, between your tears and our tears. She will *live*."

But the Taxidermist would not open the door. During the night, he gathered his gifts and threw them in the trash.

6.

We listened to the old men in Ole's Tavern suck down shots and chasers and fuss over the meeting in the school. Or the building that will soon *not* be a school.

"Not much use pretending we're still a town if the school's gone."

"We stopped pretending we were a town after the grain elevator closed."

"And when the butcher shop shut its doors. Can't call yourself a town if you can't get a fresh hock for supper. If you don't have a locker to put your winter's buck."

"Taxidermist's got a lot of damn gall closing the school mid year. If he was any sort of a man, he'd set aside his own salary rather than pull the rug out from underneath a bunch of little kids."

"Not much of a bunch. Just fifty. On a good day. When was the last good day?"

"We stopped pretending we were a town when the hardware store closed. And the seed store. And the gas station. And the green grocer. And the shoe shop. At least we still can pickle ourselves at Ole's. Soon, he'll just shove each one of us into a bunch of damn mason jars and line us up on the shelf. He'll keep us topped up with nice, clear vodka so we can see. Folk'll come in looking for the town and find it looking right back at 'em, shelves and shelves of blinking eyes." Arne says this. He's always been a morbid fellow.

"The Taxidermist'll like it though," Zeke Hanson says. "He'll like it very much."

We agree.

7.

Night falls early in November. In those waning moments of light, the sky paints its face like a harlot (overripe rouge, stained lips, unbuttoned taffeta spreading outwards like wings), before opening itself wide to the void of space. Each jagged shard of light in the darkness is a tiny message sent from the recesses of time. "You are alone," the stars say. "You are alone. You are still alone."

We pull our coats tightly against the howl of the wind and start our cars.

The school is slightly outside the town, and it sits on a small rectangle cut out of Martin Hovde's sod farm. The schoolyard is packed earth with a single metal swingset for the children to play on. The yard is dusty from their feet, every speck of green crushed by the insistence of play. Nothing grows. Just outside the schoolyard is the endless grass of the Hovde farm. He steamrolls it twice a year to keep it as flat as any floor and then he burns it, again and again, to give the grass a good, rich start. It is green as snakes, and softer than a lie. The children are not allowed to play on it. Indeed, if they so much as set one foot upon that green, green grass, they will be sent home with a note explaining the rules of their suspension.

Once, a year ago, the children broke free in one large mass, moving in a joy of arm and leg and muscle, feeling the gooey give of the sod under their feet. They were all suspended. They spent their day off home and in bed, vomiting bile and blood. Martin Hovde denied that the fertilizer had sickened the children. He said, most likely, it was guilt.

We park our cars next to the school but do not lock them. No one locks their doors. This is a small town. A good town. Or it was, anyway. We hold our coats closed tightly at our throats and bend our backs against the wind. The stars are cold and sharp above our heads and the wind howls across the wide, empty fields.

8.

Taxidermy must embrace imperfection. It is a weak practitioner who feels the need to extend the leg of a lamed cougar cub, or repair the jagged scar above the eye of an ancient wolf. Taxidermy, in its soul, is the celebration of life, the recreation of a single moment in a sea of moments. The taxidermist must build motivation, history, consequence, action, reaction, into one, perfect gesture.

The taxidermist's diorama is a poem.

A song.

A short story.

"We are all just a collection of faults," the Taxidermist told us once. "A myriad of imperfections through which shines divine Perfection. You see? It is our flaws that make us beloved by heaven. It is our scars and handicaps and *lack* of symmetry that proves that we are—or once were—alive. The more we attempt to force our corrupted idea of the Perfect and the Good upon what is *actually* and *deeply* perfect and good, the further we are from the divine. Reveal the subject as the subject *was,* and you reveal the fingerprints of God."

We have shut our ears to the Taxidermist. We have stopped listening to his hypocrisy.

We cannot bear to tell him that this is the very reason why we can never love his other wife.

9.

The Taxidermist's other wife greets us while we come in. Her eyes light upon each coming person and dim when they pass. Her lips spread open into a smile. We shudder at those straight, white teeth. We turn our gaze from that flawless skin. She tilts her head to one side and blinks her large eyes.

(*There!* We gasp. We grab one another's shirts and pull. We whisper in one another's ears. *Did you hear that? The whir of metal. The click of motor. She doesn't clear her throat. She doesn't sigh. She doesn't lick her lips, or adjust her skirt. She doesn't pass gas, or snort when she laughs, or cough.*) We have examined her skin. We have watched her pass. We've looked for clues but have come away with nothing.

"The efficient preservationist leaves no trace of his hand," the Taxidermist told us once. "It is a dim fellow who has the tools of the trade, who has centuries of experience to guide his practice, and still leaves evidence of stitching. Who still leaves a seam to mar the life that he sets out to create. Do not repeat the blunder of that poor fool in Austria. Do not let the Doctor's mistakes be your mistakes."

We would not expect to see scars.

We would not expect to see seams.

The Taxidermist's other wife lays her hand upon our arms as we pass. We shiver. Even through our coats we can feel the stony cold of those fingers. Even through our scarves, we can smell the formaldehyde on her breath.

10.

The Taxidermist takes the podium. His other wife sits in a folding chair just behind. She crosses, then uncrosses, then crosses her legs again. She rests her hands, one on top of the other, on her knees. She cocks her head to one side. A studied look of wifely admiration on her face.

(*We know! We know what she is. Look in her eyes. Look under her skin. We know what we'll find.*)

The Taxidermist taps his microphone three times. He smiles at the audience. The audience does not smile back.

"My friends," the Taxidermist says.

(*You are no one's friend. You closed the library. You're closing the school. We are pickled with memory, preserved on porches and church basements and bars. We blink through worlds of liquor and mason jars. You have frozen us in time.*)

"This isn't easy for me to say," the Taxidermist says easily. "We are down to fifty students. That's all. What we get from the state isn't enough to cover the heat for the building. It doesn't cover the health insurance for the employees. Our school, once the pride of the county, is falling apart. It is dying."

(*We are dying. We are dying and we don't know why.*)

"Now, I recognize that, with the school closed, we will be forced to bus our children all the way to Harris, and I recognize that it is a long ride for little ones, but I'm afraid it cannot be helped. Those who do not want their children going so far away can consider homeschooling. We can all come together to help make that happen. This is a *community*."

(*It was a community. Now it is a cold, dead thing. We are alone, we are alone, we are so alone.*)

"It is true that we loved the school."

(*No. We loved Margaret.*)

"And it is true that we will mourn its passing."

(*We wanted to mourn her. We wanted our grief to prove that we aren't alone. We wanted our grief to show that we are—or were—alive.*)

"But we now have an opportunity. Preservation, my friends. The dead are not gone when we preserve what is left."

The Taxidermist's other wife lifts her hands, preparing to clap. Her lips unfurl in a mechanical smile. Our eyes dazzle and spin in the glare of those perfect teeth. She splays her fingers out and brings her hands together.

But once her palms are a half an inch apart from one another, they stutter and halt. The lights behind her eyes flicker and dim. Her lips freeze in that lovely smile—pink lips insinuating themselves into the white mounds of her cheeks. She is porcelain. She is glass. She is petal and stone and milk. She doesn't move. The Taxidermist doesn't notice.

"We, right now, are sitting on holy ground. How many of us first fell in love on this very schoolyard? And here in these halls, how many of us first discovered the tools that would make us the men and women that we are today? Our lives are written on memory. We preserve the memory—in its perfection, in its state of bliss, and we preserve our*selves*."

The Taxidermist's other wife does not move. She does not blink. She is lifeless, breathless, perfect. She is memory and history and longing.

There are stitches hidden under her collarbone.

(*We know! We know what's in there! We know what we'll find!*)

There are seams sliding along the curve of her spine.

(*A gesture. A moment. Proof of life, or the memory of life.*)

Margaret.

(*We wanted to mourn you. We wanted to grieve. We wanted his tears on our shoulders, his hands in our hands. We wanted to sing songs and tell stories and let you live in the spaces between word and word, between breath and breath.*)

"My wife," the Taxidermist says.

(*Margaret.*)

"Thinks I'm crazy."

(*She doesn't think. She simply is. A memory. A state of bliss.*)

"But it can work. We can preserve what we have. We can turn our loss into a single perfect moment. We can turn this school into a memory of a school. A moment in time. The fingerprints of a thousand hands, and the mingling of a thousand breaths. And it will be proof forever that we are not alone."

(*We are alone.*)

"We are not alone."

(We are alone. We are still alone.)

The Taxidermist's other wife does not move.

(Margaret.)

She does not clap.

(Margaret.)

And we feel ourselves lifting. We feel our souls unfurling like wings. We feel the howl of the wind and the vastness of space and the tiny voices of the distant stars. We feel our stitching and our seams, the clean line of empty bones, the weight of plaster and spun glass. We taste arsenic and salt, the grease of leather, the dust of hair. We feel the beat and the longing of our broken, paper hearts. And we love the Taxidermists's other wife.

Love her.

On the Banks of the River Lex

N. K. JEMISIN

Death lay under the water-tower on a sagging rooftop, watching the slow condensation of water along the tower's metal belly. Occasionally one of the water beads would grow pregnant enough to spawn a droplet, which would then fall around—and occasionally onto—Death's forehead. He had counted over seven hundred hits in the past few days.

Sleep appeared and crouched beside Death, looking hopeful. "You look bored. I don't suppose you'd care for a little oblivion?"

"No, thank you," said Death. He was always scrupulously polite, to counter his reputation. He waited until another drop fell—a miss, alas—and then turned his head to regard Sleep. "You're looking a little detached yourself."

At the refusal, Sleep had sighed and sat down beside him. "I thought I would be all right," she said. "I should be all right. Animals sleep, even plants in their way. But it just isn't the same."

Death reached out to touch her hand. It was his own silent offer.

"No thanks," she said, though she did take his hand. He was glad. Others rarely touched him, if they could help it. By this gesture he understood: *not yet.*

He sat up. The sun had just risen above the city. Clouds like strings of pearls girded the sky. A flock of tiny birds—Death guessed hummingbirds, migrating back from the south—passed through the rust-rimmed hole in the Met Life Building.

"What's that?" asked Sleep.

Death followed her finger and saw a cluster of flowers. The rooftop on which he lay was thick with meadowgrass, and one very determined ailanthus grew in the dust and silt of one corner. There were many flowers amid the meadowgrass, which was why Death liked this roof so much. He would be sorry when it finally caved in.

"Just a daisy," he replied.

"No, beyond that."

They got up and walked around the roof's holes for a better look. Beyond the daisy, fighting its way up through the grass in the shadows of the roof-wall, was a flower Death had never seen before. Its shape was something like that of a crocus, but its roots were shallow, like all rooftop flora. There was no bulb. And its petals were a lush, deep matte black.

"That's different," said Sleep.

Death crouched to peer at the flower, then reached out to stroke the satin softness of one petal. Not just different. New.

Something tickled his cheek. He reached up to brush it away and found his fingers wet. Glancing back at the water-tower, he wondered how he could've missed his count.

Death liked to walk across bridges. For this reason he had claimed a home for himself relatively far from the center of town. This was in a big ugly gray stone of a building that had once been a factory, and then had been colonized by artists, and then by trend-obsessed young professionals. Now it was ruled by cats. Death passed perhaps a dozen of them on his way down the stairs, including one mother briskly carrying a mouse and trailed by two gangling adolescents. As usual they ignored his presence, merely slinking out of the way as he passed. On the rare occasions when one would deign to look at him, he nodded in polite greeting. Sometimes they even nodded back.

He had attempted, once, to entice a kitten to live with him. This was something he knew humans had done. But he kept forgetting to bring food, and because he did not sleep, the kitten was unable to cuddle with him at night. After a few days the kitten had left in a huff. He still saw its descendants around the building, and felt lingering regret.

The Williamsburg Bridge had not yet begun to warp and sag like the Manhattan and Brooklyn Bridges. Death suspected there was some logical reason for this—perhaps the Williamsburg had been renovated more recently, or built more sturdily in the first place. But in his heart, Death believed that *he* helped to keep the bridge intact. By walking across it, he gave the bridge purpose. For all things created by humankind, purpose was the quintessence of existence.

So Death walked into town every day.

There was much activity in town when Death arrived.

"The twins have opened a Starbucks at Union Square!" said a stranger, when Death stepped off the bridge on Delancey. He nodded in pleasant response to this, though he was not certain what a Starbucks was or why the twins would have bothered with it.

Still, everyone seemed so excited about the Starbucks that Death wandered uptown, curious. Most of the streets were empty, except for cats and a few coyotes. The coyotes were not as bold as the cats; they mostly tried to keep out of sight. At 14th Street and Avenue A, Death found the Dragon King of the Western Ocean playing bagpipes on the corner stoop. He sat on the gnarled root of a young oak that was slowly crushing an ancient, spindly cherry, and destroying the sidewalk in the process. Skirting around the growing sinkhole, Death sat down to listen until the Dragon King was done.

"Thanks," the Dragon King said. "It's good to have listeners."

"You're very good," said Death.

"Always wanted to learn this thing. It's just so ugly, you have to love it. I looked all over the mainland, even in Hong Kong, and couldn't find one. Had to come here, finally. Thank little apples for the Chinese Diaspora." The Dragon King set down the bagpipes carefully. "Are you going to Starbucks?"

"I was thinking about it, yes. Are you?"

"Course not. I hate coffee. People used to offer it to me all the time—nasty, vile stuff. Now, a Krispy Kreme doughnut? Got one of those once, thought I would die of joy." He let out a wistful sigh.

"I've never tried coffee." People, in the time before, had made very different offerings to Death.

"You probably won't have any today, either. Mawu only found a few bricks of the freeze-dried stuff; I bet they'll run out by noon."

"Oh." Death felt mildly disappointed.

"Let's go anyhow. I'm bored."

They walked over to Union Square, where as usual the south-end steps were filled with worshippers. Not people, for all that most of them had adopted the forms of people in homage. Just others of their kind who were willing and had the strength to assist those in need. But this time the line *around* the square, trailing from the Starbucks all the way to the collapsed bank on the opposite corner, was long enough to rival the crowd on the steps.

The Dragon King clapped Death on the shoulder. "See what I mean? Good luck getting a taste."

"Anything new is worth trying," Death replied with a shrug.

The Dragon King sighed. "I know you don't need it, man, but you really ought to try a service." He nodded toward the square. "Way better than coffee."

"Others need it more than me." They both fell silent, embarrassed, as a thin, waiflike creature shuffled past. It was difficult to tell if this one was male or female or one of the androgynes, because its clothing was ragged and its face too hollow for easy recognition. Its gaze was fixed on the square. As Death and the Dragon King watched, the creature crossed the street; the worshippers there opened their ranks at once to admit the newcomer.

"Damn," said the Dragon King. "I think that was one of the Bodhisattvas. I used to know all those guys. Girls. Them."

Death nodded, solemn. He had known them too.

The Dragon King glanced at him, guiltily. "Look, I know I don't need it either. The oceans are still around, the rain still falls. But it's not the same, you know?"

"I know that," Death said, a little taken aback. "You don't have to justify it to me."

"Damn straight I don't." The Dragon King glared at him for a moment; in the distance, clouds rumbled with faint thunder. But almost as quickly as the Dragon's anger had come, it seemed to fade, and he sighed. "Well . . . anyway. Thanks for listening to the music."

The Dragon King then crossed the street to join the throng on the steps. Death watched him for a moment, contemplating. They would help the ones who needed it most first, but beyond that they helped everyone, offering worship in whatever form necessary—blood, prayer, sex—for hour-long increments. If not for them and other groups like them, many would have given up, or faded away, by now.

Would they die for him, if he asked it? Death wondered idly.

Then he turned and went to the end of the Starbucks line. They ran out of coffee before he got halfway there.

But the twins had attempted another experiment, which Death did get to try: cookies. He sat at one of the small tables in the crowded cafe, and peered dubiously at the plate that Lise had set in front of him.

"They're good," she said.

"They're green," he replied.

"That's because we made the flour from crabgrass seeds," she said. "It makes them a little bitter, but otherwise they're good. Look, real raisins."

Wild grapevines had overrun Brooklyn Heights. "Ah. As I recall, Mawu did make passable wine for libations, once."

"Yes, the bottles that didn't explode or turn to vinegar. He's still working on the technique. But raisins are easy. Grow some grapes and ignore them. *Try* it."

Death picked up the cookie and nibbled. It was, to his great surprise, good. He said as much, and meant it.

"You don't have to sound so shocked," Lise said, annoyed. She stormed away behind the counter and resumed work on some contraption that she must have rigged to bake the cookies. She and her twin brother, Mawu, were good at creating new things. Almost as good as people had been.

"I need to talk to you," said an angel, coming over to sit across from him. She did not ask to sit, but angels did not ask permission.

"Of course," he said. Lise glared at him from behind the dusty old counter, and he remembered the ritual of sitting in a cafe. Small talk was necessary before business could be conducted. It was respectful to treat the twins' endeavor in the spirit it was meant. "How have you been? Is, er, is life good for you?" He had not meant that the way it came out. Hopefully she would not think he wanted to kill her.

"The life of mankind has passed on, and we are but shadows in its wake," she said truthfully, ignoring the polite fiction that the ritual demanded. He winced. At the counter, Lise sucked her teeth. "I came to tell you that the Lex has overflowed its banks. I talked to Ogun; the pumping system is completely unsalvageable. Took everything he had to keep it going this long. He thinks the entire Upper East Side will be underwater within a year."

Death spat out a raisin-pit, and fished in his mouth for a bit of grass-seed hull that seemed to have gotten stuck in his teeth. He did not have to have teeth, he supposed, but he generally liked them, except at times like this. "Why is that a problem?"

"The English Nursery Rhymes. They all live on the Upper East Side."

"Why can't they move?"

She looked at him with annoyance, though this was mild, her being an angel. He thought she might be Gabriel; the rest were less tolerant of those outside their circle. "There are more kindergartens and schools in that part of town than any other."

Which explained why the Rhymes had claimed that neighborhood. Death considered. "What about Park Slope?" This was a neighborhood in Brooklyn not far from his home in Williamsburg. He remembered visiting there often, in the old days. It had been a hotbed of gang activity once, but later, before the people had gone, there had been many children.

"They can't make it that far. They're not like the rest of us that had thousands of years and dozens of cultures to strengthen them. To get to Brooklyn, they'd have to travel through several neighborhoods that didn't have many kids, and across the East River. It's too much for them."

Death frowned, a slow suspicion eating into his enjoyment of the cookies. He sat back, silent for a long moment, and gazed at her until she sighed and said it out loud.

"You need to help them," she said. She spoke softly. A rarity. "It's worse to wither away. You know that."

"My help is always available. To those who *ask*."

"They're children! They sing and rhyme and bounce around—they don't know to ask!"

He remained silent, not bothering to point out the obvious. The Nursery Rhymes weren't children, any more than he was a man, or she a woman. There were no more children.

"It isn't right." She looked away. Her hand lay on the table. Her fingers tightened into a fist, then relaxed, then tightened again. Her wings, which dragged the floor behind her chair, fluffed and settled. "Letting them suffer when they don't have to. You know it's not right."

It was not. Inadvertently he thought of the Bodhisattva he had seen, shambling its way toward survival. "They might want to try."

"They don't think that far, Death. They're full of nonsense. But they suffer as much as the rest of us. It's amazing they've managed to hang on this long."

He shook his head slowly, but sighed. "I'll speak to them," he said at last. "I'll try to make them understand, and then ask what *they* want. Life—even its shadow—deserves that much consideration." He leveled a hard look at her. "And I will abide by their decision."

She nodded slowly. "That's all I ask." With a heavy sigh, she got up, and finally yielded to propriety. "Thank you. Er, have a nice day." At this, Lise looked pleased.

Death finished his cookie and got up. He walked uptown, which took the rest of the day. By the time he reached the Upper East Side, night had begun to fall. He traveled more slowly along the banks of the river, because the sidewalks and streets were treacherous here. The water flowing through the subway lines had undermined the whole area, and it was obvious that this part of the island would soon be reclaimed by the sea. But at 66th Street he found a downed Victorian turret fetched up against several cars, which formed a precarious bridge. After climbing over this, Death made his way further north, following the old sense that had always led him to wherever he needed to be.

He found the Nursery Rhymes in the garden of an ancient school. Though it was pitch dark, they were still running about and playing, chasing fireflies, their peals of laughter making Death feel lonely and nostalgic. There were peacocks and peahens in the garden too, some of them roosting sleepily in the trees as he passed underneath. They cooed challenges at him, less indifferent than his building's cats. But then he stopped, surprised to find one peacock down on the ground, directly in his path. As he stared at it, he realized it was not blue and green like the others. Its head was a fierce, iridescent red, shading to gold on the neck and below. When it suddenly fanned and shivered its great tail, he saw that all the eye-spots were a baleful, white-rimmed black.

Then, as if satisfied that he had noticed its strangeness, the peacock dropped its tail and flew away.

When the children ran over to Death, still giggling and delighted to meet someone new, he could not help noticing how thin they were.

One day Death began to feel restless, which was strange. He was Death, the inevitability of all living things. He should never have felt restless. Yet he did.

He wondered: was his dissolution beginning, as had happened to so many others? But there was still death in the world, all around him, every day. The cats in his building. The rats and mice and birds that they fed on. The plants that grew from cracks in the concrete. His own kind, when they faltered. Yet he also knew the truth: that death might exist in the absence of humankind, but not *Death*.

He felt no weaker. There was no perceptible thinning of his substance. But something troubled him, nevertheless.

He began to walk, picking a direction at random. South. The streets in Brooklyn were less damaged and flooded than those in Manhattan, but there were other problems, especially in the poorer neighborhoods. He had to go slowest in Flatbush, which had been in a state of disrepair long before the end of humanity. The sinkholes and downed facades got so bad that eventually he simply willed himself over to Kensington. (He preferred to walk, but physicality was not always convenient.) Strolling along tree-lined streets and gazing at brownstones that still looked as beautiful as the year they'd been built was marvelous, though it felt a bit like cheating.

Because Death did not tire, he walked well into the night, and reached Coney Island by morning. It was nice to watch the sunrise from the beach. The ocean hummed with its own cycles, hardly changed by the presence or absence of humanity. He spent an hour or two just listening to the surge and sough of the waves, and remembering all that had been. He was not like many of his fellows, who were confined to the places where they had been conceived and nurtured. Where there was life, there was death, and where there was death, was his domain. He was one of the few who could, if he wished, travel the whole world. It was good to be Death.

When the sun was well-risen, he turned away from the sagging roller coaster and the midway, with its stands full of mildewed lumps that had once been stuffed animals. The Aquarium stood open, the glass of its doors long since shattered and washed away in the hurricane that had hit the city not long after its abandonment. Inside the Alien Stingers exhibit—the only building still standing—Death found mostly darkness and silence. He moved quietly between the still, dark tanks, looking for nothing in particular. Just walking. Listening. He sensed now that something had drawn him to this place. He didn't know what, but he knew this: it was a sensation he had not felt since before people had gone. That in itself was enough to merit his attention.

As Death reached the south end of the building, he found that it had been torn open by long-gone wind and rain, leaving a great, gaping, splintered hole. Debris, itself mostly buried in sand with the passage of time, paved the way across the tumbled wall of the sea lion tank, between the man-made hills (now flat) which had bordered the site, and through the crazily leaning pillars which were all that remained of the Boardwalk. The building's guts trailed away in a clear path all the way down to the water.

Here, Death found something odd. A series of peculiar, curlicued scuff-marks moved along this trail of lathing and salt-rotted wood, cutting across the windblown drifts of sand. Following them, he found that the marks petered out a few dozen meters from the water's edge, washed away by the tide-line. Backtracking instead, he found them continuing into the aquarium—but where the sand gave way to the building's cheap, nearly-indestructible carpeting, there were no marks for him to follow.

Death did not have much imagination. He did not require it. He was patient, however, so lacking any other means of fathoming the mystery, he sat down beside the trail. The marks were fresh, after all. Perhaps whatever had made them would eventually return.

And finally, as dusk fell, he saw movement down near the beach. An animal, dragging itself out of the surf. At first he thought that it was another new thing, like the black flower, and the red peacock. Then it drew closer, and belatedly he realized it was just a small, dark blue octopus, walking its way along the lathing and sand. As it came, he saw that it carried an old blue plastic cup that read SLURPEE in faded letters, balanced carefully atop two of its tentacles. Water sloshed over the cup's lip now and again, though it was clear the creature was making an effort not to spill the liquid. It used the other six tentacles to walk, Death saw, leaving behind that familiar curling pattern.

Now and again the creature stopped, set the cup on some flat surface or against a rock, and thrust its head into the water. Death watched it breathe in and out, its color flickering momentarily lighter blue, like the cup. When it had finished this procedure, it withdrew from the cup and resumed walking.

It paused when Death rose to follow it into the Aquarium. He stopped when it did, and felt himself actively considered by the creature's strange bar-pupilled eyes. When he did not approach more closely, however, the creature finally resumed its laborious march.

Inside, they both proceeded to one of the building's vast, double-walled tanks. Here, unlike the rest of the tanks—most of which no longer had any need of his services—this one still flickered in glowing, vibrant blue. There was a hole in the tank's uppermost corner, where the glass met the plaster of its display case, and something had cleared away the killing algae from the water's surface. Above the tank was a skylight in the aquarium's ceiling, which let in plenty of the setting sun's rays. Thanks to this, Death could see that the tank was still halfway full with water, the water-mark just at his eye level. The water had gone murky, the glass speckling with age and wear—but beyond the speckling, he could see many small things darting and moving.

Before he could identify this, the octopus stopped beside this tank, then laboriously climbed the glass wall, still carting the cup. It poured the water into the tank, dropped the cup—Death had already noticed many other cups, cans, and coconut shells littering the floor here—then wriggled through the gap in the glass. Here it paused, clinging to the glass above the water-line, gazing through a clear patch at Death. Again, Death felt himself *considered.*

Then one of the darting things in the water flicked up and attached itself to the plastic too, and he understood. It was a tiny copy of the larger octopus—a baby. There were likely hundreds of them, if not thousands, in the tank.

Death leaned close to the glass, looking the elder octopus in its—her—odd little eye. He considered her in return.

"Shall I kill you?" he asked. "Is that what you want?"

He felt her deep weariness. This was the way of things, he knew then: the mother died, her flesh granting the young a last bit of strength so that they might survive. It had happened for countless generations already, since the destruction of the Aquarium had provided her ancestors with such a convenient, safe nursery for their young. How many more octopi had survived their youth, thanks to this happenstance, than there would have been in the wild? How many more adults had learned to leave the ocean, carrying their water with them as they found safer shelter somewhere along the empty seaside?

The octopus did not answer. She could not speak. Yet he knew, because he was what he was, that she *understood* what he was. She was not a red peacock or a black flower, yet she was, in a similar way, a new thing. Or an old thing, taking advantage of a new opportunity. It did not matter. Of such opportunities, embraced and exploited, were new things born.

One of the mother octopus's wet, attenuated tentacles curled over the edge of the broken glass, twitching slightly. Nodding, Death touched this. A moment later the octopus turned gray and dropped into the water. The tank roiled with movement as her children swarmed in for a last loving taste of her.

The small octopus that had leapt out of the water, and which had continued to cling to the glass, observing, while Death killed its mother, remained where it was. Death nodded to it, solemn, then turned to go.

Movement caught his eye. The small octopus had begun to scurry up toward the hole in the glass. Death stopped.

"No," he said, recalling that its mother had not come ashore 'til dusk, with the tide. "Wait until morning, near dawn. Bring water with you."

The baby octopus stopped, its sides heaving with the effort to breathe out of the water. He had no idea whether it understood him. If it did, it would wait, and have that much better a chance of surviving the trek to the ocean. Perhaps a few of its siblings would attempt and survive the journey too, and in turn they would pass on the necessary skill, and the intelligence to use it, to the young who came after them. And in time, with luck and other opportunities . . .

It was how people had begun. It was how all new things began. He understood this, the life and death of species, as he had always understood the life and death of individuals. But perhaps he had been too preoccupied with the latter, as a result failing to notice the former.

The little octopus detached itself from the side of the tank and dropped back into the water, darting in for its own share of the mother's corpse. Death felt himself ignored and forgotten—but that was all right. The young did not often think about Death, but Death was no less eternal for their disinterest.

He smiled with the realization that some concepts would always be the same, no matter who conceptualized them. Still . . . lifting his hand, he contemplated the shape and structure of tentacles. They would be very versatile, he decided, though they would take some getting used to.

Then he turned and headed for home.

A few days later, Death went to Union Square. He walked over to the worshippers on the south-end steps, and asked them what to do.

"Just . . . think about the one you're trying to help," said the Dragon King, who had been looking at him oddly since his arrival. "That's all any of us really needs, y'know. But if you don't mind me saying so, buddy, I never expected to see you here. I figured—" He paused, abruptly looking embarrassed. "Well, I figured you didn't mind seeing the rest of us crash and burn."

Death understood. Others usually assumed worse. "Death comes on its own," he said. "I don't have to do anything to facilitate it. But everyone deserves a chance to *try* and survive." Even us, he had decided.

"Well, sure. But . . . " The Dragon King scratched his long, curling moustache, finally letting out a weak laugh. "Man, you're weird."

Death smiled. It pleased him to be called "man," though eventually there would be other names and other manifestations for him. He would not be the same, filtered through such different imaginations. None of them would be—but it was now important to him that his fellows hold on, take the opportunity to adapt if they could. The world had not ended, after all. The stuff of which he and his kind had been made, had not vanished. The thinker did not matter, so long as thought remained.

"Thank you," Death said, and then he clapped the Dragon King on the shoulder. (The Dragon King started and threw him a puzzled look.) "Now tell me: are bagpipes easy to learn?"

While he still had fingers, he would need a way to pass the time.

Signals in the Deep
GREG MELLOR

Earth

There's a place in our future where we are all heading, driven by our instincts and the deep heritage of our genes. It is a place where we are more at peace, in harmony with the universal fabric from which we were born. It's what I was taught, and it's what I believe. Our past provides a foundation, a platform from which we can achieve great things: growth, meaning, *enlightenment.*

I tried to instill this belief into Matthew as any good mother would—show, don't tell. But it seems that the young are both deaf and blind to old-world values. I rationalized his anger at first. Looking beyond the veil of testosterone, it was his imperative to experience life for himself and to sometimes learn things the hard way. After all, there is no manual when you are born into the skin you live in.

Then, as Matt blossomed from boy to teenager, I began to doubt myself and wondered what I had done to estrange him. The genome patent meant he didn't need a father, but there were plenty of male role models during his semesters at the private didactic havens. He developed incredible skills in languages and mathematics, and although the complex problem solving could make him so detached, in hindsight it was a source of comfort for him. He was gifted from the start—before he was even born—and if I was honest with myself, it had raised my expectations into the stratosphere.

And therein lay the irony: in providing for everything perhaps I had unwittingly given him little cause to look back. There was no sense of the past for his generation; everything was about the here and now, and the future was something to worry about when it arrived. I realized, too late, that I must have come across as so set in my ways: stern, reflective, always grounded.

The chill autumn nights are spent pondering these things under the spatter-painted veil of stars. The motor on the tracking dish hummed quietly, the barrel of the telescope cold in my hands. Ancient light shone into my eyes, translating into images, connecting me again—the past was always with me.

But did Matt see it now? Was there such a thing in his world?

I wasn't sure. Heaven help me, after two years with no word or sign from him, I wasn't sure at all.

And there was only one way to find out.

Earth + 100km

My journey began with cold sweat beading on my skin as the elevator rose up and up on a white-knuckled ride into vacuum. I had never been good with heights, but this was ludicrous. Nothing should be this high—it seemed physically impossible—yet the elevator kept going until the cerulean sky turned indigo and the stars shone more intensely.

The steward had been keeping a watchful eye over me on the way up. He had a ceaseless capacity for small talk, which was harmless enough, but now a worried frown creased his face as I clumsily disembarked.

"Are you okay, Beth?"

I didn't reply, preoccupied with weightlessness and being towed across the bridge to the shuttle port by an usherbot the size and shape of a dustbin. I glanced through the viewing ports, trying to keep my eyes away from the cloud deck far, far below. There were several more elevators in the distance, rising like needles along the curvature of the world.

"They're impressive," the steward said, a cheeky smile playing at the corners of his lips.

Please go away. I nodded and smiled as best I could. "There are so many of them, and it's all happened so quickly."

"I guess that's why they call it the Quickening." His lips turned down as my face darkened at his pun. I had used affordable nanotech to create Matt's genome and I often blamed the technology for my predicament, but it was just a classic case of denial.

As we entered the bustling port I began checking for signs to the shuttle departure lounge, but this was a damn confusing place. No doubt there were a thousand data casts flying about, but what I needed was a *physical* sign.

The steward's eyes widened, convinced, I am sure, that I was a complete anachronism. Then to my surprise he tucked his arm through mine with that same familiarity. "Where are you traveling, Beth?"

Okay, so maybe I do need your help. "Pluto . . . Charon Relay Station, actually."

His eyes widened even further. "The back of beyond. I've always wanted to go there, they say the stars are . . . " He caught my look again. "The departure lounge is just this way."

Earth + 2AU

It is said that you can make friends in the most unlikely places. And this shuttle was one of those places: a cold, disorienting cavern, with row upon row of rockbusters reeking like a metal refinery.

The rockbuster next to me tried to strike up a conversation, his third attempt. "You're a long way from home . . . ?"

"Beth." My feet dangled, child-like, over the edge of the seat.

"I'm Ryan."

A rockbuster named Ryan; what stories your mother could tell.

He turned his enormous plated head, gyros whirring, metal creaking, and leant over me. His massive bicep brushed dangerously close to my head. "Are you management?"

"Do I look like management?"

"No." He seemed unphased by my terseness, but I doubted that anything could bother these giants. "And you're not a tourist. Not that we get many out this way. Some engineers, a few scientists, and management . . . sometimes."

"So you work the belt?" It was an infantile deflection, but home seemed so far away, my worry now consuming more hours of each day that passed. Maybe that was a mother's lot in life, but then again, it seemed that I had more than my fair share—a constant, gut churning state. And it was starting to show.

"What do *you* think?" His eyes gleamed mischief deep beneath the edge of his cheek plates.

"Judging by your pitted armor, three-meter frame and stubborn demeanor, I'd say so."

He half turned in his seat, his plates sliding across each other like an avalanche, a smile on his segmented lips. With a hint of conspiracy in his voice, he said, "So you must be looking for something . . . or *escaping* something."

My exasperated sigh misted the air. "I'm looking for my son."

"Ah." He relaxed back in his seat, another avalanche. "The truth. We're all searching for it in our own way. You find a vein of ore; it's an achievement, a vindication that you serve a purpose. There's truth in that. If your friends speak plain words, you know you can depend on them—truth again."

"You're quite the philosophical one."

His eyes swiveled. "For a robot?"

"No, I wasn't going to say that."

"But you thought it."

Maybe. I let out a long breath. "Okay, yes." Ryan was human deep down. And I had no doubt that his decision to work in vacuum, to go through the physical torture of bio-metal skin grafts, was not an easy one. I knew this, yet to listen to him, to look at him . . . "I'm sorry."

He shrugged. "Maybe I come across like one: irrefutable, irritating logic and all. But space does that to you. There's no room for shades of grey, at least not in my line of work." Then, "I take it you haven't seen him for a while?"

I nodded, trying to stop the surge of emotion, the pent up frustration. This man's presence was calming, but at the same time he was a stark reminder to me, raking my fear, gathering up a storm of dreadful possibilities. I began to wonder how much Matt had changed. What had he gone through to adapt?

What decisions had he made—*life-changing* decisions? Would I even recognize him? And more importantly, was he happy in himself, accepting, like Ryan, or was he still the angry young man I remembered?

Ryan patted me gently, his hand completely covering my forearm. "Solar winds and empty space, it shouldn't be too hard to find him."

My tears floated up and away from my face, tiny spheres drifting.

Earth + 6AU

Chartering the light sail had cost me the rest of my savings. The cabin was very small and beige and although it had all the necessary facilities, it would become a lonely prison during the long months ahead. The fixed autopilot's lights blinked occasionally from a tiny alcove, its bland chrome head rotating on a stalk, constantly monitoring.

Ahead, through the viewing cells, the sail stretched out like delicate foil reflecting sunlight into shards. But photonic pressure alone could not drive this tiny ship, and so it needed supplementing from the orbital laser array at Jupiter to bring it up to the velocity necessary to reach the outer solar system.

And behind: the Sun so remote now that I had forgotten its warmth. But then it is hard to feel warmth of any kind when one's soul is locked in ice.

I had sent a message out to Matt on my departure from Earth, and again at the asteroid belt. The only thing I received was a silence that spoke volumes. My anxiety shifted then, became anger.

He was the communications expert. The outer system relay stations were being constructed to assist with the exploration and population of the Kuiper Belt. So if he could communicate with the settlers, *why* was it so hard to stay in touch with me? If he had no time for a personal message he could have arranged an automated update or blog. Hell, he could have sent something by solar snail mail by now.

I looked down at my jiggling legs and placed my hands on my knees. Peering into the dark, hoping that it might calm me somehow, I saw a light appear beyond the edge of the sail, tracking against the star field. It was on the same vector; perhaps it was a tourist yacht. But something about it didn't feel right. It was tracking quickly now, which meant its relative velocity must be enormous, well beyond anything I had heard about.

"Pilot, what is that to port?"

The pilot's head rotated and two lights blinked on its chrome head. After a few seconds there was a metallic reply: "Unknown."

"Your best estimate?"

Another few seconds: "Experimental space probe or military craft."

"Military? But there's nothing out here."

Solar winds and empty space.

Earth + 38AU

I had taken to roaming the methane ice wastes of Charon during the days. The baroque spacesuit had good power, large spotlights and was insulated enough to stave off the incredible cold. Even so, it was still reckless of me to wander the hills and valleys. But not so reckless that I didn't steer clear of the cryo-geyser fields, though on my darker days I thought that being trapped in the geysers might provide a fitting end to my foolishness.

The backlit crescent of Pluto peaked above the horizon, casting long shadows across the ground, stretching out towards me—raven wings of a kind. My mind was playing tricks, and all I could do was let it run wild. What else was there in this hell hole?

I think I was a distraction for the grizzled scientists and technicians at the relay station for, oh, ten minutes or so. They were as perplexed as I was when I drifted in like flotsam, a random event that upset their daily routine. They had no idea where Matt was, nor were they willing to answer my questions about what he was actually doing if he wasn't at the station. After some grumbling they sent a message to him then hastily located me in a habitat dome away from the main nest of the station to wait for the reply. Three weeks later, my mind turning lethargic in the stale air, the walks were providing a reprieve of sorts.

Today I had ventured further than before, taking languid strides out to a low ridgeline south of the habitat. The suit's external crampons gave me purchase, but occasionally I tripped until I got into the ludicrous rhythm of moon walking: walk, sprawl, slide, stand, walk.

By the time I made it to the ridgeline I was gulping for oxygen. I checked the suit monitor: still green. Then something caught my eye and I crouched down instinctively. The valley beyond was covered with domes with square lit windows, radio dishes at the perimeter, a launch platform lined with the translucent delta-shapes of spaceships resting on landing stems. And there . . . rockbusters operating large equipment . . . there, humans in white skinsuits . . .

The com-channel crackled in my helmet.

"What?" I began to turn, sensing movement behind me.

"State your identity." A young man's voice, used to being obeyed.

"Don't move." A young woman now.

My spotlights swept over them . . . white skinsuits . . . sleek gold-glass helmets . . . carrying long barreled vac-weapons . . . grey static across my vision now . . . a heavy feeling in my head . . . down on one knee . . . "Wait—"

Earth + 38AU

"You were extremely lucky," Graeme said. He had permanently windswept hair and a serious frown for a fourteen-year-old.

"Those old suits are unreliable," Trace said. "And you were out there too long. You could have asphyxiated." Her eyes were palest blue and her black hair was tied up in a spiky bun, giving her an innocent look that belied a sharp wit and intelligence. I liked her a lot—an attitude tempered with a maturity beyond her years. She reminded me so much of Matt just before he left home.

I glanced around the white walls of the med-room. The single viewing port revealed one of the launch pads I had spied from a distance. "What are you doing here?"

Graeme's frown deepened. "That's classified."

I turned to Trace, my eyes pleading.

She arched an eyebrow at Graeme. "I think we can ease up a little. The approval arrived via the Jupiter Relay this morning."

He gave her a *whatever* look.

I looked at them both in turn. "You're not here to help the settlers, are you?"

Graeme sat back in his chair. "No, ma'am."

Trace lent forward and took my hand. Her skin was warm, and filled me with hope I thought I had lost, until her words cut through, grating at my naivety. "Matt doesn't work on Charon."

"It's taken me a *year* to get here. Where is he?"

She squeezed my hands and glanced through the viewing port. "He's out there, beyond the heliopause."

I began to shake and leant forward until my elbows touched my knees. The air seemed suddenly unbreathable again. "It's too far . . . how can I . . . "

Trace moved to me and put her arm around my shoulder. "We've sent a higher priority message to him, but it might take some time."

Earth + 50AU

"He didn't tell you, did he?"

It was Trace's voice, heard in my mind as if from a murky distance, echoes along the shore of a raging sea. I opened my eyes. A milky white film crawled across my vision. I made to raise my hand to rub my eyes, but I couldn't move. I tried to breath, but there was something slimy sitting heavily in my lungs.

"What—?"

"Don't panic, it's just the dampening gel." A pause. "There, that should do it."

My eyes, or the gel, cleared; then a chemical rush regulated my heart rate. I cleared my throat, adjusting to the subvocalization. "Are you licensed to administer pharmaceuticals?"

"You're hilarious, Beth."

We were suspended in a small, angular cabin with no visible controls or systems. I sensed a delta shape around us, sleek and transparent against the backdrop of space. "What is this thing?"

"It's an interceptor. Bio-ceramic hull, neural-interface circuitry, top speed in excess of 10,000 kps . . . ah, look, I really shouldn't. Beth, no parents come out here . . . ever. You're an enigma, and under any other circumstances you'd be turned around in your light sail and sent home. But we figured Matt didn't tell you about the conscription so the least we could do is arrange a meeting."

It struck me that Trace had considerable authority. "You love it here?"

I felt her inner smile . . . there was an empathic component to the com.

"I still don't get it. What could possibly be a threat here in the middle of nowhere?" *No disrespect.*

"None taken."

"Oh . . . " *More than empathic.*

"There doesn't need to be a threat, just the possibility of one." Feeling my confusion, she added, "There's more here than interstellar dust. We've discovered a communication network of unknown origin."

"You're talking about aliens?"

"We think it stays outside a system's heliosphere until its civilizations are advanced enough. Or it could be a relic network and all we're hearing is remnants of dead civilizations. Either way, we're very cautious in case there's a risk of viral data packets . . . for want of a more technical explanation."

My mind raced ahead. "Matt's an interpreter?"

I felt Trace nod, but there was apprehension.

"What is it?"

"Nothing."

"Don't fob me off, Trace."

Fair enough. "The oldies—it's an endearing term for people like Matt approaching their twenties—if they're good at what they do then they get moved into the deep. You have to *adjust* or die."

The truth. For the first time since my arrival, I had finally found a vein of ore. I rummaged around the com, trying to delve deeper into her mind. There was more; I'd only caught a glimmer.

She said, "I'm going to have to activate the gel again. There's still a long way to go."

"Has Matt changed?" But another question begged at the back of my mind. *Is he still the son I used to know?*

The gel activated. I forced myself across the com before unconsciousness took hold . . . there . . . a feeling carefully held in check . . . doubt . . .

Earth +100AU

A tingling sensation ran over my body—the after effects of the gel?—no, it was a white skinsuit, knitting with my nervous system. It felt almost intimate. Thankfully it didn't extend over my head; I'd had enough of feeling claustrophobic. Instead, fresh oxygen circulated within a gold-glass helmet.

I turned my head, expecting to see Trace. The Milky Way was a bright etching on impossibly black velvet. My arms thrashed involuntarily—I was EVA!

The com hissed and her voice filtered into my waking senses, a long way off still. She was talking to someone.

"Long time, my friend."

"You too . . ."

"What is it?"

"I haven't spoken English for a long time."

Laughter.

"Why is she here?"

"She wants to know you're okay."

Silence.

"She's a good person." *Kind of strict, in a your-best-interest way.* "I wish my parents cared as much . . . oops, I think she's awake . . . twenty kilometers to starboard."

"I know."

Silhouettes glided languidly across the star field until I could see the sheer, terrifying wonder of him. He was there—at the center—but the rest of him was strung out in many disconnected parts. What looked like advanced relay panels were stretched over delicate bio-ceramic bones, unfolding over kilometers. Titanium pivots and joints secured critical junctions of the larger pieces. The entire array ebbed and flowed, resonating to Matt's remote commands, a thousand separate parts miraculously working in synch—a dark cybernetic angel gliding down to meet me.

I extended my arms as he approached, the sheer scale of his structure more daunting as he got closer, until I was at his center, his human body encased in a sleek black bio-alloy skin. His eyes were still the same, that dark brown with green flecks, glazed with a protective covering that blended into his skin.

I held him, apprehensive at first as the massive wings seemed to bend in toward us. He was changed beyond reckoning, but still himself inside, still Matt.

"You shouldn't have come."

"Is that any way to greet—"

He laughed. "I've missed you, Mum."

I squeezed him tighter. With so many questions, after all this time and all that I had witnessed, I still couldn't move beyond the selfish ones. "Why did you leave?"

"Why do you think?"

"Was I too controlling?"

"Of course not. I'm sorry if I was angry all the time, but I did listen to you." *I just couldn't wait to experience life.* "Out here the past is more important than ever. You have to be grounded to survive. If we don't have a strong sense of who we are, then how can we face the unknown?"

I laughed inwardly. Such a blind thing I had become, journeying all this way with the answer in my back pocket. It was that paradox that all parents face at some point. He was always going to grow up despite my good intentions and overbearing guidance. It just happened a little sooner than I expected, or rather sooner than I was willing to acknowledge.

He let me float free and turned away, breaking my reverie. He was focused now upon some object that I could only just make out against the star field. His wings shuffled and folded in like a line of dominoes, quickening into a blur of movement. There was something agile about him, as if he were capable of great speed—like the interceptors.

The object came into view slowly, an odd-pointed shape distilling out of the dark. I urged the skinsuit forward and felt a slight pressure on my back. I followed, a white speck hovering above the expanse of his wings. We seemed to take forever to reach the object, until it dawned on me that it was on a different scale altogether. After about thirty minutes Matt decelerated suddenly, but my vector carried me forward and I tumbled away over one of his panels until the skinsuit righted my spin.

"Sorry," I said.

"My fault."

We fell into a geosynchronous orbit. The object was shaped like a giant black starfish, but the arms were multi-segmented, stretching out for a thousand kilometers or more. It was moving and fluttering, in a way that seemed biological or semi-sentient, as it coaxed the faintest of signals from the interstellar medium.

"How was it discovered?"

"There have been anomalies in heliospheric imaging for over a century—where the warmer ions of the solar wind meet the cold interstellar gas. We knew that the bulk of the anomalies were caused by the galactic magnetic field draping over the heliosphere. This object's magnetic field appeared as a point anomaly on the imaging in a year when the heliosphere extended much farther out than normal." He seemed mesmerized as he swung down, gliding closer over one of the arms. "You're right. It is self-aware, most likely on the low end of the Turing scale. If you concentrate hard enough you can tap into its empathic link. It knows about us; it can sense us now. They've known about us for a long time."

"They?"

"The signals are coming from Fomalhaut, and being relayed on to other systems. It's a data and com network of sorts—an interstellar internet if you will—but that's a fairly primitive analogy."

I hesitated. Something inside me desperately wanted to know, but another part of me was petrified by the possibilities. *What are they saying?*

Matt reached out and touched a finger to my helmet. Something electric shimmered through the skinsuit, up through my nervous system, images cascading into place . . .

A young, orange star surrounded by a massive dust ring extending out and out. On the inner edge of the ring, a Jovian world with swirling storms of violet and grey surrounded by a chain of satellite moons, worlds in their own right that would dwarf Earth. Each of the moons is transformed by civilization—bubble ecologies, floating cities, blue-white skies over ring worlds, with the starfish arrays connecting all in a vast hub of interaction.

And deeper down, into the network—images and empathic memories of a collective, then voices in a fantastic dialect that stretches into the upper harmonic. The citizens? . . . no, custodians . . . they are older than this world, transferred here millennia ago . . . via the network . . . biotech . . . their angular heads turn atop bodies that look like dancing blue flames.

The eyes of one entity swivel then widen in acknowledgement. I can see its indigo irises, so close now, speckled with white circuitry. The pupils dilate . . . it is looking *at me—*

The skinsuit thrusters pushed me away and the link faded. My eyelids fluttered as the treacly slide into unconsciousness took hold . . . then Matt was with me, shaking me gently. I gasped. "How is that possible?"

"We're not sure. It could be an autonomic response programmed into the starfish—a bit like an interactive interstellar greeting card. But some of us speculate that it could be a true faster-than-light relay. I've spent a lot of time analyzing this. They're survivors, and their technology is . . . well, we can't make assumptions . . . we must be vigilant."

I looked at him then, behind his technology and his vacuum-adapted skin. For the first time I realized why the motion of his massive structure seemed familiar. His new body, his entire array, moved like the starfish.

"Oh, Matt."

He arched a dark metal eyebrow, his eyes like beacons. "It was the only way. We don't know how to operate the starfish and any attempts to get inside it might destroy or disable it. But we can scan and replicate—*align* with it."

He looked at me then, in that way that he used to before bed time when he'd tell me about his day at the havens and the patterns he saw in things. Our talks helped him understand his intuition—a young boy in awe of the world around him.

I float for days in the path of the data stream.

I sighed. *There's truth out here if you listen long enough.*

Earth

Ancient light fell upon my retina as the tracking dish hummed. The autumn nights seemed colder after three years, but there was a warmth now, inside me, that pushed away the chill.

I had been living in denial, grounded in the misconceptions of my own humanity. In wanting so much for Matt, I had forgotten to listen to him. Physically, he was far from human now, but spiritually, as he touched those alien signals in the deep, he was more human than any of us could be.

And with that knowledge, I was finally able to let go, to open up my own horizons.

I turned away from the telescope as an icon flashed on my computer. A new message scrolled down the screen.

Hello, Mum.

The Fish of Lijiang
CHEN QIUFAN
TRANSLATED BY KEN LIU

Two fists are before my eyes, bright sunlight reflecting from the backs of the hands.

"Left or right?"

I see myself reaching out with a child's finger, hesitating, and pointing to the one on the left. The fist flips, opens. Empty.

The fists disappear and reappear.

"One more chance. Left or right?"

I point to the one on the right.

"You're sure? Want to change your mind?"

My finger hesitates in the air, waving left, then right, like a swimming fish.

"Final answer? Three . . . two . . . one."

My finger stops on the left.

The fist flips, opens. Other than the bright sunlight, the hand is empty.

A dream?

I open my eyes. The sun is bright, white, and hurts my eyes. I've been dozing in this Naxi-style courtyard for who knows how long. I haven't felt this comfortable in such a long time. *The sky is so fucking blue.* I stretch until my bones crack.

After ten years, everything here has changed. The only thing that remains the same is the color of the sky.

Lijiang, I'm back. This time, I'm a sick man.

Twenty-four hours ago, I had a multiplicity of identities: an office drone with a strict routine, the master of a gray Ford, the prospective owner of a moldy apartment tucked into a hidden fold of the city, a debt-ridden parasite, etc.

Now, I'm just a patient, a patient in need of rehabilitation.

It's the fault of that damned mandatory physical exam. On the last page of the report were the words: PNFD II (Psychogenic Neural-Functional Disorder II). Translated into words normal people can understand, they say that I'm messed up and I must take two weeks off to rehabilitate.

My face flushed, I asked my boss whether I could be exempted. I *felt* the stares of everyone in the office burning into the back of my neck. *Schadenfreude.* They were delighted that the "boss's pet" was shown to be human after all, weak in the head, collapsing under the stress.

I shuddered. That's office politics for you.

The boss spoke slowly, methodically: "You think I want this? I have to pay for your mandatory vacation! People working at other companies can't even get rehab even if they need it. But the new labor law requires it of us. Our company is a proper, globalized business; we have to set an example . . . Anyway, if you get worse, your disease will turn into neurosyphilis and infect the rest of us. Better that you leave now, yes?"

Ashamed, I left the boss's office and cleaned out my desk. I ignored the stares. *Keep on looking, you neurosyphilitic assholes. I'll be back in two weeks and we'll see who gets to be assistant manager at the end of the year.*

On the airplane, I listened to the snores around me, unable to fall asleep. I've been dealing with insomnia for more than a month. Actually, I've been dealing with a lot of things: upset stomach, forgetfulness, headaches, fatigue, depression, loss of libido . . . maybe it really was time for me to rest for a while.

I flipped through the in-flight magazine: the pictures of the tourist sights around Lijiang were so beautiful they almost seemed fake.

Ten years ago, I had nothing and no care. Ten years ago, Lijiang was a paradise for those who liked to exile themselves from civilization. (Or, to put it less pretentiously, that was where young people who fancied themselves "artists" slept with each other.) Ten years ago, I carried everything I owned on my back (still had some muscles then). A map of the ancient city in my pocket, I wandered through it from morning till midnight, chatted with every woman who was alone, fell asleep to the accompaniment of song and alcohol.

Now I'm back. I have a car, a house—everything a man should have, including erectile dysfunction and insomnia. If happiness and time are the two axes of a graph, then I'm afraid that the curve of my life has already passed the apex and is on its inexorable way down to the bottom.

I stay still, thinking of nothing. Sunlight falls from the top of the high walls into the yard, which smells of Chinese mahogany. I don't know how much time has passed. My watch, mobile, and any other gadget capable of displaying time have been taken away by the staff of the rehabilitation center.

The ancient city has no computers and no TV. But some of the inhabitants have decided to rent out the space on their foreheads and chests. Tiny LCDs are embedded into their skin, showing all kinds of ads, twenty-four hours a day. Like I said, this is no longer the Lijiang I knew.

Strangely, my desire to get better as soon as possible so that I can get back to the office is fading in the sunlight, like the fading smell of the Chinese mahogany.

My stomach growls, once. I decide to go find something to eat. My stomach seems the only way I have left to tell time—oh, there's also my bladder and the shifting lights in the sky.

The slate-lined street has few pedestrians—this part of the city is reserved for the use of the rehabilitating patients. There *are* many stray dogs, however: fat, thin, all kinds.

On the flight here I heard a joke. Serious economic criminals, in addition to the death penalty and life imprisonment, can now be sentenced to a third kind of punishment: become experimental subjects for consciousness transfer operations in Lijiang so that they can be turned into dogs. Normally, because these experiments often fail, no one volunteers. But the idea of living in Lijiang is so attractive—even as a dog—many have jumped at the opportunity.

Seeing how these dogs are so obsequious before pretty girls and so nervous before city inspectors, I almost think the joke is reportage.

I finish a bowl of soy chicken, find a café, and sit with a cup of black coffee. I flip through a few books I've always been meaning to read (and will never finish) and think about "the meaning of life."

Is this how you get better? Without any physical therapy, medication, special diet, yoga, yin-yang dynamics, or any other kind of professional care? Is this the meaning of the slogan plastered all over the rehabilitation center: "Healthy Minds, Happy Bodies"?

I have to admit it: I have a great appetite; I'm sleeping well; I'm relaxed; I feel better even than I did ten years ago.

Even my nose, which has been stuffed up for several weeks, can now pick out the fragrance of sachets in a coffee shop. *Wait. Sachets?*

I lift my head. A girl in a dark green dress is sitting across from me, holding a drink that smells delicious and looking at me with a big smile on her face. This is like the hook for some French film, I think, or maybe a dream, either sweet or terrifying.

"So you're in marketing?"

The woman and I are walking together in the light of the setting sun. The stone-paved street is bathed in a golden glow. Lovely smells waft from the snack bars.

"Sure. You can also say I'm in sales. How about you? Office lady? Civil service? Police? Teacher?" Then I add a bit of flattery. "Actress?"

"Ha! Keep on guessing." She seems to enjoy my attempt at humor. "I'm a special care nurse. Surprised?"

"So even nurses can get sick and need rehab."

After dinner, we go to a bar. She's disappointed by the decline in the level of service at Lijiang. "What happened to all the fun people who used to run this place?"

From one of the waiters we find out that the place is now owned by Lijiang Industries (stock code # 203845), backed by several wealthy conglomerates. The local owners she knew sold because they either could no longer afford to keep the place running or could not afford a new license. Everything is so much more expensive now. But the stock of Lijiang Industries is doing very well.

The ancient city at night is filled with the spirit of consumerism, but we can't find anywhere we want to go. She has no interest in hearing Naxi folk music played by a robot orchestra—"Sounds like a braying donkey with its balls cut off." I don't want to see a folk dance demonstration by a bonfire—"Like a human BBQ." In the end we decide to lie down on our bellies by the side of the street, watching the little fish swimming in the waterway.

In the waterways of Lijiang live schools of red fish. Whether it's dawn, dusk, or midnight, you can see them hovering in the water, facing the same direction, lined up like soldiers on a parade ground ready for inspection. But if you look closer, you'll see that they aren't really still. In fact, they're struggling against the current in order to maintain their position. Once in a while, one or two fish become tired and are pushed out of the formation by the current. But soon, tails fluttering, they struggle back into place.

It's been ten years since I last saw them. *They,* at least, haven't changed.

"Swim, swim, swim. Before you know it, life is over." I repeat the same words I said ten years ago.

"Just like us," she says.

"This is the hidden meaning of life," I say. "At least we still can choose how to live." I sound so pretentious that I want to gag.

"But the reality is that I didn't choose you, and you didn't choose me."

My heart skips a beat. I look at her. I really haven't thought about inviting her to come back to my hotel. I still don't feel the return of my libido. This is a misunderstanding.

She begins to laugh.

"I was quoting a song. You don't know it? Well, I'm pretty beat. Why don't we meet up again tomorrow? You're fun."

"But how do I find you . . . " I suddenly realize that I don't have my mobile.

"I'm staying here." She hands me the card from a hotel. "If you're too lazy to walk there, just get a dog."

"A dog?"

"You really don't know? Any stray dog would do. Take a piece of paper, write down the time and place you want to meet at and stick it in the dog's collar. Then swipe the hotel card through the collar."

"You're not kidding?"

"You need to read your Lijiang guidebook."

I don't know how long I slept.

I think it's the afternoon of the second day, but the position of the sun tells me it's morning. Except I have no way of ascertaining that it's not the morning of the third day, the fourth day, or a morning that comes after a dream that lasts a lifetime.

Maybe that's the trick to full rehab: just don't dream about business reports and my boss's fat face.

I look for a dog. But the dogs here have sharp noses. They can smell the failure on me and run away. I'm forced to buy a packet of yak jerky. I feed a dog—a real son of a bitch—until it's stuffed. Finally I get him to carry my message.

In case she forgets who I am, I sign the note "Last Night's Fish."

I wander the streets. I enjoy the sun and the idleness. No one here has any sense of time anyway, so she can come whenever she wants to.

I see an old man sitting in a corner with a falcon. The falcon and the man are both full of energy. I go up to them with my camera.

"No pictures!" the old man shouts.

"Five yuan! One dollar!" the falcon shouts in a mixture of Sichuan-accented Mandarin and English.

Fuck! They're both robots. The city has nothing authentic any more. I turn around angrily.

"Do you want to know why the sky in Lijiang is so blue? Do you want to hear the legend of the Jade Dragon Snow Mountain?" Seeing that I'm about to go away, the old man changes his pitch and even his accent. Now he sounds like a man from urbane Suzhou. "I know everything there is to know about Lijiang. One yuan only for each piece of information."

Why not? I just want to kill some time. Might as well hear his lies. I take out a coin and stick it into the falcon's beak. *Clink!* A panel opens in the falcon's chest, revealing a pink-glowing keypad.

"To hear why the sky of Lijiang is so blue, press 1. To hear the Legend of Jade Dragon Snow Mountain, press 2. . . . "

Enough. I press "1."

"Modern Lijiang relies on condensation control and scatter index standardization. The technology is able to maintain sunny days with probability above 95.426%. Through micro-adjustments to the atmospheric particle content, it is able to maintain the hue of the sky between Pantone2975c and 3035c. The system is designed by . . . "

Damn it. I feel sad. Even the sky, so beautiful it's like the pristine sky present at Creation, is fake.

"Looking for UFOs?" she asks, as she puts her hands on my shoulders from behind.

"Can you tell me if anything here is real?" I mutter.

"Sure. There's you. There's me. We're real."

"Real sick," I correct her.

"Tell me about yourself. I love getting to know someone."

We're now back in the bar. Through the window we can see the fish in the waterway below, swimming, swimming, going nowhere.

"Let's play a game," she says. "We take turns guessing facts about the other person. If the guess is right, the other person drinks. If the guess is wrong, the guesser drinks."

"Sure. We'll see who gets drunk first."

"I'll go first. You work for a big company, right?"

"Ha. My boss's favorite saying is: *We're a proper, global, modern, big*"—I lower my voice—"*factory.*"

She giggles.

I can't remember if I told her anything about my company in the past. But I take a drink anyway.

"Your patients," I ask, "are all important people, right?" She drinks.

"You're an important man at your company," she says. I drink.

"I'll ask something more interesting," I say. "You've had patients who made passes at you, haven't you?"

She blushes, and drains her glass.

"You must have many girlfriends," she says. I hesitate for a second, and drink. *"Had" is a form of "have,"* I tell myself.

"You are not married," I say.

She smiles, not answering.

I shrug, taking a drink.

Only after I'm done does she lift her glass and drink.

"Not fair! You tricked me." I say. But I'm happy.

"It's your own fault for being impatient."

"Fine, then I'm going to guess that you have insomnia, anxiety, arrhythmia, irregular periods . . . " I know I've been drinking too fast. I know I'm going to regret this but I can't stop talking.

She glares at me, and drinks. Then she adds, "Whatever symptoms you have, I don't. Whatever symptoms I have, you don't."

"We're both here, aren't we?"

She shakes her head. "You think nothing has meaning."

"That was before I met you," I say, in what I think is a seductive tone. Now I'm just shameless.

She ignores me. "You're often anxious, because you hate the feeling of the seconds slipping away from you. The world is changing every day. And every day you're getting older. But there are still so many things you haven't done. You want to hold onto the sand. But the harder you squeeze, the quicker the sand slips from the cracks between your fingers, until nothing is left . . . "

Coming from anyone else, the words would just be pop psychology, pseudo intellectualism, cheap spirituality. But somehow, coming from her, they sound like the truth. Every word strikes against my heart, making me wince.

I drink by myself in silence. Her smile begins to multiply: two, three, four of her . . . I want to ask her something, but my tongue is no longer obeying.

She looks embarrassed. She whispers to me, "You're drunk. I'll take you back."

So, I've failed again.

It takes a long time for me to remember where I am.

During the time I'm thinking, the sun shifts through six window squares. The sun marches across three more window squares before I've washed away the smell of alcohol on my body and the vomit in the bathroom.

I guess Miss Nurse hasn't taken good care of *this patient*. I have a splitting headache.

I don't want to send a dog after her. Indeed, I'm a bit scared to meet her. Maybe she's a telepath? It makes sense to have a telepath as a special care nurse, right? Especially if a patient can no longer speak.

The biggest fear is for someone else to understand what you really fear.

A Shar-Pei enters my room and barks at me. I take out the slip of paper tucked into its collar.

She wants me to go with her to listen to robots playing Naxi folk music, which she described to me as a donkey braying with its balls cut off. She signed her note "I'm No Telepath."

Screw you! You bourgeois bitch! I kick the Shar-Pai. It whimpers.

In the end, curiosity overcomes fear. I wash, get dressed, go to the concert hall. She's dressed all in yellow. I nod at her.

But she ignores my attempt to remain distant. She walks right up to me, takes my hand in hers, and drags me inside.

"Stop pretending," she whispers in my ear. I have to struggle to keep from her how aroused I am.

They begin to play. It does sound like a donkey braying. It's an insult to real Naxi music, the sort I heard ten years ago.

The robots swing back and forth, pretending to play all sorts of Naxi instruments, and recorded music streams from speakers embedded into the seats. The robots are clearly made in China: stiff, ridiculous movements, limited repertoire of gestures, monotonous expressions. Only robot Xuan Ke is made with any kind of care for detail. Once in a while he even acts as though he's completely absorbed by his performance. I worry that he'll swing so hard that his head is going to fall off.

"I thought you didn't like donkey-braying," I whisper into her ear. The fragrance of sachets surrounds me.

"This is one part of our rehabilitation."

"Yeah, right."

I try to kiss her. But she dodges out of the way and my lips meet her fingers.

"Back in your office, on your desk, there's a tiny grey alarm clock. It's shaped like a mushroom, and it often runs fast."

Her tone is calm, but I'm stupefied. That clock was a gift from the company when I won employee of the month. How does she know about it?

I lost the drinking game—maybe that was an accident. But this . . .

I continue to stare at her profile. The donkey-braying music washes over me like a tidal wave. I seem to have also become a robot musician. I strain to play my foolish song of seduction, but she sees through me with no effort. I have nothing in my chest but a mechanical heart made of iron.

We end up in bed together.

She acts as though this is nothing special. But not me. A man is such a strange animal: fear and desire are expressed by the same organ. For the former, he loses control of the organ and it lets out urine; for the latter, he loses control of the organ and it fills with blood.

Is this part of our rehab too? I can imagine myself mocking her. But I don't, because I fear how she'll answer.

"Who are you really?" I can't help myself.

Her voice is muffled, indistinct.

"I'm a nurse. My patient is time."

In the end she does tell me her story.

She works for a place called "Time Care Unit." Only the most important men of the business world get to go there.

The old men are like mummies, their bodies plugged full of tubes and wires. Twenty-four hours a day they must be watched and cared for. Every day, all kinds of people come to visit. They dress in sterile biosuits and stand around the beds, communing with the old men, reporting and receiving instructions in silence.

The old men never move. Each of their breaths takes hours. Once in a while, one of them moans like a baby, and someone makes a record of it. Looking at all the biological signs, they should all be considered dead. The numbers shown on their machines never change. But they remain in that place for years, decades.

She tells me that they are receiving "time sense dilation therapy." She calls them "the living dead."

The therapy began some twenty years ago. Back then, scientists discovered that by controlling the biological clock of an organism, it was possible to reduce the production of free radicals and slow down aging. But the decay of the mind and its eventual death could not be reversed or halted.

Someone made another discovery: the aging of the mind was intimately connected with the sense of the passage of time. By manipulating certain receptors in the pineal gland, it was possible to slow down one's sense of time, to dilate it. The body of a person receiving time sense dilation therapy remains in the normal stream of time, but his mind experiences time a hundred, a thousand times slower than the rest of us.

"But what does this have to do with you?" I ask.

"You know that women who live together synchronize their biological rhythms, like menstrual cycles?"

I nod.

"It's the same thing with us nurses who care for these living dead, day in, day out. Once a year, I have to come to Lijiang to rehabilitate, to remove the effects time dilation has on my body."

I feel dizzy. Time sense dilation is used on those old men because of the need to maintain stock prices or to delay power struggles among successors. But what if the dilation is applied to a normal person? I try to imagine experiencing a hundred years within a second. But my imagination is not up to the task. To extend time to near infinity is to slow it down until it's almost still. Then isn't the mind under such dilation immortal? What's the need for a body made of flesh?

"Remember what I told you? I didn't choose you, and you didn't choose me," she says, smiling almost apologetically.

I begin to feel anxiety again, as though my fingers are wrapped around a handful of sand, leaking sand.

"You're the other half of me, cloven by Zeus's thunderbolt."

The words sound to me like a curse.

She's leaving.

She tells me that her rehabilitation period is up.

We sit in the dark. In front of us is the imposing mass of Jade Dragon Snow Mountain, its snowy peaks reflecting the silver moonlight. Neither of us speaks.

The donkey-braying music loops again and again in my head.

"Remember that alarm clock on your desk?"

Although time sense dilation therapy is very expensive, the opposite procedure—time sense compression—is not. The procedure is cheap enough to be commercialized. Several large conglomerates have invested in it, and taking advantage of certain loopholes in China's labor laws (and the complicity of the government), they've been conducting secret trials on Chinese employees of international companies.

That alarm clock is a prototype time sense compressor.

"So we are all lab mice," I remember mocking myself at her revelation. Even my boss is a mouse—he also has one of those clocks on his desk.

"It doesn't matter if you know the truth," she says. "The theoretical basis for time sense compression does not exist."

"Does not exist?"

"Theoretical physics says it's impossible, so they had to base it on the philosophy of Henri Bergson. It's all about intuition."

"What are you talking about?"

"I don't know." She laughs. "Maybe it's all nonsense."

"You're telling me that my disease, this PNFD II or whatever it's called, is the result of time sense compression?"

She doesn't say anything.

But it makes sense. Time passes quicker in my mind than it does in the real world. Every day I'm exhausted. I'm always working overtime. I accomplish so much more in twenty-four hours than others. No wonder the company thinks I'm a model employee.

Clouds drift over and hide the moon, eliminating the reflected light on the snowy peaks. Everything grows darker like after they lower the lights in a theatre.

A bright red laser beam lands on the snowy cliffs—5600 meters above the sea—now acting as a giant screen. The laser creates shifting patterns, telling an animated tale, the creation of the world. A myth has been bowdlerized to mass entertainment. I'm not in the mood to appreciate it. The dancing lights only make my heart beat irregularly.

Time sense compression is wonderful for improving productivity and GDP. But there are many side effects. The mismatch between subjective time and physical time causes metabolic problems that accumulate into severe symptoms.

The conglomerates that invested in the technology created the rehabilitation centers in China and lobbied to change the labor laws to institutionalize the idea of "rehabilitation" so as to hide the truth.

They discovered that those suffering from the side effects of time sense dilation and those suffering from the side effects of time sense compression can help each other, be each other's cure.

"I'm the yang to your yin, is that it?" So her interest in me is limited to my value as a medical device. My middle-aged male ego is hurt.

"Sure, if you insist on thinking about it that way." Her tone, at least, is compassionate.

"What about the donkey-braying music?"

"It's a way to harmonize our biorhythms."

I wait for her to stroke my ego by telling me that compared to her previous rehabilitation biorhythm partners, I'm better looking, more interesting, more special, etc. But she says nothing of the kind.

"What about the dogs?" I'm running out of things to say before she leaves.

"They started out as regular dogs. But because they're exposed to so many patients with out-of-sync senses of time, the structures in their brain have changed."

"I have only one last wish." I stare at her bright eyes in the darkness, like a pair of fireflies. "Come and look at the fish in the waterways with me. Maybe they're the only creatures in this world who live real lives."

The fireflies brighten. She touches my face lightly. "Actually . . . "

I silence her lips with my fingers. I shake my head. I've succeeded. There's no need for her to tell me what she's going to tell me, the three heaviest words in the world.

But she gently moves my hand away, and says three words, three different words.

"Don't be stupid."

I'm alone by the waterway, staring at the fish.

She's gone, leaving behind no way to contact her. Sand pricks my palms. No matter how hard I squeeze, they slip away.

Fish, oh fish, you're the only ones left to keep me company.

Suddenly, I feel an intense jealousy of these fish. Their lives are so simple, so pure. There's only one direction—against the current. They do not have to hesitate, overwhelmed by an endless array of choices. But if I really lived a life like that, maybe I'd still complain. A man is never content with what he has.

Suddenly I want to spit at myself for my self-love, self-pity, self-obsession, self-self. But in the end I do nothing.

I look at one single fish: it's pushed away from its school by the current. Once, twice, thrice. It falls behind, waves its tail madly, and returns to its position.

Fuck. It's tough.

But wait.

Why is it always this one fish? Why is its trajectory and movement always exactly the same?

I wait, unblinking.

Two minutes later, that same little fish again drifts away from the school, again waves its tail madly, again returns to its position.

I lift the stone in my hand.

The stone falls through the holographic fish and sinks to the bottom of the waterway.

I have nothing left in my hand, not even a single grain of sand.

My rehabilitation over, I'm on my return flight with my not-so-healthy mind and not-so-happy body. The airplane hasn't taken off yet but the cabin is already filled with snores.

I guess some people at least have been fully rehabilitated.

Suddenly the idea of returning to that concrete jungle to struggle against my fellow time-compressors disgusts me.

The plane takes off. Cities, roads, mountains, rivers—everything recedes into a small chessboard composed of parti-colored squares. In every square, time flows faster or slower. The people below throng like a nest of ants controlled by an invisible hand, divide into a few groups, are stuffed into the different squares: time flies past the laborer, the poor, the "third world"; time crawls for the rich, the idle, the "developed world"; time stays still for those in charge, the idols, the gods . . .

Suddenly, two fat hands belonging to a child appear before me, holding the entire world in them, backs of the hands up.

"Left or right?"

I look to the left and then right. I'm frightened. I have no way to pick.

Mocking laughter.

I lunge and grab both fists and force the fingers open: both are empty, both lies.

"Sir, sir!"

The pretty flight attendant wakes me. Now I finally remember the origin of that dream. It was my cousin who tormented me as a child. His favorite game was to force me to guess in which hand he had hidden the candy he took away from me. He loved to tease me because I was always hesitant, always had trouble deciding.

"Sir, would you like soda, coffee, tea or something else?"

" . . . you."

She blushes.

I smile at her. "I just want coffee, black."

This is the only truly free choice I have left.

"The Fish of Lijiang" was originally published in
Science Fiction World, May 2006.
First English language publication.

Conservation of Shadows
YOON HA LEE

There is no such thing as conservation of shadows. When light destroys shadows, darkness does not gain in density elsewhere. When shadows steal over earth and across the sky, darkness is not diluted.

Hello, Inanna. You have seven inventory slots, all full. The seventh contains your heart, which cannot be removed. We will do our best to remedy this.

A feast awaits you at the end, sister. I am keeping it warm for you. You will be cold by the time you reach my hall beneath the floors of the world. Meadow honey on barley cakes, cheese and the tender flesh of goats; plums and pears brighter than the jewels in your hair; wine less sweet than birdsong and more bitter than tears. Taken together they form a nutritionally complete diet.

You think that all we eat in the underworld is dust and all we drink is the dregs of rain, but that is not the case. Come and share the feast.

You hesitate over the shadow-gun at your waist. Notice the holster, leather stamped with a lioness on each side. The leather comes from a lioness's hide. She is dead, sister. She cannot aid you here.

I can't tell you how to pass through the first gate. More accurately, I could, but I won't. We live by different laws in the underworld, we who live at all. Now you must respect those laws as well.

The gate lies there. Your fingers move toward it, then draw back. How wise of you. Gates are hungry. They demand propitiation. Once a woman put her hand in a gate and it ate her fingers. A five-legged spider with red eyes crawled out. That woman put in three fingers from her other hand, so that the spider might be complete. Do you have that integrity of purpose, sister?

No, what you feed the gate is other. It is easy for gates to be dark, maws opening to the earth's own secrets. They wonder what light is like. So you tempt it with the jewels in your hair. Poor gate: it knows nothing about symbolism. It knows only that the tinted diamonds and emeralds and lapis lazuli glint with the evening star's passion. Down you draw the golden pins from your dark hair and let that torrent free.

Eagerly, the gate lips at the diamonds' fire, the emeralds' intimation of bounty, the lapis lazuli's memory of the sky that cannot be seen. The color leaches from the diamonds, leaving them ashen. The other stones, less hardy, crumble into dust, their virtue vanished.

Sated, the gate eats no more of you as you pass through, divested of glory yet more beautiful than ever.

The fires won't hurt you unless you let them, sister. Hungry already? You'll be hungrier still. Don't roast the flesh off your bones. It's not time yet.

Did you think the underworld moved in ignorance of summer? The season that scours the earth and fills the stomachs of those aboveground while leaving us below-ground with the rotting chaff? At least we know that we are the chaff of days, the dust of time.

It is summer because you've scarcely left the world above. Just think, sister: the longer you linger here, the more the leaves shrivel gold and brown on the branches; the more the last grapes wither on the vines.

Now you are hungry again, and thirsty as well. I know. I know you so well that you could flense yourself bare of face and fingerprints and still I would recognize you. After all, I recognized you the first seventy-four times you came my way.

Does it surprise you that your inventory comes up in the shape of an eight-pointed star? Blink once and it appears; twice, and it folds out of your field of vision. It reports nothing you can't find upon you.

One slot is empty now, black as a gate, as the absence of day; black as your hair. Pick up something else if you like. Yes, that pencil will do. The graphite's luster is dark. It grows darker yet in your grasp.

I don't recognize the words you are writing on my walls, sister: graffiti, in scratchy bird-claw marks. Maybe you mean it to be illegible. That would be unkind.

Consider this. The seventy-four earlier iterations of you left no guide-star tags upon the walls, no cheat sheets, no maps tattooed upon their skins. Underneath your armor there is skin, the organ on which your boundaries are written. You'll know the instant it dissolves and opens your secrets to the air.

Nothing's left of your pencil but a stub. One point of the eight-pointed star flares diamond-bright as the inventory slot empties itself in response.

Did I speak to you of skin? The walls are my skin, the gold-painted pillars my bones. Do what you will with them. You always did.

You are silent. I don't know whether this is an improvement or not. Do you think your words will inscribe themselves upon the air like the coming frost upon fallen leaves? Twenty degrees Celsius, room temperature. You are in a room.

There is no way out of the room, except now there is. Like a hundred mutilated lips the letters—are they letters or logograms?—crack wide, wider. Gap to gap, they gape until they dissolve into a single opening.

A wind rushes through the gate. The wind chill factor is 14 degrees Celsius. You may feel that is excessive. From that number you can calculate the speed of the wind. Unfortunately, your pencil's stub will write no more for you. Perhaps you can do the figures in your head.

If you came to the feast, you would soon sate yourself with warm food. You would watch as dancers clad in feathers reenacted the descent of your first self, or the eighth, or the forty-ninth. How many gates do you think your sad, brave clones survived? Do not worry. You are different, you are special, more clever and greater of heart. I will make sure you reach the barley cakes brimming with dark honey.

Now you are singing. Your formants are rich with despair. Some languages can be recorded without stylus or pencil.

The gate swallows the holy sweetness of your voice. It cancels the waveform, replacing it with silence beyond imagining. Sister, you have not known silence until you have sat in the dark among the dead for generations.

You don't know, yet you do. These are the things you sing of: the embryos of mice, stillborn, albinos that have never known light; the needle's prick drawing blood directly from the betrayed artery; curling strands of fossil DNA, a language more legible than yours. Memory is not inherited, memory is no mirror to times past, yet you divine the experiments that I oversee here.

The gate is as still as matter ever is. Even you cannot cancel that lowest level of vibration, absolute zero thrumming. It will have to do.

Assured of the gate's momentary toothlessness, you step through, and it lets you. Silence drifts in your wake like leaves and petals, like all things ephemeral.

This time it's not so easy to ignore the fire, is it? Go deep enough and you'll meet the mantle's heat. You think of the underworld as cold and dank, inhabited by pale, eyeless creatures whose circulatory systems are written within them with ink redder than spinels. That is not the whole of us. We can kill you by fire, too.

Are you worried about dying? You shy from the fires, watch your balance on the narrow walkways. It helps to have good reflexes in death as well as life. It's good that you practice. Of course I support your efforts.

Traverse the spiraling maze and who do you find at the center? Imagine peeling the layers of yourself away. What's left when you reach your hallowed heart, when the hollows admit no shadows but what you carry with you? I forgot: with no voice, you can't answer me.

Walk and walk as you may, you only knot yourself further into the maze's pattern. Isn't this the way of the world? From the moment you first draw breath, you're woven into the world's overbearing warp.

Look: the necklace at your throat responds to the fire, capturing and releasing that warm light with its own golden gleam. In this surfeit of light I can read the inscription on your eight-pointed pendant, spider-scratch marks deep in the metal. No cipher hides you from me. I have mapped you down to your mitochondria. I can read your rate of respiration, the flush of your skin. Surely the heat isn't unbearable yet.

You unclasp the bright unknot from around your neck. Which lover gave you that necklace? Was it before or after he pressed you against the flowering earth, the leafing tree? Through the floor of the earth, I heard your demands. You were never easy to please, no matter how many lovers you dragged from bars, drugged by the honey of your voice and the heat of your mouth. Nevertheless the mares and does swelled, and the boughs curved under the weight of tender fruit.

Did the lionesses nuzzle each other, wondering over cubs to come?

Like a sleepy snake the necklace ripples over your hands, throwing bright glints across knuckles and prominent bones. I will listen when you explain to your beloved that his gift was worth nothing except as a talisman against one more nexus of shadow and insatiable envy. That's the problem, surely: not that you discarded the gift, but that it was discarded in such small cause.

There are people who would kill for fire: fire to stoke youth in the furnace beneath their skins, fire to brighten the faded cloth of their lives. Better to die burning than chilled by slow moments into the silvered dark. No? Tell that to all those whose bones embrace beneath the worm-furrowed loam.

A narrow opal flares open in the air at the maze's heart, narrow like a woman before she grows great with child. Were this gate a woman you could dance with her, span her with your hands—no. Instead, you fasten the necklace around the gate, adorning it as you once adorned yourself.

The gold shines with the warmth of the surrounding fires. The gate does not drain away the reflected light. Instead, darkness seeps into the inscription. You can't turn away from the words, sister, the seething shapes of *summer, hope, health* inverted.

The gate offers you its embrace. Without hesitation or tenderness, you accept, ducking your head so that you are briefly crowned in gold.

Do you know how deep in the earth you are, sister? You squint in the near-dark. There is only a single lantern to comfort you. Imagine: maybe that lantern is the only thing between you and utter darkness. Shall I snuff it out? Don't shiver so; it doesn't become you.

The stalactites and stalagmites grip the light in their jaws, returning only washed-out, variegated colors: poor exchange for that faint gold.

You shouldn't have sold your voice so cheaply. It makes conversation difficult. Would you like to borrow the voices that whisper in the underworld for your own? You never know who might wander here. They might remember the world's oldest hymns. They might be praising the serpentine coils of your hair, the silent cunning of your hands. They might not know who you are at all, now that you're stripped of your war-chariot, far from the morning star. For all the storms you dragged in your wake, all the rain-tossed days and nights, you craved light as your nourishment: star or moon, lightning scarring the shrouded sky. You always were one for fanfare.

Here are no drums to shake the stone columns and threaten you with the slow death of suffocation. Don't worry about the air, dear sister. You breathe as darkness does, without need of oxygen or any element but your very self. Light travels through the void without a mediating aether; why should darkness be any different?

Come to my halls, sister, and there will be no more talk of light or dark or the permutations in between. We will sit side by side on our thrones, drinking young wine and old rather than the dark, dank water that trickles just beneath the world's skin. We will bestow treasures upon those who please us, luminous cabochons and spiral emblems of gold, chains sometimes of silver and sometimes of bronze.

In the earth's hidden hoards you can taste treasure as though it were a nectar beyond price. Underground, so deep that even fungi find no nourishment, the earth fruits metal and precious stones. It is of no concern to us that living creatures starve contemplating such fruit.

You unfasten your belt, such a short, blunt length to encircle your waist. Jewels of varying cuts are set in the leather, all polished to the brilliance of river water beneath a fecund moon. They fling colored sparks across the floor and walls. Did you ever spare a thought for the underground spirits that had to be disturbed by the digging for your treasures?

With the belt you whip the largest geode in the wall, already cracked half-open to reveal its jagged amethyst heart. The jewels fall out of your belt and scatter to the floor, uncracked yet dimmer, duller. You should be more patient, sister. After all, when you reach the final gate there will be no returning. Doesn't the thought distress you even a little?

Heedless, you bunch up the belt in your fist, then thrust it into the gate that is growing from the crack in the geode. Is that how you regard the underworld's gleaming treasures? Obstacles to be destroyed?

I suppose I haven't learned anything that I didn't already know. You are all the same, all of you.

The geode's teeth scratch your skin as you enter, even through the stiff curves of your armor.

This deep in the earth, you can't hear the seasons breathing even in your dreams. Tell me true: when you close your eyes, can you smell the earthy sweetness of rotting leaves, or taste the last fruits of fall? If I set before you a feast of the finest wines and hearty porridge and roast boar, would it taste like the dust that surrounds you?

Come to me before it's too late, before you lose all ability to see color or to taste salt or sweet.

You tilt your head, listening to the laments of the dead. Their voices sound very like your own, don't they? Maybe they always have. There is no use for fertility without death, you know.

All your faces are mine. You can verify that with a mirror when we meet, except that mirrors are liars when there is no light, claiming that everything is equal to everything. Perhaps that's the sort of lie you like to tell yourself.

Here's the thing about shadows. Even at their most distorted, shadows are mathematically precise. They show you what is given to them to show. If a shadow portrays you as larger as you are, it's no fault of the shadow's. It's all a matter of light, of angles and intensity and color.

If I loom so large in your experience here, sister, you might consider what it is about you that has made me who I am.

Don't worry about the candles here, or the supply of oxygen. The ventilation is quite adequate for our purposes.

Your shadows flicker and jump in perfect time to the candles' flames, like dancers yearning after each other. Which one most truly represents your face? Or mine?

When you close your eyes, just before sleep bears you beneath the surface of the world, do you have a face at all? Can you differentiate yourself from the shadows at all?

Furiously, you pull open your jacket, unfasten your tunic. I know all the scars you bear, sister. The abrupt cuneiform shapes of scars embellish your skin. Scars from battle or love or all the jagged shapes in between, cicatrices and burn scars, round and pale and lightning-shaped.

Of course: no shadow living ever bore a scar.

You feed the shadows your scars, erasing all record of those past triumphs and defeats. As the scars smooth out, becoming invisible against the brown canvas of your body, the shadows gain in depth and form, braiding themselves together until they are a cold, tangible presence on the floor.

Unhesitating, you refasten your tunic and step through, falling without falling.

You're shielding your eyes. Surprised at how bright it is? I thought you could use a reminder. The spectrum produced by each lamp imitates that of a sun you or one of your clone-sisters has visited. Sadly, no matter how faithful a lamp is, it can never rival the real thing.

Don't look for their remnants here. Seasons in human time are one thing, but seasons in the lives of starfarers—what is a human winter to people like you or me? You've been breathing their dust, treading on their fossilized despair.

Nevertheless, you crouch, heedless of the gray grit that clings to your clothes, and draw figures on the cave's floor. If you think your calculus will save you, you are sorely mistaken. In your formula the infinitesimals come to a positive sum. Here, the sum of iterated emptiness will only be more emptiness.

Let me tell you a story to distract you from the useless fable you are telling yourself. Long ago, the people of a great and fertile land resolved to explore worlds that circled the god-stars that they had watched and worshiped since their people first set brick upon brick to build cities. But for all their ambitions, they were loyal, and did not forget their gods. They knew they would need their gods to guard them from the dangers that lie deep in space.

So they made sure that their gods would follow them into that shining darkness, a pantheon of gods for each world. They made you, all of you, and they made me.

If you must console yourself over your journey here, tell yourself that those who made you achieved their purpose, and that you are perfectly recapitulating that old story so that your world will pass into its winter rest. You will not live to see your world's renewal, but another of you will.

Don't bother scratching out a message to her. She won't read the same languages you do, won't take the same twisting path. I will tell her the same things that I have told you. You may be sure of it.

You've removed the shadow-gun from its holster and are cradling it in your hands. You knew it would come to this. We both did.

It's a beautiful weapon. It has the same coiled intensity that you do when you are intent on war, sister. And it has killed people in your hands. You are not the kind to beg forgiveness; you were made for bloodshed. I don't understand why you regard the gun with such loathing, then.

Steadily, you raise the shadow-gun and squeeze the trigger. The room explodes into utter darkness, the kind of darkness that swallows sound and stifles thought. Even the spangled otherspace behind your eyelids is brighter than this.

A moment later, your fingers close around empty air as the gun dissolves. It has served its purpose. All but one of your inventory slots is empty as well.

The entire room is a gate now. It remains only for you to take a step. It speaks well of you that you listen for a long, careful moment before moving in the direction leading downward, toward me.

Your heart thuds one-two, one-two, one-two like a march without an army. There is only you, alone before the last gate. What did you hope to accomplish when you set out, sister? Did you have some brave notion of unseating me from my dark throne, or tearing asunder all the underworld gates so the dead would roam free and outnumber the living?

I have always admired your purity of purpose, mistaken as it is. We are not so different, you and I. We play the roles that are given to us. Yours is to die, and mine is to kill you. Don't spoil the symmetry of the story.

The only reason you can see anything here, where the darkness is thicker than honey, is that you still have a heart. It shines red-bright in the final inventory slot, last remaining illumination. If I cared to, I could grow you a new, more compliant heart. But that is not my duty. Would you deny Number Seventy-Six her chance at this journey?

There is a small, angular object in your hand like a dead star. Your inventory system needs to be debugged. Why was I not informed?

You kneel again. I can hear the painful harshness of your breathing. More important is what you are scratching into the dust on the floor with your pointed fingernail. This time it is in a language I understand:

I have always known I am not the only one. You are not the only one of your kind, either. My clone-sisters and I have planned for this moment, a coordinated strike. It is the only way we can be free. I am s—

How can it be that I feel the touch of rain so deep beneath the earth, blotting out the last word you would have written?

You timed it to your traitor heart. And now that I know to look, I see it: a mass inside your heart, tangled inextricably into it.

In the end you give up your heart after all, but I am the one who loses everything, in a springtime effusion of light.

for Sonya Taaffe

The Cartographer Wasps and the Anarchist Bees

E. LILY YU

For longer than anyone could remember, the village of Yiwei had worn, in its orchards and under its eaves, clay-colored globes of paper that hissed and fizzed with wasps. The villagers maintained an uneasy peace with their neighbors for many years, exercising inimitable tact and circumspection. But it all ended the day a boy, digging in the riverbed, found a stone whose balance and weight pleased him. With this, he thought, he could hit a sparrow in flight. There were no sparrows to be seen, but a paper ball hung low and inviting nearby. He considered it for a moment, head cocked, then aimed and threw.

Much later, after he had been plastered and soothed, his mother scalded the fallen nest until the wasps seething in the paper were dead. In this way it was discovered that the wasp nests of Yiwei, dipped in hot water, unfurled into beautifully accurate maps of provinces near and far, inked in vegetable pigments and labeled in careful Mandarin that could be distinguished beneath a microscope.

The villagers' subsequent incursions with bee veils and kettles of boiling water soon diminished the prosperous population to a handful. Commanded by a single stubborn foundress, the survivors folded a new nest in the shape of a paper boat, provisioned it with fallen apricots and squash blossoms, and launched themselves onto the river. Browsing cows and children fled the riverbanks as they drifted downstream, piping sea chanteys.

At last, forty miles south from where they had begun, their craft snagged on an upthrust stick and sank. Only one drowned in the evacuation, weighed down with the remains of an apricot. They reconvened upon a stump and looked about themselves.

"It's a good place to land," the foundress said in her sweet soprano, examining the first rough maps that the scouts brought back. There were plenty of caterpillars, oaks for ink galls, fruiting brambles, and no signs of other wasps. A colony of bees had hived in a split oak two miles away. "Once we are established we will, of course, send a delegation to collect tribute.

"We will not make the same mistakes as before. Ours is a race of explorers and scientists, cartographers and philosophers, and to rest and grow slothful is to die. Once we are established here, we will expand."

It took two weeks to complete the nurseries with their paper mobiles, and then another month to reconstruct the Great Library and fill the pigeonholes with what the oldest cartographers could remember of their lost maps. Their comings and goings did not go unnoticed. An ambassador from the beehive arrived with an ultimatum and was promptly executed; her wings were made into stained-glass windows for the council chamber, and her stinger was returned to the hive in a paper envelope. The second ambassador came with altered attitude and a proposal to divide the bees' kingdom evenly between the two governments, retaining pollen and water rights for the bees—"as an acknowledgment of the preexisting claims of a free people to the natural resources of a common territory," she hummed.

The wasps of the council were gracious and only divested the envoy of her sting. She survived just long enough to deliver her account to the hive.

The third ambassador arrived with a ball of wax on the tip of her stinger and was better received.

"You understand, we are not refugees applying for recognition of a token territorial sovereignty," the foundress said, as attendants served them nectars in paper horns, "nor are we negotiating with you as equal states. Those were the assumptions of your late predecessors. They were mistaken."

"I trust I will do better," the diplomat said stiffly. She was older than the others, and the hairs of her thorax were sparse and faded.

"I do hope so."

"Unlike them, I have complete authority to speak for the hive. You have propositions for us; that is clear enough. We are prepared to listen."

"Oh, good." The foundress drained her horn and took another. "Yours is an old and highly cultured society, despite the indolence of your ruler, which we understand to be a racial rather than personal proclivity. You have laws, and traditional dances, and mathematicians, and principles, which of course we do respect."

"Your terms, please."

She smiled. "Since there is a local population of tussah moths, which we prefer for incubation, there is no need for anything so unrepublican as slavery. If you refrain from insurrection, you may keep your self-rule. But we will take a fifth of your stores in an ordinary year, and a tenth in drought years, and one of every hundred larvae."

"To eat?" Her antennae trembled with revulsion.

"Only if food is scarce. No, they will be raised among us and learn our ways and our arts, and then they will serve as officials and bureaucrats among you. It will be to your advantage, you see."

The diplomat paused for a moment, looking at nothing at all. Finally she said, "A tenth, in a good year—"

"Our terms," the foundress said, "are not negotiable."

The guards shifted among themselves, clinking the plates of their armor and shifting the gleaming points of their stings.

"I don't have a choice, do I?"

"The choice is enslavement or cooperation," the foundress said. "For your hive, I mean. You might choose something else, certainly, but they have tens of thousands to replace you with."

The diplomat bent her head. "I am old," she said. "I have served the hive all my life, in every fashion. My loyalty is to my hive and I will do what is best for it."

"I am so very glad."

"I ask you—I beg you—to wait three or four days to impose your terms. I will be dead by then, and will not see my sisters become a servile people."

The foundress clicked her claws together. "Is the delaying of business a custom of yours? We have no such practice. You will have the honor of watching us elevate your sisters to moral and technological heights you could never imagine."

The diplomat shivered.

"Go back to your queen, my dear. Tell them the good news."

It was a crisis for the constitutional monarchy. A riot broke out in District 6, destroying the royal waxworks and toppling the mouse-bone monuments before it was brutally suppressed. The queen had to be calmed with large doses of jelly after she burst into tears on her ministers' shoulders.

"Your Majesty," said one, "it's not a matter for your concern. Be at peace."

"These are my children," she said, sniffling. "You would feel for them too, were you a mother."

"Thankfully, I am not," the minister said briskly, "so to business."

"War is out of the question," another said.

"Their forces are vastly superior."

"We outnumber them three hundred to one!"

"They are experienced fighters. Sixty of us would die for each of theirs. We might drive them away, but it would cost us most of the hive and possibly our queen—"

The queen began weeping noisily again and had to be cleaned and comforted.

"Have we any alternatives?"

There was a small silence.

"Very well, then."

The terms of the relationship were copied out, at the wasps' direction, on small paper plaques embedded in propolis and wax around the hive. As paper and ink were new substances to the bees, they jostled and touched and tasted the bills until the paper fell to pieces. The wasps sent to oversee the installation did not take this kindly. Several civilians died before it was established that the bees could not read the Yiwei dialect.

Thereafter the hive's chemists were charged with compounding pheromones complex enough to encode the terms of the treaty. These were applied to the papers, so that both species could inspect them and comprehend the relationship between the two states.

Whereas the hive before the wasp infestation had been busy but content, the bees now lived in desperation. The natural terms of their lives were cut short by the need to gather enough honey for both the hive and the wasp nest. As they traveled farther and farther afield in search of nectar, they stopped singing. They danced their findings grimly, without joy. The queen herself grew gaunt and thin from breeding replacements, and certain ministers who understood such matters began feeding royal jelly to the strongest larvae.

Meanwhile, the wasps grew sleek and strong. Cadres of scholars, cartographers, botanists, and soldiers were dispatched on the river in small floating nests caulked with beeswax and loaded with rations of honeycomb to chart the unknown lands to the south. Those who returned bore beautiful maps with towns and farms and alien populations of wasps carefully noted in blue and purple ink, and these, once studied by the foundress and her generals, were carefully filed away in the depths of the Great Library for their southern advance in the new year.

The bees adopted by the wasps were first trained to clerical tasks, but once it was determined that they could be taught to read and write, they were assigned to some of the reconnaissance missions. The brightest students, gifted at trigonometry and angles, were educated beside the cartographers themselves and proved valuable assistants. They learned not to see the thick green caterpillars led on silver chains, or the dead bees fed to the wasp brood. It was easier that way.

When the old queen died, they did not mourn.

By the sheerest of accidents, one of the bees trained as a cartographer's assistant was an anarchist. It might have been the stresses on the hive, or it might have been luck; wherever it came from, the mutation was viable. She tucked a number of her own eggs in beeswax and wasp paper among the pigeonholes of the library and fed the larvae their milk and bread in secret. To her sons in their capped silk cradles—and they were all sons—she whispered the precepts she had developed while calculating flight paths and azimuths, that there should be no queen and no state, and that, as in the wasp nest, the males should labor and profit equally with the females. In their sleep and slow transformation they heard her teachings and instructions, and when they chewed their way out of their cells and out of the wasp nest, they made their way to the hive.

The damage to the nest was discovered, of course, but by then the anarchist was dead of old age. She had done impeccable work, her tutor sighed, looking over the filigree of her inscriptions, but the brilliant were subject to mental aberrations, were they not? He buried beneath grumblings and labors his fondness for her, which had become a grief to him and a political liability, and he never again took on any student from the hive who showed a glint of talent.

Though they had the bitter smell of the wasp nest in their hair, the anarchist's twenty sons were permitted to wander freely through the hive, as it was assumed that they were either spies or on official business. When the new queen emerged from her chamber, they joined unnoticed the other drones in the nuptial flight. Two succeeded in mating with her. Those who failed and survived spoke afterward in hushed tones of what had been done for the sake of the ideal. Before they died they took propolis and oak-apple ink and inscribed upon the lintels of the hive, in a shorthand they had developed, the story of the first anarchist and her twenty sons.

Anarchism being a heritable trait in bees, a number of the daughters of the new queen found themselves questioning the purpose of the monarchy. Two were taken by the wasps and taught to read and write. On one of their visits to the hive they spotted the history of their forefathers, and, being excellent scholars, soon figured out the translation.

They found their sisters in the hive who were unquiet in soul and whispered to them the strange knowledge they had learned among the wasps: astronomy, military strategy, the state of the world beyond the farthest flights of the bees. Hitherto educated as dancers and architects, nurses and foragers, the bees were full of a new wonder, stranger even than the first day they flew from the hive and felt the sun on their backs.

"Govern us," they said to the two wasp-taught anarchists, but they refused.

"A perfect society needs no rulers," they said. "Knowledge and authority ought to be held in common. In order to imagine a new existence, we must free ourselves from the structures of both our failed government and the unjustifiable hegemony of the wasp nests. Hear what you can hear and learn what you can learn while we remain among them. But be ready."

It was the first summer in Yiwei without the immemorial hum of the cartographer wasps. In the orchards, though their skins split with sweetness, fallen fruit lay unmolested, and children played barefoot with impunity. One of the villagers' daughters, in her third year at an agricultural college, came home in the back of a pickup truck at the end of July. She thumped her single suitcase against the gate before opening it, to scatter the chickens, then raised the latch and swung the iron aside, and was immediately wrapped in a flying hug.

Once she disentangled herself from brother and parents and liberally distributed kisses, she listened to the news she'd missed: how the cows were dying from drinking stonecutters' dust in the streams; how grain prices were falling everywhere, despite the drought; and how her brother, little fool that he was, had torn down a wasp nest and received a faceful of red and white lumps for it. One of the most detailed wasp's maps had reached the capital, she was told, and a bureaucrat had arrived in a sleek black car. But because the wasps were all dead, he could report little more than a prank, a freak, or a miracle. There were no further inquiries.

Her brother produced for her inspection the brittle, boiled bodies of several wasps in a glass jar, along with one of the smaller maps. She tickled him until he surrendered his trophies, promised him a basket of peaches in return, and let herself be fed to tautness. Then, to her family's dismay, she wrote an urgent letter to the Academy of Sciences and packed a satchel with clothes and cash. If she could find one more nest of wasps, she said, it would make their fortune and her name. But it had to be done quickly.

In the morning, before the cockerels woke and while the sky was still purple, she hopped onto her old bicycle and rode down the dusty path.

Bees do not fly at night or lie to each other, but the anarchists had learned both from the wasps. On a warm, clear evening they left the hive at last, flying west in a small tight cloud. Around them swelled the voices of summer insects, strange and disquieting. Several miles west of the old hive and the wasp nest, in a lightning-scarred elm, the anarchists had built up a small stock of stolen honey sealed in wax and paper. They rested there for the night, in cells of clean white wax, and in the morning they arose to the building of their city.

The first business of the new colony was the laying of eggs, which a number of workers set to, and provisions for winter. One egg from the old queen, brought from the hive in an anarchist's jaws, was hatched and raised as a new mother. Uncrowned and unconcerned, she too laid mortar and wax, chewed wood to make paper, and fanned the storerooms with her wings.

The anarchists labored secretly but rapidly, drones alongside workers, because the copper taste of autumn was in the air. None had seen a winter before, but the memory of the species is subtle and long, and in their hearts, despite the summer sun, they felt an imminent darkness.

The flowers were fading in the fields. Every day the anarchists added to their coffers of warm gold and built their white walls higher. Every day the air grew a little crisper, the grass a little drier. They sang as they worked, sometimes ballads from the old hive, sometimes anthems of their own devising, and for a time they were happy. Too soon, the leaves turned flame colors and blew from the trees, and then there were no more flowers. The anarchists pressed down the lid on the last vat of honey and wondered what was coming.

Four miles away, at the first touch of cold, the wasps licked shut their paper doors and slept in a tight knot around the foundress. In both beehives, the bees huddled together, awake and watchful, warming themselves with the thrumming of their wings. The anarchists murmured comfort to each other.

"There will be more, after us. It will breed out again."

"We are only the beginning."
"There will be more."
Snow fell silently outside.

The snow was ankle-deep and the river iced over when the girl from Yiwei reached up into the empty branches of an oak tree and plucked down the paper castle of a nest. The wasps within, drowsy with cold, murmured but did not stir. In their barracks the soldiers dreamed of the unexplored south and battles in strange cities, among strange peoples, and scouts dreamed of the corpses of starved and frozen deer. The cartographers dreamed of the changes that winter would work on the landscape, the diverted creeks and dead trees they would have to note down. They did not feel the burlap bag that settled around them, nor the crunch of tires on the frozen road.

She had spent weeks tramping through the countryside, questioning beekeepers and villagers' children, peering up into trees and into hives, before she found the last wasps from Yiwei. Then she had had to wait for winter and the anesthetizing cold. But now, back in the warmth of her own room, she broke open the soft pages of the nest and pushed aside the heaps of glistening wasps until she found the foundress herself, stumbling on uncertain legs.

When it thawed, she would breed new foundresses among the village's apricot trees. The letters she received indicated a great demand for them in the capital, particularly from army generals and the captains of scientific explorations. In years to come, the village of Yiwei would be known for its delicately inscribed maps, the legends almost too small to see, and not for its barley and oats, its velvet apricots and glassy pears.

In the spring, the old beehive awoke to find the wasps gone, like a nightmare that evaporates by day. It was difficult to believe, but when not the slightest scrap of wasp paper could be found, the whole hive sang with delight. Even the queen, who had been coached from the pupa on the details of her client state and the conditions by which she ruled, and who had felt, perhaps, more sympathy for the wasps than she should have, cleared her throat and trilled once or twice. If she did not sing so loudly or so joyously as the rest, only a few noticed, and the winter had been a hard one, anyhow.

The maps had vanished with the wasps. No more would be made. Those who had studied among the wasps began to draft memoranda and the first independent decrees of queen and council. To defend against future invasions, it was decided that a detachment of bees would fly the borders of their land and carry home reports of what they found.

It was on one of these patrols that a small hive was discovered in the fork of an elm tree. Bees lay dead and brittle around it, no identifiable queen among them. Not a trace of honey remained in the storehouse; the dark wax of its walls had been gnawed to rags. Even the brood cells had been scraped clean. But in the last intact hexagons they found, curled and capped in wax, scrawled on page after page, words of revolution. They read in silence.

Then—

"Write," one said to the other, and she did.

About the Authors

Kelly Barnhill's work has appeared in *Postscripts, Weird Tales, Fantasy, The Sun, Sybil's Garage* and other publications. She also writes high-interest nonfiction books for children (the fact that she has written books about sea monsters, sewer systems, eyeless salamanders and pee has made her very popular at children's parties). Her first novel *The Mostly True Story Of Jack,* a middle-grade fantasy set in rural Iowa (a lonely boy, and avenging girl, a mysterious house, two possibly murderous cats, a remarkable skateboard, and a nasty bit of magic) will be released next summer by Little, Brown. She is, by all accounts, ridiculously excited about it. She is a former schoolteacher, a former bartender, a former janitor, a former receptionist, a former park ranger, a former wildland firefighter, and a former waitress. The sum of these experiences have prepared her for nothing save freelance writing, which she has been happily doing for the past six years. She lives in Minneapolis with her brilliant husband, her three evil-genius children, and her emotionally unstable dog.

Jacques Barcia is a weird fiction writer and technology reporter from Recife, Brazil. A non-practicing atheist, he likes to engage in theological fights with random people in the streets. He holds a professional record of 33-1-1. He can't defeat his wife, nor his three-year-old daughter. When he's not writing or blaspheming, he serves as the lead growler of grindcore band Rabujos.

Eric Brown began writing when he was fifteen and sold his first short story to *Interzone* in 1986. He has won the British Science Fiction Award twice for his short stories and has published over thirty-five books. His latest includes the novel *Engineman* and, due out in December, *Guardians of the Phoenix.* He writes a monthly science fiction review column for the Guardian newspaper. He lives near Cambridge, England.

Jason K. Chapman lives at the intersection of Geek and Art. His two main interests come together in his job as the IT Director for *Poets & Writers* (pw. org), where he has worked for almost fifteen years. His short fiction has appeared in *Cosmos Magazine, Grantville Gazette-Universe Annex, Asimov's Science Fiction, Bullspec,* and others.

Gwendolyn Clare has a BA in Ecology, a BS in Geophysics, and is currently working to add another acronym to her collection. Away from the laboratory, she enjoys practicing martial arts, adopting feral cats, and writing speculative fiction. Her short stories have appeared or are forthcoming in *Asimov's*, Ekaterina Sedia's *Bewere the Night* anthology, *Daily Science Fiction*, and *Abyss and Apex*, among others.

Erin M. Hartshorn is a desert rat transplanted to a humid climate. Her ideal home has bookcases in every room. She is a moderator at Forward Motion for Writers, an on-line writers community. Her fiction has appeared both on-line and in print in various places, placed in the PARSEC short story contest, earned honorable mentions in the Writers of the Future contest, and been short-listed for the UPC Award. When she's not writing, she enjoys various handicrafts, though she prefers spending time with her family.

N. K. Jemisin has sold short stories to *Strange Horizons, Postscripts, Baen's Universe*, and other markets. Her first novel, *The Hundred Thousand Kingdoms*, was published by Orbit in February 2010 and she was nominated for both the Hugo and Nebula Awards for her 2009 *Clarkesworld* story, "Non-Zero Probabilities." She's lived in New Orleans, New York, Boston, and Mobile (Alabama), and has only written stories about the first two cities so far.

Yoon Ha Lee's fiction has appeared in *The Magazine of Fantasy and Science Fiction* and *Beneath Ceaseless Skies*. Her first short story collection, *Conservation of Shadows*, is currently available from Prime Books.

Ken Liu was a programmer before he became a lawyer, and he still drafts legal documents like he writes code. His fiction has appeared in *F&SF, Strange Horizons*, and *Science Fiction World*, among other places. He lives in the Greater Boston area with his wife, artist Lisa Tang Liu, and they welcomed their daughter into the world in 2010. He and Lisa are collaborating on a novel.

Greg Mellor is a science fiction writer living in Canberra with his wife and son. His work has appeared in *Cosmos Magazine, Aurealis* and *Antipodean SF* plus several print anthologies. *Wild Chrome*, his debut collection of short SF, will be released by Ticonderoga Publications in 2012.

Mari Ness lives in central Florida with two cats who think her fingers should spend less time on a keyboard and more time in their fur. Her fiction and poetry have previously appeared in numerous print and online publications, including *Fantasy Magazine, Ideomancer*, and *Shine: An Anthology of Optimistic Science Fiction*. On Thursdays, she blogs about Oz and other works of the fantastic for children over at *Tor.com*. You can also follow her on Twitter at @mari_ness.

Nnedi Okorafor is the author of the critically acclaimed novel *Who Fears Death* (a Nebula Award Nominee for "Best Novel"). Her YA novels include *Zahrah the Windseeker* (winner of the Wole Soyinka Prize), *The Shadow Speaker* (winner of the CBS Parallax Award) and *Long Juju Man* (winner of the Macmillan Prize for Africa). Her YA novel *Akata Witch* will be released in April, 2011. Okorafor is a professor at Chicago State University.

An Owomoyela, a linguistics enthusiast and denizen of the American Midwest, writes a little bit of everything, so long as it's speculative. After graduating from the Clarion West Writers Workshop in 2008, An returned to Iowa to begin case-modding consensus reality one work of fiction at a time. Fiction bearing the mark of this elusive author can be spotted in a variety of "here"s and "there"s, including *Fantasy Magazine, Asimov's Science Fiction, Apex Magazine,* and Rich Horton's *The Year's Best Science Fiction & Fantasy, 2011.*

Chen Qiufan was born in 1981, in Shantou, China. (In accordance with Chinese custom, Mr. Chen's surname is written first. He sometimes uses the English name Stanley Chan.) He is a graduate of Peking University and published his first short story in 1997 in *Science Fiction World,* China's largest science fiction magazine. Since 2004, he has published over 30 stories in *Science Fiction World, Esquire, Chutzpah* and other magazines. His first novel, *The Abyss of Vision,* came out in 2006. He won Taiwan's Dragon Fantasy Award in 2006 with "A Record of the Cave of Ning Mountain," a work written in Classical Chinese. His story, "The Tomb," was translated into English and Italian and can be found in *The Apex Book of World SF 2* and *Alias 6.* He now lives in Beijing and works for Google China.

Cat Rambo lives and writes in the Pacific Northwest. Her works have appeared in such places as *Asimov's, Tor.com,* and *Weird Tales.* Her fcollection, *Eyes Like Sky and Coal and Moonlight,* was a 2010 Endeavour Award finalist. Her latest collection is *Near + Far* (Hydra House, 2012.) She has served as the fiction editor of *Fantasy Magazine.*

Robert Reed has had eleven novels published, starting with *The Leeshore* in 1987 and most recently with *The Well of Stars* in 2004. Since winning the first annual *L. Ron Hubbard Writers of the Future* contest in 1986 (under the pen name Robert Touzalin) and being a finalist for the John W. Campbell Award for best new writer in 1987, he has had over 200 shorter works published in a variety of magazines and anthologies. Eleven of those stories were published in his critically-acclaimed first collection, *The Dragons of Springplace,* in 1999. Twelve more stories appear in his second collection, *The Cuckoo's Boys* [2005]. In addition to his success in the U.S., Reed has also been published in the

U.K., Russia, Japan, Spain and in France, where a second (French-language) collection of nine of his shorter works, *Chrysalide*, was released in 2002. Bob has had stories appear in at least one of the annual "Year's Best" anthologies in every year since 1992. Bob has received nominations for both the Nebula Award (nominated and voted upon by genre authors) and the Hugo Award (nominated and voted upon by fans), as well as numerous other literary awards (see Awards). He won his first Hugo Award for the 2006 novella "*A Billion Eves*". He is currently working on a Great Ship trilogy for Prime Books, and of course, more short pieces.

Gord Sellar is a Canadian who was born in Malawi and lived in South Korea from 2002 until early 2013. A 2006 graduate of Clarion West and a 2009 finalist for the John W. Campbell Award for Best New Writer, his work has appeared in many major SF magazines and numerous anthologies and collections, and his first screenplay ("The Music of Jo Hyeja," a Korean adaptation of an H.P. Lovecraft story) was made into an award-winning short film in 2012. For recent news, visit his website at gordsellar.com.

Rachel Swirsky's short fiction has been published in numerous magazines and anthologies and been nominated for the Hugo, the Nebula, the Sturgeon, the Million Writers Award, and the Locus Award. Her first collection, *Through the Drowsy Dark*, a slim volume of fiction and poetry, came out from Aqueduct Press in 2010. A second collection is forthcoming from Subterranean Press. She lives in Bakersfield, California, with her husband, a geologist who has never been to the moon.

Genevieve Valentine is the author of *Mechanique: A Tale of the Circus Tresaulti*. Her short fiction has appeared or is forthcoming in *Clarkesworld*, *Strange Horizons*, *Journal of Mythic Arts*, *Fantasy Magazine*, *Lightspeed*, and *Apex*, and in the anthologies *Federations*, *The Living Dead 2*, *The Way of the Wizard*, *Running with the Pack*, *Teeth*, and more. She is a co-author of the forthcoming pop-culture book *Geek Wisdom*, and her film and TV writing has appeared in *Fantasy Magazine* and *Strange Horizons*. Her appetite for bad movies is insatiable, a tragedy she tracks on her blog.

D. Elizabeth Wasden manages volunteers for a small nonprofit on the Delmarva Peninsula. Her fiction has appeared in *Fantasy Magazine*, *G.U.D.*, and *Electric Velocipede*. She is a graduate of Clarion West 2009.

A.C. Wise was born and raised in Montreal, and currently lives in the suburbs of Philadelphia. Her work has previously appeared in places like *Strange Horizons*, *Fantasy Magazine*, and *ChiZine*. For more information, or just to drop by and say hi, visit her blog at acwise.livejournal.com.

E. Lily Yu is a student at Princeton University, where she dances, makes music, keeps bees, and rarely sleeps. Her work has recently appeared in *The Kenyon Review Online, Jabberwocky 5, Electric Velocipede,* and *Goblin Fruit,* with more stories coming from *Podcastle* and *KROnline* later this year.

Clarkesworld Citizens
OFFICIAL CENSUS

We would like to thank the following Clarkesworld Citizens for their support:

Overlords

L A George, Renan Adams, Claire Alcock, Thomas Ball, Michael Blackmore, Nathalie Boisard-Beudin, Shawn Boyd, Jennifer Brozek, Karen Burnham, Barbara Capoferri, Morgan Cheryl, Gio Clairval, Dolohov, ebooks-worldwide, Sairuh Emilius, Lynne Everett, Joshua Faulkenberry, Fabio Fernandes, Thomas Fleck, Eric Francis, Bryan Green, Andrew Hatchell, Berthiaume Heidi, Bill Hughes, Gary Hunter, Theodore J. Stanulis, Marcus Jager, Jericho, jfly, jka-poetry, Lucas Jung, James Kinateder, Daniel LaPonsie, Susan Lewis, Philip Maloney, Paul Marston, Matthew the Greying, Gabriel Mayland, MJ Mercer, Achilleas Michailides, Adrian Mihaila, Adrien Mitchell, MrMovieZombie, Mike Perricone, Jody Plank, Rick Ramsey, Jo Rhett, Joseph Sconfitto, Marie Shcherbatskaya, Tara Smith, David Steffen, Elaine Williams, James Williams, Doug Young

Royalty

Paul Abbamondi, Albert Alfiler, Raymond Bair, Kathryn Baker, Nathan Blumenfeld, Marty Bonus, David Borcherding, Robert Callahan, Lady Cate, Richard Chappell, Carolyn Cooper, Tom Crosshill, Michael Cullinan, Mr D F Ryan, Sky de Jersey, David Demers, Cory Doctorow, Brian Dolton, Alexis Goble, Hilary Goldstein, Andy Herrman, Kristin Hirst, Colin Hitch, Victoria Hoke, Christopher Irwin, Mary Jo Rabe, Lukas Karl Barnes, G.J. Kressley, Jeffrey L Lewis, Jamie Lackey, Jonathan Laden, Katherine Lee, H. Lincoln Parish, David M Oswin, Sean Markey, Arun Mascarenhas, Barrett McCormick, Kevin McKean, Margaret McNally, Michelle Broadribb MEG, Nayad Monroe, James Moore, Anne Murphy, Persona Non-Grata, Charles Norton, Vincent O'Connor, Vincent P Loeffler III, Marie Parsons, Lars Pedersen, David Personette, George Peter Gatsis, Matt Phelps, Ian Powell, Rational Path, RL, John Scalzi, Stu Segal, Maurice Shaw,

Angela Slatter, Carrie Smith, Paul Smith, Richard Sorden, Chugwangle Spar-klepants, Kevin Standlee, Neal Stanifer, Josh Thomson, TK, Terhi Tormanen, Jeppe V Holm, Jasen Ward, Weyla & Gos, Graeme Williams, Jeff Xilon, Zola

Bürgermeisters

7ony, Mary A. Turzillo, Rob Abram, Frederick Amerman, Carl Anderson, Mel Anderson, Andy90, Marie Angell, Jon Arnold, Robert Avie, Erika Bailey, Brian Baker, Michael Banker, Jennifer Bartolowits, Lenni Benson, Kerry Benton, Bill Bibo Jr, Edward Blake, Samuel Blinn, Johanna Bobrow, Joan Boyle, Patricia Bray, Tim Brenner, Ken Brown, BruceC, Adam Bursey, Jeremy Butler, Robyn Butler, Roland Byrd, M. C. VanderSchaaf, Brad Campbell, Carleton45, James Carlino, Benjamin Cartwright, Evan Cassity, Lee Cavanaugh, Peter Charron, Randall Chertkow, Michael Chorman, Mary Clare, Matthew Claxton, Theodore Conti, Brian Cooksey, Brenda Cooper, Lorraine Cooper, B D Fagan, James Davies, Tessa Day, Brian Deacon, Bartley Deason, John Devenny, Fran Ditzel-Friel, Gary Dockter, Nicholas Doran, Christopher Doty, Nicholas Dowbiggin, Christine Ertell, Joanna Evans, Rare Feathers, Tea Fish, FlatFootedRat, Lynn Flewelling, Adrienne Foster, Matthew Fredrickson, Alina Fridberg, Patricia G Scott, Christopher Garry, Pierre Gauthier, Gerhen, Mark Gerrits, Lorelei Goelz, Ed Goforth, Inga Gorslar, Tony Graham, Jaq Greenspon, Eric Gregory, Laura Hake, Skeptyk/JeanneE Hand-Boniakowski, Jordan Hanie, Carl Hazen, Helixa 12, Corydon Hinton, Sheridan Hodges, Ronald Hordijk, Justin Howe, Bobby Hoyt, David Hudson, Huginn Huginn and Muninn, Chris Hurst, Kevin Ikenberry, Joseph Ilardi, Pamela J. Davis, Justin James, Patty Jansen, Cristal Java, Toni Jerrman, Audra Johnson, Erin Johnson, Russell Johnson, Patrick Joseph Sklar, Kai Juedemann, Andy Kaden, Jeff Kapustka, David Kelleher, James Kelly, Joshua Kidd, Alistair Kimble, Erin Kissane, Cecil Knight, Michelle Knowlton, JR Krebs, Andrew Lanker, James Frederick Leach, Krista Leahy, Alan Lehotsky, Walter Leroy Perkins, Philip Levin, Kevin Liebkemann, Grá Linnaea, Susan Loyal, Kristi Lozano, LUX4489, Keith M Frampton, N M Wells Foundry Creative Media, Brit Mandelo, Mark Maris, Matthew Marovich, Samuel Marzioli, Jason Maurer, Rosaleen McCarthy, Peter McClean, Michael McCormack, Tony McFee, Mark McGarry, Doug McLaughlin, Craig McMurtry, J Meijer, Geoffrey Meissner, Barry Melius, David Michalak, Robert Milson, Sharon Mock, Eric Mohring, Samuel Montgomery-Blinn, Rebekah Murphy, John Murray, Barrett Nichols, Peter Northup, Justin Palk, Norman Papernick, Richard Parks, Katherine Pendill, Eric Pierson, E. PLS, PBC Productions Inc., Lolt Proegler, Jonathan Pruett, QLM Aria X-Perienced, Robert Quinlivan, Mike R D Ashley, D Randall Kerr, Paul Rice, James Rickard, Karsten Rink, Erik Rolstad, Joseph Romel, Leena Romppainen, Michael Russo, Mark S Haney, Stefan Scheib, Alan Scheiner, Kenneth Schneyer, Bluezoo Seven, Cosma Shalizi, Jeremy Showers, siznax, Allen Snyder, David Sobyra, Jason Strawsburg,

Keffington Studios, Jerome Stueart, Robert Stutts, Maurice Termeer, Tero, Chuck Tindle, Raymond Tobaygo, Tradeblanket.com, Heather Tumey, Ann VanderMeer, Andrew Vega, Emil Volcheck, Andrew Volpe, Wendy Wagner, Jennifer Walter, Tom Waters, Tehani Wessely, Shannon White, Dan Wick, John Wienstroer, Seth Williams, Paul Wilson, Dawn Wolfe, Sarah Wright

Citizens

Pete Aldin, Elye Alexander, Richard Alison, Joshua Allen, Alllie, Imron Alston, Clifford Anderson, Kim Anderson, Randall Andrews, Author Anonymous, Therese Arkenberg, Ash, Bill B., Benjamin Baker, Jenny Barber, Johanne Barron, Jeff Bass, Aaron Begg, LaNeta Bergst, Julie Berg-Thompson, Clark Berry, Amy Billingham, Tracey Bjorksten, John Bledsoe, Mike Blevins, Adam Blomquist, Allison Bocksruker, Kevin Bokelman, Michael Bonsall, Michael Bowen, Michael Braun Hamilton, Commander Breetai, Jennifer Brissett, Kit Brown, Thomas Bull, Michael Bunkahle, Karl Bunker, Cory Burr, Jefferson Burson, Graeme Byfield, c9lewis, Darrell Cain, C.G. Cameron, Yazburg Carlberg, Michael Carr, Nance Cedar, Timothy Charlton, David Chasson, Catherine Cheek, Paige Chicklo, J.B.& Co., Elizabeth Coleman, Johne Cook, Claire Cooney, Martin Cooper, Lisa Costello, Charles Cox, Michael Cox, Yoshi Creelman, Tina Crone, Curtis42, Sarah Dalton, Ang Danieldeskbrain - Watercress Munster, Gillian Daniels, Chua Dave, Morgan Davey, Ed Davidoff, Chase Davies, Craig Davis, Gustavo de Albuquerque, Alessia De Gaspari, Maria-Isabel Deira, Daniel DeLano, Dennis DeMario, Michele Desautels, Paul DesCombaz, Aidan Doyle, dt, Alex Dunbar, Susan Duncan, Andrew Eason, David Eggli, Jesse Eisenhower, Brad Elliott, Warren Ellis, Douglas Engstrom, Lyle Enright, Peter Enyeart, Yvonne Ewing, Feather, Josiah Ferrin, TJ Fly, the Paragliding Guy, Ethan Fode, Dense Fog, Jason Frank, Michael Fratus, William Fred, Michael Frighetto, Sarah Frost, Fyrbaul, Paul Gainford, Robert Garbacz, Eleanor Gausden, Leslie Gelwicks, Susan Gibbs, Holly Glaser, Sangay Glass, Laura Goodin, Grendel, Valerie Grimm, Damien Grintalis, Nikki Guerlain, Geoffrey Guthrie, Richard Guttormson, Michael Habif, Lee Hallison, Lee Hallison, Janus Hansen, Roy Hardin, Jonathan Harnum, Harpoon, Jubal Harshaw, Darren Hawbrook, Leon Hendee, Jamie Henderson, Samantha Henderson, Dave Hendrickson, Karen Heuler, Dan Hiestand, John Higham, Renata Hill, Björn Hillreiner, Tim Hills, Peter Hogberg, Peter Hollmer, Andrea Horbinski, Clarence Horne III, Richard Horton, Fiona Howland-Rose, Jeremy Hull, John Humpton, Dwight Illk, John Imhoff, Iridum Sound Envoy, Isbell, Stephen Jacob, Radford Janssens, Michael Jarcho, Jimbo, Steve Johnson, Patrick Johnston, Gabriel Kaknes, Philip Kaldon, KarlTheGood, Sara Kathryn, Cagatay Kavukcuoglu, Lorna Keach, Keenan, Jason Keeton, Robert Keller, Mary Kellerman, Kelson, Shawn Keslar, Kate Kligman, Seymour Knowles-Barley, Matthew Koch, Will Koenig, Lutz Krebs, Derek Kunsken, Erica L. Satifka, T. L. Sherwood, Michele Laframboise, Paul

Lamarre, Gina Langridge, Darren Ledgerwood, Brittany Lehman, Terra Lemay, Pontus Liljeblad, Danielle Linder, Susan Llewellyn, Thomas Loyal, James Lyle, Allison M. Dickson, Dan Manning, Margaret, Eric Marsh, Jacque Marshall, Dominique Martel, Daniel Mathews, David Mayes, Derek McAleer, Mike McBride, T.C. McCarthy, Jeffrey McDonald, Holly McEntee, Josh McGraw, Roland McIntosh, Brent Mendelsohn, Seth Merlo, Stephen Middleton, John Midgley, Matthew Miller, Stephan Miller, Terry Miller, Alan Mimms, mjpearce, Aidan Moher, Marian Moore, Jamie Morgan, Patricia Murphy, Jack Myers Photography, Glenn Nevill, Stella Nickerson, Robyn Nielsen, David Oakley, Scott Oesterling, Rick of the North, Christopher Ogilvie, James Oliver, Lydia Ondrusek, Ruth O'Neill, Erik Ordway, Nancy Owens, Stuart P Hair, Thomas Pace, Amparo Palma Reig, Thomas Parrish, Andrea Pawley, Sidsel Pedersen, Edgar Penderghast, Tzum Pepah, Chris Perkins, Patricia Peterson, Nikki Philley, Adrian-Teodor Pienaru, Beth Plutchak, David Potter, Ed Prior, David Raco, Mahesh Raj Mohan, Adam Rakunas, Ralan, Steve Ramey, Diego Ramos, Dale Randolph Bivins, Marcel Raoul, Robert Redick, George Reilly, Joshua Reynolds, Julia Reynolds, Zach Ricks, Carl Rigney, Hank Roberts, Tansy Roberts, Kenneth Robkin, James Rowh, Roy and Norma Kloster, RPietila, Sarah Rudek, Woodworking Running Dog, Oliver Rupp, Caitlin Russell, Abigail Rustad, George S. Walker, Lior Saar, S2 Sally, Tim Sally, Jason Sanford, Steven Saus, MJ Scafati, Jan Shawyer, Espana Sheriff, Udayan Shevade, Josh Shiben, Aileen Simpson, Karen Snyder, Morgan Songi, Dr SP Conboy-Hil, Terry Squire Stone, Jennifer Stufflebeam, Kenneth Takigawa, Charles Tan, Jesse Tauriainen, David Taylor, Felix Troendle, Julia Varga, Adam Vaughan, Extranet Vendors Association, William Vennell, Vettac, Diane Walton, Robert Wamble, Lim Wee Teck, Neil Weston, Peter Wetherall, Adam White, Spencer Wightman, Jeff Williamson, Neil Williamson, Kristyn Willson, A.C. Wise, Devon Wong, Chalmer Wren, Dan Wright, Lachlan Yeates, Catherine York, Rena Zayit, Stephanie Zvan

Interested in immigrating to Clarkesworld?
Visit **clarkesworldmagazine.com** for more details.

About Clarkesworld

Clarkesworld Magazine (clarkesworldmagazine.com) is a monthly science fiction and fantasy magazine first published in October 2006. Each issue contains interviews, thought-provoking articles and at least three pieces of original fiction. Our fiction is also available in ebook editions/subscriptions, audio podcasts and in our annual print anthologies. *Clarkesworld* has been nominated for Hugo Award for Best Semiprozine four times, winning three, and our fiction has been nominated for or won the Hugo, Nebula, World Fantasy, Sturgeon, Locus, Shirley Jackson, WSFA Small Press and Stoker Awards. For information on how to subscribe to our electronic edition on your Kindle, Nook, iPad or other ereader/Android device, please visit:

clarkesworldmagazine.com/subscribe/

About the Editors

Neil Clarke (neil-clarke.com) is the publisher and editor-in-chief of *Clarkesworld Magazine,* owner of Wyrm Publishing and a two-time Hugo Award Nominee for Best Editor Short Form. He currently lives in New Jersey with his wife and two boys.

Sean Wallace is a founding editor at *Clarkesworld Magazine,* owner of Prime Books and winner of the World Fantasy Award. He currently lives in Maryland with his wife and two daughters.